THE NIGHT DRIFTER

Also by Susan Carroll

The Bride Finder
Winterbourne
The Painted Veil

The
NIGHT
DRIFTER

SUSAN CARROLL

Ballantine Books • New York

A Ballantine Book
Published by The Ballantine Publishing Group

Copyright © 1999 by Susan Coppula

All rights reserved under International and Pan-American Copyright Conventions. Published in the
United States by The Ballantine Publishing Group, a division of Random House, Inc., New York, and
simultaneously in Canada by Random House of Canada Limited, Toronto.

Ballantine and colophon are registered trademarks of Random House, Inc.

http://www.randomhouse.com/BB/

Library of Congress Cataloging-in-Publication Data

Carroll, Susan, 1952–
    The night drifter / Susan Carroll. — 1st ed.
        p.   cm.
    ISBN 0-345-43312-2 (hardcover : alk. paper)
    I. Title.
PS3553.A7654N54   1999
813'.54—dc21   98-54616
                                           CIP

Manufactured in the United States of America

First Edition: May 1999

10   9   8   7   6   5   4   3   2   1

PROLOGUE

*I*t was the kind of night when anything could happen.

Magic. Moonlight. The sea roaring like a dragon, breathing a soft mist that was slowly enveloping the land. The stalwart figure who drifted along the rocky shoreline materialized like an apparition in his glinting chain mail and dark tunic. A ghostly knight from King Arthur's court who had wandered into the nineteenth century by mistake and couldn't quite find his way back to Camelot.

But Lance St. Leger was merely a man attired in the costume he had worn to the Midsummer's Eve fest and had not yet troubled to remove. He had far weightier matters on his mind.

He scanned the dark and silent beach ahead of him, his face anxious and tense. He was possessed of strong handsome features: a square jaw, a hawk-like nose, and a deeply tanned complexion framed beneath a sweep of raven-black hair. But a certain cynicism already marred the velvet darkness of his eyes, despite the fact that he was a relatively young man, only twenty-seven. The disillusionment that tugged at the full curve of his lips made him seem older, giving his mouth a hard cast except when he smiled.

He wasn't smiling now as he studied the overturned hull of an abandoned fishing boat, the sea raking cold fingers of foam across the sand, obliterating all traces of any footsteps. But Lance was certain this was the place where he had been attacked only an hour before, surprised by some hooded brigand and rendered unconscious.

When Lance had awoken, he had found his watch and signet ring missing. But that had not been the worst of it. The thief had also taken his sword, the one that had been in his family for generations, a weapon as steeped in mystery and magic as the St. Leger name itself.

When the sword had first been handed down to Lance on his eighteenth birthday, he had sensed the power in it. Merely touching the hilt had somehow made him feel stronger, better, more noble.

He had earnestly recited the pledge that all St. Leger heirs were required to give:

I vow that I will only employ this blade in just cause. That I will never use it to shed the blood of another St. Leger. And on the day that I marry, I will offer this sword up to my bride as a symbol of my undying love along with my heart and soul forever.

But that had been a long time ago. Back when Lance still believed in such things as just causes, magic, and true love. Back when he still believed in himself . . .

Lance desperately circled the area around the boat, but he didn't know why he had bothered to come back here, what he was hoping to find.

That the thief had experienced a change of heart? That he would suddenly reappear to return the stolen treasure to Lance, scraping and bowing while he babbled, "Oh, here you are, Master Lance, here's your ancestral sword. Please forgive the impertinence."

Lance's lip curled in contempt at his own folly. He swore beneath his breath, cursing both the unknown brigand and himself. He had certainly made mistakes in the past, brought enough disgrace to his family's name, but allowing that sword to be stolen was by far the worst thing he'd ever done.

Not true, a sad voice whispered in his ear. *The worst thing was what you did to your brother, Val.*

But Lance refused to think about Val. He was already racked with enough guilt over the disappearance of that infernal sword.

Despairing of finding any clue to his attacker on the beach, Lance turned and headed up the path toward the village instead. Despite the fact that he had recently cashiered out of the service, Lance still moved with the military bearing of a man who spent nearly nine years as an officer in Wellington's army.

Slipping quietly alongside the forge next to the blacksmith's shop, he peered toward the line of whitewashed cottages. Earlier Torrecombe had been a riot of noise and laughter, alive with all the excitement of the Midsummer's Eve festival. But the village slumbered now, not a soul stirring across the green in the center of town.

Lance thought briefly of conducting a house-to-house search, only to discard the notion. He doubted that anyone from the village would have dared to attack him. The local folk were too much in awe of the St. Legers and their legends. Legends of a family descended from a notorious sorcerer. The mighty Lord Prospero might have come to a disastrous end, burned at the stake, but he had passed on a legacy of strange talents and powers to his descendants, of which Lance had inherited his share.

No. Lance was convinced. No one from the village would have trifled with a St. Leger. The thief had to have been an outsider, a stranger, and there had been plenty of those wandering through Torrecombe tonight because of the fair. Many of them were stopping over at the inn, and that seemed the most likely place for Lance to begin his search.

He stole across the village square until the Dragon's Fire Inn loomed over him. A quaint building, it still bore traces of its original Tudor construction, with mullioned windows and overhanging eaves.

An ostler bustled about the stable yard, attending to the horse of some late arrival. Lance watched, keeping to the shadows. Long ago, he had promised his father that he would never reveal the secret of his own peculiar and frightening power to anyone outside of the family. And one did not lightly break promises given to Anatole St. Leger, the dread lord of the Castle Leger.

Lance was deeply grateful that at this moment his father was far from Cornwall, traveling abroad on an extensive holiday with Lance's mother and three younger sisters. He'd already proved enough of a disappointment to Anatole St. Leger, Lance reflected grimly. With any luck at all he would be able to recover the sword before word of this latest escapade reached his father's ears. *He had to.*

Huddling behind a tree, Lance wished that he was merely a clairvoyant like his second cousin Maeve. It would certainly make his search for the sword easier . . . and safer. The ostler was taking a damned long time about disappearing into the stables. The blasted fool was doing more stroking and talking to that horse than he was attending to it.

Lance cast an uneasy glance toward the sky, trying to calculate how much time he had left until dawn. It would not do for him to be caught abroad exercising his strange gift when the sun came up. That could prove dangerous. In fact, deadly.

He was filled with relief when the ostler moved on at last, leading the horse into the stables. Stealing from his hiding place, Lance drifted toward the inn. After a moment more of hesitation, he braced himself.

And shimmered straight through the wall.

CHAPTER ONE

*L*ady Rosalind Carlyon sat with her chin perched upon her hands, her elbows resting upon the open casement. Her long hair rippled in a golden braid down the back of her fine lawn nightdress, her bare toes peeking out beneath the hem.

With eyes the serene blue of a lake in summer, she stared dreamily out the window of her second-story chamber at the Dragon's Fire Inn, past the dark and silent inn yard to where the fair had once been. She had been watching most of the evening. There had been a puppet show and a fire-eater and dancing on the green, tents gaily decked out with flags and ribbons after the fashion of a medieval tournament. At one point, she believed there had even been some manner of joust, but the men had crowded about so thick, it had been impossible to see.

Impulsively Rosalind had snatched up her shawl, preparing to dart down there and find out exactly what was going on, lose herself in all the color and excitement. She had been held back only by her maid.

As soon as she'd mentioned the fair, Jenny Grey's earnest eyes had widened with alarm.

"On no, miss," she had cried. "These country fairs can be dangerous. Full of such vulgar and rough characters. No place for a respectable young lady to be walking alone. Whatever would his lordship's—God rest his noble soul— whatever would his aunts think?"

The mere mention of Clothilde and Miranda Carlyon, with their sour disapproving scowls, had almost been enough to send Rosalind hurtling out the inn door, defiantly prepared to do as she pleased. After all, she was no longer a chit out of the schoolroom, but a twenty-one-year-old widow.

In the end, however, she had yielded to Jenny's pleas and had spent her evening curled up by the hearth with her much worn copy of Thomas Malory's *Le Morte d'Arthur*.

Rosalind regretted it now as she sat by the window, gazing out at the empty village square. The laughing crowds had long ago dispersed, the torches extinguished, the tents struck, leaving her with the forlorn sensation of having been left behind while the rest of the world moved on.

All she had wanted had been a wee bit of excitement, a shade of adventure. She had known too little of that in her life.

The sole child of a doting older couple, she had been cosseted by parents whose only fault had been loving her too much. And when Walter and Sarah Burne had fallen victim to a cholera epidemic, the task of sheltering Rosalind had passed on to her guardian, Lord Arthur Carlyon, an honorable gentleman some twenty years her senior.

Despite the difference in their ages, it had seemed the most right and natural thing to marry Arthur. It had been more than a year since his death, and she still grieved.

The village was completely silent now, the houses snug beneath their thatched roofs as though the cottages had donned nightcaps and were all peacefully asleep.

It was lonely, Rosalind thought, being the only one left awake. She had had difficulty sleeping ever since Arthur had died. Her maid had bustled off to find the inn's kitchen and brew Rosalind a posset that Jenny swore would cure her mistress's insomnia.

Rosalind only hoped the girl was right. She needed to get some rest or she would be exhausted tomorrow, and she had a special call to pay before she continued on with her journey. If she ever was fortunate enough to travel into this part of the country, she had always promised herself that she would look up an old friend of her father's, the Reverend Septimus Fitzleger.

She had only met the elderly clergyman once, years ago when he had paid a visit to their house in Hampshire, but Rosalind retained a vivid memory of the kindly old man who had dandled her upon his knee. His pockets stuffed full of sweetmeats and an ancient timepiece he had permitted her to play with, he had seemed more of a magician than a vicar to her, a regular Merlin with his snowy-white tufts of hair and wise, twinkling eyes. He told her delightful stories of the land he came from, so different from the quiet, well-ordered house and garden where she was growing up like a sheltered princess.

A country of storm-lashed cliffs, wild moors, and a fairy-tale castle perched high above the sea. *Corn Wall,* she had repeated the name after Mr. Fitzleger in accents of childish wonder, certain it must not be a part of England at all, but a magical kingdom unto itself.

"And someday when you are quite a lady grown, Miss Rosalind," Mr. Fitzleger had told her with a smile, *"you must promise to come visit me in my kingdom by the sea."*

Rosalind had slipped her small hand into his gentle aged one and solemnly given her word. But it had taken her a great many years to keep that promise. She was not even certain if the old man still lived, but on the morrow she intended to find out, so it would not do to wear herself out to the point that she overslept.

Closing the casement, Rosalind turned away from the window when she was startled by her bedchamber door crashing open. Jenny bolted back into the room, but there was no sign of any posset in the little maid's trembling hands.

She slammed the door closed and leaned up against it, her thin face as white as her mobcap, which had gone askew. She panted and shook like a frightened rabbit who'd just outrun a pack of ravenous hounds.

Recovering herself from her shock at Jenny's abrupt appearance, Rosalind rushed to the agitated maid's side.

"Jenny? My poor girl, whatever is the matter?"

Jenny moaned and shook her head, clearly unable to answer. She seemed in danger of swooning away, but somehow Rosalind managed to coax Jenny away from the door and get her settled into the large overstuffed chair by the hearth.

Hunkering down beside the trembling girl, Rosalind chafed her wrists. Heartened to see some color seeping back into the girl's face, Rosalind repeated her anxious inquiries.

"My dear Jenny, do tell me what has happened."

"Oh, m'lady . . . m'lady," was all Jenny could groan.

Rosalind squeezed her hand. "You've obviously had a dreadful fright. Did some rogue here at the inn attempt to accost you? Did someone try to do you a harm?"

"N-not someone," Jenny quavered. *"S-something."*

"What?"

Jenny recovered herself enough to straighten a little and go on in halting accents. "I—I was making my way down to the k-kitchen when I got lost. I fetched up in this—this storeroom, kind of scary and dark like, and I saw the largest, most dreadful—" The girl broke off, shuddering.

"A rat?" Rosalind asked faintly.

"No, m'lady. Far worse. A-a *ghost.*"

Rosalind gaped at the girl

" 'Tis true, m'lady." Jenny's linen cap bobbed up and down as she nodded. "I'd swear on my mum's grave. I did see a ghost, a terrible knight all in armor, like that one you was telling me about. I was so scared, I c-couldn't even scream, and then my candle blew out so I didn't get a real good look at him, but I'm certain it's that same dreadful specter that went after poor Sir Gawain."

"Dear me," Rosalind murmured. "What I told you about Sir Gawain was only a story, Jenny. Out of the tales of King Arthur and his knights."

"But you said King Arthur was real, m'lady. That's why you came to Cornwall to have a look at that ruined castle where he was born, see the caves where Merlin used to do his magic."

"Well . . . yes, I hope to do so," Rosalind said. "Arthur was indeed a real king, but—"

"Then it stands to reason, the ghost was real too and still knocking about."

Jenny was so thoroughly in earnest and so thoroughly frightened, Rosalind was not even tempted to smile. She was flooded with guilt instead.

This was all her fault. Would she never learn her lesson? Arthur had often tried to warn her. It was one thing for Rosalind to be such an avid collector of legends, but she must try to contain her enthusiasm in front of the servants. Refrain from filling their heads with such things as vampires, banshees, and knockers. Their butler, Mr. James, had complained that he could not even get a footman to fetch a bottle of port from the wine cellar unaccompanied anymore.

Rosalind had tried to be more careful after that. But her new maid, Jenny, had seemed so unflappable. She shared Rosalind's own delight in tales and legends, both wondrous and horrible.

Jenny had even chatted with the other servants at the inn when she had gone belowstairs to fetch up her mistress's supper tray and returned to Rosalind with all manner of fascinating local gossip, stories about a mysterious castle very close by and a strange family named St. Leger.

She and Jenny had had a delightful time over supper, swapping lore of sorcery, ghostly apparitions, and even darker things. But now it was clear to Rosalind that as usual she had gone too far and had frightened poor Jenny out of her wits. She tried to comfort the girl and urge her to put the matter out of her mind and go to sleep, but Jenny continued to quake.

"Oh, no m-m'lady. I'll just sit here in this chair 'til dawn. I'm sure I couldn't get a wink of sleep now. Not in this dreadful haunted inn."

Which meant that Rosalind was unlikely to get a wink of sleep either. Rosalind sighed, seeing only one way to remedy the damage she had done, although she did not exactly relish the prospect. She gave Jenny's shoulders a comforting squeeze and said, "How would it be if I go to this storeroom and have a look round? Then when I report back to you that there is no ghost, you may feel quite easy again."

"Oh!" Jenny's mouth rounded with dismay. "I couldn't let you do a thing like that, m'lady. What if that horrible specter is still there, prowling about? Aren't you afraid of ghosts?"

"I don't know," Rosalind said honestly. "I've never encountered one."

She did experience a momentary qualm. It might be better to summon the landlord, demand that one of the male servants be sent to investigate. But despite his unctuous manner, there was something about Mr. Silas Braggs's small, narrow eyes and sly smiles that Rosalind had found repellent from the first. She thought she'd far rather risk encountering a ghost than endure any more of the innkeeper's oily courtesies.

Besides, creeping about the darkened corners of an inn at night could prove an adventure. A smallish one, but an adventure all the same.

Rosalind shoved resolutely to her feet, snatching up her candle before she could change her mind. Jenny was torn between admiration and terror, begging Rosalind not to go and at the same time cautioning her to be very careful.

The girl was still quaking so badly from her fright, Rosalind settled the maid in her own bed. She draped her shawl about Jenny's trembling shoulders and plied the girl with a box of chocolates before slipping out of the room, assuring Jenny she would return very soon.

Outside her door, Rosalind hesitated, Jenny's directions having been a little incoherent. Down the hall and turn right or was it left? She would have to be careful. It would not do at all to seize upon the wrong room and blunder in on some guest who'd been imprudent enough to leave his door unbolted.

Shielding her candle from any stray drafts, Rosalind padded cautiously along. But it was not as difficult to locate the door Jenny had described as Rosalind had feared it might be. It stood at the end of another long hall, and while fleeing the ghost, Jenny had left it ajar.

Cracking the door open further, Rosalind peered at the darkness that loomed before her with some trepidation. This part of the inn seemed silent and deserted, certainly no place for a respectable young widow to be wandering alone in the dead of the night.

Bucking up her courage, she slipped inside, holding the candle before her like a Valkyrie brandishing her sword. She didn't expect to find anything more sinister than an oddly draped piece of furniture or moonlight casting eerie shadows on the wall.. The Dragon's Fire Inn seemed too cheerful and bustling a place to be haunted. Especially not the storeroom.

She found herself in a large chamber with the mullioned window allowing rays of moonlight to play across the wooden floor. During the older days of the inn, it had likely been a handsome bedchamber reserved for the most illustrious of guests. The walls still boasted beautiful linenfold paneling and ornate candle brackets.

Now it appeared to be used solely for storage, crates and chests, mismatched chairs stacked haphazardly alongside a table with a broken leg. The fire-blackened hearth looked cold and dismal from lack of use.

Rosalind shifted her candle, darting her light into every corner of the chamber. If there truly had been a ghost strolling about here, there was no sign of him now. She released a long sigh, relieved at finding nothing, yet strangely disappointed as well. She never even noticed the knight melting out of the woodwork until she collided with him.

Her entire body shuddered with the sensation as though her veins were being pierced by slivers of light, slivers of darkness, her soul torn apart by conflicting emotions, the warmth of intimacy, the chill of despair.

Staggering forward a few steps, she felt stunned, not quite certain what had just happened to her. She was trembling, gooseflesh parading along her arms, the hairs at the nape of her neck prickling.

Very carefully, she turned around.

He stood not more than a foot away, transfixing her with his eyes. His black hair, like his tunic and the dark steel of his chain mail were calculated to blend with the night, a warrior emerged straight from the halls of Camelot.

Rosalind realized what had happened to her.

She had just walked through a ghost.

She might have screamed if she still had a voice. All she could manage was a soft moan. Dropping her candle, she cowered away from him, retreating until there was no place to go. She flattened herself against the wall.

The candle snuffed out, but she was trapped in the beam of moonlight spilling through the diamond-shaped panes of glass. For what seemed like an eternity he simply stood and stared at her, a silent shadow. Recovering from her initial shock, she was almost able to breathe again when he stirred.

Coming closer.

Rosalind gulped, trying to force the air into her lungs for one mighty shriek. He drifted into her circle of moonlight, and she hardly dared raise her eyes to his face, anticipating some truly hideous countenance.

She peered fearfully up at him . . . and her racing heart stopped altogether.

Light played over the face of a hero straight from the pages of a fairy tale or a woman's most secret dreams. High cheekbones and an iron jaw, full sculpted lips, and his brows two straight slashes as lustrously black as his hair. It was a strong face, one of remarkable character and vitality for a ghost. He could not have been so very old when he died, not more than thirty.

The thought filled Rosalind with an inexplicable sorrow.

Seen up close, he no longer seemed such an alarming specter, his dark eyes less fierce than tired and sad. He could have done his haunting with that soul-weary gaze alone.

"Please. Don't be afraid," he said softly.

"I—I'm not," she stammered, astonished to realize that was almost true.

"You are not going to scream? Or faint?"

She shook her head, struggling to credit the evidence of her own eyes. Her gaze skimmed wonderingly over him. She was not sure what she would have expected a ghost to look like if she ever encountered one. More transparent, more unreal perhaps.

Yet she had actually seen him come walking straight out of the wall . . . or had she? The muscular compactness of his frame seemed far too solid. She felt as though she ought to be able to rest her hand on the hard plane of his chest, feel the cold weight of his chain mail, the tensile strength of his arms.

She reached out to touch his hand, but her fingers melted through his, sending an odd tingle through her. She snatched her hand back at once.

There was no doubt about it. Whoever and whatever he was, he was not of this world. Perhaps she would faint after all.

She sank weakly down on top of an old trunk instead. He gazed down at his hand, flexing his fingers with a slight frown. Whether he had been offended by her attempt to touch him, or merely astonished, Rosalind could not tell.

"That—that was very rude of me," she said, finding her voice at last. It came out somewhere between a gasp and a squeak. "I shouldn't have been poking at you. I'm sorry."

"That is quite all right, milady. I am sure your fingers are very gentle and soft. I'm only sorry I could not feel your touch." His smile was filled with genuine regret.

"You really *are* a ghost," she murmured, more to herself than to him, as though by admitting the fact aloud, she could convince herself she was not dreaming.

"A ghost?" he repeated, sounding surprised, as though he was just becoming aware of the fact himself. "Er . . . yes, that's exactly what I am."

"But whose? Who are—who *were* you? What is your name?"

"Lancelot."

"Lancelot? Du Lac?" she gasped.

"Er . . . ah, yes. Sir Lancelot du Lac at thy service, milady." He dropped down on one knee before her.

It was the most dashing, the most romantic thing she had ever seen any man do. He did it naturally and gracefully, as though he had paid homage to ladies this way his entire life. Which he likely had if he was who he claimed to be.

And all she could do was clutch the sides of the trunk and gawp at him like a freshly landed fish.

Sir Lancelot du Lac. *The* Sir Lancelot. The spirit of the most famous knight of King Arthur's Round Table. Could it possibly be so? What reason would a ghost have to lie?

There would have been plenty of people in her life to warn her that she would be a fool to believe him. Only her papa would have understood. Walter Burne had been something of an Arthurian scholar himself, frequently ridiculed by his learned colleagues for his insistence that there really had once been a King Arthur and his Knights of the Round Table.

But now kneeling before Rosalind was proof that her papa had not been a fool. Emotions sifted through Rosalind in quicksilver succession. Incredulity replaced by awe, replaced by a surge of unbelievable delight.

"Papa was right," she whispered.

"I beg your pardon, milady?"

"*Papa was right!*" she cried with even more conviction. "Sir Lancelot! This is too good to be true. Did you know that I traveled to Cornwall, hoping to find you?"

"You have?" He rose to his feet, clearly nonplussed. "I mean . . . thou hast?"

"Not you exactly. I was looking for anything to do with the King Arthur legends. I traveled into Cornwall for that very reason, to visit all the famous places like Tintagel and King's Wood and the Maiden Lake. You would be astonished by the number of people who refuse to believe that you and your fellow knights even existed, deeming it all a pack of nonsense."

Rosalind beamed up at him. "But here you are! What more proof could anyone ask for?"

If it was possible for a ghost to pale, Sir Lancelot did. He backed away from her, retreating into the shadows, appearing about to take flight at once.

"No! Please. I'm a shy, retiring sort of—uh—spirit. If you reveal my existence, I shall be set upon by throngs of gaping fools. I do not care for large crowds of people."

"No, of course not," she soothed. "I didn't mean I was going to tell anyone. People would think me more mad than they already do. It is enough that I have proved to myself that you exist. No one else need know if you do not wish it."

"Indeed, I do not. Though I fear I have already betrayed myself to one other, the little lass who stumbled into this room awhile ago."

"Jenny. You did give her quite a fright." Rosalind gave a rueful chuckle. "But she did not get a very good look at you. I merely came to reassure her that there was nothing here, which is exactly what I shall tell her. But you must promise not to terrify her again."

"Most readily. It grieves me much that I did the first time. Is she all right?"

"Oh, quite. I left her tucked up in my shawl, blissfully eating sweetmeats. Chocolates, I find, are a great restorer of one's nerves."

Rosalind thought he smiled a little at that. She was gratified when he trusted her enough to step back into the circle of light. Considering the bold warrior he'd once been, she was much struck by his uncertainty, his aura of vulnerability.

She found his shyness rather endearing. She'd always been a little shy herself, especially around striking young men. That was why it had been so comfortable to marry Arthur, someone she had known from the earliest years of her childhood.

If Sir Lancelot had been flesh and blood, she would have been overwhelmed, unable to stammer out two words to him. So devastatingly handsome, such a powerful specimen of a man. Though not overly tall. She would have fit nicely beneath his chin. If he were still alive.

But the fact that he was a ghost left her curiously at ease in his presence. She rose to her feet, relieved to discover that her legs no longer trembled beneath her, even when he subjected her to a rather searching inspection with his fine dark eyes.

"Thou art this Jenny's guardian angel, then?" he asked.

"Hardly. She is my abigail." Rosalind laughed, then realized with a start that she had quite forgotten to introduce herself. What must he think of her?

"I have the most rag manners," she said. "I have not even told you who I am."

"I already know who thou must be."

"You do?"

"Verily, thou art the Lady of the Lake, the fair damsel who came from the castle beneath the shimmering waters of the Maiden Lake to bestow upon my liege Arthur the wondrous sword Excalibur."

"Oh, n-no," Rosalind cried in dismay at his error.

"But thou hast the eyes of that enchantress, jewel bright, and thou art clothed in white samite."

White samite? What was he talking about? Rosalind glanced down and to her horror realized she had been prancing around before him clad only in her nightgown. After her usual impulsive fashion, she had dashed out of her room, not even remembering to snatch up a wrapper or a shawl.

Flushing, she crossed her arms over her bosom in defensive fashion. Sir Lancelot must have sensed her embarrassment, for he averted his gaze. Whether alive or dead, the man was the soul of chivalry.

Rosalind inched back so that she was not quite so fully illuminated by the moonlight.

"This is not samite, only my linen nightdress," she explained, blushing furiously.

"Then thou art not my Lady of the Lake?"

"N-no, I'm sorry."

"And thou hast no magical sword for me?"

"I'm afraid not," she said regretfully. "Do you need one?"

"Thou hast no idea how much."

Rosalind puzzled over his wry remark for a moment, wondering why a ghost, even if he was Sir Lancelot, could still have need of a sword.

When she dared glance up at him again, she saw that his eyes twinkled, his lips curved in a smile. Comprehension flooded her at once.

"Oh! You never really thought—you were only teasing me!"

"Alas, I was. Forgive me, milady."

She tried to look indignant and failed. Her late husband had been such a good man, but so serious. She had rarely been teased, but she discovered she didn't mind so much.

Sir Lancelot's gaze was not mocking, but filled with an amusement that was almost tender, his eyes lit up by his smile. Any woman in the world would have pardoned Sir Lancelot for that smile. Rosalind certainly was not proof against it.

"Forgive me," he repeated again more gently.

"I do," she said. "But only because I am pleased to see that after so many centuries, you still have a sense of humor."

"It is about all I have left." His mind seemed to wander to some reflection that deeply saddened him, but he wrenched his attention back to Rosalind.

"So if thou will not be guardian angel, nor even my Lady of the Lake, then what may I call thee?"

"I am Lady Rosalind Carlyon." She started to curtsy and extend her hand, then pulled back, remembering the futility of such a gesture. "I am one of the guests of this inn."

"Traveling through Cornwall in search of legends."

"Yes. I know it must sound odd to you because I am sure ladies did not do such things in your day. They didn't have to look for legends. They lived them.

"Such a pursuit is not even normal for ladies in my time. But my own papa was an Arthurian scholar. I suppose I inherited the madness from him. To come to Cornwall, to actually see Tintagel, where Arthur was born, and find the magic lake where he received Excalibur. It's a journey I have always dreamed of making, ever since I was a little girl."

She added wistfully, "I just never imagined I would have to make it alone."

"Your father? He is . . . gone now?" Lancelot asked.

"They all are. Mama, Papa." She could not quite suppress the small catch in her voice. "And I lost my husband only last year."

"I am sorry," he said. "You . . . thou art full young to be a widow, all alone in the world. Hast thou no brothers or sisters?"

"No. I have no one." She ducked her head, fearing that she might be revealing more than she should.

Her husband had always worried that she was far too trusting of strangers, showing a lamentable tendency to confide in anyone who showed her the smallest kindness. He had begged her to be more circumspect. Did that warning also extend to sympathetic ghosts?

Rosalind felt something brush her as though a soft breeze stirred her hair. She glanced up to discover Sir Lancelot attempting to touch her, to comfort her. Quite impossible, of course.

Looking frustrated and helpless, he allowed his hand to drift back to his side. Her eyes locked with his. In that instant, Rosalind felt a jolt of recognition, a connection so strong, she was at a loss to explain it. A feeling that he understood her grief completely. Because he, too, knew what it was like to be all alone.

The longer that Rosalind gazed into his eyes, the more she was certain. Sir Lancelot du Lac was no stranger to her. She had known him all her life through the tales and legends. Known of his nobility, his courage, his chivalry. Known him as well as her own dear Arthur.

She could see that all her talk of having no one had saddened him, and she could not allow that. Sir Lancelot had enough sorrow of his own to bear.

Seeking to cheer him, Rosalind rallied behind a bright smile. "Of course I am not entirely alone," she said. "I keep forgetting Miranda and Clothilde."

"You speak of some pets, milady? Thy dogs perhaps?"

"No, my late husband's maiden aunts. I live with them now, although"— she grimaced—"it has not always proved the happiest of arrangements."

Lancelot frowned. "They are cruel to thee, milady?"

"Oh no. They are very worthy women, but they have strict ideas of how a widow should behave." Rosalind flushed guiltily as she confessed. "They have no idea of why I really took this journey. They think I have gone off very properly to visit one of my husband's elderly cousins residing in Conway. Which I shall do presently. I have only taken a slight detour en route."

"Thy secret is quite safe with me, milady," Sir Lancelot assured her solemnly, but his eyes twinkled.

"Thank you." Rosalind's mouth twisted into a rueful smile. "Otherwise I might find myself summoned back to Kent to resume knitting socks and distributing jars of calve's-foot jelly to the deserving poor.

"And I make such dreadful jelly. You have no notion how fast the poor folk in our village have learned to run when they see me coming with my basket."

Lancelot chuckled, the sound deep and warm, as charming as his smile. He needed to laugh. Rosalind felt certain of that. She was delighted to have amused him, but worried that she might have given the wrong impression.

"It is not that I dislike helping the poor," she hastened to add. "Only I should prefer to do something more useful than poisoning people with my jelly. I don't want you to think that I am callous or hard-hearted."

"As if I ever would, milady." He continued to smile, but his eyes rested tenderly on her. "I know full well thou could never be aught but kind."

Rosalind blushed, feeling absurdly pleased by the compliment.

"You have only just met me," she protested. "You could not possibly know if I am kind."

"Could I not?" He quoted softly, "Is she kind as she is fair? For beauty lives with kindness. Love doth to her eyes repair to help him of his blindness. And being help'd, inhabits there."

"That's lovely," Rosalind said, though she was not certain if she meant the verse or the rich timbre of his voice. It drifted over her warm as a caress, leaving her oddly breathless.

"That's from Shakespeare, isn't it? I recognize—" She broke off, confusion flooding her. "But Shakespeare was not even born until long after you— you—how could *you* possibly know his work?"

The question appeared to discompose Lancelot for a moment. Then he said, "Oh, I—I have drifted through many places and times since my death. I missed the troubadours of Camelot so greatly that I frequently hovered near The Globe, absorbing the poetry of this bard you call Shakespeare."

"Then you have not always"—Rosalind hesitated, fearing he might be offended by the word "haunted"—"you have not always *lingered* in Cornwall?"

"Ah, no, milady. I fear I have ever been a most restless spirit. Just a lost soul doomed to rove the earth forever."

His words troubled her, filled her mind with images of him wandering through the ages, heartsore, weary, never able to find peace.

"Doomed?" she asked. "But why?"

"As atonement for my sins, I suppose."

"You were the bravest of Arthur's knights. I cannot believe you did anything that would merit a punishment as dreadful as this. What sin did you commit?"

"Far too many. The worst being that I fell in love with the wrong woman."

"Oh . . ."

He had to mean Guinevere, his ill-fated passion for King Arthur's beautiful queen. It was the most romantic and tragic tale Rosalind had ever heard. She had pored over the story many times, had wondered what it would be like to be swept away by such tempestuous emotion.

Of course she had loved her own husband, loved Arthur for as long as she could remember. But that was not exactly the same as falling *in* love, tumbling head over ears at first sight.

"To know a passion such as that," she mused aloud, "so powerful and strong it burns bright throughout the ages—how could such a love ever be wrong?"

"Very easily," Lancelot said bitterly. "When such passion is purchased at the price of one's honor, the betrayal of another man by bedding his wife."

"But you were a man in love. Surely your reason was overcome—"

"I was an adulterer! And that's the plain ugly truth of the matter."

The harshness of his voice caused Rosalind to flinch from him. He added more quietly, "A man always has a choice, milady. And when he makes the wrong one, he must suffer the consequences. Unfortunately the innocent suffer along with him. And that is the true sin that condemns him forever."

His words left Rosalind a little bewildered, with only one thing clear to her, the degree of pain she saw buried in his eyes. Whatever sins he spoke of, no judgment of heaven could condemn him more cruelly than Sir Lancelot condemned himself.

He fell silent. Lost in his own black thoughts, he seemed to forget she was there. Rosalind stood aside, not knowing what to say by way of comfort, acutely feeling her ignorance. Sin, passion, the torment of regret. She had no more experience of such things than if she had been a novitiate at a convent.

Lancelot said darkly, "And as if I had not committed enough folly for one lifetime, now I needs must lose that infernal sword."

Rosalind had been trying to remain unobtrusive, but her ears pricked up at this last remark. "A sword?" she repeated in astonishment. "Then you truly are looking for one? You were not jesting about that?"

"No. How I wish to God I were."

There was only one fabled sword that Rosalind had ever heard tell of. "Surely you cannot be speaking of *Excalibur*?" She pronounced the very name with awe.

"What? Oh ... er, yes. Excalibur," he replied distractedly.

"But I thought when King Arthur died, the sword was returned to the waters of the lake."

"I wish that's where the thing was. Maybe if the blade was sunk back to the bottom, I would finally know some peace. But there will be precious little rest for me until I find that blasted sword."

Rosalind pressed her hands to her brow, feeling as though all of this was beginning to get a bit much, even for her to absorb.

"I don't understand at all," she said. "What were you doing with Excalibur?"

"I am supposed to be the guardian of the sword until—until the day my liege returns. But I allowed myself to be set upon by a thief. Now the sword has fallen into the hands of who knows what sort of villain, and I have to get it back."

This was an aspect of the legend Rosalind had never come across. But before she could question him further, Sir Lancelot's attention focused sharply elsewhere.

He stared in the direction of the window, an expression of horror chasing across his features.

"Damnation!" he said.

"What is it?" Rosalind asked uneasily, glancing that way herself. But she remarked nothing beyond the fact that the sky had begun to lighten with the first streaks of dawn.

He twisted back to her, apologizing for having cursed in her presence. "I must leave thee, fair lady."

"Oh no!" she cried. "There is still so much I need to ask you. Must you go so soon?"

"I fear I must. The sun has nigh arisen, and it could be dangerous for me to be drifting abroad in the daylight. Even fatal."

Fatal? Rosalind blinked in astonishment. How much more fatal could it be? The man was already dead.

But all thought of that was swept aside as he hovered near the window, preparing to depart. "I thank thee for thy kindness. I would beg to salute thee properly, milady but . . ." He smiled sadly. "All I can do is bid thee farewell."

Rosalind darted forward anxiously. "Oh, please. Wait! You must at least tell me. Will I ever—"

But he was already fading, dissolving through the window, his eyes shimmering with regret.

"—ever see you again?" Rosalind finished in a small voice. She walked toward the window and peered out for a last glimpse of him. Her heart quickened as she thought she detected a movement, a passing shadow set against the pearly gray sky. But it turned out to be no more than a flock of gulls wheeling seaward.

Sir Lancelot was gone.

She would likely never see him again. The thought brought a curious ache to her heart. But as the sun broke over the horizon, dispelling night and all its mystery, Rosalind could not help but doubt her own senses.

Perhaps she had only been dreaming, walking abroad in her sleep. Or her too vivid imagination had once more regained command of her.

The rich fantasy life she had led as a child had often worried her parents, even Papa. For him the study of the Arthurian legends had been an intellectual exercise. But to Rosalind . . .

Tonight was not the first time she had entertained a vision of Sir Lancelot. She had frequently laid out her miniature cups and saucers in the garden, serving up tea to Lancelot, Sir Bedivere, and Sir Gawain, her favorites among the Round Table knights, sharing her cake with them on Tuesdays. Wednesdays, the fairies came calling. And Fridays had always been reserved for the little family of gnomes that lived beneath the hedgerows.

Rosalind smiled regretfully at the memory. She had dallied too much perhaps in the realms of her own fancy. But what else was a little girl supposed to do? She had no one to play with, often retreating into her imagination out of sheer loneliness.

Was that what she had done tonight—felt so desperately alone that she had once more resurrected Sir Lancelot to keep her company? But he was far different from the knight of her childhood, a vague figure, tall and noble, more like a charming older brother.

The being that she had recently conjured up was not likely to arouse sisterly feelings in any woman's breast. Not with those handsome features, broad shoulders, and sinewy arms. The generous mouth, sensual and sensitive. The changeable dark eyes, one moment bold with laughter, the next soft with regret. The deep-timbred voice that both teased and caressed.

Could even her imagination be that good? Rosalind reflected. And besides ... Jenny had seen him, too.

Jenny!

"Oh, dear lord," Rosalind murmured as remembrance shafted through her. She had left the girl alone all this time, waiting for her. If Rosalind did not want to be caught up in a welter of cumbersome explanations, she had better get belowstairs posthaste.

Whirling about, Rosalind darted away from the window, only to strike her bare toes up against something hard. She stifled a gasp of pain and stumbled, hopping about on one foot until she found a chair to sag down upon.

Raising up her foot, she examined the throbbing member, gingerly wiggling her big toe. It did not appear broken, but she wagered it would be black and blue by the morrow. She glanced reproachfully down at the object that had tripped her—a floorboard so loose, it had actually come dislodged. She really ought to have a discussion with Mr. Braggs about the sad condition of his storeroom. But then that would involve an awkward accounting of what she had been doing here in the first place.

Rosalind knelt to replace the board when the gleam of something beneath caught her eye. She squinted closer, discovering that the entire board shifted rather easily, exposing a space beneath the floor.

A hiding place for ...

Rosalind's breath snagged in her throat. She rocked back on her heels, staring, dazed by the object she had uncovered.

A sword of unsurpassed beauty with a hilt of finely wrought gold, a dazzling crystal mounted into the pommel. For long moments, she knelt there not daring even to touch the weapon.

With shaking fingers, Rosalind reached for the hilt and tugged the sword from its place of concealment. Not an easy task, for the blade was heavy, a magnificent length of steel forged from fables and dreams, in a time long ago and a place far away.

Rosalind raised the weapon to the light, the brilliance of the crystal almost blinding her, sparking a rainbow shower across the dark wood walls. Her heart thundered with a feeling of awe and triumph.

She was now certain she had not imagined one moment of this magical night, not one precious second she had spent in the company of Sir Lancelot du Lac. It had all been wondrously real. She *had* seen him, and she was fully confident she would see him again because she had found it. She had found what he was looking for.

Excalibur.

CHAPTER TWO

*L*ance was in trouble.

The realization shot through Val St. Leger like a blaze of gunfire, startling him awake. He sat bolt upright in his bed, heart pounding, caught somewhere in the shadowy world between consciousness and sleep. With trembling fingers, he raked back his dark curling hair from eyes creased with pain and care that went well beyond his twenty-seven years.

Staring about him, he sought to make sense of his situation, sprawled on top of the counterpane, sweating with fear, clad in his breeches and shirt. His bleary-eyed gaze fell upon a trail of papers and books scattered from bed to carpet to nightstand, where the remains of a burned-out candle pooled over a silver holder in a congealed lump of wax.

He'd done it again, Val realized. Stayed up too late poring over his studies until he'd fallen asleep, only to be awakened by a . . . nightmare? No, more of an alarming sense that Lance was in some kind of danger.

An irrational thought because he had no reason to suppose that Lance was not burrowed deep beneath his sheets, sleeping off whatever excesses he had indulged at the Midsummer's Eve fair. By all rights, Val should have gone with his brother, but he did not particularly care for the company Lance chose to keep these days.

He knew Lance had likely been carousing with that Rafe Mortmain again. The thought alone was enough to render Val uneasy. Somehow he feared that Lance wasn't back safe in his bed. It was only a feeling, but he was too much of a St. Leger to ignore it. His intuitions regarding his twin had never been wrong before.

Swinging his legs over the side of the bed, he winced at the stab of pain behind his right knee. He groped for his cane and hobbled off a few steps, trying to work some of the stiffness out of the joint before he limped from the room.

The hall beyond his chamber appeared gray and misty in the early morning stillness. None of the household were even up yet and stirring. Val heard nothing beyond the soft click of his cane and the anxious hitch of his own breathing as he made his way toward the bedchamber of his older brother.

Older only in the sense that he and Lance were separated by the span of a day. Lance had charged into the world seconds before the stroke of midnight, while Val had lingered, not putting in his appearance until the next morning.

Lance had often tormented him about that, jesting that Val was so busy daydreaming, even in their mother's womb, that he couldn't manage to be born on time.

But that had been back in the days when there had been a great deal of jesting between him and his brother, Val reflected sadly. Back before Lance's restless urges had taken him so far from Castle Leger, before the injury that had left Val crippled in one leg. Now his cane, light and slender as it was, seemed to cast a long shadow between them.

Leaning heavily on the ivory-handled walking stick, Val knocked on Lance's door. When there was no response, he rapped again, louder this time.

"Lance?" he called, praying to be rewarded with a curse, Lance's growl to get the devil away and let him sleep.

But there was nothing. Only the silence that sharpened Val's intuition that something was wrong, driving it deeper into his heart.

He reached for the doorknob, knowing that Lance would not welcome either his concern or his intrusion. The thought hurt worse than his throbbing knee, but it did not deter him.

Shoving open the door, he crept inside. Morning didn't seem to have reached Lance's room yet, the heavy crimson-and-gold draperies shutting out most of the light. Adjusting his eyes to the semidarkness, he looked about for any sign that his brother had come home last night, anything that would reassure him.

But all the evidence he needed lay waiting on the four-poster bed, and the sight was far from reassuring. Val's breath caught in his throat as he shuffled forward to peer down at the figure stretched out on the mattress.

Lance's dark hair fanned across the pillow, his arms folded across his chest, his body encased in what appeared to be a black tunic and shirt of chain mail. But it wasn't the strangeness of his brother's attire that caused Val's heart to still.

It was the way Lance lay there, so cursed pale. Not moving, not breathing, looking for all the world like a stone effigy carved upon some medieval knight's tomb. Looking exactly like he was . . . dead.

This was not the first time he had ever seen his brother in this trancelike state, but it never failed to alarm him. Val had done extensive studies on the St. Leger family, the supernatural talents that had cropped up generation after generation. A strange history of diviners, fortune-tellers, mind readers, and even unusually gifted healers like Val himself.

But Val had never come across any power that awed or terrified him more than this one of Lance's, this ability to separate body from soul, to send the spirit soaring out into the night while flesh, bone, and sinew remained behind.

Night drifting Lance had always called it. Dangerous was Val's term for it because no one knew how long Lance could safely maintain such a separation or even what would happen if Lance was ever caught with his spirit abroad in the full light of day.

Hoping that the morning was not as advanced as he supposed, Val stumped to the window. Twitching aside the curtains, he saw the sun hovering just below the horizon, the first rays of light beginning to streak across the garden below.

His heart sickened with dread, Val limped back to his brother's bedside. Bending down, he caught up one of Lance's hands.

Sweet lord! The fingers already felt stiff and cold, colder than Val had ever known any living flesh to be. He couldn't begin to guess how long Lance had been gone this time. Too long, Val feared, judging from the chilled feel of his skin.

"Damn it, Lance. Not even you can be this reckless. Get back here. Now!" Val muttered, chafing his brother's hand, trying to infuse some of his own heat into those icy fingers.

He glanced about him, desperate for something else to do. More blankets perhaps. If he piled enough on Lance, maybe he could retain what warmth remained in his brother's body until he returned.

And if he did not . . .

Val refused even to consider that possibility. Moving over to the wardrobe, he began to rummage for a heavy cloak or anything that he could find. Caught up in his task, he never noticed the curtains stir as though shifted by a light breeze, or the ghostlike form that shimmered into the room.

For one brief moment, Lance St. Leger hovered over his bed, experiencing the eerie sensation of staring down at his own body. He hesitated, bracing himself. The rejoining was never pleasant, and he had a strong presentiment it was going to be worse than usual this time.

He was right.

As he cast himself downward, it felt like striking a sheet of ice, his body rigid and unwelcoming. He strained with all the force of his will until the ice cracked, plunging him into a chilling river of darkness.

He remained mercifully numb for several seconds before he became aware of his hands and his feet, snapping around him like manacles, holding his restless spirit fast. The sensation spread up his legs, over his thighs, along his arms, across his shoulders, each limb binding him ever tighter until he felt entombed.

There was no air. He couldn't breathe. Panic clawed at Lance, and he writhed, struggling against the suffocating confines of his own flesh. His heart, which had been barely beating, kicked into motion with a furious thud. His entire body jerked spasmodically as his lungs filled with air.

He sank back against the mattress, drawing in grateful breaths. Slowly, his heart resumed its steady rhythm, returning warmth to his chilled frame.

Damn! That had been a narrow escape, but he was back. Safe in his own skin, although it was a mixed blessing as Lance became aware of sensations he'd escaped when he had shed his all too human flesh hours before. The sour smell of his own sweat. The sore muscles protesting the weight of the blasted armor. The dull headache left from that blow he'd taken down on the beach. He tried to hold himself very still, not wanting to move, to even think.

An impossibility because he couldn't help reflecting on the night he'd just passed. A strange one, even by St. Leger standards. Getting attacked and robbed near his own village, drifting all over in search of the culprit, trying to recover that wretched sword. And to top it all off, being mistaken for the ghost of Sir Lancelot du Lac.

That last memory was the only one he found pleasant enough to dwell upon, his meeting with the lady Rosalind. Between the two of them, he questioned who had been the more startled by their encounter. He had been, he believed. She had appeared to glide out of a ring of candlelight, walking straight through him with a sense of innocence and wonder such as he had not felt for a long time. And he had *felt* it, he who never felt any sort of physical sensation when he was in his drifting state.

He could hardly be blamed for the first thought that had popped into his head, that he'd stumbled upon a spirit himself. For what kind of mortal woman went prowling about a strange inn in the dead of night, looking for ghosts? One that was either amazingly brave or completely mad.

He'd come to the conclusion that Rosalind Carlyon must be a bit of both. After she'd blundered into him, she hadn't run off shrieking as any sane person would. No, she had lingered until dawn, engaging him in the most earnest conversation.

Quite mad. But if the lady was, then what did that make him? He had lingered as well, and at the peril of his own life, quite forgetting the time, that he should have spent those last precious moments of darkness searching for the sword.

It was as though the woman had cast a spell upon him, softening the hard edges of his soul. He had felt unusually gentle toward her, moved by the hint of sadness behind her smile, the plight of one widowed far too young. A mere slip of a girl in her white linen nightgown and bare feet. She had seemed badly in need of a champion, and he had enjoyed playing the hero for her, too much perhaps. It had all started out as a mere expedient, a way to avoid awkward explanations for who and what he was. But he'd gotten a trifle carried away.

Lance winced at the memory of the nonsense he'd spun out for Rosalind. About being doomed to wander the earth in atonement for his sins. The great wrong he had done by loving another man's wife, damaging his honor beyond all repair.

Nonsense that had skimmed uncomfortably close to truth until he was no longer certain whom he'd been talking about, Lancelot du Lac or Lance St. Leger. He had talked a great deal too much, raking up memories he was determined to forget. Now, safely back in his own bed, he had no idea what the devil had come over him.

Maybe it was doubly dangerous going night drifting after he'd taken such a whack to the head. All he wanted to do with his aching muscles and throbbing skull was lie there and die quietly.

But that privilege was clearly going to be denied him, for he realized he was not alone in the room. A floorboard creaked by his bed.

Someone . . . someone was actually tucking him in, dragging some heavy garment over him all the way up to his chin. Forcing his eyes to half-mast, Lance squinted through the thickness of his lashes at the person bending over him.

He focused on a face not identical but similar to his own. The same hawklike nose, only straighter, the same deep brown eyes, only gentler, the same square jaw except for the faint indentation in the chin. A leaner, more careworn version of himself.

Val.

Lance had thought it could not be possible for him to feel any more wretched than he already did. He was wrong. With his brother's presence, any hope of keeping the folly of this latest escapade to himself faded to nothing.

Suppressing a groan, Lance shut his eyes tight. The movement, slight as it was, must have been enough to draw his brother's attention, for Val leaned closer, whispering, "Lance? Are you there? Lance? Answer me!"

Lance popped his eyes open, wincing at the full stab of daylight.

"Yes, I'm here," he growled. "There's no damned need to shout."

Val's pale features flooded with relief. "Thank God. You made it back. You're all right."

That was entirely a matter of opinion, Lance thought dourly. He started to demand what Val was doing creeping about his room at such an hour, but the answer was all too evident from the rumpled state of Val's clothing, the haggard look on his face.

His brother had obviously been sitting up with him for half the night, maintaining a sleepless vigil over Lance while he drifted. How the blazes did Val even know he had gone?

Another stupid question. Lance gave a disgruntled sigh. Of course Val knew when he was in any kind of trouble. He always did.

Trembling from the force of his relief, Val dragged a shaky hand back through his mass of wavy black hair. "I thought you'd really done it this time. Turned yourself into a permanent ghost. For one awful moment, I really feared you were—were—"

"Dead?" Lance supplied when his brother couldn't bring himself to say the word. He struggled up onto one elbow, shoving aside the fur-trimmed greatcoat Val had draped over him. "So what were you planning to do with this? Lay me out in it? I would have preferred my black riding cloak. It would go better with the armor, don't you think?"

"Don't jest, Lance. This is nothing to laugh about."

"Do I look as though I'm laughing?" Lance hauled himself to a sitting position and swung his legs over the side of the bed, grimacing at the fresh pain that shot up his spine. Lord! He felt like he'd been sleeping on a bed of nails.

Pressing one hand to the small of his back, he grumbled, "Remind me next time I put myself into a trance, not to do it wearing chain mail."

"Why did you do it at all?"

"Wear the chain mail? If you had bothered to attend the fair, you would have known there was supposed to be this mock tournament—"

"Blast it, Lance!" A look of reproach flashed in Val's eyes. "You know what I meant. Why were you drifting? You weren't even careful to get back before daybreak. Do you have any idea how close you cut it this time?"

He limped to the window and flung the curtain open wider. Lance cursed, flinging up one hand to shield his eyes from the burst of light, a little disturbed himself to see how far the sunrise had advanced.

"Damn," he murmured. "I really did linger too long talking to my Lady of the Lake."

"W-what?"

"The Lady of the Lake," he repeated, smiling in spite of his misery, Rosalind's memory dancing across his mind. "A most wondrous enchantress with hair spun from a braid of moonlight and eyes the color of heaven. She cast a spell on me."

His voice softened. His expression must have undergone some odd change as well, for Val stared at him as though he'd lost his mind.

His brother stumped anxiously toward him. "Lance, maybe you'd better lie back down. You don't seem quite yourself."

"I'm fine." Lance said, rubbing his brow. "Just a little dizzy from sitting up too fast."

When Val continued to hover over him with an expression of deep concern, Lance sought to explain Rosalind in more rational terms, perhaps to himself as well.

"There was this pretty young widow stopping over at the Dragon's Fire. When I was out drifting, we sort of . . . bumped into each other."

"An outsider caught you night drifting?"

"Yes, but it's all right. She thought I was the ghost of Sir Lancelot du Lac."

"Why would she think a thing like that?"

"Most likely because I told her I was."

Val's frown deepened. The idea of lying for any reason was incomprehensible to Lance's honest brother.

"So you were using your power to woo this woman?" he asked in a troubled tone.

"What a delicate way of putting it," Lance mocked. "Do you mean was I planning to seduce her?"

He paused, considering the possibility himself. It would certainly go a long way to explain the depth of his attraction. And yet the thought of bed games and his lady Rosalind . . . it almost seemed profane.

"No," Lance admitted at last. "I wasn't seeking some clever ploy to lure her between the sheets. She wasn't that sort of lady. She was more your kind."

"Mine?" Val echoed.

"Yes, the maiden fair that you ride out to slay dragons for and return to kneel in homage at her feet."

Lance was amused to see a hint of red creep across his solemn brother's high cheekbones.

"And most certainly the kind of lady who should be kept far away from a lying rogue like me," Lance concluded. "Which she will be. The lovely widow will continue on her journey today, none the worse for my little jest, and I shall never see her again."

The thought sent an unexpected pang through him. But Lance was quick to thrust the emotion aside. He dragged himself to his feet and was heartened to discover that he could stand without pitching forward onto his face.

Brushing past Val, he fought his way out of the chain mail. An arduous and painful process, but when the heavy shirt dropped to the carpet, Lance issued a groan of pure relief. Even his headache had subsided to a faint throb, and he began to feel as though he might want to live after all.

If he could only get rid of Val.

But his brother threatened to become a permanent fixture in his bedchamber. Rooted to the spot, resting both hands on his cane, Val studied him with a thoughtful intensity Lance found damned uncomfortable.

"And that was your only reason for drifting again?" he asked. "To play a jest on this poor unsuspecting lady?"

"What other reason could there possibly be?" Lance replied, but he could tell from Val's grave expression he wasn't fooled.

Val knew perfectly well that something else was wrong. Lance had always been good at dissembling, evading, handing out bags of moonshine with a charming smile. But it never worked with Val, and he wondered why he even bothered to try.

That was the trouble with a man who knew you literally from the womb, Lance thought as he sank back down on the edge of the bed to tug off his boots.

He managed to get one off. Val simply stood there, silent, patient, waiting.

Lance flung the boot to the carpet with a resigned sigh. "Fine! If you must know, I went drifting because it seemed the best way to search for something I lost."

"What could you possibly have lost that would be worth risking your life for?"

"The St. Leger sword."

Val's mouth fell open. "Not—not Prospero's sword?" he faltered. "The one with the crystal in the hilt?"

"The very one."

As Val sagged down into the nearest chair he could find, Lance proceeded to relate the circumstances of the entire evening, not sparing himself in the process: his own stupidity in using the valuable weapon as a costume prop, flashing it about the village square as though the ages-old sword were some tinker's trinket, drinking far too much ale at the Dragon's Fire Inn, weaving his way alone down the darkened beach, allowing himself to be surprised and taken down without even putting up a fight.

He told his story in a flat indifferent tone, all the while reflecting that he had been trying for years to destroy his brother's persistent faith in him. This should finally do it. For there was no one more steeped in the legends and history of the St. Leger family than Val was. He set a far higher value on that sword than Lance ever could.

And yet as he concluded his tale, Lance read no sign of condemnation in Val's features. "My God, Lance," he breathed. "You could have been killed."

He had lost the St. Leger sword, and that was all Val was worried about? Lance scowled at his brother, torn between annoyance and amazement.

"That would have been no great loss, I assure you," he said. "Then you could have inherited Castle Leger."

"I don't want to inherit Castle Leger," Val replied quietly.

"What a coincidence. Neither do I." Lance removed his other boot with a savage tug and slammed it down. Ever since he'd regained consciousness to find that sword gone, he'd been calling himself every kind of blockhead imaginable. It would have been a relief to have someone else take up the task.

But his brother was not about to oblige him. Val didn't even look angry.

"You said you didn't get a good look at the man who attacked you?" he asked.

"No, I was too drunk," Lance said bluntly. "I would have been lucky to recognize my own hand if I'd held it in front of my face."

"Do you think it could have been one of those smugglers that have been operating off the coast of late?"

"Smugglers don't usually ply their trade under a full moon and with a fair going on within shouting distance. No, this was nothing but a common footpad."

"Footpads in our village," Val mused with a doleful shake of his head. "Thieves operating within the boundary of St. Leger lands. We never had anything like that happen before—before—"

Val hesitated with an uneasy glance in Lance's direction, but Lance was sure he understood his brother well enough.

"Before Father went away?" he finished with a hard edge to his voice. "Before I was left in charge here?"

"No! I didn't mean anything like that. But I'm afraid what I did mean you will like even less."

He fretted with his cane handle before continuing, "I was going to say that we never seemed to have much trouble here before . . . before Rafe Mortmain's return."

Lance stared at his brother, dumbfounded. "Rafe? What's Rafe got to do with any of this?"

"Nothing I hope. I just can't help wondering . . . where was he when all of this was going on last night?"

"I don't know. We parted company early in the evening. Rafe had to ride out on patrol. He received some sort of tip that—" Lance broke off, frowning at the implications of his brother's question. "You can't think that Rafe had anything to do with the attack on me. Good Lord! The man is a customs officer, charged with protecting the coast."

"Still . . . Rafe's involvement is a possibility that has to be considered," Val returned gravely.

"I'll be damned if it does! What the devil would Rafe Mortmain want with my sword?"

"Everyone knows the St. Leger sword is invested with some sort of unusual power. And power is something the Mortmains have always coveted."

"Bloody nonsense," Lance growled. He shot to his feet, slapping his thigh with a gesture of pure disgust. "We're not going to play this game, Val."

"What game?" his brother asked, clearly bewildered.

"The favorite St. Leger pastime for generations. When something goes wrong, let's find a Mortmain to blame it on."

"There is a good reason for that. If you'd ever studied the history between our two families, as I have—"

"I have no interest in ancient history."

"Not so ancient," Val reminded him. "Rafe's own mother once plotted to murder both our parents."

"And the woman paid for it with her own life," Lance said impatiently. "That all happened long before either of us was even born, and Rafe was only a child himself. I assure you he feels no great love for Evelyn Mortmain either. The woman abandoned him in Paris."

"Or so he says," Val murmured.

"And," Lance went on, tersely ignoring the interruption, "I don't believe either of our parents ever perceived Rafe as a threat. They allowed him to live with us that one summer he was sixteen."

"Until you almost drowned in the Maiden Lake."

"That was an accident!" Lance said. "How many times do I have to tell people that? I recall quite clearly that it was my own fault that I slipped and fell in. It was Rafe who pulled me back to safety. He saved my life that day."

"It seemed to me that he only dived in to do so when Father and I rode into sight."

"Then your memory is greatly at fault like everyone else's around here, too blasted ready to suspect the man of any crime simply because of his family's reputation.

"Bad 'cess to all Mortmains!" Lance sneered out the St. Leger family toast for generations. "Well, excuse me if I don't raise my glass. I have only ever known one Mortmain, and he happens to be my friend."

"Friends shouldn't bring out the worst in each other," Val persisted.

"And exactly what the devil is that supposed to mean?"

Val examined the tip of his cane, looking sad and thoughtful. "Only that I have observed there is a darkness in Rafe Mortmain, and he seems to bring that darkness out in others. I can scarce explain it, but you are different in his company somehow. More hardened, more cynical, more reckless."

Lance shook his head, finding his brother completely unbelievable.

"When are you going to get it through that hard head of yours?" he demanded harshly. "No one influences me. If I act like an irresponsible rake when I'm with Rafe, it's because that's what I bloody well am."

Striding over to his wardrobe, Lance tore off the remains of his sweat-stained costume, the chill morning air in his room cooling his bared flesh but not his temper.

As he wrenched open the wardrobe door, flinging garments about until he found his dressing gown, he wasn't entirely sure why he was so blasted angry: because Val was attempting to put doubts in his mind about a man he liked and admired, or because he'd offered Val proof time and time again of his own worthlessness and yet his brother was still at it. Always determined to forgive him, make excuses for him, find someone else to blame his folly on.

Lance shrugged himself into the robe, knotting the belt with a savage tug. Behind him, he heard Val struggle to his feet.

"I'm sorry, Lance," he said quietly.

Oh, great. Now, as usual, Val was apologizing to him. Lance gritted his teeth.

"You are right, of course," Val continued. "I should be ashamed of suspecting a man merely because of the misdeeds of his ancestors. I'm sure there are many far more likely suspects we should be questioning."

Lance whipped around to glare at his brother. "What do you mean, *we?*"

"Naturally, I assumed—"

"You assumed wrong." Lance interrupted, slamming the wardrobe door shut with a brutal kick. "Every time I get myself into some sort of trouble, I don't need you charging to the rescue."

"I'm not. I only—"

"Nor do I need you wearing yourself to a shadow, mounting sleepless vigils at my bedside like some overprotective nursemaid!"

"I didn't," Val protested. "Lance, I only want to help."

"I think you've helped me more than enough for one lifetime, *brother,* don't you?" He dropped his gaze significantly toward Val's injured leg.

Val flinched. He limped over to the window, but not swiftly enough to conceal the flash of hurt in his eyes. Then again, it was so easy to hurt Val. There was practically no art to it.

As his brother gazed down at the garden below, the sunlight played across Val's tired countenance, exposing every pain-etched furrow that marred his youthful features.

Lance thought he could almost count every one of those lines he was responsible for. Damn near all of them.

A man always has a choice, milady. And when he makes the wrong one, he must suffer the consequences. Unfortunately the innocent suffer along with him. . . .

The words Lance had spoken to Rosalind came back to haunt him. He told her he had to wander the earth to pay for his sins. But in reality, he didn't have to wander very far.

Merely being around Val was like being forced to wear a hair shirt. Lance's anger melted away, the all too familiar guilt taking its place, chafing him raw. He wondered for perhaps the millionth time what had ever possessed him to come back here.

Perhaps because after the victory at Waterloo, the final defeat of Bonaparte, Lance had simply run out of excuses for remaining with the army and staying away from home. As the oldest son and heir, it had been more than time for Lance to cease his rambling, to settle at Castle Leger and learn to assume the responsibilities that would one day be his, to become the kind of man his entire family presumed him to be, not the kind of man that he was. And there was such a damnably wide gulf between the two.

He stalked over to the pitcher and basin perched on the washstand, pouring out some cold water to dash against his face, as though he could somehow cleanse his guilt away and his ill humor along with it.

The icy liquid stung his bare skin awake, and he felt better for it—until he caught a glimpse of himself in the small mirror mounted above the washstand.

Lance grimaced, wondering what his Lady of the Lake would think if she could see her bold Sir Lancelot now in his all too human form: badly in want of a bath and a shave, his hair a disordered tangle, dark shadows beneath his eyes, that hard ugly set to his mouth.

A dishonored knight.

He didn't know why such a foolish phrase should pop into his head, but it suited him amazingly well.

He toweled his face dry, slicking the damp ends of his hair back before coming about to deal with his brother. He still wanted nothing so much as to tell Val to get out and leave him alone.

Instead he heard himself saying gruffly, "Look, Val. Don't worry about the sword. I'll find the damned thing even if I have to ride to hell and back."

Val gave a sad smile. "I know you will."

"So you don't need to exhaust yourself worrying about it . . . or me. You should go back to bed, try to get some sleep. You look worse than I do, which is saying a lot."

"Yes, it is," Val agreed with a weak laugh. "But I want you to understand one thing. I didn't 'wear myself to a shadow,' as you put it, keeping watch over you while you drifted. I only came into your room a short while ago. There was another reason I was up most of the night."

Lance was relieved to hear it. It eased a little of the guilt he felt, although he groused, "Not your infernal books again. I know Mama always hoped to make at least one of us a scholar, but she wouldn't want you killing yourself over some musty old volume either."

"I know that, but it's so aggravating. I've been working so hard to compile a complete history of our family, hoping to have it done before Father and Mother return." Val limped off a few steps, the movement conveying his frustration. He waxed passionate on few subjects, but this was one of them.

"I've gone through every archive, every record, every history of Cornwall I can find and yet—" He checked himself, casting an apologetic look at Lance. "Well, I know you're not interested."

"That's never stopped you before."

Val gave a sheepish laugh. "No, I suppose it hasn't." He sighed and continued, "It's that blasted Prospero. How can I complete a history of the St. Legers when I can find so little information about the man who supposedly founded our family? It's as though practically every mention of him has been deliberately erased."

"It probably has been." Lance shrugged. "A knight who was rumored to have been a sorcerer, reckless, making ill use of his power, seducing every woman within sight. Hellfire, he sounds a lot like me. They'll likely expunge my name after I'm dead, too."

"Not if I can help it," Val retorted. "Seriously, Lance, don't you ever wonder what kind of man could have spawned a family as unusual as ours? What was his life really like? Was he happy?"

"He was burned at the stake. That would tend to make a man damned unhappy."

"I mean *before* that. For all the intelligence, all the power he was supposed to have possessed, was he content? Out of all those women he was said to have had, was there never one that meant more to him than the others? If only Mama hadn't driven his spirit away, I could have asked him."

That was but another of his family's many legends, Lance thought wryly, that Prospero's ghost had once haunted the old keep. He had supposedly been exorcised, not by Lance's formidable father, but by his petite flame-haired mother. Madeline St. Leger was a practical woman, holding firm sway over one fierce husband and five unruly children. She was not the sort to tolerate the peace of her home being disrupted by the spirit of a mischievous sorcerer.

Lance folded his arms across his chest, regarding his earnest brother with amusement. "Even if Prospero's ghost was still hanging about, what do you think he'd do? Invite you to crack a bottle of port while he discussed his amours with you?"

"I suppose not," Val conceded. "But it would please me to know that he eventually found someone. That he didn't end up dying embittered . . . alone."

Lance couldn't begin to imagine why Val should even care, but this was a side of his brother he'd never fully understood. "You're an incurable romantic. That's what comes of a man being born on St. Valentine's Day."

"Perhaps it is. I fear I've been thinking too much lately about matters such as—"

Val's eyes skittered away from Lance, staring fixedly down at the carpet in a way that aroused Lance's curiosity. It wasn't like Val to be evasive or secretive about anything.

"Thinking about matters such as what?" he prodded.

"Oh . . . about being alone. Being in love." He avoided looking at Lance, toying with the tip of his cane for so long, it began to work on Lance's nerves.

He was on the verge of closing his hand over Val's to still his infernal fidgeting when Val finally confessed, "It's not the books that have been keeping me awake at night, Lance. It's something else. I think my time has come."

"Your time for what?"

Val flushed bright red. "To take a wife."

Lance stared at him. Always so absorbed with his books, his writings, the medical studies he was engaged in with the local doctor, Marius St. Leger, Val had never even evinced any interest in the ladies. Not in that way. In fact, there were even times when Lance wondered if his saintly brother might not still be a virgin.

Squirming with embarrassment, Val went on, "You remember the discussion Father had with us that one autumn day in his study? About marriage. And—and women."

"Vaguely. Since I already knew all about the fairer sex, I fear I paid little attention."

"I did. And I remember well what he said about how a St. Leger male knows when his time has come to mate. The sleepless nights, the fire in the blood, the restlessness, the almost unbearable feeling of longing . . . I have all those symptoms, Lance."

Lance rolled his eyes. From the misery in his face, Val might have been speaking of some fatal disease. And as for these so-called symptoms of his, they weren't any different from what Lance himself had lately.

Lance stiffened, oddly disquieted by the unexpected comparison. He was quick to dismiss it, resting his hand on Val's shoulder with a condescending smile.

"Listen, little brother, all you need is a quick trip down the beach. I know this delectable fisherman's daughter—"

"That's not what I need, Lance," Val said tersely. "I need a proper bride."

"All right!" Lance flung up his hands, backing off. For all his gentleness, Val could be cursed stubborn when he took a notion into his head.

"What lady do you have in mind?" Lance asked.

Val looked shocked that he could even ask such a thing. "You know that isn't for me to decide."

"If not you, then who—" Lance stopped as he gazed deep into his brother's earnest eyes, realizing his meaning. Lance cringed.

"Oh no," he said. "Val, please . . . *please* tell me you are not thinking of consulting the Bride Finder."

"I already have."

When Lance groaned, Val bristled defensively. "You know I have no other choice, Lance. This is one aspect of our family traditions even you have to understand."

"Oh, yes, I'm familiar enough with the legend," Lance muttered, then began to recite in mock imitation of a schoolboy reeling off his lesson: "All St. Legers are considered too odd or too stupid to be entrusted with the task of finding their own mate. If any St. Leger attempts to do so, he will meet with nothing but disaster.

"But if he entrusts the mystical being appointed as Bride Finder to fetch him a wife, he will find true love that will last through all eternity."

"Aye, indeed," Val cried. "And I don't see how you can sneer about it when we have our own parents for an example."

Lance couldn't argue with Val on that score. It was true. There could not possibly be any more devoted husband and wife than Madeline and Anatole St. Leger.

But he scowled, pointing out to his brother, "Our parents were of another generation. Look who they had for their matchmaker. An elderly clergyman who was noted for his learning and wisdom. But when he passed on, who succeeded to his power? Who is supposed to be our Bride Finder, Val?"

Val fidgeted beneath Lance's hard stare but at last admitted unhappily, "Effie. Effie Fitzleger."

"That's right. Elfreda Fitzleger, a woman so scatterbrained, she has trouble choosing what color feathers to put on her own bonnet, let alone select a wife for anyone."

"But she has made some successful matches. Look at our cousin Caleb St. Leger and his wife."

"They fight like a pair of bad-tempered alley cats!"

"I know, but they actually seem to enjoy it. Especially the mending part that comes after the quarrel."

"But is that really what you want, Val?" Lance asked. "A wife who will throw china at your head when she's angry?"

"No, Effie will find a bride that's more suited to me."

Lance rubbed the bridge of his nose in sheer frustration. He knew it was really none of his concern what Val decided to do, but he couldn't help making one last effort to reason with his brother.

"Don't you think you'd do far better simply relying on your own heart?"

"But—but isn't—" Val hesitated, then went on diffidently, "Forgive me, Lance. But isn't that what you tried to do?"

His brother's question left Lance momentarily thunderstruck, for he couldn't deny it. His own wayward eye and hot-blooded passions had certainly led him to fix his heart upon Adele Monteroy. *His commanding officer's wife.*

"Yes, I was a fool," Lance admitted reluctantly. "I always assumed you had better judgment, Val. But if you feel you need to rely on the services of some so-called Bride Finder, that's your decision. You don't need my approval."

"No . . . but I could use your help."

"Help with what?"

"You know what Effie is like. She's always been very reluctant to perform her bride-finding duties. I've been to see her almost every afternoon for a fortnight, and she keeps putting me off."

"So what do you expect me to do about it?"

"You could talk to her, persuade her. People listen to you, Lance. You command their attention and their obedience. You are like Father in that respect."

No, that was his chief problem, Lance thought. He was nothing like the legendary Anatole St. Leger. And he already had enough difficulties with that blasted sword gone missing. The last thing he needed was to get involved in any bride-finding nonsense with Elfreda Fitzleger.

He wanted to refuse Val's request, but one look into his brother's pleading dark eyes, another glance toward that damned cane, and of course he was unable to do so.

"All right," he said grudgingly. "I'll talk to the ridiculous woman. I'm sure I owe you at least that much."

"I would rather you did it just because you are my brother," Val said sadly. "But thank you."

His eyes brightened with a gratitude that only rendered Lance more uncomfortable because he knew he'd done nothing to deserve it.

But Val beamed at him. "You'll never know how much I appreciate this, Lance. I'll be sure to christen my firstborn son after you."

"Good God, no!" Lance exclaimed in sheer horror. "As if it wasn't bad enough our father allowed Mother to saddle us with such ridiculous names. *Saint* Valentine."

"*Sir* Lancelot!"

There had been a time in their youth when adding these teasing titles to the names they already both hated would have resulted in a mock-fierce exchange of blows, descending into an all-out wrestling match.

Lance almost forgot himself for a moment, was about to deliver a playful buffet to Val's shoulder when he caught himself, remembering his brother's crippled frame just in time.

He let his hand drop awkwardly back to his side. Val, too, appeared extremely self-conscious. With a taut smile, he excused himself on the grounds of having already taken up enough of Lance's time.

As he moved to leave, Lance rushed ahead to get the door for him. Head bent, Val hobbled from the room. Holding the door slightly ajar, Lance watched him through the crack.

Observing his brother's progress down the hall, he feared that for once in his life Val might have been less than truthful. That his leg was bothering him seemed a far more likely explanation for his sleeplessness than any St. Leger mating urge.

His brother's limp was more pronounced this morning, and it made Lance all the more aware of his own limbs, so straight and strong beneath him. Absent of any pain, of the injury that should have rightfully been his if not for Val's interference. Closing the door with a dull click, Lance wondered, as he often did, whether he loved his brother or hated him more.

But not nearly as much as Lance St. Leger hated himself.

CHAPTER THREE

———

*M*iss Elfreda Fitzleger poured out more tea for her afternoon caller, her brassy gold ringlets bobbing around sharp features well past the first blush of maidenhood. Crow's-feet stalked the corners of her hazel eyes, greatly at odds with her youthful manner of dressing her hair and the girlish simplicity of her white muslin gown.

Despite the fact that she would never see her thirtieth birthday again, Miss Fitzleger simpered at her visitor like a young miss on the brink of her coming out as she maintained a constant flow of chatter. Afternoon callers, especially such genteel ones from the vast world outside of Torrecombe, were a scarce commodity. And like a merry spider with a reluctant guest caught in her web, Effie was determined not to let this one get away.

Rosalind stifled a yawn behind her gloved hand, appalled by her own rudeness. But she felt nigh overcome, between having so little sleep the night before and the closeness of Miss Fitzleger's parlor.

Despite the warm summer afternoon, all the windows were shut and a blazing fire crackled on the hearth. Rosalind perched uncomfortably on a stiff chaise, her black gown wilted to her body, her damp curls clinging to her forehead, perspiring beneath the layers of her lace-trimmed cap and dark crepe bonnet.

She marveled that the heat appeared to have no effect whatsoever on her hostess. Miss Fitzleger had even draped a shawl about her own thin shoulders.

When Miss Fitzleger attempted to press upon Rosalind yet another cup of tea, her eyes strayed longingly toward the door.

"Oh, no thank you, ma'am," she said. "I fear I have trespassed upon your kindness long enough."

"I declare!" the woman exclaimed. "You have only just arrived."

One half hour ago. Rosalind had counted out every sweltering minute with the aide of the clocks in the room, and there seemed to be dozens of them, ticking incessantly.

"It was very good of you to receive me at all," Rosalind murmured, attempting to rise. "Arriving on your doorstep, unannounced, with no claim upon your acquaintance."

"No claim indeed!" Miss Fitzleger interrupted, thrusting Rosalind back into her seat. "Were you not acquainted with my own dear departed grandpapa? And I am an excellent judge of character. All my admirers say so.

"Mr. Josiah Gramble said just the other day, 'Miss Effie'—he calls me Effie." She paused to giggle. "For a vicar, he's such a cheeky rogue—he says, 'Miss Effie, you are as perceptive as you are lovely.' And it is true. I am blessed with a remarkable degree of intuition. I saw at once you were a respectable woman, and besides, any old friend of my grandpapa is a friend of mine."

Rosalind sighed. She had tried in all honesty to explain to Miss Fitzleger that her acquaintance with the late Mr. Fitzleger had been a brief one. But it was as useless as trying to avoid the tea that her hostess forced into her hands.

"Dearest Grandpapa," Miss Fitzleger went on, stirring her own tea with a sentimental expression on her face. "He would have been so glad to see you, too. What a pity you were not able to come sooner."

"Yes," Rosalind agreed sadly. She took a sip of the tepid liquid and tried not to choke. The tea seemed to be the only thing in the place that wasn't hot. "Is Mr. Fitzleger's demise a recent one?"

"Oh, Lord, bless you, no! The dear man has been gone these ten years and more, and I still miss him dreadfully." Miss Fitzleger batted her lashes in a coy manner, but the tears she suppressed seemed genuine enough. "I was quite his favorite grandchild, you know. He raised me himself after my mama died in childbirth. I was his sole heiress."

"Then you inherited this cottage from Mr. Fitzleger?"

"I inherited a great deal too much from him."

The tartness of the remark surprised Rosalind, as well as the bitter look that momentarily hardened the spinster's features. But it was buried in a flash behind another of Effie's simpering smiles.

She swiftly changed the subject to her gentlemen admirers, and according to Miss Fitzleger, she possessed a great number of them. She went rattling away, and Rosalind despaired of making her escape for at least another quarter hour.

She set her tea cup aside on a piecrust table, and her gaze fell upon yet another of Miss Fitzleger's collection of timepieces. This was a plain gold pocket watch sealed beneath a glass dome, but it triggered for Rosalind a flood of memories: of a sunny afternoon in her childhood when the watch had not been a knickknack gathering dust but an old man's treasured possession, one that he had permitted an awed little girl to examine with her chubby fingers.

It had not surprised Rosalind to learn of the good vicar's demise, but she was astonished by the depth of loss she felt. She had only known Mr. Fitzleger for the space of a few hours, and yet she retained an impression of him as one of the wisest men she had ever met.

And she could have used a bit of wisdom just now, Rosalind thought ruefully. The adventurous madcap who had pranced about the inn in her nightgown hunting for ghosts was long gone. In her place was the all too familiar timid and uncertain young widow. A widow with a stolen sword tucked beneath the mattress of her bed.

Rosalind had felt nothing but triumph when she had managed to successfully spirit the heavy weapon back to her bedchamber without being detected. But in the ensuing hours, she had been left with too much time to reflect upon what she had done.

Whatever villain had been bold enough to lay hands upon Excalibur would not be pleased when he discovered his prize missing from its hiding place.

The thief surely had to be someone staying at the inn, and if this desperate rogue should discover that Rosalind had been the one to thwart him . . . She suppressed a shudder.

According to the gossip Jenny had gleaned, the Dragon's Fire was full of despicable characters. From the sly-faced Mr. Braggs to a customs officer who maintained permanent lodgings at the inn. A sinfully handsome man, but extremely dangerous by all accounts.

"One of those Mortmains, milady," Jenny had informed her in a hushed whisper. "And you can't imagine what murderous scoundrels everyone in the village says they are."

Unfortunately Rosalind could imagine and did. Enough so that she almost considered turning the sword over to the nearest magistrate. But she could just hear herself trying to explain to some stern-faced official.

"This sword is Excalibur, the property of its rightful guardian, Sir Lancelot

du Lac. I found it at the inn and have been trying to keep it safe until it can be restored to him."

Rosalind would be fortunate if she didn't end up being mistaken for a thief herself. Even if she didn't land in the nearest gaol, Bedlam would be her final destination for sure. She was beginning to wonder herself if that was not where she belonged.

It had all seemed so different this morning when her hands had first closed upon the hilt of that wondrous sword, the soft light of dawn playing over the gleaming blade. She had felt stronger somehow, braver, capable of dealing with anything, ghosts, villains, legendary swords. A far cry from the shy girl who had been so pampered and protected all her life.

But now . . . all she felt was frightened and confused. The safest thing she could do was simply put that sword right back beneath the floorboard and forget she had ever found it. But even as the thought occurred to her, she knew she couldn't do that.

Because of *him.* Sir Lancelot du Lac.

The gallant knight who had knelt so humbly at her feet, a haunted soul with weary eyes and a gentle smile, condemned to an eternal search for forgiveness, his own redemption. In those dreamlike moments she had spent in his company, she had obtained a glimpse of the man behind the legend with his all too human regrets. He'd become more real to her than many a living person she had known.

Despite the desperation of his quest, he had taken the time to offer a sympathetic smile, a kind word to a young widow who felt as though she had become somewhat of a lonely traveler herself. Was she then to repay such chivalry with cowardice? Tamely return the sword to the enemy who had robbed him of it? No! Such an ignoble course was not even to be thought of. Rosalind firmed her lips, silently vowing that she would sit up in that storeroom every night for the rest of her life if she had to, waiting for Lancelot until she could place Excalibur safely back in his keeping.

It would have been comforting if he had at least left her with some hint of his eventual return. But his parting had seemed distressingly final. She thought she would never forget the sorrow in his eyes, that deep note of regret in his voice.

"I would beg to salute thee properly, milady, but all I can do is bid thee farewell."

Salute thee . . . such an elegant old-fashioned way of speaking. The mere sound of the words had so charmed her, she had scarce given thought to their meaning. But now she puzzled over the phrase, trying to recollect its place among the Arthurian legends she'd read.

Bold knights frequently asked that question of their ladies fair. "May I salute thee, demoiselle?" They had always been begging for the favor of . . . of a *kiss.*

Rosalind stiffened as the import of Lancelot's parting words struck her at last. If it had been possible, he would have asked to kiss her good-bye. And would she have granted his request?

She touched one finger hesitantly to her lips as she considered the possibility. The mere notion of such a thing seemed disloyal to the memory of her late husband, almost as though she were betraying Arthur with Sir Lancelot.

The irony of that was not lost on her, and Rosalind's mouth formed into a wry half smile. But she couldn't stop herself from thinking about Lancelot's kiss, what it would have been like.

Warm and gentle, she was sure. And flavored with all the romance of one of history's most noble lovers. She could almost feel the tender pressure of his mouth on hers. A heat flooded into her cheeks that had nothing to do with the temperature of the room, and a delicious shiver worked through her.

"Is anything the matter, my lady?" Miss Fitzleger's voice broke rudely in on Rosalind's imagined embrace.

Startled back to her surroundings, she realized that her hostess's amiable flow of gossip had ceased and the woman was staring at her with an inquiring smile. But Rosalind did not have the least idea what the question had been.

"Well, I—I—" she stammered.

"Poor dear! A moment ago you shivered, and now your teeth are chattering," Miss Fitzleger cooed. "There is a terrible draft in this room. I feel it myself. I'll just throw a few more logs on the fire."

"Oh no!" Rosalind cried, but her faint protest fell on deaf ears as Miss Fitzleger leapt cheerfully to her feet. Effie heaped more wood upon the inferno that already blazed upon the hearth, but at least the woman's actions helped to snap Rosalind out of her foolish daydreaming about Sir Lancelot and back to the grim reality of her present situation.

She stole a glance at the hodgepodge of clocks upon the mantel and feared she had already been absent from the inn for too long, leaving her poor maid guarding a most dangerous treasure.

When Miss Fitzleger's back was turned, Rosalind stifled an ignoble impulse to snatch up her reticule and dart out the parlor door. She inched to the edge of the chaise, once more trying to marshal her excuses when Miss Fitzleger startled her with a delighted shriek.

"I declare. I hear a carriage arriving." The woman beamed from ear to ear. "More callers!"

Rosalind didn't know how Miss Fitzleger could hear anything with the windows closed and the clocks setting up a din, all of them now bonging and chiming out the hour. But as her hostess darted across the room to peer past the draperies, Rosalind shot to her feet, her spirits lifting.

With the arrival of fresh victims for Effie—or rather she should say *visitors*, Rosalind amended, she at last saw her golden opportunity for escape.

But as Miss Fitzleger stared out the parlor's front window, her look of joyful expectancy fled.

"Merciful heavens. It's him!" She wrenched the curtains closed, pressing her trembling hands to her thin bosom. Her alarm was so palpable, it communicated itself to Rosalind.

"Who is it, Miss Fitzleger?" she asked anxiously.

"That dratted Valentine St. Leger!" Effie whipped around and risked another peek through the curtains. She moaned, "He's coming to plague the life out of me with his incessant demands. And this time he's even brought his devil of a brother with him. The heartless pair of villains!"

"V-villains?" The word set Rosalind on edge, conscious as she was of the sacred sword she had sworn to keep safe. And the name St. Leger . . . she was certain she'd heard it before.

Jenny had mentioned them. They were the principal landholders hereabouts, a rather infamous family by all accounts, inhabiting a haunted manor bearing the title of Castle Leger.

Rosalind had absorbed the gossip from her maid with all her usual delight in anything new and curious. But swapping deliciously eerie and frightening legends was one thing. It was quite another to have the object of those dark tales come hammering at the door.

"Oh dear! Oh dear!" Effie fretted, alternating between stealing glances through the slit in the curtains and wringing her hands.

Rosalind crept to the distraught woman's side. "Miss Fitzleger, what do these St. Legers want from you?"

"What those infernal St. Leger men always want! *Women!*"

"I beg your pardon," Rosalind said faintly. "I don't quite understand."

"I have never understood it either." Effie sniffed. "Some sort of moon madness seems to steal over them, and their blood gets all fired up, positively seething until they become quite insatiable. Then I am given no peace until I go fetch them some wives."

"Wives? You are their matchmaker, then?"

"What I am is a slave to those St. Legers and their passions. It is so exhausting, my dear. First using my magical talent to find the bride, then persuading the lady to marry into a strange family like the St. Legers. Often the silly chit doesn't want to be thrust into the arms of some lusty dark lord who can scarce wait to wed and bed her."

"I should imagine not," Rosalind faltered, her mind filling with images of some wild-eyed Cornishman flinging a terrified lady over his burly shoulder and carrying her off to his castle. She had heard that people could be a little rough-hewn in this part of the world, a little less than civilized.

"But surely, these are no longer medieval times," she couldn't help protesting to Miss Fitzleger. "No woman can be forced into marriage against her will. Not in this day and age."

"Humph! You don't know these St. Legers, my lady. They can be quite ruthless about getting what they want. Only look how they force me to go bride hunting for them."

"Why don't they find their own wives and court them in decent gentlemanly fashion?"

"They can't do that. Not with their peculiar family heritage and customs. They are utterly dependent upon me. I am their one and only true Bride Finder." Effie drew herself up with an air of self-importance, at the same time a bleak expression chased across her face. "But you have no idea what it is like to be burdened with such an awful power, Lady Carlyon. It has quite blighted my life."

Rosalind nodded sympathetically but retreated a wary step. She had no idea what sort of fresh trouble she might have stumbled into here, but it promised to be more than she could handle. Miss Fitzleger apparently believed that she possessed some sort of magic power to find brides, and these St. Legers were mad enough to agree with her. Lust-ridden young men, ready to pounce upon whomever Effie pointed out to them as a likely wife, be she young, old, rich or poor, a trembling girl, a respectable matron or . . . or even a virtuous widow.

Rosalind swallowed nervously and inched toward the parlor door, but to her dismay, Effie got there first.

"I'll just command Hurst to deny I'm at home," Effie said. "If we are very quiet, they'll never guess we're here."

"Miss Fitzleger, please—" Rosalind began, but with a conspiratorial wink, the woman whisked open the door to summon her housekeeper.

Rosalind pressed one hand to her brow, fearing the heat might have addled her wits more than she supposed. Surely she must have misunderstood Effie's odd remarks, or the woman had grossly exaggerated. But whatever was going on between her hostess and the St. Legers, Rosalind had a sinking feeling she should have made her escape while she still had the chance.

*   *   *

His curly-brimmed beaver tipped at a rakish angle, Lance St. Leger stared at
the vine-covered cottage before him, the taut set of his mouth revealing how
little he relished the prospect of this visit. He was in no humor to be dealing
with a recalcitrant Bride Finder. Especially when he should have been orga-
nizing a hunt for the thief who'd attacked him last night. But it was damned
near impossible to mount a proper search when he couldn't even admit to
anyone that he'd been robbed of his own sword.

Just one more part of the curse of being a St. Leger, this need to appear infallible in the eyes of the local folk. Lance wondered how his father had managed all these years. Probably because Anatole St. Leger *was* infallible. He
would never have allowed anything like this to happen.

That bitter reflection did nothing to ease Lance's black mood. As he
reached Effie's front door, he cast a brusque look over his shoulder, annoyed to
realize that Val had lagged behind, not having gone much farther than the
garden gate. But it was not his brother's bad knee that impeded his progress
so much as the scrawny girl that clung to his waist, threatening to topple Val
over into a bed of roses.

Kate . . . Effie Fitzleger's ward, another of the woman's foolish whims. When
Effie had gone to take the waters at Bath some years back, she had apparently
plucked the child from some foundling home and returned cooing over the
prospect of playing "mama."

The rambunctious Kate had fast cured Effie of that notion, which was just
as well—or they'd have had Effie collecting up children the way she did
clocks.

Kate clutched at Val with all her strength. She was a regular gypsy with
her mass of thick black straight hair, dirt-smudged cheeks, and flashing
dark eyes.

"No, Val!" she cried. "Don't do it. Don't!"

Attempting to maintain his balance, Val said gently, "Katie, you know that I
must—"

"No! Don't you dare do it. Don't ask that damned old Effie to get you a
bride."

Unable to loosen her grip on him, Val bent and wrapped his arm around
her thin shoulders. But neither his remonstrances with Kate not to swear or
his efforts to reason with her had any effect. The girl's countenance grew
stormier by the moment.

Lance finally felt compelled to intervene. Striding down the walk, he peeled

Kate away from his brother in one swift movement, ignoring both Val's soft protest and the girl's shrill cry.

As he dragged her away from Val, she turned on Lance like a fury, punching and kicking. Lance half lifted her off her feet and plunked her down outside the gate. Grasping her wrists in one hand, he subdued her with a bout of strategically placed tickling aimed at her rib cage.

Kate collapsed in the lane at his feet, breathless with furious laughter. "Damn you—Lance St. Leger," she panted. "You—don't—fight—fair. Let me go."

"Not until you behave yourself, Miss Katherine."

"Go to the devil!"

"Very likely I will," Lance agreed amicably. "And you with me, if you don't mend your ways, hoyden."

She struggled to wrench herself free. When she found herself unable to do so, she glared up at him, her eyes black pools of fury. Lance maintained a firm but careful grip on her wrists. For all her wiry strength, Kate was a rather delicate girl with fine bone structure. Her smallness made it all but impossible to guess her age. The girl herself didn't seem to know what it was.

About twelve or thirteen, Lance judged, although there was *that* in Kate's gaze that always gave him pause. An expression so old, so world-weary, it pained him to find it in the eyes of one so young. Wherever the orphaned girl had spent the early years of her life, she had clearly seen and experienced far too much of the misery to be found in this world.

Lance returned her fierce stare with a steady regard, not slackening his grasp until she regained some measure of control over her temper.

"Let me go," she repeated through clenched teeth.

Lance cautiously released her. "Now, what the blazes is all this fuss about, Miss Katherine?"

Kate stood up, brushing the dust from her elbows. She took a long time about replying but finally confessed sullenly, "I don't want Val marrying some dumb old bride Effie finds for him."

"Why not, babe?"

"Because." Kate ducked her head, disappearing behind the heavy curtain of her gypsy dark hair. "I mean to marry Val myself someday."

"What!" Lance tipped up her chin, forcing her to look at him. The girl's expressive eyes were shaded with a hint of defiance and a look so forlorn, it curbed in Lance any urge to smile.

"Don't you think my brother's a little old for you?" he asked.

Kate vigorously shook her head. "I will catch up to him if he'll only wait for me."

"That's a rather hard thing to demand, Miss Kate. For poor Val to wait for a bride until you've finished growing."

"He has to! If he doesn't, I'll never marry anybody. I'll end up an old maid like Effie."

"Nonsense. You'll have lots of beaux. Especially if you ever decide to wash your face." Lance pinched her chin playfully. "And if you ever get that desperate, you can always marry me."

"Humph!" Kate gave a dignified sniff. "I wouldn't have you. You'd make the very devil of a husband."

"So I would," Lance chuckled. But he eventually managed to coax a smile from the girl, especially when he slipped several coins into her hand.

She trudged off down the lane, only pausing long enough to shake her fist and holler back at his brother, "You haven't heard the last of me, Val St. Leger. Even if Effie does find you a bride, I'll shoot her dead."

Lance laughed, but he turned to find Val horrified. The encounter with Kate had done a great deal to restore Lance's good humor, and he strolled back through the gate toward his brother, wickedly arching one brow.

"Ah, the devastating effect your charms have on the ladies, Valentine."

"Poor child." Val stared after Kate with a worried frown. "I only ever meant to be kind to her. I had no idea she'd take such an odd notion into her head about marrying me."

"Merely a childish infatuation. Don't you remember when Leonie insisted she was going to wed that acrobat that came here for the fair one year?"

"Aye, but Kate is a deal more intense in her emotions than our sister ever was."

"More hot-tempered, you mean. Well, I wouldn't worry overmuch. I doubt Kate has saved up enough to buy herself a pair of dueling pistols, *yet.*"

"More likely she'll just borrow yours," Val said, turning a stern look on Lance. "You know the girl runs wild enough without you encouraging her."

"Me! What the devil do I do?"

"You always tease her, laugh when she curses. Fill her apron pockets full of coins. And all she does with it is buy so many sweets, she makes herself ill."

Lance frowned. He harbored a soft corner in his heart for the fierce orphan, alternately overindulged or neglected, according to Effie's moods. But it had never occurred to him that he might be doing Kate more harm than good with his careless generosity.

"I fear I have little understanding of children," he said ruefully.

"You'll learn fast enough after you've fathered a few of your own."

"Never intend to, Valentine," Lance drawled. "I leave it entirely up to you to fill the cradle of Castle Leger with heirs."

Val looked disturbed as he always did when Lance made remarks like that, but Lance's words appeared to recall him to some sense of his mission.

As they traced their way down the walk, together this time, Lance was amused to observe Val's nervousness. His absentminded brother, usually so careless of his appearance, alternately fidgeted with his cravat and shifted the low-crowned beaver perched atop his disorderly waves of hair.

"You don't need to look so blasted tense," Lance said. "It is not as though I'm going to be able to make Effie fetch you a bride out of her closet this very afternoon."

But despite his teasing, Lance paused himself on the front step to help Val straighten his cravat. His own claret-colored frock coat immaculate, Lance could never understand how Val always contrived to appear as if he dressed himself in the dark.

"Hold still," Lance growled, wrestling with the haphazardly tied linen.

Val sighed but obeyed, submitting patiently to Lance's ministrations. It struck Lance that this was one of those moments when his twin seemed a great deal younger than he, strands of dark hair drooping stubbornly over Val's brow, his soft eyes dream-ridden with notions of love eternal and all those happily-ever-afters Lance had long since ceased to believe in. His brother's hopeful face aroused in Lance an embarrassing surge of protectiveness.

"There. That will have to do," he said gruffly, giving Val's appearance one last critical appraisal. "But before Effie does produce this wife of yours, remind me to send my own man to give your hair a trim. Your bride might object to wedding someone who resembles a spaniel caught in a windstorm."

"Yes, thank you. I will remind you." Val smiled, but a shadow fell across his gentle features.

"Do you think my bride will—will object to this?" His gaze dropped to the ivory-handled cane he clutched in his right hand.

Val rarely ever revealed that he minded himself about the injury that had left him permanently crippled. But for a brief moment, there was a wistfulness in his eyes, a vulnerability he could not quite disguise. And it left Lance pierced clean through.

He forced a hard laugh, saying, "No, I'm sure your bride will be suitably impressed, especially after you explain to her how nobly you acquired your wound, saving your worthless brother. Ladies are always thrilled by such heroics."

"Lance—" Val began with a pained look, but Lance had already turned away, his brief spate of brotherly feeling curtailed by the far more familiar one of guilt.

Seizing Effie's brass door knocker, he rapped it with more force than necessary, eager to have this damn fool business over and done with it.

His first summons went unanswered. Likewise his second. Swearing under his breath, Lance started to resort to his fist when the door finally swung open a crack.

Effie's housekeeper peeked out, wiping one meaty fist in the folds of her apron.

"What d'ye want?"

"Be so good as to inform Miss Fitzleger that my brother and I desire—"

"Mistress be not at home." The dour Miss Hurst moved to slam the door in his face, but Lance prevented her. Behind him, he heard Val heave a disappointed sigh, preparing to go away. But Lance was not so easily deterred.

"My dear Hurst," he said in a voice of deceptively soft patience. "Perhaps you had best check again. When I rode up just now, I saw Miss Fitzleger at one of the windows."

Hurst glared at him, wisps of her gray hair straggling from beneath her mobcap. "The mistress be not at home t'callers. Which any *gentl'mun* would understand."

"When I find one, I'll be sure to tell him." Lance forced his way into the house, leaving Val with no choice but to follow.

Hands propped on her ample hips, Miss Hurst hissed like a furious cat, but Lance ignored the woman. Sweeping off his hat, he tossed it onto the nearest chair, his gaze tracking around the hall, whose walls were cluttered with more of Effie's endless timepiece collection, two long case clocks guarding the foot of the stairs like a pair of solemn sentinels.

"So where has Effie gone to ground this time?" he demanded. "The breakfast room? The parlor?"

The sullen housekeeper compressed her lips, but a furtive glance of her small, tight eyes told Lance all he needed to know.

"Ah, the parlor, then."

Over Hurst's vociferous protest, Lance stalked in that direction, but before he'd taken many steps, Effie herself burst out of the room, slamming the door closed behind her.

Splaying both hands against Lance's chest, she drove him back with a shrill cry: "Go away! Both of you!"

Lance paused, momentarily startled, finding this agitated greeting rather extreme, even for Effie.

"I did my best to keep 'em out, ma'am," the housekeeper said. "But this here impert'nent rogue—"

"That'll do, Hurst." Lance cut her off in a tone he rarely used, but one the most brash privates in his regiment had never been foolhardy enough to disobey. He dismissed the woman with a curt nod. The housekeeper glowered at him but slunk away.

Turning back to Effie, Lance summoned up his most charming smile. "Now, Effie, is this any way to address your most ardent admirer?" He caught one of her hands, carrying it to his lips in a practiced gesture. "How can you be so cruel as to send me away?"

Effie pouted, but she said in mollified tones, "I am always glad to see you, Lance. You make no unreasonable demands upon a poor woman. But I won't have *him.*" She leveled an accusing finger at his brother.

"But, Effie," Val said, coming forward, hat in hand. "Only yesterday, you told me to come back tomorrow."

"This wasn't the tomorrow I meant. I am already occupied entertaining a lady, a friend of mine from out of town."

"And I'm sure she'll be pleased to make our acquaintance," Lance said silkily.

"Indeed she won't. She's not the least interested in either one of you."

"Isn't she, by God?" Lance murmured. Behind Effie, he could see the parlor door move the barest fraction, assuring him that Effie's uninterested caller was likely eavesdropping for all she was worth.

A mischievous smile hovering at the corner of his mouth, Lance slipped around Effie in one fluid motion and wrenched the door open. With a tiny gasp, the woman staggered out into the hall, tumbling into Lance's arms. His hands shot out to steady her.

"Good afternoon." He grinned. "I've never had a lady fling herself at my feet before, but I daresay I could grow accustomed to ..."

His words trailed off as the woman raised startled eyes to his. Underneath the lace trim of a grim black bonnet, Lance found his Lady of the Lake.

His hands froze on her shoulders, and for a moment even Effie's infernal clocks seemed to go still. He stared with disbelief at features that already seemed achingly familiar to him: the soft bow-shaped mouth, the pert nose, the gold-fringed lashes framing impossibly blue eyes.

Rosalind ... Rosalind Carlyon. What the blazes was she doing here? She should have been far away by now, continuing her journey through Cornwall to find King Arthur's birthplace or the ruins of Camelot or whatever the deuce she was looking for.

But she wasn't. She was right here, hardly more than a heartbeat from falling straight into his arms, and he felt inexplicably glad of the fact.

Scarce thinking what he did, he started to pull her closer, only a small, frightened cry from the lady snapped him back to his senses. All the color drained from Rosalind's cheeks. She stared up at him, as though she were looking at . . . a ghost.

Which she likely thought she was. Lance winced. He let his hands fall away from her, dimly aware that Effie was performing some sort of disgruntled introduction.

But Lance barely heard a word of it as he racked his brain for some glib excuse, some clever explanation as to why he was the image of the phantom Sir Lancelot du Lac. He was usually so good at talking his way out of any kind of awkward situation. But as he gazed deep into Rosalind's stricken eyes, for the first time in his life, Lance St. Leger had run out of moonshine.

"Lady Carlyon . . . Rosalind," he faltered. "I—I can explain—"

Hell! No, he couldn't. But it hardly mattered, for Rosalind didn't seem to be listening to him anyway. She looked like she had fallen into a state of shock, her breath coming quick and shallow.

Raising trembling fingers, she reached toward him as though she expected her hand to go clean through him. When her palm collided with his chest, a soft moan escaped her. And the lady who had scarce turned a hair at finding a ghost prowling through the Dragon's Fire Inn, fainted dead away into Lance's arms.

Lance caught her with a startled oath, sweeping her off her feet. She wasn't so much of a slip of a girl as he'd supposed last night. As he cradled her high in his arms, he was disturbingly aware that the soft curves pressed tight against him were those of a woman.

A tangle of confused emotions raced through him, but the one that surfaced uppermost was alarm. Lance had seen ladies burst into hysterics or temper tantrums, had had china and curses flung at his head. There'd even been a fiery opera dancer who'd tried to shoot him. But never once had a woman actually swooned on him.

What he clearly needed right now was another lady, a practical one like his mother with her reticule stuffed full of smelling salts. But it was Lance's ill luck to have only Effie Fitzleger at hand, and the flighty creature showed signs of going off herself.

"Oh, I declare, I declare, I declare!" Effie moaned, pressing her hands to her mouth as she swayed back and forth, staring at Lance and Rosalind.

Shifting the inert lady in his arms, Lance appealed to his brother for assistance instead. "Val?"

But to Lance's dismay, Val appeared in little better case. Usually so quick to react in any sort of medical crisis, Val simply stood there, gaping at Rosalind with a dazed expression on his face.

"Val!" Lance snapped.

The sharpness of his tone jarred Val out of his trance. With a concerned frown, he hastened forward only to be stopped by Effie groaning and clutching at his arm for support.

"Oh! Oh! Oh, it's her. Why didn't I feel it before?"

"Effie, this is no time for hysterics," Lance said. "Will you please do something useful? Summon Hurst to fetch some water or—or—"

"But it's her, I tell you," Effie cried, giving Val's arm a vehement shake. *"Your chosen bride!"*

Effie's words left even Lance stunned for a moment. As for Val, he dropped his cane, the ivory-tipped walking stick clattering to the floor. He looked at Rosalind, and an expression stole over his solemn features such as Lance had never seen on his brother's face before.

Awe, tenderness, and a dawning joy that made Val's eyes glisten fever bright. His injured leg unheeded, his limp barely perceptible, he walked toward Lance with his arms outstretched, for all the world like he'd turned into some god-cursed prince out of a fairy tale, preparing to swoop up the lady and revive her with a kiss.

Lance's Lady of the Lake.

His arms tightened involuntarily around Rosalind, a sense of unreasonable possessiveness coursing through him. He backed away from Val, his lip starting to curl into something resembling a snarl when Lance blinked, catching himself.

What the devil was he doing? He reminded himself sharply that this is exactly what he'd come here for. To force Effie to use her powers to find Val a bride. He just hadn't expected that it would happen so soon or that the bride would turn out to be . . . Rosalind.

But why the blazes should that matter to him? Reluctantly, Lance prepared to surrender Rosalind into Val's eager arms when Effie shrieked out again.

"No! What are you doing?" she demanded.

Lance glowered at the woman. "You said Lady Carlyon is to be Val's wife."

"Not Valentine's chosen bride, you impossibly stupid man," Effie cried, stomping her foot at Lance. *"Yours!"*

"What!" Lance came damned close to dropping Rosalind. He shifted her to a more secure position in his arms, her head lolling against his shoulder as if she belonged there. He gazed down at her pale face, experiencing a quickening in his veins, a rush to his heart that felt strangely like tenderness. He was swift to quell the disturbing sensation.

"Here!" Lance thrust Rosalind toward his brother as though the lady had suddenly turned into an armful of hot coals.

But Val's arms fell back to his side, the light dying from his eyes. "No, Lance," he said quietly. "She's not my bride. She's yours."

"What the woman is—is unconscious," Lance sputtered. "As far as I'm concerned, if you'd just take her and revive her, you can have her."

But Val retreated with a sad shake of his head. "You heard what Effie said."

"I did and as usual, the blasted woman is quite mistaken."

"I am not," Effie wailed indignantly. "I never make mistakes."

"No? What about when—" Lance began, then broke off, unable to believe that he was engaging in such a ridiculous argument while he stood with a swooning woman in his arms.

Since he appeared to be the only person left with any degree of sense, it was clearly up to him to deal with Rosalind. Brushing past Effie, he strode through the parlor door, looking for some comfortable place to lay the lady down.

He eased Rosalind gently onto a backless chaise that more resembled something to be found in a Roman emperor's palace than an Englishwoman's drawing room. As he did so, the stifling heat of the room assailed him in one great wave.

That fool Effie actually had a roaring fire going in here and all the windows closed, in the dead of summer.

"Damnation," Lance muttered. No wonder his Lady of the Lake had fainted.

Hearing someone enter the parlor behind him, he assumed it was his brother and called out, "Val, go open the windows or I'll be passing out myself in a moment."

But it was Effie's aggrieved voice who answered him. "Valentine isn't here. I told him to go away."

"What the deuce did you do that for?" Lance snapped.

Effie hovered at his shoulder, craning her neck to peer down at Rosalind with a wounded sniff. "Well, one can hardly expect me to find any more brides today. I am so done in, I have no idea when my power may ever function again. I declare! I believe I may faint myself."

"If you do, I swear I'll cart you out to the garden and dump you in the fish pond. Now stop acting like a blasted fool and help me with this woman."

"Ohhh!" Effie wailed. "Of all the ungrateful wretches. And after I found you a wife!"

"I don't want a wife!"

"Then you shouldn't have come barging in here, should you?" Effie regarded him with reproachful tear-filled eyes. "But 'tis too late now. So you just get that woman out of here and marry her. And don't you St. Legers even think of asking me to be b-bridesmaid again."

Bursting into sobs, she rushed out of the room. Lance let her go, far too exasperated to try to stop her. Storming to his feet, he charged across the parlor to shove aside the curtains and open the windows himself.

As he fought with the casement, he caught a glimpse of his brother trudging down the lane back toward the inn where they had left their horses. Shoulders slumped, Val hobbled along, looking as though whatever castle in the clouds he'd woven in those few seconds he'd thought Rosalind was his had crashed down around his ears.

Lance watched him go, nonplussed. He'd never known Val to turn his back on anyone who needed help before. He could scarce imagine how badly disappointed, how hurt his brother must be to have done so. And Lance felt that once again he was somehow to blame.

He wanted to go after Val, make things right for him. But with Effie off somewhere having the vapors and his Lady of the Lake still out cold, what the devil was he supposed to do?

Forcing open the rest of the windows, he charged back into the hall bellowing for one of the servants. But as usual in Effie's feckless household, there was no one to be found, even the formidable Miss Hurst inexplicably absent.

Hurrying back to the parlor, Lance glanced distractedly around for a fan, smelling salts, some brandy, anything that might help. In sheer desperation, he flung a bouquet of wilting roses out of a Sèvres vase and used the water he found at the bottom to dampen his handkerchief.

Perching beside Rosalind on the chaise, he fumbled with the ribbons of her bonnet, tugging it off and her lace cap along with it. Tendrils of her golden hair escaped from her tight chignon, straggling across her eyes. Lance brushed them aside, regarding her anxiously: so pale, she still showed no signs of coming around.

Likely it was the fault of all those blasted layers of clothing women insisted upon burying themselves in. Val would have shrunk from such ungentlemanly behavior, but Lance stripped away the gauzy scarf that served as her modesty piece without a second thought.

Shifting her to her side, he undid the buttons of her bodice and unlaced the corset he found beneath. As he exposed the dainty lace of Rosalind's chemise, he thought she seemed to breathe easier.

Easing her onto her back, he felt for her pulse. To his relief, he found it faint but steady. He made a heroic effort to keep his eyes averted, but assessing a woman's charms came as naturally to him as breathing. And Rosalind Carlyon had charms aplenty....

His gaze dipped down, taking in a glimpse of delicate collarbone, a tantalizing beauty mark just above the swell of her breasts, the sweat-dampened linen of her chemise outlining round, perfect globes, the dusky shadow of her nipples.

Disgusted with himself, Lance wrenched his eyes back to her face. Using some of the water in the glass, he dampened his handkerchief and pressed it to Rosalind's brow, trying to keep his movements brisk and businesslike.

But his fingers gentled in spite of himself as he studied her face. She was no beauty, not by the classical standards that were the fashion now. Her nose was too snub, her chin too decided, her cheeks dusted with a hint of freckles.

And yet there was a sweetness and harmony in her countenance any man would find captivating. It was a gentle face, a face fresh as springtime flowers, a face spun from fairy tales and long-ago days, of golden-haired maidens who waited in rose-covered bowers, humming and dreaming of the prince who would come for her on his white charger.

It was the face of the kind of woman who ... who could cause a man a great deal of trouble if he wasn't careful. Lance grimaced. And hadn't this one managed to do so already? Taking him by surprise at the inn last night, walking straight through his very soul, distracting him from his search for the sword.

And now with Effie Fitzleger declaring Rosalind to be his chosen bride ... Lance might have little respect for Effie's powers as Bride Finder, but he knew his family would not agree with him. If word of Effie's latest pronouncement leaked out, he'd have the entire St. Leger clan swooping down upon him, demanding a wedding, and that, Lance reflected grimly, would be the last thing he bloody well needed.

His only hope was to convince Effie she'd made a mistake this time, which Lance was blasted sure she had. Rosalind was a gentle lady who would require a gentle lover, a knight whose soul shone as brightly as his armor. Someone noble, honest, and true. Someone exactly like his brother Val.

As he chafed her wrists and called her name, she began to stir at last. Rosalind whimpered softly. Her head shifted and her eyes fluttered open.

Her bewildered gaze roved about the room, finally coming to rest on Lance's face, and her eyes lit up with such undisguised joy, it sent an odd pang straight to his heart. Never could he recall any woman looking at him in such a way, as though he truly were some valiant hero come to answer all her prayers.

Her lips curved, a hint of color stealing back into her pale cheeks. When she smiled, she made him feel like a blind man first beholding the radiance of the sun. So much wonder and delight, so many dreams to be found shimmering in one pair of blue eyes.

She really ought to be Val's bride. She was perfect for him. But even as that stubborn thought crossed Lance's mind, he found himself drawn forward.

Scarce realizing himself what he was about to do, he brushed Rosalind's mouth with his kiss.

CHAPTER FOUR

ir Lancelot's kiss was warm and tender, just as she'd imagined it would be. Rosalind sighed, still feeling as though she groped her way through a swirling haze. Her mind remained clouded, uncertain where she was or how she'd got there, but it didn't matter because she was no longer alone.

He had returned to her. Sir Lancelot du Lac.

He wore a beleaguered expression, as though he'd fought his way back to her side through an army of hostile knights, a score of fire-breathing dragons. But as she peered up at him, his features relaxed into a look of profound relief.

"Rosalind," he murmured. "Thank God!"

Her name sounded so sweet on his lips. Rosalind issued a soft sigh. Every morning since Arthur had died, she'd been roused from her sleep to a heavy feeling of being all alone in the world, sorrow pressing like a weight upon her heart.

This was the first time that she'd opened her eyes in a long while to a far different sensation, something so light and fluttery, it took her a moment to remember what it was.

Happiness. It rushed to her heart leaving her giddy with the sensation. She gazed up at Sir Lancelot, whispering in joyous disbelief, "You've come back to me."

"Have I?" He smiled. "I thought it was the other way around."

She returned his smile, her fingers trembling as she threaded them through his dark, silky lengths of hair. She'd never imagined a man's hair could be so cool and soft in marked contrast to the rugged warmth of his skin. She continued her dazed exploration, stroking the curve of his cheek and the iron-willed jaw with its hint of roughness that she doubted any razor could ever entirely tame.

He appeared surprised by her touch at first; then something in his eyes darkened. He caught her hand and pressed his lips to her palm in a kiss that was bold, passionate, searing.

The tremor of heat unleashed through her body shocked her fully back to her senses and the realization that something was terribly wrong.

The man bending over her was no ghost of some long-ago hero. The hand that imprisoned hers was gentle enough, but beneath that gentleness, she could feel the heat, the strength, the pulsing vitality.

Her eyes roved over him, taking in details she should have noted from the first. No armor, no tunic, his hair neatly arranged to rest against his collar. Or at least it had been until she had disturbed the dark waves. The intricate folds of a cravat cascaded like snow down a crisp shirtfront, a silk-striped waist-coat. His frock coat strained over his powerful shoulders to the bursting point while his breeches . . . Rosalind's stunned gaze dipped down, then quickly back. His breeches molded to his muscular thighs like a second skin.

This . . . this wasn't Sir Lancelot, this man with his languid smile, smoldering gaze, and overly bold mouth. The warm glow faded, replaced by such an aching disappointment, she wanted to cry. It was like being rudely awakened from the most beautiful dream she'd ever known.

Rosalind's gaze roved bleakly around the room as she strained to recollect where she was, how she'd got here, exactly what she had been doing. She . . . she was lying on a chaise in Effie Fitzleger's parlor. She remembered having tea with the woman, and then someone else had arrived that Miss Fitzleger had seemed determined to avoid. Visitors whose description had alarmed Rosalind. The St. Legers, men with their passions out of control, who apparently ranged around the countryside, demanding brides like those hot-blooded Romans who'd carried off the unfortunate Sabine women.

And this particular St. Leger had already taken possession of her hand like he never meant to let her go. Rosalind stared up at him, her pulse taking a frightened leap. But he didn't look like some uncivilized marauder. The cut of his clothes, too sophisticated for a simple country village, proclaimed him to be every inch the gentleman.

Yet the danger was there, inherent in the sensual curve of his mouth, in those impossibly dark eyes—eyes that seemed to devour her with a look that could have melted a candle into nothing more than a pool of molten wax and scorched wick.

And there was no sign of Effie Fitzleger or even one of the servants. She'd obviously been left quite alone with this man, and for what reason, Rosalind was too frightened to think.

Wriggling her fingers free of his strong grip, she struggled to a sitting position. When he would have stroked her cheek, she shrank back, crying, "Don't touch me! Please!"

His brows rose in astonishment, and she trembled, hardly knowing what she would do if he didn't heed her frantic command. But to her relief, he drew his hand away.

"All right," he said with a hint of a roguish smile. "Although I do feel compelled to point out you were also touching me and *I* didn't object."

To her deep mortification, Rosalind realized that was true. Touch him? She'd even allowed him to kiss her. A perfect stranger, and all because he bore such an uncanny resemblance to her phantom Sir Lancelot. Now that she realized he wasn't, that kiss no longer seemed so sweet . . . or innocent.

"I—I thought you were someone else," she faltered.

"Oh? And who would that be?" He framed his question with the most polite interest, but there was an intensity in his gaze she found unnerving.

"No one you'd know. A friend," she said sadly. A gallant friend that she wished were with her now, to shield her from this man's alarming attention.

He leaned closer, his physical presence overwhelming, the broad shoulders, the long arms, the powerful hands. His scent filled her nostrils, bay rum mingling with something darker, more masculine.

"I wish you would also regard me as a friend," he murmured.

Him? A man whose very voice was calculated to intimidate, whiskey-warm with seduction.

She inched farther away. "I—I know who you are. You're one of those dreadful St. Legers."

"My reputation precedes me. But yes, I am Lance St. Leger."

"Lance? As—as in Lancelot?"

"Unfortunately, yes."

Even his name was the same? She found such a coincidence bewildering, disturbing, even rather cruel. She pressed her hand to her brow, trying to clear away the webs of confusion. When her fingers struck up against damp tendrils of hair escaping her chignon, she frowned, becoming aware that her bonnet was missing. Likewise her lace cap.

But that realization paled by a discovery far more alarming. Her scarf was also gone. She peered down, dismayed to discover her gown and corset half-falling to her waist, exposing the swell of her breasts thrusting against the thin fabric of her chemise.

Merciful heavens! The St. Leger had unlaced her. To assess her charms as a prospective bride? Or even worse, to sample them?

"You still look rather shaken, sweet. Perhaps you'd better lie back down," he said.

Why? So that he could finish what he'd started while she was unconscious? When he reached for her to ease her down, a wave of pure panic swept over her.

She struck his hands away and scrambled off the side of the chaise, finding her feet. She heard his startled oath but never paused to look back. Heart pounding, she bolted for the door. But she had scarce taken more than a few steps when her head swam.

She would have tumbled headlong, but he was already there, springing after her with all the speed of a pouncing wolf, catching her hard against him.

"Rosalind!" His voice rasped in her ear. "What the devil do you think you're doing?"

She struggled feebly, attempting to fight off her own weakness, attempting to fight off *him*. "Let me go!"

"To do what? Fall on the floor?"

He was right, she realized with dismay. He was supporting her as much as restraining her, her body melting against his, absorbing the full impact of his heat and strength. The sensitive tips of her breasts pressing hard against him, veiled only by a whisper of lawn. So shockingly intimate, as though she were on the verge of becoming his lover.

Her eyes locked with his, and something strange seemed to flash between them, something dark and hot and heavy. And Lance St. Leger no longer looked the least bit civilized, but fully capable of sweeping a woman ruthlessly off her feet and to his bed.

With one wild frantic movement, Rosalind managed to jerk free and staggered back, bracing herself against the fireplace mantel.

When he stalked toward her, she panted, "If you touch me again, sir, I will scream loud enough to bring the entire village."

"I wouldn't advise you to do that, my lady."

"W-why not?"

"Because I know of only one way to stop a woman from screaming. And that would be to kiss you again."

"Oh!" Rosalind gave a frightened gasp and groped for something to fend him off. She seized the fireplace poker, but he closed in on her, easily forcing it from her grasp before she could even lift it.

"Damnation, Rosalind," he growled. "I was only teasing you. You take things even more seriously than my brother does."

His brother? Rosalind remembered there had been another man in the hall, a quiet-looking one with a cane, but he, too, seemed to have vanished. She would have far preferred his somber presence to this St. Leger's more overpowering one.

His hands gripping her shoulders, Lance forced her back toward a chair. "Sit down," he commanded.

She had no choice but to comply, sinking down onto the tapestry-covered seat. Her legs were trembling. *She* was trembling.

He towered over her, hands placed on the flat of his hips, regarding her with a frown. "Now, what the blazes has come over you, woman?"

Rosalind clutched the loosened corset and bodice tight to her bosom and huddled further down in the chair. "Nothing much, sir! Merely the small matter that while I was fainted, you tried to undress me."

"Purely for medicinal purposes." He didn't even have the grace to look abashed. "I had no other choice. You did swoon in my arms, remember?"

She remembered, but not the way he made it sound. Intimate yet arrogant, he described it as though she'd been overcome by his physical charms.

"But where is Miss Fitzleger?" she demanded. "Why didn't she attend me?"

"Because she's up in her room, very likely swooning herself. She can't bear to be outdone in anything by another woman. And as for that housekeeper of hers, I'll be hanged if I could find the wench."

"I doubt you tried very hard." Rosalind dragged the ends of fabric higher over her exposed décolletage. "You should be ashamed of yourself!"

"Very likely I should be, most of the time. But for once, my intentions were perfectly honorable." The scoundrel actually had the nerve to sound aggrieved.

Rosalind quivered with outrage. "You call it honorable to undo a lady's corset?"

"No, I call it reviving her. When any of the silly young clunches in my regiment locked up their knees while at attention and keeled over, loosening their collars was always one of the first things I did."

"Indeed? And then did you kiss them, too?"

A red flush stained his high cheekbones, but it appeared to be more from annoyance than embarrassment.

"I don't know why I kissed you," he said. "Out of relief most likely, that you'd finally come around. It was only the slightest peck. Nothing for you to get so distressed about. Surely you didn't think I was preparing to ravish you or—" He broke off, peering down at her. "My God, that's exactly what you thought."

To Rosalind's indignation, the depraved wretch actually laughed. She bristled defensively. "Well, what else was there—what could I think?"

"My dear girl!" He chuckled. "Ravish you beside the tea table? In broad daylight in Effie Fitzleger's parlor with all the village passing by in the lane outside the window?"

"Well, I—I—" When he put it *that* way, it did sound ridiculous.

"If I was going to have my wicked way with you, I'd at least have carted you off to a bedchamber and revived you. It wouldn't be very entertaining ravishing a woman who's like a dead weight in your arms. And besides that . . ."

His voice lowered to that intimate, suggestive timbre she found so disconcerting. ". . . I would never ravish any woman. I don't have to."

Rosalind didn't know what was worse, his arrogance or the amused way he glanced down at her, making her feel inexperienced and foolish.

Perhaps she had overreacted, but she was not accustomed to dealing with such things as casual kisses and a man undoing her laces for any reason. Even her own dear Arthur had never undressed her. His conjugal visits to her bedchamber had always been conducted with the utmost modesty and decorum, just a discreet lifting of her nightgown.

She longed to heap reproaches upon Lance St. Leger, inform him that he could have found a more gentlemanly way of handling this situation. Sir Lancelot du Lac would certainly have done so. *He* would never have behaved so unchivalrously if she'd fainted in his arms.

He would have found some way to spare her embarrassment. Some way that was gentle and considerate. The reflection brought an unexpected stinging of tears to her eyes, and she ducked her head to hide them, blinking furiously.

It only made matters worse when Lance St. Leger made a belated effort to be kind to her. He hunkered down in front of her, reaching for her hand.

"Rosalind, my dear—"

"Lady Carlyon." She flinched away from him. "I never gave you leave to use my name, sir." A foolish quibble perhaps, considering the liberties he'd already taken.

Apparently, he thought so, too, for he rolled his eyes. "Lady Carlyon, then. I am sorry if I have offended you. You are obviously suffering from a great shock. Now, if you will just sit here like a good girl, I'll go fetch something to help you feel better."

Rosalind found the way he patted her shoulder almost as insufferable as his patronizing tone of voice. As he straightened and strode from the room, she would have given all she possessed to have fled from this place.

But she still didn't trust the steadiness of her own legs. It would only mean further mortification if he was obliged to catch her again, and she could scarce leave the house in her current stage of undress.

She spent the time of his absence straining to redo laces and buttons, reflecting upon how much she detested the man. Lance St. Leger was exactly that sort of rakish male who had always rendered her most uncomfortable.

Too handsome for any lady's good. Insufferably arrogant, far too sure of himself. Under the protection of Arthur's wing, Rosalind had often observed men of Lance's stamp from a safe distance. Dancing and flirting, flattering and teasing, bringing laughter and blushes to other ladies' cheeks.

But let such a man once turn his wicked, assessing gaze in her direction, and Rosalind had always longed to dive under the nearest table.

It was exactly what she wished she could do now when Lance returned to her, far too soon. Her corset was barely tied, but if she could get her bodice adjusted, hopefully it would conceal the deficiency. Observing her struggles, Lance murmured wickedly, "Do you need any help?"

"No!" Rosalind shot him a fierce glower. Although she could not reach the last few buttons, she would have died before allowing him to touch her again.

Sauntering across the room, he held out a tumbler of some amber colored liquid. "Here," he said. "Drink this."

Rosalind accepted the glass and sniffed it suspiciously. She recoiled from the potent odor. "Oh, no. I never drink brandy."

"It will make you feel better." A thread of impatience crept into his voice. "It's not drugged, if that's what you're afraid of. So come along now and drink up."

He wasn't the sort of man to brook refusal. Closing his hand over hers, he guided the glass to her lips, compelling her to sip. Rosalind did so resentfully, thinking that her Sir Lancelot would never have forced spirits down a lady's throat.

The fiery liquid almost caused her to choke. But as Lance compelled her to take another swallow, the brandy began to have its effect, sending a reviving warmth coursing through her veins.

"Better?" he demanded.

Rosalind hated to admit it, but if she did not, the brute would likely oblige her to consume an entire bottle of the hateful stuff. She nodded grudgingly, pushing the glass away, wishing she could thrust him away as well. He hovered far too close.

As he set the glass down on the tea table, he said, "Here. You're probably going to want this as well."

Rosalind glanced up and was appalled to see her scarf dangling from his fingers.

"You wouldn't want to go about exposing your . . . er—beauty mark," he said with a teasing smile.

Her cheeks flaming, she snatched the gauzy fabric from him. "You looked at me when you undressed me?"

"You're a lovely woman. I couldn't help myself. I'm sorry."

But from the gleam in his eye, Rosalind didn't think he was remorseful at all. She struggled to her feet and this time was relieved to discover she could remain upright.

Taking several tentative steps away, she turned her back on him and arranged the scarf around her neck, tucking the ends firmly down inside her bodice, all the while thinking furiously, *Sir Lancelot never would have looked.*

Whipping around, Rosalind demanded to know what Lance had done with her bonnet. He looked around the scrolled legs of the chaise for it and eventually produced the missing apparel, but he seemed unable to locate the lace cap.

"You don't need it." He handed over the bonnet. "It didn't become you anyway. You're far too young to be going about attired in such matronly caps."

Rosalind shot him a blistering look and half started to argue with him but saw it was pointless. She had plenty of other lace caps, and all she wanted to do was get out of here as quickly as possible.

Jamming the bonnet on her head, she jerked the ribbons into a haphazard bow beneath her chin.

Sir Lancelot would never have misplaced her cap. He would not be so discourteous as to criticize her mode of apparel.

Drawing herself up with as much composure as she could muster, Rosalind prepared to take her leave. "Will you please convey my regrets to Miss Fitzleger and tell her I shall call to inquire after her health in a day or two when I am feeling more myself."

"A day or two? How long do you intend to remain in Torrecombe?" he demanded.

"I fail to see how that concerns you, sir. Good day." She dropped a stiff curtsy and flounced toward the door.

But the icy dignity of her exit was interrupted as he caught hold of her arm.

"I shall escort you back to the inn," he said with one of his hateful insinuating smiles. "I'm certain you do not travel alone. Perhaps one of your servants will be far more obliging about answering my question."

"How—how dare you, sir!" Rosalind huffed, but her fierce glower barely concealed her alarm at the thought of this man pursuing her to the inn. Though she hated being bullied, she realized she had little choice but to give him some sort of an answer.

"My stay in Torrecombe is of an indefinite nature, sir. Perhaps a week or only a few days."

However long it took her to figure out what to do with the legendary sword. Rosalind wondered why the length of her stay should even matter to Lance St. Leger, but clearly it did.

He released her, a faint crease forming between his brows. "A few days," he muttered. "Damn! That would be long enough."

"Long enough for what?" she asked fearfully.

"Long enough for you to hear every blasted rumor floating around this village if Effie is stubborn enough to—" He broke off, subjecting her face to a disquieting inspection through narrowed eyes.

"Perhaps you already have heard a deal too much about me and my family?" he asked, stalking a step closer.

"N-no, I—I've heard nothing," Rosalind stammered, ducking her head and retreating from him. But she never had been a good liar.

Lance pursued, cornering her against the wall, trapping her in place by bracing one sinewy arm on either side of her.

"Earlier you referred to me as 'one of those dreadful St. Legers.' Exactly what have you heard?"

Rosalind shook her head in denial, but Lance only leaned in closer. He crooked his fingers beneath her chin, forcing her to look up at him.

"Effie must have told you something," he insisted. "What was it?"

Rosalind squirmed, thinking Lance St. Leger would have made an excellent Grand Inquisitor. Those eyes that offered no quarter. That voice, so silken soft yet able to convey a great deal of menace.

"Miss Fitzleger only told me a good amount of nonsense I didn't properly understand," Rosalind said. "Something odd about you and your brother needing wives when the moon was full and you got this overwhelming urge to marry.

"And then Miss Fitzleger seems to think she possesses this magic power to find you a bride and when she does, it hardly matters if the lady she designates is willing or not. You St. Legers just—just . . ."

"Seize the poor girl by the hair and drag her to the altar?"

"Yes!" Rosalind cringed.

Some of the tension seemed to melt out of Lance St. Leger. He gave her chin a playful pinch and released her.

"My dear Lady Carlyon, St. Leger brides are always willing. I have never heard tell of a single St. Leger who ever had to take a wife by force. Usually our women wax so passionate, the poor bridegroom is hard-pressed to keep the lady from diving into his bed before the ceremony can be performed."

A hot blush seared Rosalind's cheeks. Sir Lancelot du Lac could certainly have taught this St. Leger a thing or two about the virtue of humility. And to refrain from making such bawdy comments in the presence of a lady.

"So then Effie did not fully explain to you about the legend?" he persisted.

Rosalind contemplated the possibility of ducking beneath his arm, making a bolt for the door, but her attention was arrested, dragged back to him by a single tantalizing word.

Legend.

Although she despised herself for showing interest in anything this arrogant man might have to say, she couldn't seem to help herself.

"Legend?" she asked. "What legend?"

"The one that has plagued my family for generations. The blasted notion that for each St. Leger, there exists one perfect mate, the partner of the soul. The ideal love that will last for all eternity."

"Oh!" Rosalind breathed. "That does not sound like much of a plague. It's wonderfully romantic."

"You may not think so when I tell you the rest of it," he replied grimly. "According to the legend, we St. Legers must not attempt to find this perfect love for ourselves. We have to rely on the services of a person blessed with a special gift for locating our mates, our Bride Finder. And currently—God help us—our Bride Finder is Effie Fitzleger."

"Then Effie did not exaggerate what she told me. You truly are obliged to marry whoever she chooses?"

"Yes, unless we want to bring the ancient curse crashing down upon our heads."

There was a curse as well? A delicious quiver worked through Rosalind, and she almost forgot how much she disliked Lance St. Leger as she hung upon his every word.

"In the past," Lance continued, "it seems that any St. Leger who chose to ignore the power of the Bride Finder and seek out his own mate met with nothing but disaster."

"What kind of disaster?" Rosalind asked eagerly.

"My brother could probably tell you better. He's made a study of our family history. But I do recollect one poor lady, Deidre St. Leger, who lived during the time of Cromwell." Lance frowned as though in effort of memory. "She refused to marry the man who was chosen for her and insisted upon taking another lover instead."

"And what happened to her?"

"Apparently she met with some manner of hideous death. All that was left of her was her heart, which was buried beneath the church floor."

Rosalind pressed her hands to the region of her own heart, a dark shiver coursing through her. It was as thrilling a legend as any she had ever heard. It only amazed her to be hearing it from the lips of a man like Lance St. Leger. Nothing of the dreamer about him, fast grounded in his own time and place from the gleaming tips of his boots to the starch in his cravat. Not at all the kind of person to go about relating fairy tales. In fact, he sounded impatient and more than a little annoyed with the entire story.

"Forgive my asking, Mr. St. Leger," Rosalind said timidly. "But do *you* actually put any faith in this legend?"

He shrugged, then admitted, "Not a great deal."

"Then why have you bothered telling it to me?"

For once Lance's bold eyes seemed incapable of meeting her own. "Because if you insist upon staying in Torrecombe, I thought you should be warned before word spreads through the entire village."

"Word of what?" Rosalind asked warily.

"That Effie's power has been at work again. That she believes she has found me the perfect bride."

"And—and who would that be?" Rosalind's heart squeezed with dread. She knew the answer even before Lance St. Leger pinned her with a single dark look.

"You," he said softly.

"Oh no!" she cried. "Never. I'd sooner wed the devil himself."

"Thank you," the devil replied dryly.

Rosalind winced. She had been far too blunt, although it was little more than he deserved. Still . . . she had a strong presentiment that it might be less than wise to anger a St. Leger.

"I am sorry," she said, scooting her back along the wall, nearly bumping her head against the weight dangling from one of Effie's clocks as she evaded the trap formed by Lance's powerful body. "It's just that I'm a widow. A recent one, and I was very devoted to my late husband. Lord Arthur Carlyon was the best and most kind man in the entire world."

"*Arthur*? This paragon's name was Arthur?" Lance muttered more to himself than to her. "Of course. It *would* be."

"So you see, I am not at all interested in being married again. Not now. Not ever." Rosalind risked a dread-filled glance up at him, Effie Fitzleger's words returning to haunt her.

You don't know these St. Legers, my lady. They can be quite ruthless about getting what they want.

But Lance seemed to take her rejection calmly enough. "There is no need for you to distress yourself, my dear. I quite understand."

He levered himself away from her, much to her vast relief, until he added with a tiny sigh, "I'm sure I shall grow accustomed to being doomed."

"Doomed?" Rosalind said. Oh, lord, she had entirely forgotten about the curse. "But surely, you don't really think that—that—"

"That I shall meet with some hideous disaster if you don't wed me? Who knows?" Lance made a valiant effort to smile. "At the very least, I shall be condemned to a lifetime, nay, an eternity of drifting through the world all alone."

His voice sounded light enough, but there was that in his eyes that reminded Rosalind poignantly of Lancelot du Lac. Something a little wistful, a little lost, a little sad.

Scarce thinking what she did, she impulsively held out her hand to Lance. "Oh no! You can marry someone else. It is only a legend, after all."

"And you don't believe in legends?"

"Well, yes, but only ones like Camelot or the fall of Troy."

"Ah, I see. You only believe in legends when they are long ago and far away. How very convenient . . . and safe."

"No! I didn't mean—I—I . . ." Rosalind trailed off, dismayed at how easily Lance St. Leger could get her flustered and confused. He'd taken possession of her hand again, and the things he was doing to it with his mouth . . .

Warm kisses. Soft kisses. Just the whisper of his lips against each fingertip, sending her nerve endings ajangle like chimes caught in the wind. She wondered why she didn't simply pull away from him, but his very gentleness took her by surprise, somehow disarmed her.

"I am sure there is nothing to this legend of the chosen bride. I am sure you will be all right," she said breathlessly, the brush of his mouth against her wrist causing her heart to pound faster, and suddenly she didn't feel sure of much of anything.

She regarded Lance with deep distress. "If only you hadn't come here today. If only you hadn't tempted the curse by asking Effie to find you a bride."

"I didn't."

"But you said—"

"No, I didn't. Actually it was my brother, Val, who came to consult Effie's power. I only bore him company. I'm not the least bit interested in acquiring a wife."

Rosalind stared at him, stunned. Still bending over her hand, he peered at her through the thickness of his dark lashes. She saw the glint and realized how wickedly he'd taken advantage of her concern, how easily he'd made a fool of her again.

She snatched her hand away. "You—you villain! Legends! Curses," she sputtered. "You never believed a word of this chosen bride story. I daresay you made up the whole thing just to tease me. Do you take nothing seriously?"

"No, I fear I don't," he drawled. "And you'd do well to remember that, lady."

"I don't need to remember anything because I never want to set eyes on you again!" She felt her face flame with humiliation and choked, "To think I ever fancied you could be in the least like him! Even for a moment!"

"Like him?" Lance looked confused; then his eyes lit up. "Ah, that mysterious friend of yours that I resemble." His lips twitched with an odd smile. "He must be a devilishly handsome fellow."

"He is! Far more handsome than you!"

Lance blinked in astonishment.

"The more I look at you, the more I realize there is no likeness at all," Rosalind went on, her words propelled by a mixture of fury and wounded pride. "He is by far taller than you and broader through the shoulders. His brow is more noble, his hair darker and more lustrous, his chin far stronger and more manly. And as for his eyes—they are at least a dozen times finer and more expressive than yours."

Lance swiveled toward the oval mirror that hung near the door. He rubbed one hand along the line of his jaw, studying his own reflection with a startled look on his face, as though it came as quite a shock to the conceited man to hear that there might exist someone better-looking than himself.

Rosalind wagered that it wasn't often anyone could give the arrogant Lance St. Leger such a set-down, let alone a lady usually as shy as herself.

She continued with a savage sense of satisfaction. "And as for manners, my friend's are far superior. So kind and courteous, and he recites poetry."

"Poetry?" Lance pulled one more wry face at himself, then wrenched his gaze from the mirror. "This fellow actually minced about spouting verses at you? He sounds like an incredible ass."

"Well, he's not," Rosalind snapped. "He's courageous and brave, yet so gentle. He would never pounce upon a half-conscious lady and steal a kiss. He would never embrace her at all without asking."

"This fool goes about asking women for kisses?" Lance's eyes danced with a mocking amusement.

"Yes! And in the most tender way possible." Despite her anger with Lance, Rosalind's voice softened at the memory of her gallant knight. "He would say something romantic like . . . 'I beg the honor of saluting you, lady.' "

She fixed Lance with a scornful glare. "That is the proper way to go about it. That is the gentlemanly way."

"So let me get this clear. If I were only to ask you for a kiss, you would give it to me?"

"Certainly not!" Rosalind thrust her chin high into the air. "Not even if you begged!"

Having dealt him this final crushing blow, she prepared to sweep triumphantly from the room. But she should have known it would not be so easy to quell Lance St. Leger.

She'd scarce taken a step when his arm lashed around her waist, drawing her back to him.

"There's only one problem with that, my lady," he murmured, his eyes glimmering dangerously. *"I never ask."*

Before she could even draw breath, he bent her back over his arm, setting her off balance. A startled cry escaped Rosalind, but he smothered it with his lips, his mouth taking hers in a hard fierce kiss.

Frightened, furious, she struggled in his embrace, flailing her fists against his back, helpless against the iron strength of his arms, the insistent pressure of his lips. If Lance St. Leger had determined to terrify her, alarm her into fleeing the village, he could not have been more ruthless.

His mouth bruised, plundered, ravaged hers, rendering her so giddy, she whimpered in protest. If it had been at all possible to have summoned Sir Lancelot from his grave to defend her, she would have done so. But all she could do was submit, trembling in Lance's arms.

Just as she feared she might faint all over again, he suddenly broke the contact, hauling her upright. He regarded her with a strange frown, and when she returned his stare, reproachfully, she was surprised to see a hint of regret in his eyes.

But not enough to stop him from holding her fast in his arms, preparing to kiss her again.

"Please don't!" she begged, trying to insinuate her hands between them, hold him off.

But he caught her wrists, sweeping her arms behind her back, crushing her breasts against the wall of his chest. She cast him a pleading look only to shut her eyes tight as his mouth claimed hers again. Not quite so ruthlessly this time. He was more gentle, more coaxing. His lips slanted over hers, tasting, exploring the texture of her mouth, forcing her to taste of his.

A taste that was hot, strangely sweet. She tried to hold herself rigid, feel nothing but the ice of her outrage, but it was impossible as his kiss waxed more seductive.

To her dismay, she felt her body quicken with involuntary response, something stirring deep within her. Perhaps she had gone too long unkissed. Perhaps she had never been kissed quite this way before. . . .

His lips teased hers apart, his tongue slipping into the hollows of her mouth, filling her with a moist secret heat. Unleashing hungers she never knew herself capable of, flinging open dark corridors of her heart she had never dared peer into before. Arousing her, awakening her, *frightening* her.

When he finally drew back, her breath was coming quick and fast. But then . . . so was his.

"Rosalind," he murmured her name in a husky whisper. His dark eyes glowed with unexpected tenderness, passion, and desire—and the triumph of a man who knew exactly what he'd done to her.

Her heat became the flush of shame, and she jerked to one side, desperate to free herself. Her frantic movement caught him off guard, and she wrenched one wrist out of his grip.

She struck out blindly at his face, pain spiking up her fist. He staggered back with a muffled roar, clutching his nose, his eyes flying wide with astonishment. Rosalind whirled and fled from the parlor, running as though her very soul depended upon it.

Val limped up Effie's cobblestone walk, so troubled by remorse, he didn't even register the fact that her front door stood wide open.

He could scarce believe what he'd done, abandoning Lance that way, turning his back upon a lady who required his assistance. A lady who for several heart-stopping moments he'd thought was to be his.

But when he'd realized his mistake, heard Effie declare she was to be Lance's bride, Lance who didn't even want a wife, who seemed incapable of appreciating such blessed fortune . . . It had aroused such a dark bitterness in Val, such a savage jealousy of his brother, he'd been deeply shaken by it.

He'd had to trudge several times around the village before he'd been able to subdue his demons and return. But now he was prepared, he hoped, to do the decent and honorable thing and wish his brother every happiness.

As he stumped through Effie's foyer, it did occur to Val that the house had fallen unusually silent. The parlor door stood ajar, and he approached hesitantly, not wanting to blunder in on any lovers' embrace.

The passion between a St. Leger and his chosen bride was supposed to come on rather swiftly, an instant reckoning of hearts. As soon as Lance experienced it, Val doubted his brother would waste much time.

He poked his head cautiously inside the parlor door. There was no sign of

Lady Carlyon, but Lance stood by the tea table, his back to Val. Clutching one hand to the side of his head, he appeared to be draining a tumbler of brandy.

"Lance?" Val called.

"Wha' the devil do you want?" Lance's voice was oddly muffled.

Val stole farther into the room, a feeling of foreboding creeping over him. Something had gone terribly wrong here.

"Where is Lady Carlyon?" he asked anxiously. "Am I not to wish you joy?"

"Wish me joy!" Lance's snort turned into a smothered oath.

He whirled and Val gasped at the sight of the bloodied handkerchief Lance pressed to his face. His dark eyes glared at Val from above a swelling nose.

"Frankly," he said, "I don't envision much *joy* with a woman who likes me a great deal better as a ghost!"

CHAPTER FIVE

Ominous clouds lowered over the village during the week that followed, turning the sea cold and gray, rough with whitecaps. Thunder occasionally grumbled in the distance, threatening but never delivering the promised storm, producing an unbearable tension in the air.

And no one felt it more keenly than Lance St. Leger. Irritable and brooding by turns, he sought an outlet for his pent-up emotion by crossing swords with Rafe Mortmain. Stalking a brief distance up the beach from the Dragon's Fire Inn, the two men stripped down to their shirtsleeves and drew out a magnificent matched set of dueling foils from Rafe's velvet-lined case.

Boots braced against the rocky shingle of beach, they faced each other, saluting briefly before striking a pose. Then steel hissed against steel.

It was only a lark, the sort of friendly rivalry Lance and Rafe frequently engaged in. But any folk peering down from the nearby village might have been pardoned for fearing that the St. Leger–Mortmain feud had broken out all over again.

Rafe dueled with a feral grace, his aquiline features cool and collected, his dark hair cropped after the fashion of a Roman soldier, his mustache neatly trimmed. A tall man, he had the advantage of Lance both in inches and in the steely precision of his movements.

Lance fought with his usual recklessness, venting all of his recent frustration in every lunge and parry he made. Frustration of nearly a week spent riding out every day, pursuing futile leads and still no trace of his ancestral sword.

And frustration of a far different sort brought on by a memory he could not seem to shake . . . the memory of a stolen kiss. His gaze flickered past Rafe to the distant outline of the inn, the row of mullioned windows on the upper floor.

Even now Rosalind might be peering out at him— "Oof!" Lance grunted as the tip of Rafe's foil slipped past his guard and rammed hard against his shoulder.

"A hit," Rafe sang out softly.

"Damnation, Mortmain," Lance growled, flexing his bruised shoulder. "If you hit me any harder, I think you'd have run me through even with the end blunted."

"Then stop mooning over your lady love and pay attention."

Lance started to blurt out a hot denial, only to check himself. Insisting he hadn't been thinking about Rosalind would only confirm the fact. Besides, he knew Rafe's tactics too well. The man wielded his tongue as sharply as he did his sword. Too often he'd won these little contests between them simply by goading Lance into losing his temper.

But not this time, Lance vowed. Not this time. Assuming a defensive stance, he braced himself for Rafe's next onslaught. Rafe circled him, with all the loose-limbed grace of a wolf stalking his prey.

"Lady Carlyon is still there, residing at the inn," he purred. "If that is what you are fretting about. I saw her myself only this morning."

As if Lance needed Rafe to inform him of that. He was all too keenly aware that Lady Carlyon had not left Torrecombe, had spent far too many sleepless nights this past week, tossing and turning, thinking of Rosalind at the Dragon's Fire, alone in her bed. . . .

Lance attacked, getting in several fierce strokes, which Rafe easily parried. "I don't give a damn about Lady Carlyon!"

"Of course you don't," Rafe soothed. "No doubt that is why you have been avoiding drinking with me in the taproom all week. It might be awkward running into a lady one is—er—so indifferent to."

Lance gritted his teeth, trying to ignore Rafe's silken voice. He pressed in harder with a series of reckless slashes, all of which Rafe deftly blocked.

"Never known you to run from a woman before. Not that I blame you, with all that talk Effie has been spreading about Lady Carlyon being your chosen bride—"

"Will you just shut your mouth and fight?" Lance snapped.

"Before you know where you are at, you could end up leg-shackled. Especially if you get overcome by one of those strange St. Leger urges I've heard tell of."

"The only urge I'm getting is to throttle you, Mortmain."

Lance struck out savagely, but Rafe leapt nimbly back with an infuriating smile.

"I'll tell you what, Sir Lancelot. Just in case your lady might be watching us from one of yon windows, I could let you win. Just this once."

Lance cursed and made a wild rush at Rafe. In one skilled movement, Rafe knocked the sword from his grasp. Lance tripped over a piece of driftwood, only to sprawl ignominiously on his back.

Lance struggled up to his elbows, fighting to regain his breath, disgusted. Despite his best resolve, he'd done it again, allowed Rafe to goad him into losing his temper.

"Surrender, St. Leger," Rafe said with a dramatic flourish, lowering the tip of his sword until it pointed directly at Lance's throat.

Lance glowered up at him. "Go to the devil, Mortmain."

Rafe merely smiled. The clouds shifted across the sky, casting a strange shadow over his face, his eyes glittering with a wolflike intensity. Lance experienced a frisson of inexplicable unease—as though for a moment they had both forgotten that the tip of Rafe's foil was blunted and this was only a game, one they had played many times before.

Then Rafe lowered the sword, the odd expression dissolving into a hearty laugh. He reached down one hand to Lance and hauled him to his feet. Feeling more disgruntled than angry, Lance dusted sand off the seat of his breeches while Rafe consulted his pocket watch.

"Seventeen minutes," Rafe pronounced with a mock sigh. "Usually I can manage to get you disarmed within ten. I must be losing my touch."

"Perhaps those eight years you have on me are beginning to take their toll, *old man*," Lance shot back. "One of these days, I might actually manage to get the better of you."

"Perhaps. Assuming you live long enough to see the day," Rafe said softly.

Anyone else might have taken the remark and the look that accompanied it to have sinister overtones. But Lance had discovered early on in his friendship with Rafe Mortmain that the man enjoyed nothing so much as unsettling people.

Lance returned the comment with a rude gesture, moving to retrieve his sword from where it had fallen. As he did so, he couldn't resist sneaking another glance back toward the windows of the inn, and he cursed under his breath.

He couldn't seem to go five minutes without his thoughts straying back to Rosalind Carlyon. Why the devil was the woman still lingering here in

Torrecombe anyway? She had scarce set foot out of her room this past week, but her mere presence in the village had been enough to cause Lance no end of trouble.

That and Effie's wagging tongue, boasting to anyone who would listen that she had found Lance St. Leger's chosen bride. The word had gotten out just as Lance had feared. He had been besieged by a horde of St. Legers, distant relatives Lance hadn't clapped eyes on for years, all calling in at Castle Leger, demanding to know when the wedding would be.

And the worst by far was Lance's own brother. Val simply could not understand what could have possibly gone wrong, why Rosalind had not immediately surrendered her heart to Lance. Lance was not about to enlighten him, to confess that instead of wooing his destined bride, Lance had done his utmost to frighten her into fleeing his side forever.

At least that's what he had started out to do. But at what point had he forgotten his only intention had been to terrify her? Perhaps as soon as their lips had met. Such a rush of desire had coursed through him, sweet and hot and almost overpowering. Not so surprising a reaction, since Rosalind was a lovely woman.

What had been surprising and disturbing were the other emotions that had stirred inside him, the unexpected wonder and pleasure of feeling her response. His kiss had aroused Rosalind, whether she'd wanted it to or not. He'd been able to taste the longing on her lips, see it in her eyes. Somewhere beyond the Lady of the Lake, beyond the prim and proper widow, was a woman Rosalind herself had yet to discover. A woman warm, vibrant, and passionate.

And somehow he couldn't stop wondering what it would be like to help Rosalind find her. . . .

"Take care, Sir Lancelot," Rafe's amused voice broke in on Lance's wayward thoughts, dragging his attention back to the windswept beach.

He was startled to find Rafe at his elbow, reaching for the dueling foil that Lance held in a careless grip.

"Perhaps you had better give me that before you do yourself harm. I am not sure dueling was such a good idea. You seem a trifle . . ." Rafe paused to direct a significant smile in the direction of the inn. "A trifle . . . shall we say, distracted?"

Lance scowled at him, and he thrust the foil into Rafe's grasp, but he was more annoyed with himself than with his friend, irritated that he'd allowed Rosalind to invade his mind again.

Deliberately turning his back on the Dragon's Fire, he growled at Rafe, "If I am distracted, you know damn well why, and it has nothing to do with any woman. I shouldn't be here playing games. I should be out looking—"

Rafe cut him off with a low groan. "Oh, please. Can we not go one afternoon without mentioning that damned crystal sword?"

"No, I can't. I should be searching—"

"Lance, we *have* searched. Every rock and cranny between here and Penrith. Between the two of us, we've covered the entire coast, tracked down every tinker and farmer who attended the fair that night. We've simply run out of places to look."

"So then what am I supposed to do, Rafe? Simply forget about it?"

Rafe didn't answer. He gathered up both the foils and hunkered down, taking his time about placing them back in the case. At last, he said, "Is that sword really so important, Lance? You St. Legers have so many other treasures. Oh, I'll admit it is a magnificent blade. I admired it myself, but when all's said and done, it's nothing more than an old sword, isn't it?

"Unless you believe all that superstition about the crystal possessing some strange power." Rafe cast him a sharp searching glance. "You don't, do you?"

Lance shrugged. "What I believe doesn't matter. But to my family, that sword *is* magic, tradition, honor, everything the St. Leger name is supposed to represent. My father especially. If I don't find the bloody thing before he returns, I don't know how I'll face him."

Rafe slowly straightened, arching one dark brow. "What? Afraid of a tongue-lashing from Papa?"

"It is not his temper I dread, but his disappointment. The fact that once again I—" Lance broke off, flushing under Rafe's sardonic smile. "It isn't always easy being the son of a legend. *You* couldn't possibly understand."

Rafe's smile faded. "No, I don't suppose I could," he replied coldly. "Since I don't have the least notion who my father was."

"Damn it, Rafe, you know I didn't mean—" Lance said, but Rafe was already turning away, stalking up the beach to where he'd left his naval coat, his back assuming that familiar rigid line.

Rafe was usually the most unruffled of men. Only on one subject was he unusually sensitive, the circumstances of his birth.

Lance stalked after him. "Rafe, I'm sorry—" Lance began awkwardly, but Rafe cut him off.

"What for?" Rafe scooped up his coat, slinging it over one shoulder in a stance that was a shade too careless. "It's scarcely your fault that my mother was a sometime actress and a full-time whore. And a cursed Mortmain to boot. According to everyone in the village, you should not even be my friend."

"Don't be ridiculous."

"And I am sure your brother, the saintly Valentine, tells you the same."

"You know how little heed I pay to what Val says," Lance said impatiently. "Especially when he starts nattering on about the Mortmain–St. Leger feud. All those tales about how an argument over land led to the Mortmains attacking the St. Legers and the St. Legers returning the favor. A pack of old nonsense."

"My mother apparently didn't think so," Rafe replied tersely. "She plotted to destroy your entire family."

"She didn't succeed, and anyway, that all happened before I was born." Lance had always felt uncomfortable discussing the past with Rafe. Evelyn Mortmain had been a murderess and a madwoman, but she still had been Rafe's mother. However, since Rafe had been the one to broach the subject, Lance couldn't help asking.

"You were only about eight years old when your mother died. Do . . . do you remember much about her?"

"Only that she could be wildly affectionate one minute and boxing my ears the next." Rafe's jaw hardened. "And that she abandoned me in France while she pursued her crazed schemes of vengeance against your family."

"I am sure she would have returned for you if—if—"

If Evelyn Mortmain hadn't been killed herself in her attempt to murder Lance's own parents.

Lance faltered to silence, and a dark brooding expression settled over Rafe's handsome features. They were both treading too near matters that might have rendered their friendship awkward, and as usual Lance was swift to shy away from it.

Rifling through the pocket of his own discarded waistcoat, Lance produced a small flask, which he extended to Rafe.

Rafe took a grateful swallow, only to draw back, squinting down at the bottle with a suspicious frown. "This is some damn fine French brandy you've got here, St. Leger."

"It ought to be," Lance said. "It's yours."

Rafe shot him an indignant look, which Lance returned with a grin. "You dropped the flask last night when we were out searching for my sword."

"How good of you to eventually remember to return it to me." But Rafe's feigned umbrage vanished in the wake of a quick laugh. As he passed the bottle back to Lance, any tension between them seemed to dissolve.

Lance took a pull at the flask, the amber liquid sliding smoothly over his tongue. He remarked teasingly, "This *is* excellent brandy. Enough to make me wonder if instead of pursuing those smugglers of yours, you have been purchasing their wares."

"I might as well join them," Rafe said. "For all the more luck I have had in apprehending anyone."

Rafe's grumbling sounded more light than serious, but Lance's conscience still pricked him. He knew better than anyone how much Rafe despised his post as a riding officer, the assignment that had brought him to this isolated stretch of Cornwall.

Rafe's heart had ever belonged to the sea, glorying in the command he'd once had of a custom vessel. But with the end of the war against France, so many of those sloops had been retired, including Rafe's. Rafe was now land-locked, and he hated it.

If Rafe managed to bring a halt to the smuggling activity that had plagued this stretch of coast lately, he might once more have a chance of a better position in the customs department. Lance felt a stab of guilt for all the nights he'd involved Rafe in the fruitless quest for the missing sword, all the time Rafe had spent away from his official duties.

He attempted to apologize, to express some of his gratitude for Rafe's help, but as usual Rafe would have none of it, and Lance was forced to subside.

They stood sharing the flask of brandy, both of them staring out toward the churning waters. A companionable silence settled between them.

Lance was seldom given to reflect upon such things, but he couldn't help marveling at the ease of his friendship with Rafe Mortmain. Not because of the ancient feud but more because of how little he really knew about the man.

They had spent the one summer together as boys. When Rafe had turned sixteen, he had finally managed to make his way to Cornwall, looking for his heritage. He had led a hard life, from what little Lance knew of it. Abandoned in Paris by Evelyn Mortmain during the terrors of the French Revolution, Rafe had somehow survived, only to discover his mother long dead. Evelyn had been the last of the Mortmains, and Rafe had no other kin.

Despite the bad blood between their families, the orphaned boy had briefly been taken in by Lance's own father and mother. And Lance recalled trailing after the brooding youth like an adoring puppy. But that had all ended abruptly after the accident in which Lance had almost lost his life, and Rafe had run off to sea without even saying good-bye.

Lance had eventually pursued his own career in the army, and their paths had not crossed again until recently, when Lance had returned to Cornwall. Yet despite the passage of time, Lance had been amazed at how easily they had resumed their friendship.

Why was that? Lance wondered. Because he could relax when he was with Rafe, be himself? No reminders of his failings, no expectations, no disappointment. Or was it simply the restlessness that often consumed both of them? Drifters, the pair of them. Lance was aware that even now they both regarded the far horizon with the same hungry gaze.

Lance nudged Rafe's arm, pointing to a stretch of beach that was now all but obscured by the foam-capped sea nipping greedily at the land.

"Remember when we were boys, how we used to race along there when the tide was out?"

"You raced," Rafe said. "As I recall, I was simply trying to get away from you. Infernal little pest, always trailing after me on that pony you so optimistically named Charger."

"Charger!" Lance mused with a soft smile. "I'd half forgotten him. He was a noble steed."

"He was a fat slug."

"Good enough to keep pace with you, Mortmain. Unless you weren't riding away as fast as you pretended. Besides, you couldn't have loathed my company as much as you claim. You did save my life out at the Maiden Lake that day." Lance always took great pleasure in reminding Rafe of that fact.

"Damned puppy." Rafe snorted. "I warned you if you tried swimming in that stagnant pond, you would get tangled in the reeds."

"Lord, how you cursed when you had to wade in and cut me free."

"I ruined the new pair of boots your mother had given me. I should have let you drown. Can't think why I didn't." But Rafe's mouth twitched into a reluctant smile. Different from his usual smirk, it eased the hardness from his sharp, chiseled features, softening his cold gray eyes.

It was a rare glimpse of the warmth that Rafe was capable of, and Lance feared he was the only one ever to see it, which was a pity. If Rafe could occasionally let down his guard with the folk in the village, it would have made him better liked, might even have been enough to make people forget he bore the cursed surname of Mortmain.

But Rafe was already fidgeting with the end of his mustache, retreating behind his customary urbane mask. "Well, St. Leger," he drawled. "As charming as I find your company, I fear I must tear myself away. Since I am not likely to inherit a castle from anyone, I must be about my work."

Ignoring Rafe's gibe about his inheritance, Lance said scornfully, "What! Hunting smugglers in broad daylight? Small wonder you haven't caught them."

"It so happens that a paid informant has given me a tip. There is a farmer hereabouts who might know more about the local smuggling trade than he is telling."

"The devil you say! Who would that be?"

"Andrew Taylor."

"Andrew Taylor!" Lance exclaimed. "No, surely not. He is one of my tenants and too honest to even take a sip of smuggled brandy. I have always found him completely trustworthy."

"Ah, but then you have a lamentable tendency to trust everyone, Sir Lancelot," Rafe mocked. He shrugged into his frock coat, navy with brass buttons. It was part of the official uniform of the captains who commanded customs vessels, and Rafe was no longer truly entitled to wear it.

Lance watched with a troubled frown as Rafe lovingly smoothed down the sleeve. He said hesitantly, "Rafe, you will have a care, won't you? Yours is not the most popular occupation. Riding officers have been known to meet with—with unexpected accidents, and you make a damn fine target riding out through the countryside attired in that coat."

Rafe merely smiled at his warning. "If I am ever found lying facedown with a bullet in my back, it will not be because of my profession but more likely because I am a scurvy Mortmain. Sometimes I think I would have been better off if I had given over trying to be respectable and simply pursued the trade I always dreamed of when we were young."

"What was that?"

"I was going to be a pirate, remember?"

"Oh, aye." Lance laughed. "And in your more mellow moments, you even promised me I could be your cabin boy."

"The offer is still open."

"Thank you," Lance said dryly. "When my father returns home and discovers I've lost the St. Leger sword, I may have to take you up on that."

Although Rafe continued to smile, he turned away, gathering up the case that held his dueling foils. When he came about again, Lance saw that Rafe's amusement had vanished, his gray eyes suddenly intent and serious.

"Don't fret over that damned sword, Lance," he growled. "I . . . I will help you recover the blasted thing somehow."

Before Lance could reply, Rafe pivoted on his heel and stalked away, back up the beach, heading toward the Dragon's Fire Inn. Lance watched him go, suppressing his smile, not in the least disconcerted by Rafe's abrupt departure.

Rafe had always had trouble revealing the more tender side of his nature. Lance was both amused and touched by Rafe's gruff concern, his offer to help

Lance keep searching for the sword even though he obviously thought the quest futile.

Lance himself was beginning to despair of recovering the weapon, at least through conventional means. But considering who he was, there was always another way, the *St. Leger* way.

Lance had hoped to keep his unusual family out of this affair. But the time had come, he thought grimly. He no longer had any choice.

CHAPTER SIX

*C*astle Leger perched high atop the rugged cliffs, the medieval aspect of the old keep with its soaring towers shadowing the more modern wing of the manor. But even in the newer portion of the house, the walls seemed to bear down upon Lance, steeped in ancient tradition, reminding him of promises he had failed to keep.

Avoiding even the servants, he barricaded himself in the library, the chamber lined floor to ceiling with shelves of books, most of which he had never been able to sit still long enough to read. He only retreated there now because he knew it would be one of the last places anyone would think to look for him and he might be able to complete his task uninterrupted.

A grim task that he did not at all relish . . .

The gloom-ridden afternoon already necessitated the lighting of candles, and Lance moved the candelabrum to the massive desk that dominated one corner of the room. The soft light spilled over the paper, ink, and quill that awaited. Only one item on the desk appeared incongruous in this peaceful setting. Like a warrior attempting to hunker down uncomfortably in a schoolroom, the empty scabbard perched precariously on the edge of the desk.

The scabbard that should have been heavier by the weight of a sword, the very symbol of Lance's failure. He fingered the leather sheath wearily, wistfully, knowing that Rafe was right in what he had said.

They had searched everywhere. It was as though the thief had appeared in a puff of sea mist and vanished the same way, taking the St. Leger sword along with him. The weapon would never be recovered by ordinary means. As much as it chafed him to do so, Lance was going to have to ask for help.

There was a distant cousin, a daughter of Hadrian St. Leger who'd emigrated to Ireland after she'd married her chosen lord. Maeve O'Donnell was said to possess a power very similiar to one Lance's own grandfather had had: the ability to divine the whereabouts of lost things.

Maeve's gift might well be Lance's only remaining hope, though it would involve confessing his own folly in losing the sword. Word of it would surely spread through the other St. Legers, the tale eventually bound to reach his father's ears.

Lance felt himself sicken with shame at the thought, though he hardly knew why it should continue to matter. It wasn't as though Anatole St. Leger had ever been led to expect any better from his oldest son.

Sighing, Lance settled himself behind the desk and reached for a blank sheet of vellum. This was undoubtedly the hardest letter he'd ever had to write, his own fierce pride battling against him with every stroke of the pen.

He dipped his quill into the inkwell, forcing himself to begin,

My dear Maeve,
    After all these years, you will scarce remember me as more than the annoying little cousin who once slipped a snake into your reticule, but —

The library door crashing open startled Lance, nearly causing him to smear ink down the length of the page. He glanced up in annoyance to see his brother charge into the room.

"Damn it, Val," Lance growled. "Haven't you ever heard of knocking first?"

But Val took no heed of his complaint. He had not even bothered to shed his mud-spattered boots or his travel-stained tan riding cape. Closing the door behind him, he marched straight up to Lance, his determined stride little impeded by his injured leg.

Val leaned across the desk and announced without preamble, "I've just come back from the village, Lance. She's ordered up her horses. She's planning to leave tomorrow."

Lance tensed, not even having to ask which *she* Val meant.

Rosalind . . . leaving. It was tidings Lance should have been glad to hear. But an odd sensation passed through him, as though cold fingers wrapped around his heart and squeezed. He ignored it and went on with his letter.

"Blast it, Lance! Did you hear me?" Val demanded. "I said that Lady Carlyon—"

"Is leaving," Lance interrupted, never lifting his eyes from the paper. "So what do you want me to do about it? Send her some flowers and wish her Godspeed?"

"No, damn it!" Val slapped his palm down on the table so hard, he nearly overset the ink pot. "I want you to go see her. Now! Before it's too late."

"Too late for what?" Lance asked, moving the ink safely beyond Val's reach. "For the infernal woman to have another chance to break my nose? She nearly succeeded the last time."

"And I am quite sure you deserved it."

"Very likely I did." Lance forced an unconcerned shrug. "You know what I'm like with women."

"Aye, too well. You tease, you flirt, you torment. You attempt to seduce. But somehow I thought you might be different with Rosalind."

Lance kept on with his letter, but inwardly he squirmed beneath Val's reproachful gaze. For somehow he had thought he might be different with Rosalind, too. His sweet and gentle maiden. His Lady of the Lake.

But it hardly mattered, for she was finally going. And Lance was relieved. It was only the fact that Val had taken to pacing in front of the table that was making Lance feel so damned tense.

"For the love of heaven," Val said. "You can't just sit there and allow this woman to slip away from you. Your chosen bride, the lady you were born to love."

"According to Effie Fitzleger," Lance reminded his brother.

"According to your own heart. St. Legers are always supposed to know when they've found their one true love. Are you going to tell me you felt nothing when you were with Rosalind?"

Lance crinkled his nose. "Yes, I felt pain. A great deal of it."

And the overwhelming need to touch her, to go on touching her . . .

Frowning with annoyance, Lance went back to his letter. He congratulated himself on having completed the arduous task, despite all of Val's haranguing.

Until he glanced down at the bottom of the page. There, he discovered that where his own signature should have been scrawled, he had distractedly inked in another name.

Rosalind.

Swearing savagely, Lance crumpled the letter into a ball. He shoved to his feet and stormed over to the fireplace, consigning his ruined effort to the fire that had been lit to take some of the dampness out of the room.

To his complete aggravation, Val trailed after him, like an annoying burr stuck to his coattails.

"Why won't you even go see her, Lance? And at least apologize for whatever you did to upset her. What are you afraid of?"

The unexpected question took Lance aback for a moment, but he made a quick recovery.

"I'm not afraid of anything," he said, snatching up the poker and jabbing it at the half-hearted flames. "Rosalind Carlyon might swing a mean fist, but I think I could defend myself against the woman."

"Especially since you always manage to keep your heart well out of the action. Are you so afraid Effie is wrong? Is that what is is?"

"No, I'm dead certain she is." Lance shot his brother an exasperated look. "Rosalind doesn't even want me. She wants some ... some damned fool knight in shining armor. *Sir Lancelot du Lac*," Lance attempted to sneer, but found he couldn't quite manage it. Strange that it should still rankle so much, Rosalind's obvious preference for the ghostly legend he had created for her.

"You should have heard her flaming description of her great hero. By the time she was done, *I* wasn't even sure it was me she met that night."

"Then go tell her the truth."

"That shows all the more you know about women, St. Valentine," Lance replied acidly, jamming the poker back into its iron boot. "They don't want the truth. They want fairy tales, and I don't have time for such god-cursed nonsense. I have more important matters on my mind."

"What could be more important than the woman you are meant to love for all eternity?"

"How about the sword I was sworn to protect for a slightly shorter duration?" Lance seized the empty scabbard and shook it under his brother's nose. "Or have you entirely forgotten about that? Even with Rafe's help, I haven't—"

"*Rafe?* Rafe Mortmain?" Val interrupted. "You've been allowing *him* to help you look for the sword?"

"Yes. What of it?" Lance asked, glaring.

"N-nothing," Val said, although a worried frown creased his brow. He made a quick recovery, however, returning to the subject of Rosalind.

"Lance ... if you lose your chosen bride, you'll have no use for the sword."

"I don't have any bloody use for it now." Lance slammed the scabbard back on the table, his brother's persistence fraying at already raw nerves. "I didn't come back to Castle Leger to fall prey to some infernal legend."

"Then why did you come back?"

"The devil if I know!" Lance paced over to the desk, grinding his teeth when Val followed.

"And what about the curse, Lance?" his brother continued to argue. "You know what sort of terrible things happen to St. Legers who turn away from their chosen mates. Remember the story of Lady Deirdre?"

"Aye, she ended up with her heart buried beneath the church floor. I hardly think I need worry about that. I don't have a heart." Lance all but flung himself back into the chair, dragging another sheet of vellum toward him. If he could have but five minutes of peace, he could redo the letter, but it was an all but impossible task with Val hovering over him.

"Then you are determined to let the greatest miracle any St. Leger could ever know just vanish from your life?" he asked in disbelief. "You won't lift one finger to stop Rosalind?"

"No!" Lance snapped. "If you think the woman's such a blasted miracle, go . . . go court her yourself."

Val paled. "You don't know how much I wish—how often I—Don't even tempt me, Lance" he said hoarsely.

"You've taken such a dislike to Rosalind, then?"

"Good God, no. She's an angel. What makes you even ask me such a thing?"

"Because I reckon you must detest the unfortunate lady a great deal," Lance said, "to be wishing her wed to a bastard like me. You know I'm never serious with any woman. I've never been faithful to a single one of them."

"Not since Adele Monteroy—" Val began, but Lance cut him off with a dark look.

"Leave it alone, Val," he warned softly. "Leave *me* alone."

Val stared at him for a long moment, his eyes seething with the frustration of all the things he clearly wanted to say. But he compressed his lips together and stumped toward the door.

He only paused on the threshhold to add in accents of rare bitterness, "I'll never understand you, Lance. You've always been blessed with so much. Yet I've never seen any man so determined to throw it all away."

He let himself out, the sharp click of the door somehow more of a reproof than if he'd slammed it.

Lance clenched his jaw, going back to his letter, trying to put Val's intrusion out of his mind. But the peace he had so craved seemed to have turned deafening, and he could scarce string two words together.

Lance flung down his pen with a frustrated oath and dropped his head into his hands.

It had to be one of the greatest ironies of his existence, he thought. He'd spent most of his life trying to provoke his brother, doing his best to make Val think ill of him. And yet there was no one whose disapproval could disturb him more.

Damn St. Valentine anyway. He could not really have expected Lance to up and marry Rosalind Carlyon because of some family legend.

"Just go see the woman. Tell her the truth," Lance muttered, mimicking his brother's tone. Sweep her up on some white charger and live happily ever after.

If only it were that blasted simple. It would have been for Val, with all his earnest beliefs and romantic illusions. But for someone who'd grown as cynical and jaded as Lance . . .

He was actually doing Rosalind Carlyon a favor by staying away from her. Frowning, he shifted and groped in the pocket of the frock coat he had left draped over the back of the chair. He found the object he sought and dragged it out, keeping it clutched in his fists.

Cautiously, Lance opened his hands and smoothed out what he held, a lady's white linen cap. He stole a furtive glance toward the door, half fearing Val might decide to barge back in on him. That would be all he'd need, for his brother to realize Lance had been carrying Rosalind Carlyon's cap around in his pocket all this week. Like some idiotic knight cherishing a token of his lady fair.

He didn't know what had induced him to hide the cap from her in the first place. One of his devil's pranks, he supposed. He'd hated seeing her wear the damned thing, covering up every last wisp of her glorious moon-spun hair, his Lady of the Lake transforming herself into a starched and proper matron. Those widow's weeds of hers were bad enough, all those yards of black hiding her willowy charms. She was far too young to go about buried in mourning for some blasted noble idiot named Arthur.

But Lance was not the man to remedy the situation. His knight errant days had been ended a long time ago. Ended by his disastrous affair with Adele Monteroy, along with all his stupid boyish dreams of love and glory.

He'd been in and out of too many women's beds since then, fought in too many meaningless battles. Bouts of lust and reckless carousing interspersed with the blaze of cannonfire and the screams of dying men. Not the career of any valiant hero, only that of a common soldier. A little more jaded than most.

It wouldn't even have mattered if Effie was right about Rosalind Carlyon being destined to be Lance's bride. The Lady of the Lake had come looking for her shining Sir Lancelot years too late.

With a sigh of something close to regret, Lance finished folding the cap and tucked it away, intending to see it returned to Rosalind first thing in the morning.

And as for the missing sword, if he ever *did* manage to find it, the best thing he could do was surrender it to his brother, along with his birthright, and ride away again. Once he had longed for nothing more than that, to escape from Castle Leger, but now the thought left him strangely dispirited.

He was tired, that was all, Lance told himself. Sweeping paper, pen, and ink aside, he braced his head upon his forearms, resting them on the table, intending to close his eyes for only a few moments.

In less than that, Lance had fallen asleep, but not a restful repose, one clouded with disturbing dreams. Of himself mounted upon a white charger, racing frantically through the village toward the spires of St. Gothian's Church.

He was late, damn it. Late for his own wedding.

He galloped through the throngs of cheering villagers tossing flowers and all but hurled himself from the back of his horse, trying to run. But he was weighted down by the armor he wore, heavy plates of gleaming metal.

Each dragging step he took seemed to bring him no closer, and yet when he glanced up, she was waiting for him on the steps of the church. Rosalind, his Lady of the Lake, clad in her flowing white nightgown, a wreath of lilies of the valley entwined in her golden hair.

He stumbled forward at last to kneel at her feet. She beamed down upon him, her blue eyes shining, and he groped for the sword at his side, to offer it up to her, along with his heart and soul, forever.

But as he drew forth the St. Leger sword, he was horrified to discover the magnificent blade broken and tarnished, the crystal cracked. Rosalind shrank away from him, her face clouding with disappointment.

"No, milady," Lance cried. "Wait! I beg you."

She merely cast him a sorrowful look, enshrouding herself in a cloak of midnight. Pulling up the hood, she drifted across the churchyard, becoming lost to him in the gathering mist.

"Rosalind! Please. Don't go!"

Lance thrashed wildly, fighting the heavy armor. In his efforts to struggle to his feet, he all but fell off the library chair, snapping himself abruptly awake.

He clutched at the edge of the oak desk and blinked, feeling disoriented for a moment. Then he released a long breath.

A dream. It had only been a damn ridiculous dream. And yet why did there still seem to be mist, shifting like wisps of smoke before his eyes?

His heart gave a sudden lurch. Mere yards away, a figure cloaked all in black stood silhouetted by the far wall, examining one of the books.

"R-rosalind?" Lance called uncertainly, trying to sort out the confusion of his dream from the reality posed before his eyes.

The cloaked figure replaced the volume on the shelf and turned, enough for Lance to realize this was not his Lady of the Lake but a man, tall and powerfully built, his features shadowed by a hood pulled far forward over his face. The last vestige of sleep dashed from his brain, Lance shot to his feet.

"Who are you?" he demanded. "How the devil did you get in here?"

"You're a St. Leger," a deep voice purred from the concealing depths of the hood. "You figure it out."

Lance stalked around the table, muscles tensing, bracing himself for any sudden attack. "Stand still and put your hands where I can see them. Then I'll give you five seconds to answer my question before I—"

The menacing figure cut him off with a silky laugh.

Jaw clenched, Lance rushed him, intending to wrench back the hood himself. His hands closed on nothing but air. Scowling, Lance seized the intruder by the shoulder. But the black cloak seemed to melt from between his fingers.

A prickle of unease iced up Lance's spine. He pulled back his fist, more in experiment than in anger. He swung as hard as he could.

As he'd feared, his arm passed right through the cloaked figure, setting Lance off balance. A chill rippled through his veins as cold as the grave. Lance staggered away from the man, his jaw dropping open in amazement.

The stranger did not appear in the least fazed by Lance's efforts. He simply stood there, arms folded.

"Are you quite through?" he intoned.

Lance nodded, managing to close his mouth.

"By God," he breathed. "You—you're a ghost."

"A young man of infinite perception." A pair of strong, elegant hands shifted from beneath the cloak to fling back the hood, affording Lance his first clear view of his visitor's face.

He had a swarthy complexion, not the pallor Lance would have expected from such a spectral presence but a countenance full of life and vigor, dominated by a hawklike nose and lips with a wicked sensual curve. Ebony hair flowed down past his neck, his neatly trimmed beard equally as black and lustrous. But most compelling were the eyes, dark, mesmerizing with a slightly exotic slant.

Beneath the cloak, Lance caught the flash of a scarlet tunic, the woolen hose and soft pointed shoes fashioned for a man who'd stepped out of another age. Exactly like the portrait that hung in the old keep and had fascinated

Lance and his siblings since childhood: the painting of the strange man who had founded the St. Leger family, the dreaded knight who had been rumored to be more sorcerer than warrior.

"Well, Lancelot St. Leger," the ghost said softly. "Do you know me now?"

"Prospero!" Lance pronounced the name with awe.

"Very good." Those exotic dark eyes took on a sardonic glint. "It is always so flattering to be recognized by one's own descendants."

"Of course I recognize you," Lance said. "When we were children, Val, Leonie, and I used to hide for nights on end in your tower, hoping for a glimpse of you, terrifying each other by whispering the most bloodcurdling stories of your sorcery."

"I know," Prospero said dryly. "I heard you. Infernal little nuisances."

"You heard us? But you were supposed to be gone. My mother exorcised you."

"The lovely Madeline has many charming abilities, but the power of exorcism is not one of them. We struck a bargain 'twixt us, she and I. As long as matters at Castle Leger remained well in hand, I agreed to stay away."

"But where have you been all these years?"

"That hardly matters. I am here now."

"Aye, so you are." Lance said, unable to stop staring. Even as a boy, he'd only half believed in the tales of Prospero's ghost. "But my father told me you were always confined to the old hall and not allowed to venture into this part of the house."

"Your father frequently harbors mistaken notions."

"I'll be damned if he does." Lance bridled at this slighting reference to his sire. "You were never permitted beyond the castle keep."

"I never *chose* to go beyond the door of the old keep. Now, if we are entirely through debating the rules of my existence?" Prospero arched one thin black brow.

"Oh—er—ah, yes, of course," Lance stammered. A ripple of excitement coursed through him such as he'd not experienced for a long time, making him almost feel like a boy again.

"Damn!" he said. "Val . . . I have to go tell my brother. I can scarce wait to see the look on St. Valentine's face."

His quarrel with his brother forgotten, Lance started eagerly for the door. But as he opened it, Prospero made a sweeping gesture with his hand.

The door slammed shut as though propelled by a gale force wind. Lance leapt back with a startled oath.

"You will tell no one," Prospero said. "You have no need to be afraid of me."

"I'm not afraid. I only wanted you to meet my brother. You have no idea how anxious Val—"

"I have no interest in Valentine at the moment. It is you I am here to see."

"Me?" Lance's brief spurt of excitement faded. He regarded his ancestor with a shade more wariness. "What the blazes do you want with me?"

"As charmingly direct as ever your noble sire was, I see," Prospero drawled. "What do I want?" He drifted toward the desk, examining the empty scabbard. "Well, to begin with, there is the small matter of what you have done with my sword."

"I believe it is *my* sword now."

"Not if you're going to go about playacting with it and allow yourself to be robbed on some dark beach."

Lance frowned at him. "How the devil did you know about that?"

Prospero did not deign to answer. Instead he went on, "It would also appear you have other problems as well." He pointed toward Lance's frock coat, and the garment fluttered as though caught in a light breeze. To Lance's horror, Rosalind's cap came floating out of the pocket and wafted to Prospero's hand.

"Problems of the heart?" Prospero inquired with a taunting lift of his brows, dangling the frilled cap by its strings.

A hot tide of embarrassment surged into Lance's cheeks. He strode forward and snatched the garment out of Prospero's grasp.

"What have you been doing, spying upon me?" he demanded angrily. "Did my brother Val conjure you up for this?"

"No one conjures *me*, boy."

"Well, I wouldn't put it past St. Valentine to start raiding the grave." Lance drew back, whisking Rosalind's cap almost jealously out of sight, tucking it in the desk drawer. "He's stirred up every other St. Leger he could find to harass me about this chosen bride nonsense."

"Nonsense? What!" Prospero regarded him mockingly. "You do not believe in your family's most cherished legend? And you call yourself a St. Leger."

"I don't know what the devil I believe anymore," Lance muttered. "But I've already known the pain of having once loved the wrong woman. I'll not be risking such disaster again merely on the word of Effie Fitzleger."

"Elfreda Fitzleger may be a very silly woman, but there is nothing wrong with her bride-finding skills. And somewhere in that obstinate St. Leger heart of yours, I think you already know that, Lancelot."

Lance glowered and turned away. He was beginning to understand why his father had been so glad to have Prospero gone. The ghost was damned annoying.

"Of course, you understand there is also a curse involved with refusing one's chosen bride," Prospero went on. "Perhaps to be offered such a gift afforded to few mortals, a love that would last for an eternity, and then to fling it away . . . the heavens themselves might be justified in demanding retribution."

"I'll take my chances."

"Are you also prepared to take chances with your Lady of the Lake?"

Lance's heart clenched, and he whipped around to glare at the sorcerer. "Are you threatening Rosalind in some way?"

"No, I'm trying to warn you. Have you never heard the tale of what happened to Marius St. Leger's chosen bride?"

"Dr. Marius?" Lance frowned at this mention of his father's cousin, a quiet reserved man. "He's a confirmed bachelor. He never had any bride."

"Precisely. Because he, too, delayed marrying when his mate was found for him. Too busy with his medical studies, trying to save the world single-handed, was our Marius. When he finally did make up his mind to wed, it was too late. His Anne died in his arms."

"Bah!" Lance paced across the room, wanting to refute Prospero's words. He had never heard any such story, and yet . . . There always had been this haunting sorrow in Marius St. Leger's eyes that Lance had been at a loss to account for.

He leaned up against the mantel, stubbornly crossing his arms over his chest. "I would prove a worse curse to Rosalind Carlyon if I married her. I simply don't deserve her."

"Ah, well, as to that . . ." Prospero smiled. "If every St. Leger was only to get what he deserved, he would end up—"

"Being burned at the stake?" Lance suggested.

Prospero's smile vanished. He shot Lance a dark look. "Mind your insolent tongue, boy. Unless you'd like to be turned into a frog and spend the rest of your days inhabiting the old moat."

"Go ahead. It would be a vast improvement, the way my life has been going lately. Just as long as I'm not expected to take charge of any lily pad or go hunting about for a chosen lady frog."

The sorcerer's brows crashed together in an ominous line, and Lance braced himself, fearing he'd gone too far. But slowly his ancestor's grim features relaxed, and Prospero gave a reluctant chuckle.

"I see far too much of myself in you."

"Is that supposed to be a compliment?"

"No," Prospero said, an odd look sifting through his eyes, no longer so amused, one of infinite sadness. It was gone in a flash to be replaced by a more inscrutable expression. He drifted away from Lance to stare into the gloom-ridden shadows gathering beyond the windows.

Despite how irritating Lance was finding the ghost's intrusion into his life, he couldn't help watching Prospero with a certain grudging admiration.

He was a magnificent devil, his every movement possessing the grace and arrogance of some medieval king, an aura of magic and mystery, of untold power. Lance began to understand why Val was so obsessed with learning more of this elusive ancestor of theirs.

As Prospero continued to gaze out the window as though peering into some long-lost time only he could see, Lance said, "Forgive me, sir, but I have to ask why you feel so qualified to advise me on the subject of brides. Who was your great forever love? No one has ever found any reference to such a lady or any memorial to her among the family tombs."

Prospero wrenched his eyes from the window. "The history of my life is none of your concern, boy."

"As mine is none of yours."

"Mayhap not." Prospero folded his hands together with a heavy sigh. "Ah, well. If you will not venture nigh your fair Rosalind out of love, perchance you will seek her to recover your sword."

"My sword?" Lance echoed in astonishment. "What on earth does Rosalind Carlyon have to do with my sword?"

Prospero merely gave him the most aggravating smile and glided over to the bookcase, pulling down a volume. A folio of *The Tempest*.

"Ah, Shakespeare," he murmured, leafing through the pages. "The fellow didn't even come close to getting my story set down correctly, except for my name. But some of the lines are quite good. Listen to this. . . . *This rough magic I here abjure—*"

He was cut off in midsentence as Lance strode across the room and jerked the book from his hands, thrusting it back on the shelf.

"What do you know about my sword?" Lance demanded, not even troubling to hide his anxiety or impatience. "You know where it is? Who took it?"

"I have no idea who took it. But I do know who has it now." Prospero's eyes shifted slyly toward the desk drawer where Lance had hidden the linen cap.

"Rosalind Carlyon?" Lance asked in pure disbelief. "You are trying to tell me that Rosalind had something to do with the theft of my sword?"

"No, fool. I am merely telling you that she now has it in her possession."

"How the devil could you know that? How could my sword have possibly fallen into Rosalind's hands?"

"You must go ask the lady yourself," was the sorcerer's infuriating and vague reply. He stalked away from Lance and adjusted his hood over his face. To his anger and consternation, Lance realized the specter was preparing to take his leave.

"Damn you, Prospero," he said. "Don't you even think of going anywhere until you've given me an answer."

But a light mist was issuing from beneath the sorcerer's dark cloak. Prospero's voice already sounded fainter as he gave an annoying laugh.

"If you want your sword back, Sir Lancelot," he mocked, "then you had best seek out the Lady of the Lake."

"Blast it all! Prospero!" Lance lunged forward as though he could somehow prevent the phantom from fading from his grasp. But he was driven off with a blinding flash.

Lance staggered back, swearing and clutching his hands to his eyes. He rubbed at them furiously, and it was several moments before he could clear away the spots of dancing light.

When he finally lowered his hands, it was to find the library empty. Prospero was gone, only a wisp of smoke remaining. The great sorcerer vanished in such a way as made Lance's own ability to drift look like a fairground conjurer's paltry trick.

Lance released a long unsteady breath, finding the whole experience so strange, he wondered if it all might just have been an extension of his dream. But as he gazed down at the library desk, he realized Prospero had amused himself with a parting jest.

There, seared into the surface of the wood, was the emblem of the St. Leger dragon, and the mythical beast seemed to be smirking up at him.

Lance sank weakly into the chair behind the desk. What next? he thought. First the missing sword, then the chosen bride he was refusing to marry. And now thanks to him, the spirit of a centuries-old ghost had returned to plague the St. Legers with his damnable sense of humor.

"I'm not going to have to surrender my inheritance," Lance muttered grimly. "When my father returns home, he's going to kill me!"

He dragged his hand back through his hair and was annoyed to find his fingers a little less than steady. The encounter with Prospero had unnerved him more than he cared to admit, and he was a St. Leger. He should be well steeled against any such strange goings-on.

The experience filled him with a new admiration for Rosalind Carlyon, for the complete aplomb that gentle lady had displayed when she had mistaken Lance for a ghost.

But any thought of Rosalind caused his brow to furrow in a deep frown.

Could there possibly be any truth to what Prospero had said? That Rosalind did indeed have Lance's sword? What would she be doing with it, and how could Prospero even know such a thing?

Lance grimaced. The damned man seemed to know just about everything else, and he clearly *was* a sorcerer, with more than five centuries to perfect his devilment.

Perhaps that's all it was, devilment. Perhaps Prospero had only made up the tale about Rosalind having the sword in an effort to trick Lance into rushing to her side. Lance had pulled off enough jests of his own to be mighty suspicious.

But it hardly mattered if it was a hoax or not. Lance would never be sure unless he went to the Dragon's Fire Inn and checked the sorcerer's story out for himself. He shoved to his feet, his lips pursed in annoyance, realizing that Prospero had accomplished what neither Val nor all his St. Leger relatives could do: He had forced Lance to go pay a call on Rosalind Carlyon.

But his pulse quickened, and he was disturbed to realize the notion did not displease him as much as it should have.

Lance's jaw flexed in a hard line as he cantered toward the Dragon's Fire Inn. The overcast day with its threat of a storm left the lane all but deserted, but he was keenly aware of window curtains being twitched aside as he passed, heads poking out of cottage doorways.

This was an aspect of his visit to Rosalind that Lance had failed to reckon with, the stir that he might cause. The tidings would likely be all over Torre-combe by nightfall. Lance St. Leger had finally come to woo his chosen bride.

No doubt there would be sighs of relief all around, as superstitious as these people were, with their own unshakable beliefs in legends and curses. Unfortunately they were all doomed to disappointment. Lance wondered how much relief anyone would feel if they realized that far from coming to court his bride, he might actually be forced to clap irons upon the woman.

He'd had far too much time to think on the ride over from Castle Leger, too much time to consider all the implications if Prospero was correct about Rosalind having the St. Leger sword. No matter what the sorcerer might claim, Lance could see no other explanation than that she was somehow involved with the brigand who'd robbed him. What did he truly know of the woman, after all? He'd never set eyes upon her above a week ago.

Lance prided himself on being toughened beyond any blow a woman might deal him, but the thought that his Lady of the Lake might prove to be a common thief left a hollow, aching sensation within his chest, such as he'd not experienced for years. Not since Adele's betrayal.

He remembered too clearly standing on the field of his first battle, tears coursing down his cheeks, but not from the acrid whiff of cannonfire. It was because the fighting was done, and after hurling himself so recklessly into the fray, he was still alive and unscathed. All he'd wanted to do was die after he'd discovered the truth about his beloved Adele.

But he'd been a fool of eighteen. He hoped that he'd gained some wisdom since then and a better judgment of character. If Rosalind, with her wide innocent eyes and sweet smile, was a hardened schemer, then she was the most consummate actress Lance had ever met.

He'd know the truth soon enough, he thought grimly. He wheeled into the stable yard of the Dragon's Fire Inn and dismounted, tossing off the reins to one of the stable lads. Lance ducked his head as he marched beneath the inn's low-slung door, his eyes straining to adjust to the inn's gloom-ridden interior. Even the candlelight was hard-pressed to drive away the shadows cast by such a sunless day and the dark beams of the original Tudor construction.

As Lance entered the taproom, he was dismayed to find the rough-hewn tables so crowded. For such a dismal evening, half the St. Leger tenants and farmhands from the outlying area seemed to be here, bending over their ale and puffing at their pipes.

At Lance's entrance, a hush of anticipation fell over the smoke-filled room. Some nodded in respectful greeting while others hid smiles and nudged their neighbors, causing Lance to grit his teeth.

He was grateful to see that Rafe Mortmain was not present. The amusement in his friend's sardonic eyes might have been more than Lance's temper could bear. He felt damnably self-conscious as it was, wending his way through the tables to seek out the inn's landlord. Mr. Braggs whipped himself out from behind the bar counter, wiping his hands upon his apron and greeting Lance with an oily smirk.

Lance's lip curled with contempt. He'd never had much of a taste for all of Silas Braggs's scraping and bowing.

Cutting off the landlord's effusive greeting, Lance inquired after Rosalind in the lowest tones he could manage. But Braggs responded in a booming voice, "Lady Carlyon? Why certainly, sir. Shall I have one of the maids fetch her down to you?"

"Just tell me where I may find her," Lance snapped.

"The first room to the left abovestairs—"

"Thank you." Lance cut him off and stalked away before Braggs could even complete the sentence. As he strode out the taproom door and started up the stairs to the gallery on the second floor, he was followed by a tide of hushed voices.

"Lordy! Did you see the look on Master Lance's face?"

"The lad's St. Leger blood be stirred up at last."

"You there, Braggs! You best send someone to fetch the vicar and his prayer book double quick. Afore Master Lance gets his beddin' and his marryin' a trifle backwards."

"I trow he wouldn't be the first St. Leger to do so," Bragg's sneering voice replied.

This last remark was greeted with a raucous burst of laughter. His ears burning, Lance paused midstairs, seized with a strong urge to go back down and give Braggs a sharp cuff to the head. But it would only make the situation worse.

Perhaps it would have been better to have one of the maids fetch Lady Carlyon down to the private dining room at the back of the inn. But Lance felt pushed well past any such proprieties. Doggedly he kept going until he reached Rosalind's door and rapped his knuckles against the wood.

He shifted from foot to foot, disturbed to discover that the mere thought of seeing Rosalind again *was* doing something strange to his St. Leger blood. His heart pumped just a little harder, his pulses quickening with a sensation that was almost primitive and entirely out of his control.

A throbbing response that felt as old as time, the anticipation of a man who'd come to claim—

Nothing. He'd come to claim nothing. Except perhaps his sword. Lance fought to suppress the unsettling emotion and knocked harder. It seemed an eternity before there was any response, and Lance prepared to hammer again when the door inched open.

The frightened face of Rosalind's maid peeked out. Remembering that Jenny had encountered him once before in his ghostly form, Lance braced himself for a piercing shriek.

But the young woman apparently did not recognize him, for all she did was quaver, "Y-yes, sir?"

"I need to see your mistress, Lady Carlyon," Lance said.

"S-she's not here." Jenny attempted to shut the door, but Lance caught hold of the edge and forced his way into the room, ignoring the girl's alarmed squeak.

"Rosalind?" he called.

But a quick glance around the small bedchamber assured him the maid had spoken the truth. Lance saw nothing beyond the room's simple accoutrements, the bed, the washstand, Rosalind's half-opened traveling trunk.

His jaw knotted with sheer vexation.

But where? Where would she go at such an hour, the sky heavy with the promise of an oncoming storm? Not to take an idle stroll down the beach, Lance thought grimly, judging from her maid's appearance.

Strands of strawberry-colored hair escaped from beneath Jenny's mobcap, hanging limply about her frazzled countenance, her wrinkled apron looking as if it had been worried nigh to a thread by the wringing of her nervous hands.

Stalking back to confront the girl, Lance demanded, "Where is your mistress?"

Jenny cowered near the door, but she tipped up her small pointed chin in a valiant effort. "That—that is no concern of yours, sir. Now you—you just get out of here before I summon Mr. Braggs and have you thrown out."

"I mean you no harm, girl. But it is urgent I speak with Lady Carlyon at once. Now *where* the devil is she?"

Jenny shrank from him. "I—I'll not tell you. You could be a desperate brigand."

"Do I look like a desperate brigand?" Lance snapped, then grimaced, raking his hand back through his wild, windblown hair, realizing that perhaps he did.

Apparently Jenny thought so, for she swept a shaky finger toward the door. "Get out of here," she shrilled. "Or I—I'll have you taken up before the nearest magistrate."

"I *am* the acting magistrate. And if you don't believe me, I'll summon Braggs myself to tell you so."

"O-ooh!" Jenny's fair skin turned the color of ash.

Lance planted his hands on his hips and assumed his sternest expression. "Now, are you going to tell me what I need to know, or shall I have *you* arrested? I only want to ask your mistress a few questions. Regarding a certain missing sword."

Jenny pressed trembling fingers to her lips, any defiance she possessed crumbling completely. She sank down onto the edge of the bed, her eyes filling with tears. "Oh, lordy! I—I told my lady nothing good could come of keeping that terrible crystal sword. The night she found that dreadful thing, I said we should turn it over to the constable."

Crystal sword? Lance's eyes narrowed. So the old devil Prospero was right.

Rosalind did have the St. Leger blade. But the sweetest part of Jenny's communication played over again in his mind. The night Rosalind had found that dreadful thing . . . *found* it. He heaved a deep sigh, feeling as though the weight of the world had just rolled off his shoulders.

There was still much left unanswered, but Lance had learned the most important thing. His Rosalind was no thief. He focused his attention back on Jenny with a renewed patience, which was just as well, for the girl showed signs of going off into hysterics.

Her nerves clearly pushed to the snapping point, she burst into tears. Lance bent over her, offering his handkerchief in place of her much abused apron.

"Th-thank you, sir," she gulped, but it was several moments before she could tell Lance anything more and then such a garbled account made little sense to him. Something about Rosalind finding a sword hidden beneath the floor, spiriting the stolen weapon away to guard it, hiding it under—under—

"Under her bed?" Lance asked in disbelief, attempting to peer into Jenny's tear-streaked countenance. "Did you say Lady Carlyon has been keeping the sword under her bed?"

Jenny hiccuped and nodded. " 'N-neath mattress."

Lance pulled a wry face at the irony of it. For once in his life he'd avoided a woman's bed, and the object he'd been riding to hell and back looking for had been tucked safely beneath Rosalind's sheets all this time.

His gaze dropped ruefully to the mattress Jenny was perched upon. "And is that where the sword is now?"

She blew her nose gustily into his handkerchief and shook her head. "N-no. Mistress took—took it with her to r-restore—"

"To restore it to its owner?" Lance prompted when Jenny threatened to be overcome again.

"N-no, sir." Jenny's moist eyes widened in surprise. "How c-could she do that when Excalibur's owner is so long dead?"

"Excalibur?" Lance exclaimed, dumbfounded.

"Aye, 'tis that sword that King Arthur—"

"I know what it is," Lance interrupted. "But what the blazes does that have to do with—" He broke off, his mouth clamping abruptly shut. Oh, lord, surely not even Rosalind, with her head stuffed full of so many romantic stories . . . surely not even she could be so credulous to believe that she'd found—

But one look at Jenny's awed face assured him that Rosalind did indeed believe she'd found the legendary Excalibur, and she'd managed to convince her maid as well.

Lance rolled his eyes, torn between exasperation and amusement. What could have put such a damn fool notion into Rosalind's head?

Perhaps the lies of a certain dishonest rogue, masquerading as the ghost of Lancelot du Lac, filling her head full of nonsense?

Lance's amusement faded. He flinched with guilt and said, "The sword your mistress found is not—er—ah, well, never mind about that right now. Just tell me where Lady Carlyon has taken the weapon."

Jenny sniffed, taking another wipe at her eyes. "Well, sir, 'twas clearly not safe to keep it at the inn any longer. Not with that rogue as what stole the sword prowling about."

Lance stiffened. "You know who stole the sword?"

"No, sir, but mistress is fair certain she's been spied upon the past few days. That the villain must have guessed somehow that she's the one as took Excalibur from its hiding place."

Jenny shivered. "Once—once when we went out, just for a breath of air, my lady thinks that someone actually tried to break into our room. After that, neither of us barely got a wink of sleep or dared stir a step out of doors."

Lance's brow furrowed into a deep frown. Was this all more of Rosalind's fertile imagination, or was it possible that his Lady of the Lake had stumbled into a great deal of danger?

Highly possible, Lance thought, the more he considered the matter. Anyone ruthless and bold enough to have dared attack him, a St. Leger, would not easily surrender a prize gained at such risk. And how hard would it have been for his assailant to guess who had thwarted him as soon as he found the sword missing?

Not very hard at all, especially since the thief must have free access to the Dragon's Fire Inn, and it would not have taken any great perception to observe that Lady Carlyon and her maid were behaving strangely.

Jenny's nervousness was transparent as glass, and as for Rosalind . . . Lance winced. His Lady of the Lake did not strike him as a woman over-burdened with discretion. Her very furtiveness would have aroused suspicion, caused her every movement to be closely watched.

Frowning, he peered out the window. The pale sun was already starting to set upon a day that had been no more than restless shadows. The narrow lane through the village appeared empty and deserted, as most of the rugged countryside hereabouts soon would be.

And somewhere out there in this wild and isolated land of his, Lance reflected anxiously, was Rosalind, alone, unprotected, that dangerous sword clutched to her side. But no more dangerous than the threat that might be melting out of the darkness behind her.

Hitching in his breath, he caught Jenny fiercely by the shoulders, his demand taking on an entirely new urgency.

"Jenny, you have got to tell me. Where the devil has she gone?"

CHAPTER SEVEN

*B*illows of mist drifted across the surface of the lake, the last pale rays of daylight turning the smooth waters into a shield of polished steel. Rosalind huddled on the shore, knee-deep in tangled grasses, the damp seeping through the thin soles of her shoes. She shivered a little at her own reflection in the silvery pool below.

She made an eerie figure, swathed in her midnight-colored cloak, the black veil draped over her bonnet, obscuring her features. The dark wraith of a woman mirrored below her seemed somehow quite in keeping with her lonely surroundings.

Rosalind found it hard to remember that she was but a few miles from the snug confines of the village, the land having assumed a wilder, harsher aspect. No sign of any human habitation, no sound to break the twilight except for the piercing cry of a nightjar and the occasional stirring of the reeds.

Her guidebook had led her to believe the Maiden Lake would be a friendlier place, sparkling waters of spellbinding blue set in a charming clearing of ancient oaks. But even the trees took on a sinister appearance, the leaves clinging to the gnarled branches with a desperate tenacity.

Yet perhaps it was fitting that the spot where a great and noble king was rumored to have breathed his last should speak more of ghosts than enchantment, a melancholy tale of a kingdom and dreams lost. The young ostler from the Dragon's Fire Inn, who had brought Rosalind out here in his pony cart, had warned her what an isolated place it was.

Jem Sparkins had appeared much astonished by her urgent need to visit an old pond in the middle of nowhere at such an hour, but since he had been venturing in this direction anyway, the good-natured lad had willingly obliged. He had almost insisted upon staying with her, much to her alarm. What she had come to do here, she needed to be alone. It had taken a great deal of persuading to get him to set her down and be on his way.

After she had alighted from the cart, he had driven off with a perplexed frown on his face, promising to fetch her on his way back to the village. But it was abundantly plain he thought her quite mad.

And perhaps she was, Rosalind reflected as she lifted her veil and gazed out over the gloom-ridden waters. But it was a madness born out of sheer desperation.

She had spent a nerve-racking week, doing her best to keep the sword Excalibur safe, praying that Sir Lancelot would come back to relieve her of the dreadful burden. Night after night, she had kept her vigil, sometimes staring out her window at an indifferent and empty sky, sometimes creeping back to that storeroom, pacing in her bare feet until she became chilled with the wee hours of the morning.

But he had not returned, her ghostly hero with the haunting eyes and gentle smile, and she'd finally despaired of his ever doing so. Worn to the point of exhaustion, she'd taken to starting at her own shadow, jumping at any sudden noise, plagued by the feeling that her comings and goings were being spied upon by someone at the inn.

She scarce knew what frightened her most, the terror that some savage thief might eventually track down his stolen prize and attack her to reclaim it, or another meeting with the ruthless libertine, Lance St. Leger.

Ever since she had fled from Effie's, Rosalind had dreaded that Lance might come after her to exact some dark retribution for the way she had rebuffed him. But to her vast relief, he appeared to have forgotten all about her, despite the fact that everyone from the local vicar to the bootblack at the inn buzzed with the tidings that Effie Fitzleger had declared her to be Lance St. Leger's destined bride.

Ordinarily Rosalind would have been fascinated by it, an entire village that believed heart and soul in a legend as romantic as the St. Legers and their Bride Finder. But it was distressing and embarrassing to have everyone thinking Rosalind would actually marry the despicable rakehell.

She had kept to her room most of the time, not wanting to risk even a chance encounter with Lance, knowing she would be mortified by his mocking smile, unable to look him in the eye. For the man was in possession of her most shameful secret.

He *knew* that she had responded to his heated kiss, knew that she was not as virtuous as she pretended to be. Rosalind had spent many hours fretting over it, trying to find excuses for herself. She had been in a state of great distress and confusion. She had been lonely and vulnerable, missing her late husband, missing the intimacies of marriage.

But had she ever returned Arthur's gentle kisses with such sharp stirrings of desire, such naked longing? The distressing answer was no, but she had reacted wantonly to the embrace of a man she didn't even admire or like.

Perhaps . . . perhaps it was the fault of this strange land itself, so wild and rough, it somehow got into one's blood, aroused primitive impulses one would never feel elsewhere. Long ago Mr. Fitzleger had told her his distant country by the sea harbored its own unique kind of magic. Perhaps he had failed to warn her that some of that magic could be of a darker kind.

Whatever spell had come over her that day, it was not important, Rosalind assured herself. Tomorrow morning she and Jenny would climb into the hired chaise and be gone from this place, abandoning memories of disturbing rogues and their even more disturbing kisses, leaving Bride Finders and curses, sword-stealing brigands and St. Legers all behind them.

But before she could go, she had one more legend to lay to rest. . . .

Parting the folds of her cloak, she reached for the sword that felt so awkward and unwieldy strapped to her side. Jenny had fashioned a makeshift belt for the mighty weapon, and it took Rosalind a moment to disentangle the heavy blade.

She drew Excalibur forth into the waning light. As she clutched the hilt and gazed out across the mist-spun waters, she wondered. Was there some sort of ritual for returning a legendary sword to the mystic lake from whence it had sprung? Should she wait for the complete darkness to fall and the moon to rise?

All she remembered of the old tale was that as Arthur lay dying upon the shore, he had consigned Excalibur to Sir Bedivere. That redoubtable knight had then given the weapon a mighty fling into the center of the lake. Of course, he had been helped along by the obliging hand that had broken the surface and caught the blade, drawing it down into the fathomless depths.

As terrifying as such an apparition would be, she would have welcomed it, reassuring her that she was in the right place, that returning Excalibur to this particular lake was the correct thing to do. That she had not merely taken leave of her senses.

She gazed down at the weapon in her hands, caressing the pommel as though the magnificently wrought blade itself could somehow ease her doubts. But the crystal seemed to glint up at her through the gathering darkness like a reproachful eye. As though silently rebuking her for abandoning her sacred trust.

"But I don't know what else to do with you," Rosalind murmured. "I was never meant to be the guardian of an ancient treasure. I am no legendary heroine. I am nobody of any great importance. I'm only a—a poor foolish widow."

She traced the gold trim on the hilt, trying to call up the image of Sir Lancelot to her mind, trying to think what he would want her to do.

She could almost hear the sad echo of his voice. *Mayhap if the blade was sunk back to the bottom of the lake, I would finally know some peace.*

Rosalind realized if she went through with this, she would most certainly put an end to any hope that she would ever see Sir Lancelot again. Not that there seemed much hope now.

She felt tears start to her eyes, but she blinked them aside. Firming her mouth in a resolute line, she raised the sword.

"I'll take that, my lady." The harsh voice hissed from the dark line of trees behind her.

Rosalind lowered the blade and whirled around, her breath hitching in her throat. She'd heard no one approach, not even the cracking of a twig. The tall shape that advanced upon her seemed to have come from nowhere, melting out of the shadows of a towering oak.

Her heart beat wildly with hope, believing for a moment that it was indeed *he*, Sir Lancelot du Lac, come back to her at last. But that hope turned quickly to fear as the figure stalked nearer, assuming a more menacing shape.

No heroic phantom . . . his heavy boots crunched the bracken beneath his feet, the need for stealth gone. He was garbed all in black, a silken hood pulled over his face, allowing only narrow slits for his eyes. A faceless terror straight from her worst nightmares.

Rosalind froze, so frightened she could scarce move or breathe. She shuddered, wondering how long he'd been lurking there, lying in wait for her. Surely a ridiculous consideration at a moment such as this, but her mind seemed to have gone numb with panic, rendering her unable to think clearly.

As he closed in on her, her fingers tightened on the sword. She raised the heavy weapon to hold him at bay.

"Who—who are you?" she quavered.

He came to an abrupt halt, keeping a wary distance from the tip of the blade. "I'm the owner of that sword. Give it to me!" The roughness of his voice matched the cold cruelty of his eyes glittering beneath the mask.

Rosalind shrank back a step. She felt the mighty weapon quiver in her hands and fought to keep it steady. "N-no. You're the villain who stole the sword from Lancelot."

"Aye, so I did," he rasped. "And at far too great a risk to be thwarted by the meddling of some infernal woman."

Her heart lurched as he attempted to come closer. She flourished the blade at him. "K-keep back or . . . or I swear I'll run you through."

She wondered if the fear and desperation in her voice were as evident to him as they were to her. Apparently they were, for he gave a guttural chuckle.

"I have no wish to harm you, lady. But I *will* have that sword, and all I have to do is wait. You have not the strength to wield that blade against me forever."

He was right, Rosalind realized with dismay. She could already feel the strain in her forearms and up her shoulders. As soon as she wavered, she knew he would pounce. And he had all the time in the world. The brigand could not have found a better place to reclaim the sword from her if he'd chosen it himself.

What a blasted fool she'd been to come out here by herself, so concerned that if anyone saw what she was about to do, they would think her mad. She should have ordered Jem to stay. She should at least have brought her maid, though what use Jenny would have been, she couldn't imagine. The girl would have succumbed to hysterics by now. Rosalind felt like doing so herself, but there was no one to hear her scream.

Could she possibly come about fast enough and toss the sword into the lake before he could stop her? Or would such an action only make him furious enough to strangle her on the spot?

While she hesitated, the villain had begun to toy with her. Eyes glinting with amusement, he shifted from side to side, attempting to circle around her. She drove him back with short panicked thrusts that he playfully avoided. And after each thrust, he seemed to loom a little closer. The ache in her arms grew unbearable. She had to grit her teeth to keep her hands from trembling.

A sob of pure despair caught in her throat. Just as she was certain she could not hold out much longer, a miraculous sound reached her ears. Faint at first, then louder. The thud of approaching hooves on the lane just beyond the line of trees. Coming this way.

Her assailant heard it, too, for he suddenly stiffened.

Rosalind gripped the sword with a renewed burst of strength. "T-there," she said. "That would be Jem Sparkins coming back for me. A fierce man. V-very big. Very mean. You—you'd best get out of here."

The villain's eyes narrowed, and she had a feeling he was no longer smiling beneath that hood. "This tiresome game is over, madam." He drew forth a pistol from his belt and leveled it at her. "Give me that sword!"

Rosalind stared down the gleaming barrel and swallowed hard. The sound of hoofbeats thundered closer. Somehow she found the courage to shake her head.

The lane was no more than a narrow track cutting through a field. But despite the descending darkness, Lance had no difficulty in following it. He had ridden out this way many times in his youth, though it had been a long time since Lance had set a foot near the old King's Wood. It had never been a proper woods at all, more like a thick stand of trees with the pond in the clearing just beyond.

As he guided his mount impatiently toward the shadowy cluster of oaks, he wondered if Jenny could not have been mistaken. What woman in her right mind would ask to be brought out here with night coming on and fearing that some desperate thief might be watching her every movement?

Only Rosalind, he thought grimly. As soon as he found the infernal woman, made certain she was safe, he'd have a great deal to say to her on the subject of—

A sharp crack cut through the stillness of the twilight. Lance's horse shied beneath him. Bringing the gelding back under control, Lance scowled. That sounded like . . . like gunfire coming from the direction of the woods.

One thought superseded all others, making his heart constrict with alarm, making him forget every caution.

Rosalind.

Pulse thudding as hard as the gelding's hoofbeats, Lance urged his mount into the line of trees. The branches closed like a canopy overhead, rendering it darker. But Lance's eyes had adjusted by the time he burst into the clearing, bracing himself for the possibility of ambush, a pistol or rifle aimed at his head.

But he saw no sign of any weapon except the one that was the object of the desperate struggle down by the lake. Two dark figures swayed back and forth, the man cursing, the woman crying out. Some villainous bastard in a black hood was doing his best to wrest something free of Rosalind's clutching fingers.

The St. Leger sword.

Lance reined in sharply, then leapt down from the saddle, rushing to his lady's rescue. The brigand snarled at Lance's approach and abruptly released Rosalind, apparently deciding to cut his losses. He plunged into the trees with Lance hard after him.

Lance batted aside twigs that threatened his face and tore at his coat, his pursuit hindered by the darkness and low-hanging branches. The rogue was swift, but Lance was closing the distance when his foot caught on a tree root.

He fell headlong. Lance scrambled to his feet. He took two steps and was brought up short by a shooting pain in his ankle. It was too late anyway. He could see well enough to tell the fellow had a horse waiting just ahead.

He watched, fuming helplessly as the bastard leapt into the saddle and vanished into the darkness. With a frustrated curse, Lance turned and limped back to the clearing to find Rosalind.

To his relief, she appeared unharmed, although much shaken. She leaned up against the trunk of a gnarled oak near the edge of the pond, still clutching the hilt of the St. Leger sword as though her life depended upon it.

Her bonnet had been knocked askew in the struggle. But as he approached, she lifted her head and he could see her face. Pale . . . wary. It occurred to him that she didn't look much happier to see him than if he'd been a masked brigand himself.

Lance couldn't say as he blamed her, considering the way they had last parted. He pulled up short, still trying to catch his breath. He winced as he tried to work the soreness out of his ankle.

"It's all—all over now, Rosalind," he panted. "Just—just hand the sword over to me before you end up getting hurt, and everything will be all right."

He'd meant to sound reassuring, but somehow he must have said the wrong thing. She gave a horrified gasp and shrank away from him, backing toward the edge of the lake.

She whirled about, raising the sword. Before he could even guess what she meant to do, she hurled the weapon with all her remaining strength. Out, over the lake.

"No!" Lance roared, charging forward, hearing a sickening splash. He stopped barely in time to keep from falling in himself, seeing nothing but dark ripples where the sword had vanished beyond the reeds.

Rosalind's shoulders slumped with a strange air of finality. For a moment, all Lance could do was gape, no words coming. Then he shifted to glare at Rosalind, sputtering, "Bloody hell, woman! What did you do *that* for?"

"I had no choice," she said in a small voice. "It was the only way to keep it safe. From both you villains."

"*Safe?* At the bottom of the damned pond?"

"That—that's where Excalibur belongs. Back in the enchanted lake."

"Blast it all, woman! That was the St. Leger sword. It's been in my family for generations."

Her eyes widened with a flicker of uncertainty, but then she stubbornly shook her head. "No. You're lying. It is . . . it *was* Excalibur."

Lance clenched his jaw, not certain if he was more exasperated with himself or her, for being credulous enough to believe in his absurd masquerade and all this Arthurian nonsense. But now was hardly the time or place to argue with her. The light was nearly gone and it could only get darker still, rendering his task of retrieving the sword that much more difficult.

He peered down at the pond with little enthusiasm, knowing from experience how damned cold and murky that water was going to be. Gritting his teeth, he stripped off his riding cape, his coat and waistcoat and cravat quickly following.

Rosalind huddled on the bank, watching him roll up his sleeves with wide troubled eyes. "What—what are you going to do?"

"It's a lovely evening. I thought I'd go for a swim," Lance growled. "What the blazes do you think I'm going to do? I have to retrieve my damned sword."

"You c-can't. The lake is fathomless."

Lance shot her an impatient look as he sat down to wrench off his boots and stockings. "It's five feet at its deepest point. I ought to know," he muttered. "I nearly drowned here as a boy."

He shoved to his feet. Ignoring Rosalind's soft cry of protest, he waded in, sucking in his breath. The dark pool was every bit as icy as he'd anticipated. He grimaced at the feel of mud oozing between his toes, the water quickly seeping through the calves of his breeches, then up to his knees.

Heaving a disgruntled sigh, he supposed he should consider himself lucky Rosalind hadn't had the strength to heave it very far. Making his best guess where the sword had gone down, he bent and began to grope through the treacherous reeds.

It was a messy business, mud and slime and murky cold water. He cursed savagely when he nearly lost his footing, staggering back, soaking the rest of his breeches as well. It was so dark by now, he could scarce see a bloody thing, and as the moments passed and he found nothing, he was no longer even sure he was searching the right spot.

Losing patience, he thrashed about in his efforts, splashing chill droplets up over his shirt, his face, his hair. As one icy trickle cascaded down the back of his neck, he muttered imprecations against all damned legends. Cursing King Arthur and his rotten knights along with St. Legers and their infernal chosen brides. Irritating women who unsettled you by walking through your soul, almost breaking your nose, then heaving your ancestral sword into a god-cursed pond.

By the time Lance's fingers finally struck up against the hilt, he was wet through and thoroughly out of temper. He dragged the heavy weapon up out of the water, and he sloshed his way toward the bank, still muttering under his breath.

Rosalind greeted his return with a cry of dismay. Clutching a tree trunk for support, she said hoarsely, "No, put—put it back. You have no right—"

"I have every right." Lance clambered ashore, dripping like a drenched hound. "Open your eyes, you little fool. There's no magic lake, just a slime-ridden pool full of damned cold water. No Excalibur. Just a cursed old sword with a bit of glass shoved in the hilt," he said, all but throwing the weapon at her feet.

The moon broke from the cloud cover enough to reveal the sword's sorry state. Spattered with mud and draped with bracken from the pond, even the luster of the crystal was dimmed.

Something seemed to dim in Rosalind's eyes, too. She pressed her hand to her mouth and began to weep softly.

Lance flung himself down the bank, groping for his boots and hose. Clenching his jaw, he tried to ignore her as he jammed the garments back on. But he'd never heard any woman weep the way Rosalind did, loud inelegant sniffs, sobs she tried heroically to suppress, but couldn't quite.

"Aw, don't do that," he groaned at last.

She turned away from him, burying her face against the trunk of the tree, her bonnet falling back to hang by its strings, its black veil trailing like a streamer, her hair a glint of gold in the darkness. Her shoulders shook with the force of her grief.

"Look, I'm sorry," he said, levering himself after her. "It's just you don't know what a nuisance that useless old sword has been already. You throwing it into the lake was the final straw."

She merely cried harder as though her very heart would break, her ragged sobs seeming to tear at him, making him feel lower than something that had slithered from the bottom of the pond.

"Rosalind?" Softening his voice, he rested one hand on her shoulder, trying to peer into her face. "Please . . . we can pretend the damned sword is any-thing you want it to be. Just don't cry any—"

He broke off, his hand coming away from her. Warm, sticky. Frowning, he brought his fingers closer to his face for a better look.

Blood!

"Rosalind? Are you hurt?" he demanded sharply.

"L-leave me alone," she replied in an unsteady whisper. But he caught her by the forearm, gently yet firmly forcing her to turn around.

He drew her close enough to see what he had failed to notice before in the darkness. The damp stain spread across one shoulder, blending with the black of her cloak.

"My God! What have you done to yourself?"

"N-nothing." She hiccuped, attempting to thrust him away. "It's n-none of your concern."

But he swept both her protests and her hands aside. Peeling back her cloak, his alarm mounted. Her bodice was soaked through as much as his own shirt, but with a darker substance. Without hesitation, he tore open the front of her gown.

"N-no," she quavered, slapping weakly at his fingers. "M-must you always be un-undressing me?"

"Only for medicinal reasons, remember?" He tried to flash her a reassuring grin, but the smile never came. His face stilled as he laid bare the injured shoulder, a sliver of moonlight playing over the ugly wound, the tide of crimson staining her white skin.

Lance remembered the sound that had brought him charging into the clearing in the first place, and his gut clenched.

"My God! Rosalind, you've been shot!"

She was still trying to wriggle away from him, but she froze. "I—I have?" She twisted to peer down at her own shoulder, a soft gasp escaping her.

"Oh . . ." Rosalind trembled and swayed suddenly, barely giving Lance enough time to catch her. He eased her down to the bank, using her cloak as a cushion as he propped her back against the tree.

Before the moon faded behind the clouds, the silvery light illuminated her tear-streaked face, her skin so deathly pale, her eyes dilated with a look Lance had seen before—on the battlefield, dazed men stumbling about, scarce realizing they'd had an ear shot off or part of an arm blown away.

Rosalind was fairly in a state of shock, and if he hadn't been such a block-head, he would have noticed that something was wrong far sooner. He tried gently to examine the wound, but when she flinched and cried out, he stopped at once. He had no way of telling how bad it was, but it seemed to him that she had already lost a deal too much blood. The best he could do was contrive a makeshift bandage and get her the devil away from here. As swiftly as possible.

He pawed urgently through the other garments he had discarded earlier, fumbling for his cravat, a handkerchief, anything that he could use to bind the wound. He could hear her quickened breathing as she watched him.

"It—it must have happened when that man with the hood pointed his pistol at me," she murmured. "He—he wanted the sword, but I s-said no, and I hit the pistol with the tip of the blade and it—it went off. There was noise and smoke and I f-felt something burn, but—but I didn't think . . ."

"You silly chit," Lance chided gruffly. "Why didn't you just give him the damned sword?"

"C-couldn't. After I found . . . it—it was my duty to keep it safe."

Her duty? Lance felt something thicken in his throat, something vile and bitter that tasted like shame. He swallowed hard.

"Fool! Bloody damned fool," he muttered, but it was himself he cursed as he folded his handkerchief carefully against her shoulder, preparing to use his cravat to hold the linen fast. "I'm sorry, but this is going to hurt like the devil. I have to make it tight."

She tensed but nodded bravely at his warning. As he knotted the cravat around her shoulder, he felt her body arc with tension. She sucked in her breath with a tiny moan that Lance found somehow worse than if she had screamed.

By the time he finished applying the bandage, Lance was disturbed to discover his hands were shaking. "T-there," he said. "That will have to do until I get you to Castle Leger."

When he felt her stiffen with alarm, he hastened to add, "Only to turn you over to my brother's care. Val is almost a doctor. Better than one. He'll see that you're set to rights."

As he arranged his own frock coat around her shoulders instead of the bloodstained cloak, she disconcerted him yet again by asking, "Then—then you don't think I'm going to die?"

"Good God, no! Don't be a little idiot," he said, but her words struck a chill through him.

He scooped his hands beneath her knees, preparing to lift her as carefully as possible. He could tell she didn't want him to, didn't want to be that close to him, hated it in fact, but her head sagged against his shoulder.

Although he fought to block the memory, Prospero's grim voice returned to haunt Lance, the sorcerer whispering of ancient curses and tragedy, the dire fate of Marius St. Leger's neglected bride.

She died in his arms.

As he swept Rosalind off her feet, Lance stole one glance down at her pale face and felt a strange constriction in his chest. The soldier who had hazarded his own life in countless battles suddenly remembered what it was to be afraid.

CHAPTER EIGHT

*N*ight settled over Castle Leger, the sky of such unrelenting blackness, it was as though nothing existed beyond the windows of Lance's bedchamber except a great dark void. He paced in the shadows by the heavy brocade curtains, feeling as though all the light left in the world centered on the young woman lying amidst a halo of candlelight.

Rosalind Carlyon looked swallowed up in the vastness of his four-poster bed, her golden hair spilling across a mound of pillows. She had dragged the end of a sheet across her exposed breast to retain some part of modesty while Val examined her.

Whatever emotion had so dazed Val the first time he saw Rosalind at Effie's was no longer in evidence. He appeared his usual dependable self when confronted with a medical emergency, that transformation stealing over Val that always amazed Lance whenever he beheld it. The dream-ridden expression that usually clouded his brother's eyes vanished before a look far more firm and steady, his orders handed out with a quiet authority.

One of the young housemaids hovered nearby to serve him, moving the candles closer at Val's request, holding the basin as he sponged the wound. The sight of blood apparently in no way discomposed Sally Sparkins, who'd grown up among an entire horde of breakneck brothers, including the feckless Jem.

It was Lance who found himself shaken. He'd seen far more gruesome injuries upon the field of battle, but he was obliged to look away from the ugly wound marring Rosalind's fair skin. He focused on her face instead. His valiant Lady of the Lake seemed to have dwindled back into a child, her eyes huge and frightened, her cheeks gone deadly pale.

And all Lance could do was pace, clenching his hands into fists, every muscle knotted with a sense of frustration, of helplessness. When he heard her stifle a cry at Val's gentle probing, Lance nearly bolted across the room, only to bring himself up short. Knowing there was nothing he could do, nothing but make matters worse.

Rosalind would only shrink from the sight of Lance as she had done before when he'd wanted to hold her hand, offer her what comfort he could. Or failing that, allow her to dig her nails into his flesh, scream and curse at him.

But Rosalind had wanted none of those things, choosing to bear her sufferings in a stoic silence. She'd turned her head toward Val and begged in a broken whisper that had lodged itself deep in Lance's heart, "Please . . . just make *him* go away."

Val had cast Lance a rueful glance but jerked his head toward the far corner of the room, and Lance had been left with no choice but to wait and watch from the shadows until he thought he'd run mad.

He realized that he was the last person on earth who could offer any aid or comfort to Rosalind Carlyon now. The man who'd already done his best to terrify her into leaving the village, who had cursed and raged at her for throwing his sword in the lake, shattering all her romantic illusions, then crowned everything by dragging her back to Castle Leger against her will.

It was a miracle that she was still conscious after what she'd been through. That mad gallop back from the King's Wood would ever remain a nightmare in Lance's mind, his arms straining to hold Rosalind secure in the saddle over the stretches of rough ground, the moon vanishing behind threatening clouds, the rugged landscape becoming no more than a blur, his fears and hers mingling in the dark.

Rosalind had wept and pleaded with him to take her back to the inn, to fetch her a doctor in the village. But Lance had been afraid to risk it. Dr. Marius St. Leger's practice ranged all up and down the coast. One could never be certain of finding the man at home. Ignoring all of Rosalind's pleas, Lance had galloped relentlessly on toward Castle Leger, sweeping her almost by instinct to the one person he'd always been able to depend upon.

No matter how much Lance might resent it, no matter how it angered and exasperated him, for all his life whenever he had been in his deepest trouble, there was always . . . Val.

He felt as though he'd never needed his brother more than he did tonight.

Yet it was the hardest thing Lance had ever done, to surrender Rosalind to Val's care, to stand uselessly aside while his brother sought to work his healing skills.

Her continued consciousness no longer seemed like such a great blessing. She finally admitted to Val what she had stubbornly refused to confess to Lance.

"It—it hurts," she whispered, tears leaking from her eyes. "I—I don't know why men are always so eager to be shooting each other. It is m-most unpleasant."

"I know. I have never understood it myself," Val replied with a wry smile. "But we'll soon have you set to rights."

She made a valiant effort to smile back, which Lance found somehow worse than if she had cried out. Val beckoned to Sally to continue sponging the wound while he rose, wiping his hands on a towel.

Unaided by his cane, he crossed the room to Lance, his limp more awkward than usual. The gentle smile Val had worn for Rosalind's benefit faded to an expression far more grave, and Lance felt his gut clench.

"Well?" he demanded sharply. "How bad is it?"

Val murmured, "Bad enough. The shot passed too high to have hit any fatal spot, but the ball is still lodged in her shoulder, and she has lost a deal of blood."

"Damnation," Lance groaned.

"Fortunately, the ball is not in deep. You should not have any difficulty extracting it, Lance."

"What!" Lance stared at his brother. His exclamation caused Rosalind to flinch and glance fearfully in their direction. Lance forced himself to lower his voice. "What the devil are you talking about? I'm no doctor. You're the one who's been studying with Marius."

"Yes, but I've had little experience with gunshot wounds. You've handled far more of this kind of thing than I ever have."

"Only on the battlefield when surgeons were scarce," Lance blustered. "Only among poor wounded bastards so desperate, they didn't care what kind of cow-handed idiot operated on them as long you poured enough whiskey down their throats."

Soldiers accustomed to hazarding life and limb. Burly men with hides as thick as his own, who roared and cursed and spat when their wounds were probed and cauterized. But the mere thought of visiting such agony upon his gentle Lady of the Lake turned Lance's veins to ice.

"I can't do it," Lance rasped.

"You have to." Val tugged at his sleeve with an urgent whisper. "If Marius were here . . . but he's not and there's no time to fetch him."

Lance glared at his brother. "And while I'm torturing her, what the deuce are you going to be doing?"

"I'm going to hold her hand," Val said quietly.

Lance had not thought it possible to feel any more horror at this situation than he already did. But the dread resolve he read in Val's eyes showed Lance how much he was mistaken.

"No!" he breathed. When Val's lips folded into that stubborn line Lance recognized all too well, he seized his twin's arm and gave it a rough shake. "Are you listening to me, Valentine? I am telling you, no!"

"Why else did you bring her to me, then?" Val demanded.

"Not—not for *that*, damn it! Surely you must have some laudanum or—or—"

"I don't use laudanum to treat my patients anymore."

Lance regarded his brother, aghast. "You mean to tell me you're risking using that infernal power of yours all the time now? After . . . after—" Lance swallowed hard, finding himself unable even to speak of that terrible day that had left Val crippled.

"You're a bloody madman," he finished harshly.

"No, I've simply learned how much I can risk," Val said, his face calm with that same sort of fortitude martyrs must have displayed before casting themselves into the flames.

"I can control my power better now," he insisted, seeking gently to pry Lance's fingers from his arm. "You have to trust me, Lance. Nothing will go wrong this time."

"And if it does?" Lance hissed.

"Then I can bear the consequences far better than she can." Val's eyes traveled toward Rosalind with an expression that was at once tender and wistful. "You would not want your lady to suffer any more if you could prevent it, would you?"

"No, damn it, but—"

"Then stop arguing with me. We've no time for it. All you're doing is frightening her."

Lance started to retort, but he saw that what Val said was true. Rosalind had clearly been trying to follow their conversation. She could not possibly hear what was being said, but she must have sensed the tension between them, for her face appeared more white and drawn.

Lance reluctantly released him, and Val all but bolted back to the bedside.

Lance followed hard after, by no means reconciled to what Val intended to do, but short of using brute force, Lance didn't see how he could prevent him.

There was never any stopping St. Valentine, he thought bitterly. Lance hovered near the foot of the bed, feeling torn, desperate as though he were being asked to choose between the pale young woman on the bed and his own brother. A choice that Lance feared he'd already made just by bringing Rosalind to Val.

He watched as Val settled himself on the edge of the bed and gathered Rosalind's hand into his own, murmuring some soft word of reassurance. Lance started to protest, but he looked down at her pain-racked features, and somehow the words stuck in his throat.

It was too late anyway. He saw her eyes flicker in surprise, and he knew she was already starting to sense it, Val's own warm dark brand of the St. Leger magic, coursing through the strength of his fingertips to hers.

Lance's hand clenched around the bedpost, the scene before him dredging up pain-filled memories, the kind he'd fought so hard to forget. But it was as though he could feel time itself slipping away from him, the bedchamber blurring into a battlefield, and it wasn't Rosalind's hand Val clasped but his own . . .

"Hold on to me Lance. I'm here," Val urged, *his soot-streaked face appearing through the acrid haze of smoke, his gentle voice carrying above the blaze of cannonfire, the screams of dying men.*

"N-no!" Lance writhed in his own blood, agony spiraling from the shattered mass of bone and muscle that had once been his right knee. Pain . . . he was nigh out of his mind with it, but not so much that he didn't realize what Val was planning to do.

"Leave me alone, damn it!"

"Lance, please . . . lie still. I only want to help you."

"No!" Lance cursed and struggled to pull free. Didn't Val understand? He didn't want to be helped. He merely wanted to die. But he was too weak and Val far too strong. His brother tightened his grip.

"It's all right, Lance. I can take it. Just keep holding on to me."

"No, damn you, Val! Let go of me." Lance's breath escaped in a ragged cry of despair. "Let me go!"

"Lance? Lance!"

The urgent sound of Val's voice wrenched Lance back to the present. As he focused on the bed, he saw that Rosalind's eyes had closed, the lines of her face relaxing, her breathing coming light and quick.

It was Val's breath that was labored. He maintained a firm grip on

Rosalind's hand, but his face was drained white, beads of perspiration dotting his brow.

Nonetheless he managed to flash Lance a strained smile. "Th—there. I'm ready, but would . . . would appreciate it . . . if you made haste, Lance."

Val's pain-clouded eyes traveled toward the young housemaid. All he said was, "Sally?"

But the girl seemed to understand him well enough. She fetched Val's instrument case and somberly held it out to Lance. She'd been in service at Castle Leger far too long to question or even be surprised by these proceedings.

Lance recoiled from the gleaming surgical knives, wanting to curse Val, wanting to refuse, but he couldn't even afford the luxury of hesitation. They were both depending upon him now, Rosalind and Val, indelibly linked by the fragile bond of clasped hands and the strength of Val's terrifying power.

Lance tightened his jaw and steadied his fingers. As he grasped the steel handles of the probe, he reflected darkly on the perverseness of fate and Valentine St. Leger.

For the second time in his life, Lance was about to become the instrument of inflicting pain upon his brother. And just as it had happened so long ago, Val had left him damned little choice.

The storm that had threatened for so many days had finally broken with flashes of lightning and cannonades of thunder. Wind and rain battered against the house with the kind of fury that could only be hurled landward by an angry sea. But the tempest outside seemed as nothing compared to the one that raged in Lance as he trudged downstairs—a veritable maelstrom of fear, guilt, and painful memories.

He headed for the library, where a decanter of whiskey had been left waiting for him. Reaching for the bottle, he was disconcerted by how badly his hands were shaking. It was nearly an hour since he had extracted the ball from Rosalind's delicate shoulder, but he was still trembling like a raw recruit staggering back from the terrors of his first battle.

By some mercy of God, he hadn't killed either Rosalind or his brother with his clumsy efforts. The lady seemed pale and weak, but no longer in pain. As for Val, he had recovered enough to tend to the cleaning and bandaging of Rosalind's wound himself. As soon as her eyes had fluttered open, Lance had realized his presence at her bedside was no longer welcome or needed. He'd backed off and slipped out of the room . . . to find some place where he could fall apart in private, alone and unobserved.

Disgusted by his own weakness, Lance tossed the whiskey down his throat and felt somewhat better as the fiery liquid flowed through his veins. Enough so that when he poured out his second cup, the lip of the decanter barely rattled against the glass.

Clutching his drink, he sank down in the chair behind the desk with a weary sigh. As he did so, his fingers brushed up against something hard resting upon the desk's surface . . . the St. Leger sword, polished to a state of gleaming magnificence.

Lance stared at the weapon in bewilderment. The last he'd seen of the blade, it had been coated with mud and discarded on the hall table. One of the footmen must have cleaned it and fetched it in here. Or . . .

He stole an uneasy glance around him, the burst of lightning that cracked outside the window forcing him to consider another possibility. He peered intently, half expecting Prospero to emerge from the shadows, mocking him.

But to his relief, he found himself quite alone. Whatever tempest raged outside was clearly the work of nature and not the further tricks of a long-dead sorcerer.

Setting down his glass, Lance touched the sword, as though needing to reassure himself that the ancient weapon truly had been restored to Castle Leger.

Small thanks to him, he thought with self-contempt. Even half swooning from the pistol shot lodged in her shoulder, Rosalind had been the one to remember the blade Lance had abandoned at the pool's edge. He hadn't been thinking of anything but getting Rosalind to Castle Leger, but she had refused to leave without the sword, even when he'd cursed and railed at her to stop struggling and be still. Afraid that she'd do herself further harm, he'd been forced to pause long enough to tie the blasted weapon to his saddle.

Lance fingered the crystal mounted in the pommel. He supposed that he should feel more joy at the sword's recovery, but all he seemed able to think of was how close Rosalind had come to losing her life, fiercely protecting the weapon that should have been his charge.

He thrust the sword away from him, only to wince when something sharp jabbed his thumb. Frowning, he bent to examine the hilt more closely for the cause of his injury. The crystal, once so polished, the diamondlike sides so smooth, was chipped, a small fragment broken away. When or how it had happened Lance had no idea, but that seemed of small importance, he thought dourly.

It had been his intention to surrender the sword to his father upon Anatole St. Leger's return. Something that would have been difficult enough to do, but now with the magnificent crystal marred . . .

"Hell and the devil confound it," Lance muttered. That blasted sword had descended safely from generation to generation in his family, never sustaining any damage until it had passed through his hands.

It was enough to make him start to wonder if he was cursed. But why couldn't he be the one to bear the brunt of it? Why did someone else always have to endure the consequence of his folly?

First Rosalind had been horribly wounded, then Val had had to suffer again, and now his family's treasured sword would be forever flawed. But as usual Lance St. Leger emerged unscathed. Considering what a bastard he was, he seemed to lead a remarkably charmed life.

Gulping down the rest of his whiskey in one huge bitter swallow, Lance was distracted from his dark reflections when the library door creaked open.

Twisting round to see who it was, Lance forgot all about the sword as Val crept into the room. Lance had seen enough of pistol wounds to know that his Lady of the Lake was by no means out of danger. He leapt to his feet, fearing what his brother might have come to tell him.

As haggard and bone-weary as he looked, Val summoned up a reassuring smile. "Everything is all right, Lance. I've finished bandaging Rosalind's shoulder and given her a cordial."

"And how . . ." Lance could scarce find the courage to voice the question. "How is she?"

"Much better. Enough so that she can sleep. I treated her wound with basilicon ointment, and barring the risk of infection, I believe we shall have her up and about by the end of the week."

"Thank God," Lance murmured, feeling some of the tension melt out of him. But he scrutinized Val's every movement as he limped across the room. Was it his imagination? he wondered anxiously. Or was Val now carrying his right shoulder more stiffly?

"And you?" Lance demanded. "How are you faring?"

"Oh, I . . . I am well enough."

Lance's doubt must have showed, for Val thrust his shoulder forward. "Look. See for yourself. No wound. No blood. If you don't believe me, go ahead. Give me a good hard jab."

"So you can pretend that it doesn't hurt? No, thank you."

Val flushed, a rare hint of irritation creeping into his voice. "I may be a trifle tender in that shoulder, that is all. I *told* you there would be no permanent damage done."

No, not much, Lance thought grimly. Only the deep brackets that framed Val's mouth, the lines that feathered his dark brown eyes. It was aging him, this reckless use of his power, this cursed ability of Val's to absorb another person's pain. But he would never stop to count the cost of that. Not St. Valentine.

Lance felt his chest constrict with the love, anger, and frustration his brother always inspired in him. It occurred to him that he'd never once thanked Val for all that he had done. Not all those years ago, not tonight.

He'd never be grateful for what happened on that battlefield, but what his brother had done for Rosalind was another matter. Lance experienced a strong urge to clasp Val by the hand, to try to express some measure of his gratitude. But that would be tantamount to confessing that he was capable of caring deeply about his brother and about Rosalind as well.

And God forbid that the callous rakehell, Lance St. Leger, should do a thing like that.

He sank back down behind the desk and poured out another whiskey instead, thrusting it into Val's hand. He was a little surprised when his brother took it without protest. Val rarely imbibed anything stronger than claret.

But he settled into a wing chair opposite and quaffed the whiskey with a deep sigh. He set the empty glass back on the desk, his grateful smile fading as he studied Lance, as though taking in the details of his sodden breeches and shirt for the first time.

"My God, Lance. You look like something that crawled from the depths of a stagnant pond." Val sniffed, pulling a face. "And you smell like it, too."

"Thank you very much."

"Perhaps now that Rosalind is taken care of, you wouldn't mind vouchsafing me some sort of explanation. What the blazes have you been doing? Where did you find the sword, and what happened to Rosalind?"

Lance hunched his shoulders in imitation of his usual careless shrug. "You told me to go fetch my bride, didn't you? She wouldn't come. So I had to shoot her."

"Damn it, Lance—" Val began in annoyance, then broke off with a reluctant laugh. At least for once Val seemed to know he was jesting. It was Lance who found it impossible to smile.

"Maybe I didn't actually shoot her," he said. "But I might as well have."

The exasperation melted from Val's eyes.

"Tell me what happened," he said gently.

Lance sagged his head back against the top of the chair, feeling loath to recall the evening's events. As usual, the tale would not redound to his credit. But there was no resisting St. Valentine. It was those father confessor eyes of his, full of such long-suffering wisdom, patience, and compassion.

In a flat expressionless voice, Lance found himself telling Val about all that had happened since that afternoon, finding Rosalind in the clutches of that villain, her extraordinary belief she was protecting Excalibur, how she'd even tossed the sword into the lake to save it.

Lance told his brother everything, save for one small detail: who had sent him seeking Rosalind in the first place. He scarce knew why he was reluctant to speak of Prospero. Perhaps because now that the sword was recovered, Lance hoped never to see his disturbing ancestor again; perhaps because he knew how chagrined Val would be to have missed such an opportunity.

And there was enough already in Lance's tale to disappoint: his failure to capture the thief, the damage sustained by the St. Leger sword, and most of all . . . the cavalier way he'd treated Rosalind.

"I was a perfect bastard to her," he murmured. "She was practically in shock, and I didn't even notice. I was too busy cursing at her for throwing the sword in the pond, shouting what a fool she was to believe in Excalibur and enchanted lakes.

"But then that's something I've always been good at," he added with a bitter twist of his lips. "Disillusioning people, shattering their dreams."

"After how fiercely Rosalind fought to protect that sword, I believe your Lady of the Lake is far more resilient than either of us gave her credit for," Val said with a slight smile. "Not easily daunted, even by you, Lance. I am sure she will recover."

Would she? Lance wondered. From the pistol ball certainly, but from the far deeper wound that he had dealt her . . . Lance remembered the devastated look in her eyes and wasn't so sure.

"Anyway," he concluded with a deep sigh. "That's about all there is to the story. Or at least all I know of it. I still have no idea how Rosalind became involved in the entire affair or how the sword got damaged."

Val reached across the desk and lifted the sword to inspect the crystal for himself. His dark brows drew together in a puzzled furrow. "It almost looks as though whoever stole the sword deliberately nicked away a shard with all the precision of a gem cutter at work."

"Why would anyone do a thing like that?"

"I don't know. When you find the thief, you'd best ask him."

"If I ever find him, now."

"So you still have no idea of who this thief might be?" Val asked.

"No, it was too dark and I was too damned slow to catch up with him. All I know is that he was about my height and build. Perhaps a little taller."

Val hesitated. "About . . . about Rafe Mortmain's height?"

When Lance shot him a black scowl, he mumbled, "Sorry."

Val replaced the ancient weapon on the desk, saying, "Well, perhaps Rosalind knows something that will help to identify the man. You can ask her to-morrow when you discuss the arrangements for the wedding."

Lance scowled, thinking he must not have heard his brother correctly, fearing that he had.

"*Whose* wedding?" he asked in an ominous tone.

"Yours and Rosalind's."

For a long moment, all Lance could do was stare at Val, not knowing whether he wanted to laugh or strangle his dream-ridden brother. He slowly shook his head in pure disbelief. "You really are incorrigible, Valentine. After all that's happened, after all I've said on the subject, to be *still* harping on that chosen bride legend, still planning my wedding—"

"I'd hoped you were ready to do so yourself. You're the one who fetched Rosalind back here to Castle Leger. You placed her in your bed."

"The woman was wounded, remember? What the devil else was I supposed to do with her?"

"We usually treat injuries in the stillroom off the kitchen," Val reminded him.

"That place? It's—it's too small and grim. I wasn't dumping her down on some blasted hard oak table."

"Then, there are other beds in this house besides yours."

"Damn it, Val! What are you getting at? You can't think I brought Rosalind here out of any amorous motives. I was only trying to make her comfortable, keep her safe until you—you could—"

"I know that," Val said gently. "But perhaps not everyone else will."

"What the deuce do you mean?"

Val sighed, then proceeded to explain as patiently as if he were addressing a particularly slow child. "Lance, the entire village has been waiting with bated breath for you to fulfill the Bride Finder legend by sweeping Rosalind up in your arms and away to your bed. Which is exactly what you've done."

"Because the woman was wounded, damn it! No one could imagine I'd be making love to her with a bullet in her shoulder. What kind of bastard do they think I am?"

"They think you are a St. Leger. A man whose passions are bound to rage out of control when he finds that one special woman destined to be his for-ever love."

"Nonsense," Lance muttered.

"Even without the legend, there is still the problem that you brought an unmarried lady to a house where there is no proper chaperon for her. I'll wager you didn't even think to dispatch someone to fetch Rosalind's maid."

"No, I didn't. Forgive me if I failed to think of the proprieties while Rosalind bled to death."

"You're going to have to think of them now, Lance. You've placed Lady Carlyon in an unfortunate situation, enough to bring any woman to ruin and unhappiness if she leaves here unwed."

"I'd make her a damn sight more unhappy if I married her. There has to be a less drastic solution." Lance raked his hand back through his hair with a frustrated sigh, scarce able to believe this. He'd barely had time to feel relieved from escaping one disaster, only to find himself teetering on the brink of another.

"As soon as the storm eases up, I'll send for her maid," he announced.

"That won't be good enough, Lance."

"Then, tomorrow I'll force Effie to come here and play chaperon as well. Will that satisfy you?"

"But what about tonight?"

"What about it?" Lance asked impatiently. "Rosalind's reputation can surely survive one night beneath our roof. No one besides a handful of the servants even know she's here, and I think I can command their silence."

"That's not what I meant, Lance. Someone needs to sit up with her tonight in case she develops a fever."

"Have Sally do it. She's a sensible girl."

"It should be you, Lance," Val said stubbornly.

"Me?" Lance's brows shot up in outraged astonishment at the suggestion. "After the way you've been preaching propriety at me? Now you want me to be alone with her in the bedchamber?" His eyes narrowed with sudden suspicion. "Anyone would almost think you wanted me to compromise Rosalind so I'd have to marry her."

"Of course not," Val denied hotly, although he seemed to have difficulty meeting Lance's eyes. "But what if she wakes up in the middle of the night in a strange place to find a stranger bending over her?

"After what she's already been through, she'd feel frightened." Val heaved a deep sigh. "And so desperately alone."

Lance cast his brother a dark look. He was fairly certain Val was deliberately trying to play upon Lance's emotions regarding Rosalind, and was annoyed by it. Mainly because it was working. The image Val conjured up of Rosalind awakening in the night, feeling lost, alone, terrified, affected Lance more powerfully than he cared to admit.

"Rosalind doesn't know Sally or me," Val persisted. "She only knows you, Lance."

"Like she knows the devil. And I think she'd find Satan a deal more welcome than me. In fact, there's only one man in all of Cornwall that Rosalind would be delighted to find by her bedside, and that would be her beloved hero, Sir Lancelot—"

Lance had started to sneer the name, but he found himself strangely unable to do so. He finished in softer, more thoughtful tones.

"Sir Lancelot du Lac," he murmured as the idea struck him more forcibly than a lightning bolt from the storm. Perhaps he would never have even entertained such an insane notion if he wasn't a little mad or a little drunk. Imbibing whiskey on an empty stomach was never a good thing.

And yet the more Lance thought about it, the less crazed the idea seemed. To don his guise of Sir Lancelot du Lac, to play the hero for her one last time, make her feel safe, comforted if she awoke in the night. In some strange way, Lance almost felt he owed it to her.

His unfortunate Lady of the Lake had already become entangled in his family's own mad legends and Lance's reckless escapade with the sword. She'd be leaving Cornwall with a scarred shoulder. Did he have to send her away with a scarred heart as well, all her romantic illusions in ashes? He'd taken Excalibur away from her. But he could give her back Sir Lancelot, spin for her a memory she could press forever between the pages of her books on Camelot.

Some of his thoughts must have been visible in Lance's face. Val stiffened, regarding Lance warily.

"No, Lance!" he said. "I can guess what you're thinking, and it wouldn't be a good idea."

"Why not?" Lance asked. "It seems to me the perfect solution. I can keep vigil over Rosalind without compromising her honor. No lady's virtue can be threatened by a ghost."

"But it's dangerous for you, your blasted night drifting. He who has great power must use it wisely."

"That's rich, coming from you."

Val had the grace to blush. "It's not only that. For you to deceive Rosalind again in this way, to keep up this absurd pretense, it can only make matters worse between you."

"I don't see how that's possible, do you?"

When Val continued to argue, Lance cut him off and shoved to his feet. "My mind is quite made up. Now are you going to help me or not?"

Val regarded him for a long moment, his eyes clouded with apprehension and frustration. But he heaved a resigned sigh. "What do you want me to do?"

"I thought that would be obvious," Lance said with a wry smile. "Come and help me find the damned chain mail."

CHAPTER NINE

osalind sank deeper against the pillows, her eyes darting fearfully past the bed curtains to the unfamiliar chamber that yawned before her, a dark uncharted territory lit only by intermittent flashes of lightning. When a loud clap of thunder shook the windows, she flinched and dragged the sheet closer to her chin. She had never been afraid of storms before and yet even the wind and rain seemed rougher here than those soothing downpours that had watered her garden in Kent.

The thunder raged and the lightning tore jagged slashes in the sky with a violent grandeur that matched this wild land, this formidable house perched high atop the cliffs. She had caught terrifying glimpses of the place from the shelter of Lance's arms when he'd lifted her down from the saddle. Through the haze of her pain, she'd obtained night-darkened impressions of a sprawling manor adjoined to the towering battlements and ancient keep of an old castle. As though time itself had blurred here, centuries shifting with the blink of an eye.

Castle Leger. The name itself whispered of a certain dark mystery, and now she was a virtual prisoner within its walls, held fast by her own weakened condition. She had dozed fitfully for a while, only to be awakened by the storm. The cordial that Val St. Leger had coaxed her to drink must have contained some tincture of laudanum because the throb in her shoulder had eased.

But without the pain to distract her, she was left with nothing to do but stare into the darkness, fretting about her maid, thinking how alarmed Jenny would be when her mistress did not return to the inn tonight. The poor girl would have no way of knowing that Rosalind had landed squarely in the last place in the world she wished to be.

Lance St. Leger's bed.

When the storm lit up the room, she could see traces of his presence everywhere. The man's very aura seemed to cling to the sheets, musky and disturbingly masculine. As intimate as if he'd taken those strong bold hands of his and caressed them down the length of her body, Rosalind thought with a dark shiver.

Why had he insisted upon bringing her here instead of back to the village, as she had begged him to do? He'd made it perfectly clear that he'd only followed her out to the lake tonight to recover his sword, that even her getting wounded had been nothing but a confounded nuisance to him.

She remembered the fury in his voice, the scathing things he'd shouted at her.

Open your eyes, you little fool. There's no magic lake . . . no Excalibur . . .

And gazing down at that mud-spattered sword, looking suddenly quite ordinary in the pale moonlight, she'd realized he was right. To have ever imagined otherwise was absurd . . . as absurd as a grown woman who still couldn't tell the difference between fantasy and reality, who wasn't even sure she wanted to.

Despite all her fear and anxiety this past week, she had been strangely happy, feeling more alive than she had since Arthur had died. Cherishing and protecting that old sword, believing she was on some sort of quest to help Sir Lancelot du Lac. Was her head truly that empty, her life so barren that she had to fill it with such foolish dreams? Rosalind feared that it was.

Otherwise it wouldn't hurt so much to surrender her romantic illusions about Sir Lancelot. But it did. Because without them she'd become exactly what she was when she'd first ventured into Cornwall.

A lonely widow, nothing more.

The thought brought a lump to Rosalind's throat, and she tossed restlessly on the pillow. The movement caused the bandage on her shoulder to shift a little and she froze. Feeling gingerly beneath the loose bodice of the overlarge nightgown loaned to her by one of the St. Leger housemaids, Rosalind sought to adjust the thick wad of linen, making certain it remain fixed over her wound.

She was surprised when her gropings did not cost her a fresh spasm. Even a splinter removed from a thumb left some tenderness behind. She'd had a bullet dug from her shoulder, and yet she felt nothing.

Lance had claimed his brother was a gifted healer, but this was nothing short of miraculous, the more so because Rosalind could not recall exactly what Val St. Leger had done. From the moment he had sat beside her on the bed and gathered her hands into his, Rosalind's memory became a blur. She thought she must have fainted, and yet it had felt more like drifting off to sleep, a golden warmth seeping slowly through her veins, breaking up the darkness of her pain.

When she had opened her eyes, it had been all over, the pistol ball removed from her shoulder, the unbearable ache gone. She had found both Lance and Val St. Leger bending gravely over her. Val had looked pale and drawn, and yet all the anguish seemed to have settled deep in Lance's eyes. . . .

Ridiculous, of course, especially the notion that she'd seen anything on Lance's face other than mockery and impatience. Only another instance of her imagination running wild. One would think that after all that had happened tonight, she would have finally learned her lesson.

But it seemed that she hadn't.

Otherwise she wouldn't have fancied that she just saw something move beyond the bedposts. Her pulse gave a frightened leap, and her fingers dug deep into the coverlet.

Where was a burst of lightning when one needed it? she wondered desperately. Even as she struggled up onto one elbow to peer into the darkness, she tried to tell herself, Don't be silly. It was nothing, only the shadow cast by the wardrobe in the far corner.

But wardrobes, as a general rule, didn't have the ability to shift position, coming closer. Until they reached the foot of the bed and assumed the shape of a man. Tall, broad-shouldered.

Rosalind's heart leapt into her throat, and for one moment she thought it was Lance who'd stolen back to her bedside, the idea at once alarming her and causing her blood to quicken with a strange excitement.

Then lightning flared outside the window, throwing him into sharp relief. The flowing dark hair, the hard angles of the profile were Lance's, but the hesitancy of manner, the sadness of expression belonged to another man entirely. As did the coat of gleaming mail that encased his powerful frame.

"My lady?" called that deep voice she had longed for so many nights to hear. "Art thou awake?"

A half-strangled sob of joy snagged in Rosalind's throat, to be immediately swallowed in the wake of an even stronger despair. She sank back against the pillows, tears starting in her eyes.

"Go away," she whispered. "You're not real."

"My lady, I vow to you that I am," he said. "Else my heart could not ache to see you thus, so pale and forlorn."

Rosalind clapped her hands resolutely over her ears and closed her eyes so tight, the tears leaked out and trickled down her cheeks. She remained that way for several moments, before she dared open her eyes again, despairingly certain he would be gone.

He was still there, gazing down at her with such tenderness, it was enough to make her heart break. When she scrambled to a sitting position, he cried out in alarm, "Nay, my lady. You must lie still. You have been most grievously injured."

Ignoring him, Rosalind groped frantically for the candle and tinder box that had been left on the bedside table, muttering, "You're not real. You—are—not! Only a figment of my imagination. And as soon as I get this candle lit, you'll be gone."

"Nay, my lady. I assure you. . . ." His protest died away as she struggled with the flint and tinder. Her hands were shaking so badly, it took her long moments to strike up a spark. But she managed to coax the wick to light. As the candle spilled forth its soft glow, she held it up so that the light fell over him, detailing the black woolen tunic, the chain mail that belonged to a warrior of another age, but his face, the generous mouth with its perpetual hint of sadness, the firm jaw, the hawklike nose, the eyes that glowed with so many dark facets were possessed of a masculine beauty that was timeless.

Rosalind stretched one trembling hand toward him, and he reached for her. She could sense how badly he wanted to catch up her fingers, carry them to his lips. But as he attempted to grasp her hand, his fingers passed through, melting into hers, as though their flesh had become one.

No, not flesh, she realized, but spirit. All that he was, all his warmth, passion and courage, all his sorrow, loneliness and despair blending with her own, to become unbearable joy, unbearable pain.

With a soft cry, Rosalind shrank back, nearly dropping the candle she clutched in her other hand. Somehow she managed to set the wrought iron holder back upon the table. Then she buried her face in her hands with a shuddering sob.

"Oh, God, I—I *have* gone utterly mad."

She could almost feel his hand flutter past her hair, wanting to give comfort, helpless to do so. "Milady, please do not weep. I swear your mind is as healthy as my own."

"That is hardly reassuring," she sniffed. "For I am completely delusional and you . . . you're dead."

"Aye, but other than that I am quite sound."

Rosalind choked on a laugh that bordered on hysteria. She forced herself to take deep breaths, struggling to compose herself. She raised her head, blinking away a blur of tears as she studied his darkly handsome face, the face of a man who could not possibly exist outside her dreams. That is certainly what Lance St. Leger would have told her and yet . . .

"You are still here," she faltered, her eyes traveling wonderingly over him.

"Aye, milady, to keep watch over you. I never meant to cause you such distress. If it is truly what you wish, I will go."

Rosalind stared at him, knowing she should command him to do so. That would be the sane thing to do, banish him from this room and her mind forever.

When she said nothing, his shoulders slumped in defeat. He turned slowly, sadly away from her.

"No! Wait," Rosalind cried.

"Yes, milady?" He came about at once, his eyes so eager, his mouth lifted in such a hopeful smile, it settled somewhere deep in her heart. If this was indeed madness, she realized in that instant she didn't want to be cured.

"Please don't go."

"I will stay with you the entire night through if that is your wish. I only beg one boon of thee."

"What is that?"

"That you dry your eyes and lie back against the pillows to take thy rest."

It was not a brusque command such as Lance would have rapped out, but a gentle request she was powerless to resist. Mopping hastily at her moist eyelashes, she settled back against the pillows, relaxing with a deep sigh.

She was rewarded with another of his heart-melting smiles, and she found herself smiling back at Sir Lancelot. But she could not keep the note of reproach from her voice as she asked, "Oh, where have you been? I waited at the inn, night after night for you to come back. I found this old sword hidden beneath the floorboards in the storeroom, and I thought it was the one you were looking for, I thought it was Excalibur."

"I know, milady," he said sadly.

"You knew?" she repeated, stunned. "And still you did not come?"

"Forgive me, milady." He dropped to one knee by the bedside. The humble pose had the effect of bringing his face at a level with her own, so close she could see every sorrow that darkened his eyes, every regret carved deep into his noble brow. Rosalind found herself forgiving him even before he offered up his explanation.

"I only realized the truth tonight. Had I guessed sooner you had strayed into such peril, nothing would have kept me from your side. Though I scarce know what good I might have done you."

He held up his hands ruefully. "In this ghostly state, I cannot even wield a sword on your behalf. Yet I would have given up my very soul before I allowed any harm to befall thee."

Such stirring words, moving and passionate. A far cry from all of Lance's grumbling and cursing.

"I wish it could have been you riding to my rescue." Rosalind sighed. "And not that dreadful man."

"Dreadful man?" Sir Lancelot looked confused for a moment then he said. "Er . . . you mean Lance St. Leger."

"You know him?"

He grimaced. "Intimately."

"I thought that you must." In her excitement, Rosalind struggled upright only to be stopped by an admonishing glance from Sir Lancelot. She sank meekly back down.

"The resemblance between you and Lance St. Leger is positively uncanny. Although I don't mean to insult you," she added hastily.

"I am sure you do not, milady," Sir Lancelot muttered, pulling an odd face.

"But it is too strange to be mere coincidence. I *knew* there had to be some connection between you."

"Aye, there is." Sir Lancelot rose slowly to his feet and paced off a few steps, starting to run his hand back through his hair only to bring himself up short. At times he seemed to forget himself that he was a ghost, a fact that Rosalind found rather poignant and endearing.

"The truth is . . ." He hesitated like a man on the brink of some painful revelation. "The truth about Lance St. Leger and myself is—that I am—that we—"

When he faltered again, Rosalind nodded encouragingly, "Yes?"

He cast her an indecisive look, then finally blurted out, "The truth is that Lance St. Leger is—is a descendant of mine."

Somehow Rosalind had a feeling that was not at all what he'd meant to say, but she was too intrigued by the information to puzzle over the matter for long.

"Your descendant. I guessed as much," she said. "But the legends I've read are so conflicting. Some claim that you died childless while others say that Sir Galahad was your son."

"Ah . . . yes. He was."

"But I never remember reading anywhere that he married."

"Well . . . he—he did. He settled down quite nicely after his quest to find the Holy Grail. Met a sweet young lady, purchased a magnificent castle, and— and one of his daughters, eventually married a St. Leger.

"I suppose it did not get recorded in the tales because—because it is not the sort of thing one considers heroic. Weddings, babies, the changing of nappies."

"It sounds wonderful to me," she said wistfully. "I have often thought that if only Arthur and I could have had a child—"

Rosalind ducked her head in embarrassment, such a sorrow far too intimate to have confided to any man. Yet from the first she had felt a kinship with Sir Lancelot she could not explain. As though he were no stranger, but a close and valued friend.

His eyes glowed with a quiet sympathy. "Thou cannot conceive, milady?"

"I don't know," Rosalind said miserably. "Our marriage was so brief, and we were separated so often by Arthur's work in Parliament. We hoped for a child, we planned, but it never happened and then . . . then time simply ran out for us."

"Time has a way of doing that."

And who should know that better than he? Rosalind thought with a pang. One whose life had ended in the full vigor of his manhood. She gazed deep into his haunted dark eyes and wondered. Besides his tragic love for Guinevere, what other dreams had he seen go awry and remain unfulfilled?

Dwelling on such regrets was making them both melancholy, and Rosalind sought to return to the original subject.

"We were speaking of your descendants," she reminded him.

"Oh, yes, the St. Legers," he said, wrenching himself back from whatever unhappy memories consumed him. "I believe you were telling me how much you disliked them."

"Well, not Valentine St. Leger. He seems a most kind and gentle man. I like him a great deal better than I do his brother."

"So do I," Lancelot agreed with a sad smile.

"But that Lance St. Leger!" Rosalind pursed her lips, having no wish to offend her courtly friend by criticizing his namesake, but she was unable to refrain from venting her indignation.

"He's arrogant and tormenting, bad-tempered and overbearing. He has no respect for a lady's wishes. I begged him to take me back to the inn, but he dragged me here to Castle Leger and thrust me into his bed. And—and I'm a little afraid."

"You have no reason to be. I would never . . . I mean he would never harm you."

"He already forced me to kiss him once. Now I am completely at his mercy." Rosalind added in a small voice, "And I am not sure he has any."

"By God's blood, milady! If he should ever forget himself so far as to threaten your virtue again, I vow I would smite him down myself."

Sir Lancelot looked so savagely protective of her, Rosalind was both thrilled and alarmed.

"Oh no!" she cried. "Please don't do that."

The knight eyed her with an expression that was at once curious and strangely hopeful. "Then you do like this Lance? Just a little?"

"No!"

Sir Lancelot flinched.

Perhaps her denial had been too vehement, Rosalind thought guiltily. Despite all of Lance's angry bluster, she couldn't help remembering other things, the gentle way he had lifted her onto the saddle, how strong and secure his arms had felt, holding her fast against him, all that long and terrible ride back to Castle Leger.

"Lance St. Leger did save my life," she conceded. "But he was perfectly horrid about it. Shouting and bellowing at me."

"Ah, these modern young men." Sir Lancelot sighed. "They have no notion how to rescue a damsel in distress."

"No, they don't!"

But despite Sir Lancelot's solemn expression, Rosalind detected a twinkle in his eyes, and she couldn't help laughing herself.

"It is a trifle ridiculous," she chuckled, "when a man saves you, to be complaining about the manner of it. But your infamous descendant could have been a bit more chivalrous. He swears far too much."

"That's because he's a damn—he's a dastardly villain."

Sir Lancelot's hearty endorsement of her estimate of Lance's character should have pleased Rosalind. She didn't know why she kept feeling this ridiculous urge to defend the rogue.

"I suppose Lance had some reason to be angry with me," she said. "After all, I did throw his ancestral sword into the lake."

She regarded Sir Lancelot rather wistfully. "It truly was his sword, wasn't it? And not Excalibur?"

"Alas, my lady, that is so. I crave thy pardon. It was solely my doing that thou were so grievously misled."

Rosalind nestled her cheek against the pillow with a heavy sigh. "It is no one's fault but my own. I fear I have a most impulsive imagination. But Lance St. Leger set me straight quickly enough. He doesn't believe in Excalibur or the enchanted lake."

She offered Sir Lancelot an apologetic smile. "I don't think he would even believe in you."

"I am sure he wouldn't. The man puts no faith in any of the legends of Camelot."

"He doesn't even believe in his own legends," Rosalind said. "I think that's rather sad, don't you?"

"Infinitely," Sir Lancelot murmured with a wry twist of his lips.

"He would have abandoned his sword by the lake if I hadn't made him go back for it. He even threatened to throw me in the water if I didn't stop struggling."

"Men behave strangely when frightened, milady," Sir Lancelot said gravely.

"Frightened? Lance St. Leger? What could he possibly have had to be afraid of? He wasn't wounded."

"No, but you were." Sir Lancelot averted his face, staring fixedly toward the rain-washed windows. He hesitated before finishing. "Perhaps . . . perhaps he was afraid of losing you."

"But I'm not his to lose. Unless you also believe in this legend of the chosen bride, that I am somehow destined for Lance St. Leger." She added anxiously, "You don't, do you?"

"I fear I am long past the point of having anything to do with legends or love, milady." He came about slowly. "Perhaps the more important question is, what do you believe?"

"Oh!" Rosalind gave a half-embarrassed laugh. "Usually I am far too ready to believe anything. But it seems quite impossible that I should ever fall in love with Lance St. Leger. Although—"

She broke off in horror at what she'd almost been about to confess. But Sir Lancelot's eyes were filled with the weary understanding of a man who knew far more about the ways of the world than she ever could: passion, temptation, the longings of the flesh.

"Although what, milady?" he prompted.

Her cheeks flushing hotly, she blurted out, "When Lance forced me to kiss him, I—I was not entirely indifferent to him."

An odd smile played about the corners of Sir Lancelot's mouth. "I have heard that kissing is one of the few things the rogue excels at. It is not surprising he managed to fluster you."

"It was more than being flustered. It was this rush of desire so powerful,

I scarce trusted myself with Lance St. Leger. For one moment, I felt as though I could have been his for the asking. Was that not terribly wicked of me?"

Sir Lancelot regarded her with a strange, almost unnerving intensity. At last he averted his gaze, saying, "No, milady. Whatever wicked thoughts are present in this house, they are certainly none of yours."

He heaved a deep sigh. "Mayhap it would be wiser if you did not confide so much in me."

"But why not? I trust you completely." She added shyly, "Are you not my friend?"

"Would that I could be worthy of such an honor."

"I am certain that you are. And it is not as though you would fly straight to Lance St. Leger and betray my confidence, would you?"

"No," he said, but he frowned and Rosalind feared that as usual she had been too impulsive. She had presumed too much on their brief acquaintance, unburdening herself to him, perhaps even giving him a disgust of her unmaidenly behavior.

She watched him anxiously, feeling mortified. But when he returned to the bedside, she was relieved to see that his eyes were more kind and gentle than ever.

"You should try to rest now, milady," he said. "You've been through a terrible ordeal."

"But if I fall asleep, you . . . you will—" She paused, fretting her lower lip, but he readily understood her unspoken fear.

"I'll be here," he said. "Did I not swear to keep watch over thee tonight?"

And what about tomorrow? But Rosalind refused to spoil the moment by asking such a melancholy question. She tried to comfort herself with the thought that it was enough he was with her here, now.

Even the storm seemed to have abated with his arrival, the rain pattering soothingly down the windows. He perched on the edge of the bed, the mattress not even shifting beneath his phantom weight. He was a formidable figure of a man, powerful of shoulder, sinewy of limb, and yet she felt none of those flutters Lance's presence aroused in her, the overwhelming sense of physical awareness.

"It does not alarm you, then?" Sir Lancelot asked. "To be sharing your bedchamber with a ghost?"

"Not at all. I feel completely safe with you."

She could hardly imagine why her remark should have made him look so sad. But he forced a smile to his lips. Unable to touch her, he contented himself by resting his fingers near hers atop the coverlet, his strong bronzed hand in marked contrast to her own smaller one.

"You should try to sleep now, milady."

"But I am not tired," Rosalind said, even though she was well nigh exhausted. To close her eyes, to sleep, would bring the morning, and her gallant phantom would be gone.

"Talk to me, please," she begged.

"About what?"

"About everything. Tell me all about your life in Camelot."

"Er . . . ah, well . . ." Sir Lancelot looked extremely discomfited. Perhaps he feared she was seeking to pry into the more painful aspects of his past, his ill-fated affair with Guinevere. Rosalind hastened to reassure him.

"I meant could you please tell me all about your glorious deeds."

"My glorious deeds?" He pulled a rueful face. "I fear I do not have many of those to boast of, milady."

The greatest knight who ever sat at King Arthur's Round Table, who was a legend for his feats of daring and skill at arms, and yet he believed he had done nothing of note? She was much moved by Lancelot's humility, but she persisted eagerly, "Oh, please, what of your quests, your battles? If only half the stories written of you are true, you must be the most courageous man who ever lived."

He shook his head deprecatingly. "Any fool with enough brawn and too little brains can dash about, hacking away with a sword. The truest bravery I have ever witnessed was after the battle was over, the smoke cleared away, the last drop of blood spilled."

Lancelot's eyes darkened at some inner vision, not one of any glory, but one that rendered him hauntingly sad. " 'Twas then the women would come to find their dead, husbands, sons, brothers. To wash their wounds and lay them out for burial. To shoulder their own grief and then soldier on with their lives. Women of courage . . . like you."

"Like me?"

"Aye, you are the fairest and bravest woman I have ever known."

His words and the fervent look that accompanied them made Rosalind momentarily forget to breathe. It was painful to have to disillusion him.

"Oh no," she said. "I have always been rather shy and timid, not—not brave at all. I'm so afraid of—of—"

"Of what, milady?" he asked when she hesitated.

"Of dying," she whispered. "I have been afraid of dying ever since I lost my husband, ever since I had to sleep in the mourning bed."

"The what?"

"It is a custom in my late husband's family. After Arthur died, his maiden aunts, Clothilde and Miranda, prepared a special bed for me. The hangings were draped with crape, and the sheets and pillowcases were all of black."

"Good lord!"

"Of course, I wanted to honor Arthur's memory. He was such a good and noble man, but I felt like I was resting in a tomb. That my life was also over. For so many nights, I lay awake like a frightened child, snuffling into my pillow."

"By God," Sir Lancelot cried passionately. "I would never have permitted such a thing. If only I could have been there with you."

"I wish you had been, too. When I am with you, I don't feel afraid of anything. Not even death. It does not seem like it would be such a terrible thing to join you on the other side."

"Nay, milady! Never let me hear you say such a thing again."

"I suppose you would not wish to be plagued with me through all eternity." She meant her words to sound light, almost teasing, but she must have failed, for a tormented look sprang to Lancelot's eyes.

"What I wish is—is—" He levered himself abruptly from the bed, saying in an agonized voice most unlike his own, "Oh, God, Rosalind, why . . . why couldn't you have left that sword alone when you found it? Why didn't you just go home?"

"I don't know," she said with a soft break in her voice. "Perhaps because I don't really have a home anymore."

"Surely you have the house where you lived with your husband."

"No, the entire estate was entailed upon a distant male cousin."

"What! You mean you inherited nothing? Not even a widow's jointure? At least some capital left in keeping for you, safely invested in the funds?"

Rosalind's eyes widened. For such a dashing phantom, Sir Lancelot was possessed of an astonishing businesslike streak, far more so than her idealistic husband had been.

"No, there was nothing like that," she said. "Arthur always meant to establish a trust for me, but he never got around to altering his will."

"*Never got around to it?*"

Something in Sir Lancelot's tone caused Rosalind to feel a trifle defensive.

"My late husband was preoccupied with a very noble cause," she said proudly. "He was a reformer, dedicated to improving conditions for the poor."

"Such as his own wife?" The caustic comment sounded exactly like something Lance St. Leger might have said.

When Rosalind regarded Sir Lancelot in pained surprise, he immediately said, "Forgive me, milady. I intended no disrespect to your late husband. If my passions betray me, it is only because of my concern for you."

Rosalind was deeply moved by this, but she could not allow him to believe that Arthur had neglected her, a thought she found too painful herself to consider.

"I was not left destitute. I have a small competence I inherited from my parents, an income of nearly fifty pounds a year," she said. "And Arthur's aunts very kindly permitted me to live with them. Although . . ." She pulled a wry face. "I am not certain even Miranda and Clothilde will want me now."

"Why not?"

"Arthur's aunts have never truly approved of me. They have always found me sadly scatterbrained, and this latest disaster only proves them right. If they ever find out that I ended up in a rake's bed instead of properly visiting cousin Dora, as I was supposed to do, they'll likely toss me into the streets and fling all my legend books right after me."

She attempted to smile, but Sir Lancelot's brows had drawn together in a heavy scowl.

"Nay, milady," he protested. "I cannot believe even the most hard-hearted of dames would treat you thus."

"They would and I would not blame them. I fear I may have created a dreadful scandal and sullied the Carlyon name."

Sir Lancelot muttered something beneath his breath. If it had been anyone else but her chivalrous hero, Rosalind would have thought it was an extremely ungentlemanlike description of Arthur's aunts. He took to pacing furiously, looking so disturbed, Rosalind regretted she had told him anything.

Her noble phantom had enough else to torment him: his own bitter memories, the sins that kept him a drifter for all eternity. She could not allow him to add her troubles to his burden.

She spoke up, seeking to reassure him, "Even if Arthur's aunts should turn me away, I know what I would do. I have often thought before of setting up my own establishment."

Sir Lancelot stopped his pacing long enough to regard her with a hint of impatience. "On fifty pounds a year, milady?"

"Surely I could afford to rent a small cottage, if I were very frugal. And— and I could take in sewing. I am very handy with a needle."

If Sir Lancelot had appeared disturbed before, he now looked positively horror-stricken by her suggestion.

"It is something impecunious widows often do, isn't it?" she asked. "I believe it is considered respectable."

"Respectable, perhaps, but what a devil of a life!" Lancelot said, then flinched and immediately added, "Your pardon, lady, but you have no idea. You would be entirely cut off from any society worthy of you. No dinner parties, no balls, no invitations of any kind."

"I don't attend parties now."

"But you should. You are far too young to be left so all alone."

"I still have my books." She smiled cheerfully up at him. "And my legends."

But rather than giving him comfort, she only seemed to be making matters worse. He gazed back at her, his mouth pinched hard, his eyes stricken with . . . with guilt? But why should Sir Lancelot feel any guilt over her?

Before she could even begin to fathom the odd expression, his lashes swept down, veiling it, and he murmured, "There is no reason for you to reach any drastic decisions tonight. You really should sleep now. You are looking incredibly tired."

Rosalind could not deny it. Her exhaustion did finally seem to be catching up with her. Perhaps it was all this talk of her future, which even in her most optimistic frame of mind had never seemed anything but bleak.

She snuggled deeper beneath the covers. But before she closed her eyes, she stole one last glance at Sir Lancelot. He appeared to have fallen into such a dark state of distraction, that she couldn't help reminding him of his pledge.

"And you will stay with me the entire night through?"

"Aye, milady." The darkness fell from his eyes to be replaced by an infinitely tender look. "I will be here and for as many other nights as you wish."

Rosalind's own eyes widened with a delighted wonder. "That is a very reckless promise," she warned. "I might wish for a good many nights, even though it is very selfish of me. But I did try to free you. That is why I went to the lake tonight."

When Sir Lancelot appeared thoroughly confused, she said, "The sword, remember? You told me if it was sunk back to the bottom of the lake, you might finally know peace."

Lancelot cringed. "I tend to say so many stupid things, milady, sometimes I think my tongue should be cut out."

"Then even if the sword had been Excalibur and I had restored it to the enchanted lake, it would not have helped you?"

"Nay, milady, I am past all hope of redemption unless . . ."

"Unless what?"

"Unless one day instead of attempting to steal away another man's bride, I were to find a love that was all my own. Quite impossible now, I fear."

His eyes smiled into hers with a longing that was both poignant and unbearable, and found an answering echo in Rosalind's own heart. As though she, too, were reaching for the impossible, she stretched her fingers toward him.

He hesitated, then reached for her as well, until his larger hand rested against hers, palm to palm in an unearthly glow of light, as though for that one fleeting moment, they could actually touch each other, not flesh to flesh, but one lonely soul briefly joined to another, in a rare feeling of peace, warmth, and complete happiness.

All too soon, Sir Lancelot drew back, commanding her to take her rest. Rosalind obediently closed her eyes, but as she was drifting off to sleep, Lancelot's voice came to her one last time.

"Milady, there is a very great favor you could do for me."

"Anything," she mumbled drowsily.

"Would . . . would you be willing to give Lance St. Leger another chance?"

The request startled her enough that she forced her heavy eyelids open a fraction. "Another chance to do what?"

"To make amends for his behavior. To right the wrongs he has done you."

"Do you think the rogue would be likely to do so?"

"I believe that he would. Perhaps he is not so black as either of us have thought him to be. At least if you would be willing to listen to him, allow him to try."

Rosalind nestled her head deeper in the pillow, confused by exactly what Sir Lancelot was attempting to say. But she could refuse him nothing, and she mumbled a sleep-blurred promise, though she was scarce aware of what she had pledged herself to do.

Her eyes fluttered closed again, her last thought being that somehow her future did not seem so grim anymore. She knew with sudden certainty she would not be going back to stay with the aunts in Kent. Miranda and Clothilde would most decidedly not want her now, for she had finally committed the most unpardonable folly of all.

She had lost her heart to a ghost.

Long after Rosalind had gone to sleep, the ghost of Sir Lancelot du Lac paced by her bedside, a valiant figure from another age in chain mail and black tunic, but when he gazed down at her, it was with Lance St. Leger's troubled eyes.

Did the woman have to look so blasted sweet and vulnerable? Lance reflected gloomily. Rosalind hugged his pillow as though she were embracing a lover, her golden hair fanning about her shoulders, a soft rose blushing her cheeks as though she were lost deep in the most blissful of dreams.

Of Camelot and knights in shining armor, no doubt. Lance expelled a deep sigh. Valentine had, as usual, been right. Lance should never have continued this ridiculous masquerade. It had gotten him in far deeper with Rosalind than he'd ever imagined possible.

What folly had possessed him to promise her that Sir Lancelot would come to her again, for as many nights as she wished? The woman already believed in him too entirely, trusted him too completely. Imagining he was her friend, confiding in him more about herself than he'd ever wanted to know. Especially the most daunting confession of all.

. . . I could scarce trust myself with Lance St. Leger. For one moment I felt as though I could have been his for the asking.

It was a dangerous admission to make to any man, let alone a rake as notorious as himself. Lance had never been noted for his self-denial. He could be grateful at this moment that he was only spirit, not flesh. But come the morning . . .

He observed her with hungry eyes, the way she curled up in his bed, so innocently unaware of the temptation she presented to him. As soon as she was healed enough to travel, the best thing he could do would be to send her away from here.

But send her away to what? If Lance was unable to cast a mantle of propriety over this ill-fated adventure, if Rosalind did end up being cast out by those two old witches, if she were indeed forced to strike out all on her own . . .

The mere thought of such a thing made Lance's blood run cold. His dreamy-eyed Rosalind clearly had no idea of the sort of grim fates that could befall an unprotected woman, especially one who was branded "ruined goods." Anything from the soul-wearying drudgery of so-called genteel poverty to the complete degradation of being forced into prostitution in order to survive.

Yet even if he succeeded in saving Rosalind's reputation, was the destiny that awaited her any better? To return to a dismal existence of sleeping in beds with black sheets and being bullied to death by two spinsterish harpies.

He felt an almost suffocating rage against the late Lord Carlyon, an idealistic idiot out to save the world, but obviously with little thought to spare for his own bride. If her beloved Arthur had failed to provide for Rosalind, Lance didn't know why he should feel as though it had become his responsibility or why he should care so much.

But it had. And he did.

He hovered by the bedside, observing Rosalind with a tender exasperation. A lady who possessed far more courage and enthusiasm than she did good sense. Someone who, no matter how bleak and cold the world turned around her, would always find a way to believe in dreams and cherish legends.

Just like Val, Lance realized with some amazement. Was that why he felt this fierce sense of protectiveness toward Rosalind that he'd always experienced toward his twin? No matter how much his brother's dreamy-eyed optimism often irritated Lance, he'd never wanted to see Valentine changed, poisoned with the disillusionment that darkened Lance's veins.

And now he felt exactly the same about Rosalind. Perhaps that had been the real reason he'd swept her back to Castle Leger: the instinctive urge of a man when he found something that precious to tuck it away in the one place he might feel sure of keeping it safe. In his own home, behind the security of his own castle walls.

Lance would have sworn such noble impulses were no longer a part of his makeup. That perhaps was the most dangerous thing about Rosalind Carlyon. She would always be looking for a hero, and Lance doubted he could ever be what she wanted.

But sweet heaven! How she made a man long to try.

"You truly did become my Lady of the Lake tonight," he murmured. "Restoring to me my sword."

Now he found himself wondering if his innocent enchantress might not be capable of restoring other things as well. Lost honor, lost love, lost dreams.

Foolish thoughts, he chided himself, for it hardly made any difference. He had already reached a grim conclusion. Despite everything he'd already visited upon Rosalind, the dangers, the deceptions, the wounds both of body and spirit, he was obliged to inflict upon her one thing more. Perhaps the worst of all.

He was going to have to force her to marry him.

A daunting decision and one that should have him in considerable turmoil. Yet once he'd made up his mind, Lance felt strangely at peace.

He settled himself into a chair to await the first heralds of dawn, for once in his life, his restless spirit content to do nothing more than watch his lady sleep.

CHAPTER TEN

*R*osalind awakened late the next morning to a flood of sunlight and a strange sense of well-being for a woman who had been shot only the night before. Every effort had been made to see to her comfort, both her maid Jenny and her belongings fetched to her from the inn, the entire staff at Castle Leger put at Rosalind's disposal to bring her anything she desired, from books from the library to dainty morsels designed to tempt her appetite.

When Val St. Leger changed the dressing on her wound, the earnest young man pronounced himself pleased with her progress. But he advised her to spend the remainder of the day in bed. Rosalind meekly accepted his gentle orders, all the while privately thinking that Val could have used some rest himself, as pale and tired as the poor man looked.

No sooner had he left the room than she flung back the covers. Although she felt a twinge in her shoulder, she managed to swing her legs over the edge of her bed and groped for her muslin shawl. She wrapped the black-dyed garment over her borrowed nightgown and struggled cautiously to her feet.

Rosalind made it as far as the window. There she was obliged to sink down into a wing chair, but she leaned toward the casement, determined to take stock of her surroundings, bracing herself for . . . what? A castle wall with pikes on the top? A moat swarming with gigantic snakes?

But Castle Leger did not appear quite so alarming a place by day. In fact, the view from Lance's bedchamber window was breathtaking. The land sloped away before her, sweeping off into the distance to become a dramatic vista of cliffside and hazy blue sea. And just below her was a pretty wilderness of garden, trees heavy with lush pink rhododendrons, standing shepherd over herds of flowers, primroses, bluebells, foxglove, and daisies.

Only one thing marred her delight in the scene, the realization she could never explore the garden with the one person she wanted most at her side. At least not in the sunlight.

She cast a troubled glance at the bright blue sky, wondering what time it was, how much longer until sunset. Would Sir Lancelot return to her this evening? He had promised, and he was not the sort of man . . . or spirit to break his word.

Rosalind felt her pulse quicken. Was this what it was like, then, to fall passionately in love? This inability to think of anyone else, this unbearable longing for the sight of that one beloved face . . . so different from the gentle affection she had felt for her late husband.

One moment swept up in a transport of pure joy, the next flung down into the darkest pit of desolation. And she had more reason than most lovers to despair. Could there be anything more hopeless than tumbling in love with a man who could never be anything more to her than a haunting dream in the darkness?

She could not even be certain of being loved in return. Who was she to suppose that she could win the heart of one of the greatest heroes that had ever lived? A man who had once loved a queen of such dazzling charm and beauty, he had sacrificed both his honor and his immortal soul for her. Who was Rosalind Carlyon to compete with the memory of a Guinevere? No one at all, just a shy widow with a snub nose and freckles.

And yet if Sir Lancelot consented to be no more than her friend, it would be enough. She could never return tamely to the dismal life she had been leading since Arthur had died. She could not fathom her knight in shining armor making his bow to her beneath the roof of Miranda and Clothilde Carlyon. The house of two dour spinsters was not conducive to midnight assignations with any man, even if he was a centuries-old ghost.

It was in Cornwall that Lancelot clearly belonged, among the rugged hills and windswept coasts where he had once ridden his charger, engaging in quests and performing daring deeds in the service of his king. And it was here in Cornwall that Rosalind meant to remain, to be near him. No matter what the cost.

She was turning over several desperate schemes in her head, wondering if enough remained of her quarterly allowance to hire even a small cottage, when she was disturbed by a knock at the door.

She had no chance to answer before the door eased open, and she tensed when she saw who it was. Lance St. Leger appeared dauntingly virile in his gleaming boots, skin-tight breeches, and striped silk waistcoat. He wore no cravat, his white linen shirt left casually open at the neck to reveal a vee of sun-warmed skin.

He paused on the threshold and demanded, "May I come in?"

"Well, I—I—" she stammered. She'd been anticipating another encounter with the man all morning and dreading it. No doubt that was why her heart missed a beat and her hand flashed up to smooth the tousled ends of her hair.

"I promise I haven't come to bedevil you," he said with one of his most engaging smiles. "I was coming up from the stables and chanced to see you looking out at the garden, and I thought you might like to have this."

He whipped his arm from behind his back, producing a nosegay. A nosegay? No, it was more like he'd attempted to fetch the entire garden to her. His large hand barely confined a glorious blaze of colors, vibrant rhododendrons crushed up against purple heather, marigolds, day lilies, and primroses. As he crossed the room to her side, he left a trail of petals fluttering in his wake.

Stunned, Rosalind could do no more than stare.

"Here," he said, thrusting the bouquet toward her. "Take them. Not the most elegant arrangement, I fear. But I'm not accustomed to picking flowers for young ladies."

"Somehow I doubt that," Rosalind murmured.

"It's true. I usually just have my man order up a bouquet and have it sent round. With my card attached of course, jotted full of words of appropriate seduction."

Rosalind had started to reach for the flowers, only to freeze in alarm.

"Don't worry," he drawled, his eyes glinting with amusement. "I was fresh out of cards this morning."

He folded the bouquet into her reluctant hands, and she drew it closer, breathing in deeply, the mingled sweet scents as familiar and comforting to her as her books of legends, the remembrance of her papa's smile, her mother's soft caress.

She felt a prickle of tears behind her eyes and blinked them quickly away.

"Th-thank you," she said.

"You're welcome," he replied gravely.

It had to have been no more than a casual gesture to him. He could not possibly have guessed what the flowers meant to her, and yet a rare kindness had stolen into Lance St. Leger's eyes, softening the arrogant planes of his face.

Rosalind was suddenly reminded of something Sir Lancelot had said to her only last night.

Perhaps the rogue is not so black as either of us have thought him to be.

She contemplated her flowers, considering the possibility. While she did so, she heard a soft click. Glancing up, she saw that Lance had taken advantage of her distraction to close and lock the door.

Her heart did an immediate leap, all her mistrust and wariness of the man returning. When he stalked toward her, she stiffened.

"Don't be alarmed," he said in that seductive voice she found anything but soothing. "I have something of a private nature to say to you, and I would as soon not be interrupted until I've finished."

Finished what? Rosalind dropped the flowers into her lap and dragged the ends of her shawl closer together, trying to tuck her bare feet as far out of sight as possible. She might be able to entertain Sir Lancelot in her nightgown without a qualm, but Lance's mere proximity made her acutely aware that her body was draped in little more than thin linen and there was a bed looming far too close in the background.

She faltered, "My maid should at least be present. This—this is hardly proper."

"I fear it is a trifle late to be worrying about propriety, don't you?"

"Too late for you perhaps, but I—"

"Rosalind, please. I only want to talk to you. Just for a few moments. I would not press you, but the matter is rather urgent."

Rosalind shifted uneasily on her chair, unable to imagine there was anything Lance had to say that she would want to hear. Only more scolding, perhaps, about what a fool she'd made of herself last night, or some of his wicked brand of teasing. But he didn't look like a man bent on flirting or delivering another tirade.

He appeared subdued this morning . . . and determined. Knowing Lance's persistence, Rosalind did not see how she could easily be rid of him, short of feigning a spasm of pain and forcing him to go fetch his brother.

Lance made her so uncomfortable, she was tempted to do so. But she was held back by another remembrance of Sir Lancelot's voice whispering through her mind.

If you could but give Lance St. Leger a chance, milady . . . to make amends. If you would but deign to listen to him.

She squirmed, recollecting her own sleep-blurred promise. *I will do anything that you ask. . . .*

Rosalind fetched a heavy sigh at the memory. Unfortunately, Lance appeared to take this as a sign of her assent and perched one lean hip upon the window ledge, settling himself in a negligent pose. The very picture of the idle rakehell.

She found herself watching the sway of his booted foot, fascinated to note he had a grass stain on the knee of his immaculate breeches, acquired no doubt when he had bent to fetch her the flowers from the garden. Only a small flaw in his otherwise perfect appearance, but it had the curious effect of rendering him somewhat less alarming.

She relaxed a little and inquired in a reasonably calm voice, "What is it you wanted to speak to me about, sir? If it is anything more to do with what happened last night, I am afraid I have little to say. Unfortunately, I know nothing of the thief who stole your sword. I don't even have any information that will help you track—"

"I know," Lance interrupted. "Valentine already told me. He said he asked you about the man who attacked you and you have no more clue to his identity than I do."

"I'm sorry." She ducked her head, staring down at the cascade of flowers strewn across her lap.

"No reason for you to be sorry, m'dear."

"Yes, there is." To keep her hands from fretting the ends of her hair, she began to separate the blossoms and arrange them in a more tidy bouquet. "When he was changing my bandage, Val asked me if I noticed a chip was missing from the crystal of the sword and I—I am not certain. I suppose it must have happened when I threw the blade in the lake.

"And I am more sorry than you could possibly imagine," she concluded miserably.

"Oh, hang the stupid sword," he said with a hint of impatience. "It's of no great importance."

"But your brother said the sword is part of your family legends. That someday you are supposed to surrender it to the lady you love."

"Val has a tendency to talk too much. As far as I'm concerned, that blasted sword has been nothing but trouble. It is partly responsible for last night's disaster, and I'm to blame for the rest of it."

He infused a softer note into his tone. "However, you are not to worry about anything. That is what I wanted to tell you. I've already begun making arrangements."

"Arrangements?" Rosalind paused in the act of coupling a daisy with two bluebells to cast him a puzzled frown.

"Aye, this morning I've been to call upon the vicar, and I've sent for my solicitor to consult about a will."

A *will?* The mere word was enough to send a frisson of unease skittering up Rosalind's spine.

"But I'm not dying," she said. "Your brother told me I was recovering amazingly well."

"And so you are, sweetheart." Lance gave her an oddly tender smile. "The will is for me."

Rosalind felt herself flush at the unexpected endearment. "You think you are going to die?"

"Not for a while I trust, unless you decide to murder me in my bed. But it is always as well to be prepared."

Rosalind plucked a half-dead leaf off one of the primroses, her brows knitting together. She didn't know whether it was the heady scent of the flowers or the distracting way the summer breeze had teased several dark strands of Lance's hair across his forehead, but she seemed to be having a great deal of difficulty following this conversation.

Her bewilderment only increased when Lance continued, "I've also sent for a dressmaker."

"A dressmaker!"

"A local woman. She's a bit provincial with her styling, but she'll have to do until I can find you a more fashionable modiste." He fingered the ends of her shawl, making a moue of distaste. "I noticed that most of your wardrobe consists of black and . . . er—black. And I believe even wearing half mourning is considered bad luck."

"Bad luck for what?" Rosalind asked in frustrated confusion.

"To be married in."

"What are you talking about?"

"Our wedding, of course."

Her eyes flew wide open. The bouquet she had been so carefully arranging dropped from her fingers, this time tumbling to the floor. She stared at Lance for a long moment; then a hot tide of indignation swept through her.

"Oh! Why, you—you—" she sputtered, unable to think of a name bad enough to call him. "This is more of your horrid teasing."

"I assure you, my dear, I am in deadly earnest."

He smiled, but there was an edge in his voice that filled Rosalind with alarm. She scarce knew what dismayed her more, the sheer arrogance of the man to be consulting vicars, lawyers, and dressmakers without even speaking to her first, or the steely determination she read in his eyes. Not that of an ardent suitor, but more like a general marshaling his forces to take a particularly stubborn hill.

"How dare you!" Rosalind gasped. "To be making such arrangements and—and you never even troubled to ask me."

"I suppose the standard form is to go down upon one knee. I was hoping you would not require it, but—" He heaved a long-suffering sigh and, to Rosalind's horror, dropped down before her, kneeling in the fallen flowers.

"My dear Lady Carlyon," he began, reaching for her hand. "Will you do me the honor of—"

"Oh, stop it. Stop it!" She attempted to thrust him away from her. Failing that, she tugged at his shoulder in an effort to get him to rise. "Do get up . . . please. Have you run completely mad?"

"I fear that I have," he murmured, tightening his grip on her hand.

"But you don't want to be married any more than I do."

"No, I don't," he admitted frankly.

"Then why are you doing this? Is it because of that chosen bride legend? You insisted you don't believe in it."

"I'm not certain what I believe. But the problem is everyone else seems to be quite sure." He yielded to the tuggings of her hand and levered himself back to his feet. "I had hoped I could contain any scandal. I thought if I could fetch Effie Fitzleger back here to play chaperon, I could make everything all right.

"But besides the fact I couldn't even manage to roust the infernal woman from her bed this morning, it was already too late." Lance offered Rosalind an apologetic glance. "I am sorry, my dear, but the entire village seems to know you spent the night beneath my roof."

A rush of heat surged into Rosalind's cheeks. "Because I was wounded! Don't people know that? Didn't you tell them?"

"I could stand in the village square and try to proclaim the truth until I dropped from exhaustion, but I fear it would do no good. It's the damned legend. From the moment Effie declared you to be my chosen bride, everyone hereabouts has been expecting our passions to rage out of control—with or without the benefit of clergy. It's happened before. They say that one of my great-uncles spent an entire week between the sheets before—

"Well, never mind about that," Lance broke off hastily. "The point is that everyone from the vicar to the village blacksmith thinks that I must have had you last night."

"Oh, God!" Rosalind pressed her hands to her flaming cheeks. She had feared something like this, had tried to brace herself for it. But somehow accepting the reality that her reputation was destroyed was far worse than she had imagined.

Lance hovered over her, stroking a stray curl back from her brow. "It will be all right, my dear. As soon as we are married."

Rosalind thrust his hand away, shooting him a reproachful glare. "Your notions of what would be all right are clearly different from my own, sir. Do you think I would consent to marry a man like you under any circumstances?"

He flinched as though she had slapped him, but Rosalind was far too caught up in her own distress to care.

"It doesn't matter to me if I am ruined!" she cried.

"It matters to me," he said, drawing away from her, his mouth thinning into a taut line. "I know you have a bad opinion of me, and God knows, you have reason. I've done some reprehensible things in my life, but there is one thing I've never done, and that is to sully the reputation of an innocent woman."

"Exactly whose honor are you trying to save?" Rosalind asked. "Yours or mine?"

"Mine," was his unexpected reply. "You see . . . I have so little of it left."

He turned away from her, but not before she saw the bleakness that stole into his eyes. He stood by the window, looking out just as Sir Lancelot had done last night, and for one moment the resemblance between man and phantom was more marked than she'd ever seen it. The same sad eyes, the same haunted expression. Rosalind found the likeness so unbearable, she was forced to look away.

How differently she would have felt if it had been Sir Lancelot kneeling at her feet, begging her to be his bride, fulfilling all her girlish fantasies. When she thought of the happiness that would have flooded through her, the contrast was painful in the extreme.

But Lance St. Leger was not as thick-skinned as she would have supposed. She had clearly wounded his pride with her rejection, and it was not in her nature to hurt anyone.

"I'm sorry," she said gently. "I know you are trying to do right by me, and I appreciate the offer. But you must see as clearly as I do how ill-suited we would be."

She attempted to smile. "I am not a woman given to violence, and I have already hit you once. I fear I might be driven to murder you before the first year was out."

A fleeting smile touched his lips. "It would only be a marriage of convenience, Rosalind. I would not even have to come near you."

"I already had—" Rosalind broke off, appalled by what she'd been about to say. That she'd already had such a marriage and didn't want another like that. Since when had she ever thought of her union with Arthur in those cold terms?

They had wed with great affection, at least on her side. There had been times in her bleaker moments that she had wondered about Arthur, an extremely busy man, so preoccupied with all of his noble causes. That perhaps left with a young girl on his hands, the most convenient thing for him to do had been to marry her.

No, he'd loved her. Rosalind was certain of that, but she suddenly felt an unreasoning surge of anger against her dear Arthur. If he hadn't burned out his life trying to save the world, perhaps he never would have died. He wouldn't have left her so all alone, burdened with such problems and doubts.

She would still be comfortably wed to him, and not in such a dire situation, where legends and swords, heroic phantoms and sad-eyed rakes seemed to be getting all jumbled up in her head. To say nothing of her heart.

When Lance moved back to her side and took hold of her hand again, she suddenly felt far too weary to resist him.

"I might not make you the best of husbands, my dear," he said. "But I wouldn't be the worst. I could give you anything you wanted. Even if I wasn't to inherit Castle Leger, I have a fortune in my own right. While I was in the army, I had the devil's own luck. I gambled on some rather risky investments that paid off and made me a very wealthy man."

"I don't want your money, Lance," Rosalind said softly, then started a little, realizing it was the first time she'd ever used his name. It sounded dauntingly natural falling from her lips.

Lance's eyes widened, and he pressed her hand with renewed determination. "I can give you other things as well. A home and more family than you would know what to do with. My brother, Val, already adores you, and I am persuaded my parents would dote upon you. As for my sisters, they would be only too happy to join you in roundly abusing me. Leonie, Phoebe, and Mariah would welcome you as one of their own."

"Oh, please," Rosalind murmured. Did he have any idea of how he was twisting her heart, holding out such tempting possibilities to a woman as lonely as she was?

"I—I would prefer my own family," she said in a small voice.

"You mean children? I'm afraid I've never thought of myself as a father." He frowned but then shrugged. "But if you wanted a few, I suppose I could provide them."

A hint of his roguish smile surfaced. "In fact, if I really applied myself, I vow I could have you with child by Michaelmas."

Rosalind uttered a soft protest, her face searing with embarrassment, her mind seared with visions. Of herself with a dark-haired babe, curled up all warm and soft in her arms. Of the things that Lance St. Leger would have to do to her to make such a reckless promise come true.

Lance only made it worse by raising her hands to his lips, brushing her knuckles with a butterfly-soft kiss.

"You wouldn't find the getting of this child unpleasant," he murmured. "That's one of the few advantages of marrying a rake. I have certain . . . skills I would bring to the marriage bed."

"O-ohh, don't," Rosalind said, although she scarce knew what she was objecting to—what he was saying or what he was doing. Kissing each fingertip in turn, each caress of his mouth sending a fresh quiver through her.

She made a weak attempt to pull away from him, but instead of releasing her, he only leaned in closer, resting his arm along the back of her chair.

"You don't find me completely repulsive, do you?" he asked.

"No." Rosalind was forced to admit. She tried to shrink back, but there was no place to go. She could feel his hand stealing behind her, burrowing softly beneath her hair, teasing the nape of her neck, stroking shivers up and down her spine.

His face had drawn far too close, and there was nowhere else to look except into the mesmerizing haze of his eyes. She attempted to do so bravely, trying to reason with him.

"You—you are very handsome, Lance, as I'm sure you are well aware. But I'm sorry. I don't feel any sort of passion for you."

"No?" One of his dark brows lifted in almost polite inquiry. He kissed her quickly, lightly, just long enough to set her mouth tingling. "What about now?"

"N-no," she said, wishing she sounded firmer.

He nuzzled her hair, her temple, her cheek, his mouth warm and rough against her skin. She wasn't breathing in the aroma of flowers anymore, only Lance's own scent, dark, musky, and masculine.

"And now?" he whispered.

She started to shake her head, but he stopped the motion with another kiss, nibbling the curve of her jaw. His mouth moved downward to her neck, exploring and finding sensitive hollows that were so eagerly responsive. She found herself forgetting to breathe entirely.

"You—you are taking advantage of me," she faltered. "You know I am too weak to—to fend you off."

"Mmmmm, I'm a complete villain," Lance agreed with no compunction, and he fastened his lips over hers. She managed to wrench her head aside, placing her hand against his shoulder in a feeble effort to keep him at bay.

"Oh, please," she begged. "I don't want you to do this."

Lance only smiled at her, a glint springing into his eyes that was both wicked and tender. As though the rogue knew full well she was lying, that she did not find his kisses so unacceptable as she feigned.

For one awful moment, Rosalind thought Sir Lancelot must have appeared to Lance and betrayed her confidences of the night before. Ridiculous, of course. Her noble hero would never do such a thing. And what was more, he didn't have to.

As Lance bent ruthlessly to kiss her again, Rosalind realized with dismay that she was betraying herself. With her own soft sigh, with the way her lips parted to allow him greater access to the heat of her mouth.

Lance's large hand splayed against the back of her neck, holding her captive to his embrace. As his kiss deepened, her resistance grew weaker and weaker, until there was nothing she could do but clutch at his shoulder and hold on as though for her very life.

She melted into his embrace, becoming a willing prisoner. The next she knew Lance was seated on the chair, and she was cradled on his lap, their lips barely separating long enough to draw the air.

This is wrong. You don't want this to happen, her conscience insisted. But she could barely hear the whispering of her mind above the thundering of her heart. Lance's kiss waxed more passionate, his tongue teasing hers with hints of his sensual prowess, the even greater pleasures he could bestow.

She was all too aware of his powerful thighs pressing against the soft swell of her bottom, the hardness that strained against the confines of his breeches. She squirmed on his lap, the sensation both shocking and exciting her.

When her shawl drifted from her shoulders to pool with the flowers on the floor, she barely noticed or cared. Lance's hand drifted over the folds of her nightgown, roving over her hip, skimming up her rib cage to cup her breast. The heat of his palm penetrated the thin fabric, teasing her nipple, causing her entire body to quicken with a sweet, heavy anticipation. Rosalind bit down on her lip to stifle a tiny whimper of pure pleasure.

Lance buried his face in her hair, his breath coming quick and shallow, his voice hot and hoarse against her ear as he murmured endearments that she absorbed as hungrily as his caresses, like a woman starved for such tender words, such intimate touches.

She responded in kind, feverishly running her hand over the hard plane of his chest, whispering, "Lancelot . . . oh, Lancelot."

Was it the breathing of that adored name that finally shocked her to her senses? Or reaching up to stroke his cheek, so poignantly like the face of another whom she would never be able to touch, whose kiss she would never know.

She blinked as though she'd been slapped hard and snatched her hand back, recoiling not so much from Lance as from herself. Oh, God, what sort of a wanton was she? Only last night she had been silently pledging her heart to Sir Lancelot du Lac, and now she was swiftly surrendering to the seduction of his rakehell descendant.

When Lance attempted to kiss her again, she found the strength to wrench herself out of his arms. She staggered across the room and caught the bedpost for support, her legs now trembling not so much from the aftereffects of her wound but from weakness of a different sort.

Lance came hard after her, the flush of passion in his face fading to an expression of concern.

"Rosalind?"

Clinging to the post, she buried her face against her hands, too mortified to look at him.

"Whatever is the matter, my dearest?"

What was the matter? Rosalind thought, stifling a strong urge to break into sobs. Everything, but most of all she wasn't *his* dearest.

When he attempted to place his hands upon her shoulders, she flinched away from him.

"Damn," he muttered. "Is it your wound? Have I hurt you? What a cursed brute I am to have forgotten."

He slipped his arms around her waist, and she was feeling so wobbly, she was forced to accept his support, but when she realized he was guiding her toward the bed, she tensed.

"No!"

"Hush, sweetheart. I only want you to lie down, to rest, which is what you should have been doing all along."

He urged her forward, but as soon as she could break away from him, she dived for the mattress. She rolled onto her side and curled into a ball, dragging the blankets over her as though the frail coverings could somehow serve as a barrier for temptation—both his and her own.

Lance sat down on the bed beside her. She could feel the bed creak, the mattress yielding to his weight as readily as she had almost offered her own body up to his strong masculine frame.

Oh, sweet heaven! She burrowed her face in the pillow, her eyes stinging with tears, her face burning with humiliation.

Lance leaned over, anxiously trying to peer into her face. "Rosalind? Are you in pain again? Do you want me to summon Val?"

"No!" she choked out.

"Then may I fetch you some water? A glass of wine? What can I do?"

"Just go away!" She groaned, splaying her hand across her face, trying to hide from him entirely. "I am so ashamed."

"Ashamed?" He sounded genuinely confused. "Of what?" Lance paused a moment as though mulling the matter over and then exclaimed, "Oh. *That.*"

To Rosalind's indignation, the rogue actually chuckled.

"My dear, there is nothing shameful in the way you responded to my . . . er—ardor just now. It was perfectly natural. After all, you are a passionate woman and I am an irresistible man."

Rosalind peered through her fingers long enough to glare at him. Despite his teasing tone, he was smiling at her in a way that was disconcertingly tender.

"And if the legends are true," he went on, "it isn't your fault at all. If you are my destined bride, you are not going to be able to help yourself."

"I'm not your bride," she sniffed. "I—I wish I had never gone to Miss Fitzleger's that day."

His smile dimmed.

"Very likely it would be better for you if you hadn't," he agreed. "That is one thing I have never quite understood. Why did you come to Effie's? How do you know her?"

"I don't. I knew her grandfather."

"The Reverend Septimus Fitzleger?"

"Aye, he was an acquaintance of my father. Once when I was a little girl, he came to visit and he told me that I should come to Torrecombe someday to see him."

"Fitzleger told you to come here?" Lance asked in a strange voice.

"Yes, he was most insistent upon it. He said when I was quite grown up I must come to this kingdom by the sea."

"Good lord!"

Lance appeared so thunderstruck, Rosalind rolled onto her back and peered up at him.

"Is there something strange about that?" she asked anxiously.

"Yes, I fear that there is," Lance murmured. "Fitzleger was a good and wise man, perhaps the wisest I've ever known. He was also our family Bride Finder before Effie. If he is the one who told you to come here . . ."

Lance paused and reached for her hand. "Then perhaps there truly is no escaping this legend. For either one of us."

Rosalind studied him mistrustingly, but for once there was no trace of cynicism or mockery in Lance's dark eyes. Only a look of wonder so deep, Rosalind almost felt herself caught up in it.

But she shrank deeper into the pillow and cried, "No! I don't want to be a part of your legend, Lance St. Leger. I can't be. My heart belongs to someone else."

"I know you still grieve for your late husband," Lance began gently, "but in time—"

"No! God forgive me, it's not my poor Arthur I am speaking of, but—but," Rosalind swallowed hard, then confessed. "It is that same gentleman I told you of the day we first met at Effie's."

Lance looked blank for a moment, then his eyes widened. "You don't mean that—that one who is more noble and handsome than me?"

"Yes!" she said passionately. "I will love only him until the day I die. There will never be any room in my heart for anyone else."

Lance's mouth fell open and then closed again, as though for once the man could think of nothing to say, no witty remark, no teasing quip. He appeared so stunned, Rosalind was moved to some pity for the arrogant man. She had never expected he would take her rejection quite this hard.

"I am sorry," she said, giving his fingers a soft squeeze.

She wasn't sure Lance even heard her. He patted her hand absently and rose from the bed with a dazed look on his face. Mumbling something about her getting some rest now, he turned and stumbled from the room.

Only when he was out in the hallway with the door firmly closed was Lance able to let out his breath in a huge rush. He had expected that his marriage proposal to Rosalind was going to be difficult. He had expected to overcome much resistance, to have to use every last bit of his charm to persuade her.

But he had never expected anything like this. That she would turn him down because of a myth, a legendary hero, a phantom that he created first to deceive and then only to comfort her. Never in his wildest imaginings had he ever thought his Lady of the Lake was going to up and fall in love with the damned fellow.

"What have I done?" He leaned up against the door, closed his eyes, and groaned. But perhaps the far more important question was ... what the bloody hell was he going to do now?

CHAPTER ELEVEN

ance descended to the lower hall and grimaced at the activity he had set into motion only that morning. The doors to Castle Leger's most elegant drawing room had been flung open. The Long Gallery, with its tall latticed windows and walls hung with mint green Spitalsfield silk, had been the site of many St. Leger celebrations since long before Lance could remember, birthdays, christenings, betrothals, marriages.

The room had been closed up during his parents' absence, but now the chamber bustled with servants dusting, polishing, and removing the holland covers from delicate lavender-and-rose upholstered furnishings.

But he might as well tell the housemaids to put the covers right back again, Lance thought dourly. There would be no wedding celebrated anytime soon, unless it was at the local cemetery. For where else could a woman go who clearly preferred to plight her troth to a ghost?

There must be a certain grim humor to be found in the situation, but Lance was damned if he could see it. Stealing one last disgruntled look at the servants' preparations, he took himself off to the relative peace of the library.

His first impulse was to pour himself out a good stiff drink from the half-empty decanter he and Val had failed to finish last night. He found himself snatching up the St. Leger sword instead, abandoned on the library table.

Hefting the blade that seemed to be the source of all his present troubles, he peered down at the flawed crystal and saw his own image reflected back to him, slightly distorted but still amazingly clear. Lance studied his own face with a brooding intensity.

He had never thought of himself as a conceited man before, but he was dismayed to realize he must be. He had rather taken for granted that uniformity of feature, the dazzling smile that never failed to charm most women.

So what the blazes was it about Lancelot du Lac that Rosalind found more appealing? Was it merely a turn of expression, a softness in the voice? Or was there something about a man clad in chain mail that Lance completely lacked?

He expelled a frustrated sigh, fighting a strong urge to go storming back up to the bedchamber, seize hold of Rosalind, and try to shake some sense into the woman, get her head down from the clouds of Camelot and back to the realities of the nineteenth century.

Could a heroic ghost save her from ruin? Could some noble phantom provide her with a decent home and a handsome marriage settlement? Warm her bed and give her children?

No, damn it all. And even if Rosalind was not head over ears in love with Lance, she was not indifferent to him either. Had any more passion stirred between them, they both would have forgotten her wound or any notions of propriety and ended up in bed, if not for—for that damned Sir Lancelot.

The devil take the noble idiot, Lance thought angrily, then brought himself up short, realizing that he was fuming just like a jealous lover.

But jealous of whom? The rival that he'd created himself? By God, he thought, raking his hand back through his hair with a soft groan. Maybe he needed a drink after all.

But before he could even reach for the decanter, the door burst open and Val limped into the room. His brother still looked worn from the ordeal of the night before, and he was leaning more heavily on his cane than usual, but his eyes were alight with eagerness.

There had been no way to conceal from Val the nature of his visit to Rosalind, but Lance wished there had been. He winced as Val bore down upon him.

"How did it go?" he asked, then beamed at the sight of the weapon in Lance's hand. "Are you getting ready to offer her the sword? What did Rosalind say? When is the wedding to be?"

"Most likely when hell freezes over." Lance plunked the sword back on the table. "The lady turned me down. Flat."

It was almost ludicrous the way Val's face fell. He could not have appeared more stunned or dismayed if his own suit had just been rejected.

"You cannot be all that surprised," Lance continued impatiently. "What did you think? That the legend was going to triumph at last? Love and happiness ever after?"

"Well, no, not exactly." But from the way Val's face colored, it was perfectly obvious to Lance that was exactly what his romantic brother had been thinking.

"You know the woman does not exactly dote upon me," Lance said.

"Yes, but I was certain you'd be able to change that. You have such a way with the ladies, Lance."

"Your faith in my powers of seduction is touching, Valentine. But apparently the only sort of proposals I'm any good at are indecent ones."

"But didn't Rosalind understand your offer was an honorable one? That you were trying to save her reputation?"

"She did, but it doesn't matter. She would as soon go straight to the devil as wed me." Lance was surprised himself by the note of dejection that crept into his voice. It wasn't as though he had even wanted to be married in the first place. It wasn't as though he should even care.

But somehow, damn it, he did.

He stalked away to stare moodily out the windows opening onto the gardens where he had labored but an hour ago, struggling to put together that haphazard bouquet. What he had told Rosalind had been perfectly true. He never had troubled himself to pick flowers for a woman. Well . . . Lance's mouth twisted into a wry smile . . . except for his mother when he'd been a wee lad.

None of his mistresses would ever have tolerated such a humble offering still smelling of the earth of the garden, the petals yet moistened with dew. Especially not Adele Monteroy. The woman had had far too many young fools like Lance rivaling one another to present her with only the finest of roses, far too perfect to be real.

But Rosalind . . . she'd led a rather sad and lonely existence, his Lady of the Lake. No roses, no admirers, no dashing officers ready to come to blows for the merest token of her favor. Despite her natural cheerfulness, there was often a wistfulness that stole into her eyes.

But when she had breathed in the fragrance of those flowers, her face had brightened. For one fleeting moment, she had seemed genuinely happy, and Lance had been stirred by the strangest emotion—the feeling that he would ride to the ends of the earth, do anything to keep her that way.

But was he willing to continue wearing chain mail for the rest of his life?

Lance was disturbed from his glum reverie by the sound of his brother coming up behind him. He'd almost forgotten that Val was still in the room.

Val placed his hand awkwardly on Lance's shoulder and squeezed. "Lance, I'm sorry that things went so badly."

Lance shrugged, trying to summon up a smile, a quip, some clever remark to brush off his brother's sympathy, but for once he couldn't seem to think of any. He wondered if Val would have been so swift to offer comfort if he knew the reason Lance's wooing had gone so far awry.

He had warned Lance against continuing his absurd masquerade. Val was far too much of a saint to say *I told you so*, but he would be bound to come out with a remark that Lance would find equally unpalatable.

Val would certainly insist again upon Rosalind's being told the truth, and Lance considered the possibility himself. But only for a moment. He still quailed from the thought. Not only would Rosalind be crushed and humiliated, she would hate Lance for it and likely never agree to marry him.

And for a man who'd vowed to end his days as a bachelor, he was suddenly very determined to be wed.

He shook off Val's hand and squared his shoulders with fresh resolution. "There is clearly only one thing to be done. I will have to find a way to force Rosalind to marry me."

He swung around from the window to find Val regarding him, completely aghast.

"Force her? Lance, you can't do that!"

"Why not? You're the one who's insisted from the beginning that I have to save her honor, that she is my chosen bride."

"Yes, but—but—"

"What do you think I'm going to do? Simply give up and let her return to those two harpies to be buried in calve's-foot jelly and black crepe for the rest of her life? Or to be cast out into the streets, where heaven knows what might happen to her?"

Val's gaze narrowed, and he studied Lance for such a long moment, Lance grew uncomfortable.

Val finally breathed, "By God, Lance! You *have* fallen in love with her."

"No, it's just that—that I don't like to see her unhappy, that's all. I never thought to hear myself say such a thing, but even marrying me would be better than the life she's been leading since her husband died."

"I agree, but Lance, you can hardly march Rosalind down the aisle at sword point."

"Can't I?" Lance retorted, pausing by the library table to caress the hilt of the St. Leger blade. "At least I'd finally get some practical use out of this thing."

"Lance!"

Lance thrust the sword aside with a rueful grin. "Never fear, Valentine. I have no intention of offering my lady any violence. But I fear there is only one other solution."

Lance cringed at the very idea but saw no help for it. He heaved a deep sigh. "He's going to have to visit her again and persuade her. He's the only one she'll listen to."

Val's brow knit in bewilderment. "Who are you talking about?"

"Sir Lancelot du Lac," Lance said somewhat bitterly. "Rosalind would do practically anything for him, though I'm damned if I can see why."

He gave a dark scowl and muttered, "Blasted idiot in chain mail. What did he ever do but spout poetry at her? It was my kiss that fairly had her swooning."

"But Lance, you *are* . . . I mean he is . . ." Val faltered, casting him a troubled glance. "You are really starting to worry me."

That wasn't surprising, Lance thought. He was starting to worry himself. But before he could assure his brother that he was not going entirely mad, they were interrupted.

After a brisk knock, a timid housemaid poked her head in the door to announce that Captain Mortmain had arrived and was requesting a few moments of Master Lancelot's time.

Lance exchanged a startled glance with Val. As often as Lance had invited Rafe to his home, Rafe had been adamant in his refusals. Rafe had not set foot near Castle Leger since that long-ago summer when he had ended his brief stay with the St. Legers by running off to sea.

Lance couldn't imagine what had finally overcome Rafe's reluctance to visit, but he was not left to wonder for long. The trembling housemaid ushered Rafe into the library, looking as terrified as though she had allowed the devil himself to breach the walls.

As the girl vanished, Rafe hesitated on the threshold, a formidable figure in his uniform, the military cut of the navy frock coat matched by the precision of his dark cropped hair and neatly trimmed mustache.

But something in his friend's stance carried Lance back to that day so many years ago when Rafe had first been ushered into the library by Lance's own mother.

It had been employed as a schoolroom then, and Lance and his brother and sisters had lifted their heads from their books to stare wide-eyed at the creature Madeline St. Leger had brought into their midst.

A lanky youth, whose arms and legs had all but outgrown his shabby clothes, a shock of dark hair hanging over his brow, half obscuring the most hard, sullen eyes Lance had ever seen. For Lance and his siblings, it was their first glimpse of one of those terrible beings they'd heard so many dark whisperings about.

"*A Mortmain!*" Lance remembered the horrified whisper they had all exchanged until they'd been hushed by a gentle word of admonishment from his mother.

"Children," Madeline St. Leger had said with a firm but warm smile. "This is Rafe. He is a friend who has come to stay with us for a while, and I expect you to make him feel welcome."

A friend? Lance recalled it had been the first time in his eight years that he had ever questioned his mama's wisdom. The boy had loomed frighteningly over all of them, his thin features blazing defiance. Yet there had been a pride in Rafe's bearing that Lance had admired even then, and beneath the half-savage demeanor, he had found something else in Rafe's eyes: an uncertainty, the hunger of a wild thing trying to summon up enough trust to creep closer to a beckoning campfire.

That surly boy was long gone, transformed into the cool, collected man Lance saw before him, but for a brief moment, all the old uncertainties simmered in Rafe's eyes.

His mouth curved in a welcoming smile, Lance stalked forward and clapped his friend on the shoulder. "Damn, Rafe, but it's good to see you here. This is an agreeable surprise."

"A surprise certainly, but as to how agreeable . . ." Rafe's gaze traveled toward Val.

Lance was dismayed to notice how his brother had stiffened at Rafe's arrival, Val's hands clutched tightly about the handle of his cane. Val had known Rafe fully as long as Lance had, but he felt obliged to bluster out some sort of introduction.

"Rafe, you do remember my brother?"

"The noble Valentine," Rafe purred. He extended his hand, and for one awful moment, Lance thought Val intended to refuse to take it.

But his brother shuffled forward.

"Captain Mortmain," he said gravely, and the two men shook, palms barely touching in a gesture that reminded Lance of the original purpose of the handclasp between men, the assurance that one's enemy came in peace and carried no weapon.

If that was the case, neither Val nor Rafe looked particularly satisfied. The air in the room seemed to have thickened with an aura of tension and mistrust.

An uncomfortable silence descended, and Lance leapt to fill it. In his heartiest tone, Lance pressed Rafe with offers of refreshment and urgings to be seated, both of which Rafe declined.

"I don't intend to trespass on your hospitality for long," Rafe said. "I only came to inquire after Lady Carlyon. Has she recovered from her attack?"

Lance heard Val suck in his breath.

"How did you know about that?" Val asked.

"The tidings are all over the entire village by now. How else should I know?" Rafe arched one brow in an expression that was part mockery, part challenge.

"How else indeed," Lance agreed with a warning frown at his brother. "Rosalind is doing remarkably well and should fully recover."

"No thanks to the devil that shot her." Val pinned Rafe with a hard stare.

But Rafe either did not hear the remark or chose to ignore it. "I am relieved the lady has sustained no lasting harm. She was rather imprudent, to be wandering the countryside alone." Rafe fingered the end of his mustache before asking, "The gossip circulating through Torrecombe was, as usual, rather jumbled. What actually happened to the lady?"

Lance related the adventure by the lake and the events leading up to it as briefly as possible, leaving out a few salient details. Such as how Rosalind had come to be involved in the entire business in the first place, namely Lance's masquerade as the ghost of the legendary knight.

He'd never revealed the secret of his night drifting to anyone outside the family, not even Rafe. Though there had been a time or two that Lance had come close to confiding it, something had always held him back—his promise to his father, which was even stronger than friendship.

When Lance had finished his tale, Rafe shook his head in amazement. "So Lady Carlyon saved your sword from this desperate brigand. What an extraordinary woman."

Lance smiled and agreed softly. "Aye, that she is."

"And . . . she was not able to identify her assailant?"

"No, the thief was once again masked."

"How unfortunate."

"Yes, wasn't it?" Val put in. "But perhaps you can assist with the villain's identity."

"I?" Rafe regarded Val in a haughty questioning fashion, and Lance dreaded what Val might be about to say next. He had never seen his brother in such a humor. Val's face fairly radiated hostility, his warm brown eyes turned hard as agates.

"You are a representative of His Majesty's government, are you not?" Val demanded. "It is your sworn duty to uphold the law and apprehend such villains."

Rafe shrugged. "I am merely a humble customs official, sent to ferret out smugglers. Unless you believe that is who attacked her ladyship?"

"No, I'm certain it was no smuggler. In fact, I was wondering where you were last night, Captain Mortmain."

"Val!" Lance snapped at his brother.

Although Rafe smiled, his eyes narrowed. "Why should my whereabouts hold any interest for you, Valentine?"

Lance intervened hastily. "Val merely thought—er—that is, if you were out making rounds last night, perhaps you might have seen or heard something—"

"Alas, I fear I was derelict in my duties. I spent the evening carousing rather too heavily in the taproom. *All evening,*" Rafe added as though daring Val to contradict him.

Lance feared that his brother meant to do just that, but Val compressed his lips in a taut line.

"It is most regrettable that Lance was unable to apprehend the thief," Rafe continued, his eyes never leaving Val's face. "I doubt now that he will ever be caught."

"Why is that?" Val asked sharply.

"The man would have to be a fool to linger hereabouts after having committed such a crime, wouldn't he?"

"Or damnably arrogant."

"Or extremely sure of himself and his powers of deception."

"It doesn't matter how clever the blackguard imagines himself to be," Val retorted. "I intend to unmask him."

Lance followed this exchange with mounting unease, noting Rafe's expression, the thin smile, the dangerous glitter in the eyes. He'd seen Rafe fall into this ominous humor before, when he seemed purely to enjoy playing the devil, encouraging another man's worst suspicions, and Lance's usually sensible brother looked all too ready to rise to the bait.

"So you are of a mind to play thief taker, are you, noble Valentine?" Rafe asked.

"I assure you I won't be playing," Val said fiercely. "And when I catch up to that bastard—"

"Yes? What will you do then?"

Clenching his cane, Val actually took a step closer to Rafe. His friend continued to smile, but Lance recognized all too well the wolfish look settling into Rafe's eyes.

In another heartbeat, Val would be challenging Rafe's honor, and Lance would have the pair of them confronting each other with pistols at dawn.

Was this how the St. Leger–Mortmain feud had been perpetuated over the centuries? Lance wondered with exasperation. Born out of misunderstanding, suspicion, offended pride, and unyielding tempers?

It was an unusual experience for Lance, being the level-headed one in the group. He stepped quickly between the two men.

"When the villain is found, he'll be turned over to the proper authorities," Lance said firmly. "Until then, Val, I'd like a word with you. In *private*," he added through clenched teeth.

"If you'll excuse us, Rafe." Lance directed a curt nod at his friend. Before Val could protest, Lance seized him by the arm and hustled him out into the hallway.

Thrusting Val away from the library door, Lance closed it and then exploded in a harsh undertone.

"What the devil do you think you're doing, Val? Insulting a guest in our home?"

"Pardon me if I have trouble making civil conversation with the man who likely attacked my brother and nearly killed that sweet lady upstairs."

"So now you are certain Rafe is guilty. Where is your proof, Val?" Lance sneered. "Or have you merely added mind reading to your other St. Leger talents?"

"One doesn't have to be a mind reader. Good God, Lance, I have held my tongue about Rafe Mortmain until now. But surely even you have to realize. You heard him in there." Val made a furious gesture toward the library. "All those—those innuendos, the smirks, the taunts. Practically daring us to prove him a thief."

"Daring *you*. And lower your blasted voice." Lance dragged Val farther out of earshot. "Rafe has borne the brunt of unjust suspicion all his life. The mockery and sarcasm are just his way of dealing with it."

"And is it also his way to visit Castle Leger? Or is it mere coincidence that he turned up here this morning asking after a woman he barely knows?"

Rafe's unexpected visit had startled Lance as well, but he replied stubbornly, "I believe Rafe has long wanted to return to this house. Inquiring after Rosalind merely gave him his excuse."

"Aye, an excuse to find out if she could identify him."

"You seem to forget, Val, that Rafe has been the one riding out with me, night after night, searching for the very sword you're trying to prove he stole."

"*Pretending* to help you search, the same way he pretends to be your friend. For all you know, he could have been merely leading you in circles, diverting your suspicion—"

"Enough, Val!" Lance snapped. "I'm not listening to any more of these unfounded accusations against a man who has been like—like a brother to me."

"Like a brother to you?" Val echoed somewhat hoarsely. "I—I rather thought that's what I was supposed to be."

Lance shrank from the hurt he saw in Val's eyes. He muttered, "At least Rafe Mortmain doesn't plague the life out of me with constant lectures and hover at my elbow like a blasted guardian angel."

"You *are* my brother, Lance. Forgive me for being concerned about you."

"I've told you often enough before. I don't want—"

"I know. You don't need any more help from me." Val's gaze dropped to his cane, his finger flexing over the ivory tip. When he raised his eyes again to Lance, the soft brown depths were almost pleading as he asked, "Was it such a terrible thing I did to you that day?"

He and Val had barely ever discussed what had happened on that battle-field in Spain, and Lance hardly thought this an auspicious time. He tried to turn away, to head back to the library, but Val persisted, shifting to block his path.

"I used what little St. Leger talent I possess to try and save my brother's life. Was that so wrong, Lance? What if you could have taken a bullet for me? Are you telling me you wouldn't have done it?"

"That would have been different," Lance said.

"Why? Because you are the great Lancelot, named for some legendary hero, while I'm only Valentine, christened after a ridiculous saint?"

"You are a blasted saint. You ended up crippled because of me, and you don't even mind."

"Of course I mind! Every day I have to struggle just to mount the tamest old nag out in the stables; every morning when my leg's so blasted stiff, I wonder if I can manage getting out of bed on my own. And every time I look at my foils and know I'll never be able to fence again—"

Val broke off his passionate tirade, his voice softening, "But despite all that, I still don't regret what I did for you."

"I have enough regrets for both of us," Lance said. "I didn't ask you to make any kind of noble sacrifice, and I find it damned hard to forgive you for it."

"I never hoped you'd forgive me, Lance. All I ever wanted was for you to forgive yourself." Val sighed but said no more, stepping out of Lance's path to limp sorrowfully away down the hall.

Lance watched him go, churning with the familiar mingling of regret and resentment. Wondering why Val couldn't simply do as he would have when they'd argued as boys . . . deal Lance a swift knock to the head instead of those mournful looks.

He had to fight against a strong urge to go storming after Val. And do what? Have out this thing between them once and for all? There'd been a time in their youth when he and Val had understood each other so well, it had taken scarce more than a look, a friendly clap on the shoulder to heal their quarrels.

But Lance doubted there were enough words in the world ever to put things right between them.

And besides . . . he still had Rafe Mortmain to deal with.

With a weary sigh, Lance took a moment to compose himself and then pushed the library door open. It annoyed him to discover the source of his most recent rift with Val calmly thumbing through a book.

The danger had disappeared from Rafe's smooth features. He merely looked amused as he set the volume aside.

"Did you manage to soothe your brother?" he asked. "I never realized he was such a fire eater."

"He's not," Lance slammed the door closed behind him. "Not unless he's been deliberately provoked."

"Ah, but there is something a little too saintly about the noble Valentine. One cannot resist ruffling his feathers. I am sure you've done so often enough yourself."

"Yes, Rafe, but he's *my* brother, blast it. It's my right to torment him and no one else's."

"Then perhaps you'd better warn *your* brother I've little patience for thinly veiled accusations and suspicion."

"Suspicions you did your best to encourage."

"When did it ever do me any good to do otherwise?" Rafe replied, and Lance found it impossible to argue with him.

It was true. Any crime committed within a league of Castle Leger, and the St. Legers had always been too ready to hang the nearest Mortmain. It embarrassed Lance that his own twin was the one most eager to fashion the rope.

He attempted to apologize for Val's behavior, a strange undertaking for him, he reflected wryly. Usually it was the other way around.

"Val didn't mean to imply anything," Lance said. "It is only that he is exhausted, on edge from all that happened last night. We both are."

"And my coming here was obviously an unwelcome intrusion."

"Don't be a damned fool. You are always welcome in my home, and I should bloody well hope you would know that."

A ghost of a smile touched Rafe's lips. "How odd. Your mother once said very much the same thing to me. Er . . . without the swearing, of course."

Rafe's gaze roved about the library, and he confessed, "I seem to be a bit

strained myself this morning. It has been a long time since I have been back
to this house."

"Too long," Lance agreed.

Rafe strolled down the line of bookcases, lifting his fingers to stroke the
well-worn spines like a man reaching out to touch memories he wasn't certain
he cared to resurrect.

A rare softness had stolen over the usually hard planes of his face, as he
pulled out one book, then another, half smiling at some title as though at an
old forgotten friend.

"I remember little of the rest of the house," he said. "But I recall this room
very well. Perhaps because your mother spent so many summer afternoons
here, trying to make a scholar of me."

"My mother tries to do that with everyone."

"She might actually have succeeded with me. She was . . . *is* a very gentle
and patient woman. After my mother died and left me abandoned in Paris, it
was Madeline who insisted I be searched for and brought to England, did you
know that?"

"No, I did not, but it sounds like something my mother would do."

"It took your family's agents nearly eight years to find me, but your mother
would never give up."

"She's a very persistent woman."

"Sometimes I wish she hadn't been." A brooding look stole into Rafe's eyes.
"I think it might have been better if I had never been found."

Lance frowned, wondering why Rafe would say such a thing. "Better for
whom?" he asked.

"All the good folk in Torrecombe, certainly. Sleeping safely in their beds for
so many years, believing all the Mortmains were dead. Now they behave as
though a dragon had been set loose among them again."

"Perhaps it would help if you behaved less dragonlike," Lance suggested.

Rafe merely shrugged. Moving away from the bookcase, his gaze alighted
on the desk, the St. Leger sword glinting against the mahogany surface.

"Ah, St. Leger," he drawled. "Still so careless with this magnificent blade?
One would think you'd learn to treat it with more respect after its miraculous
return."

Rafe lifted the heavy weapon, cradling the hilt against his palms so that the
crystal caught the sunlight, sending fragments of a rainbow dancing across
the bookcases, refracting an even stranger light in Rafe's eyes.

An inexplicable sense of unease stole through Lance. Anyone else observing the expression on Rafe's face at this moment might have been pardoned

for supposing that he did indeed covet the St. Leger sword. And the world was already too inclined to suspect the worst of Rafe Mortmain. For Rafe's own sake, Lance was glad his friend had been able to give a good account of his whereabouts last night.

I spent the evening carousing rather too heavily in the taproom.

But Lance had been to the taproom himself when he went to inquire after Rosalind. And he now remembered distinctly.

Rafe had not been there.

The realization sent a jolt through Lance, causing his stomach to clench. As Rafe continued to admire the sword, almost caressing the hilt, Lance regarded him with a troubled frown.

"Rafe, where . . . where did you say you were last night?"

"I told you. At the Dragon's Fire."

"All evening?"

"Aye."

"But I was there myself and I didn't see you."

Rafe shrugged. "I suppose there was a brief period of time when I went out to the stables to have a word with the ostler. He's been doing a damn poor job of looking after my horse."

"Oh." Lance expelled a deep breath. He might have known Rafe would have a good explanation, but he felt relieved all the same. Small wonder his friend had managed to goad poor Val. Rafe had an evil genius for making himself appear guilty.

Something in the tone of Lance's questions must have captured Rafe's full attention at last. He cast Lance a sharp look.

"Why? What makes you ask?" Rafe demanded. "Where did you think I might have gone?"

"Oh—er nowhere in particular. I was merely curious, that is all."

"As to whether I might have actually taken a moment to nip out to the Maiden Lake to steal your sword and shoot your lady?"

"Of course not," Lance blustered, but he found himself unable to meet Rafe's eyes. Because for one terrible moment, he had suspected Rafe, and Lance feared that his doubt was all too painfully evident to his friend.

Rafe's features had gone very still. He replaced the St. Leger sword carefully back on the table. "Apparently the noble Valentine is not the only St. Leger ready to see me hanged for a thief."

"Don't be ridiculous. It was only that I am—"

"Finally reconsidering the wisdom of befriending a Mortmain?"

"No!"

"It is quite all right." Rafe looked more weary than angry, which somehow made it worse. "I was expecting this to happen eventually."

"Then you were wrong," Lance said vehemently. "You're my friend and always will be. Damnation, Rafe!" He dragged his hand back through his hair in pure frustration, ashamed of himself, angry at his brother. Damn Val and his suspicion anyway. It was like a poison, and Lance refused to be infected by it.

He crossed the room to Rafe's side. "I was merely being stupid. The only excuse I can offer is the strain I have been under of late. Forgive me."

Lance thrust his hand out firmly, forcing Rafe to take it. After a brief hesitation, Rafe yielded, returning Lance's hearty clasp, his stiff features creasing into a reluctant smile.

"Perhaps now that this wretched business of the sword is settled, you can accompany me back to the Dragon's Fire and we can raise a pint in celebration."

Lance started enthusiastically to agree, only to check himself.

"I can't," he said. "I need to meet with the vicar this afternoon."

"Planning my funeral?" Rafe jested.

"No. Hopefully, my . . . my wedding."

Rafe's expressive brows arched upward, and for a moment, he appeared rather stunned. But then he said dryly, "You plan to marry Lady Carlyon, I presume. Your chosen bride."

"Aye," Lance said somewhat sheepishly, bracing himself for a full onslaught of Rafe's teasing gibes.

To his surprise, Rafe merely murmured. "Well, well. I suppose congratulations are in order. It would seem you have finally succumbed to your family's traditions. I never thought I'd see the day.

"It appears you have turned into a true St. Leger at last."

Lance found that an odd remark, as puzzling as the hooded expression that settled over Rafe's eyes. He was left with the unsettled feeling that something had altered between him and Rafe during these past few moments. Lance's brief flare of doubt and his upcoming marriage somehow changed everything. Their friendship was never going to be quite the same again.

After Rafe had gone, Lance tried to shrug off the melancholy notion. He felt so infernally frustrated and drained, he wasn't sure what he wanted to do most: sink down into the nearest chair or bang his head up against one of the bookcases.

What a devil of an afternoon it had been. First, his rejection by Rosalind, then the quarrel with his brother, and now this friction with Rafe. Lance heaved a bitter sigh and wondered if his father had ever known days like this.

Not bloody likely. Not Anatole St. Leger, the dread lord of Castle Leger. Lance doubted his noble sire had ever let matters slip so far out of his iron control.

He stumbled over to the library window to peer out, but not at the garden this time. His gaze focused on the path that he knew meandered eventually down to the stables, and Lance felt the old restlessness rising in him, taking such a strong hold, it became almost a physical ache.

He yearned to tear down to the stables, fling himself on the back of a horse, and simply gallop out of here as he'd done so many years ago. Far away from Castle Leger with its crushing weight of expectations, including the image of the father he could never hope to live up to.

Lance wasn't even certain where he'd go. Back to his regiment perhaps. He'd long since lost any illusions about the glamour of military life, but at least things had been a deal simpler in the army.

Always certain who your enemy was. No sad-eyed brother to prod at his conscience. And best of all, no dream-ridden lady looking for a knight in shining armor. Only women interested in the size of a man's purse.

Val could surely manage the estates here until Anatole St. Leger returned. Lance stirred restively, wondering what was holding him back.

But even as the thought occurred to him, Rosalind's winsome face filled his mind. He pictured her so clearly, his blue-eyed maiden, watching and waiting eagerly tonight for her hero to return to her. And he imagined her devastation if Sir Lancelot du Lac failed her.

Lance heaved a deep sigh and turned away from the window, realizing he was going nowhere for now. He had a wedding to plan and a bride to woo.

After he had persuaded Rosalind to marry him, made sure that her future was secured, fulfilled his family's tradition, gotten her with an heir—well, then it could hardly matter to anyone if he went or stayed.

First he was going to have to slap on that damned chain mail, Lance reflected grimly. But if he could find just the right words to say to Rosalind, if he had any kind of luck at all—

Perhaps tonight would prove Sir Lancelot du Lac's final performance.

CHAPTER TWELVE

*R*osalind paced restlessly before the bedchamber windows. The glow of the candles cast dancing reflections on the darkened panes as though a dozen tiny lanterns bobbed just outside. Fairy lights, Rosalind had often thought of them as a child, but now they heralded magic of a different sort.

The coming of night, the time when the great mansion of Castle Leger would settle to silence and *he* would come.

Sir Lancelot du Lac. Her beloved friend. Her gallant knight. And never had she felt more in need of a knight in shining armor: to rescue her from the velvet folds of the trap she felt closing around her, from the lure of a legend and the temptation of a man's kiss and far too bold caress.

She had long since bathed, donning a fresh lawn nightgown, and yet the feel of Lance's touch still seemed to cling to her body, bold, intimate, tormenting her with feelings of unwanted desire. Hugging her arms tightly about herself, she sighed, torturing herself yet again with a question. What if she had not summoned up the will to stop Lance? Her gaze strayed to the bed, her mind filling with images. Of lying naked upon the cool sheets, being warmed by the dark fire of Lance's eyes. Of melting beneath one of his kisses that seemed to have the power to render her so weak. Of watching hungrily as he stripped out of his shirt, exposing the broad plane of his chest, bronzed, hard muscled.

"Oh, stop it, stop it!" Rosalind moaned at herself in dismay. What in the world was happening to her? She was a woman who'd always daydreamed about castles and knights, faraway kingdoms peopled with gentle fairy folk. Not about wild, heated tumbles between the sheets with seductive rogues who wore their breeches far too tight.

She could almost hear Lance's husky voice rumble in her ear. *You are a passionate woman, and I'm an irresistible man. If you are my destined bride, you are not going to be able to help yourself.*

What if that was true? Rosalind wondered, horrified. The St. Leger tale of the chosen bride sounded almost as old as the legends of Camelot. What if— fight it though she would—she was indeed destined to succumb to Lance St. Leger?

Effie Fitzleger had predicted it, and Effie had never been known to be wrong. Even the wise old Reverend Fitzleger appeared to have selected Rosalind to be a St. Leger bride.

No! Rosalind didn't know why Lance had been able to rouse such temptation in her. Most likely because he was an accomplished rake, far too skilled in seducing women, and Rosalind had too little experience in how to deal with such a man.

Her body might have betrayed her, but she knew full well where her heart lay, lost somewhere in the mists of time with a gentle spirit from a nobler age, when heroes were not afraid to be tender as well as courageous and bold.

"Sir Lancelot," Rosalind murmured, closing her eyes. "Please don't fail me tonight. I feel so frightened and alone. I need you more than ever."

Even though the prayer had been no more than a fervent whisper, it fortified her, enabled her to banish Lance's troubling image from her mind. Rosalind padded across the carpet, taking care not to make a deal of noise.

Everyone from her maid to her earnest doctor, Val, assumed she had already gone to bed. She had no desire to alert anyone into coming to check on her. Drifting back to the dressing table, she settled before the mirror. It would likely be hours before Sir Lancelot arrived. He had yet to appear earlier than midnight, but Rosalind was determined to prepare herself.

Although she had already combed out her hair thrice, she reached for the brush again, running it through the silken strands until her hair shimmered like a curtain of moonlight down her back. Rosalind pulled a wry face at her own image. She looked wide-eyed as ever, ridiculously young, with a countenance her Arthur had always described as sweet.

Sweet was the last thing she desired to be tonight. She wanted to be dazzling, radiant, the kind of enchantress that could entice a weary warrior into staying with her forever. Rosalind's gaze roved disconsolately over the imperfections of her figure draped beneath the nightgown. Light, slender perhaps, but hardly seductive. And the padding of her bandage thickening one shoulder did little to help her appear more alluring.

Was her wound healed over enough to risk removing the thing? Squeamish at the thought of what she might see, Rosalind had closed her eyes when Val had changed the dressing earlier. But now she loosened her nightgown and eased it off her shoulders.

The lawn fabric pooled to the chair, baring her to the waist. With fingers that trembled slightly, Rosalind began to undo the layers of linen. She was heartened by the fact that she no longer felt even so much as a twinge of pain.

Whatever sort of medicine Val St. Leger practiced, it was nothing short of miraculous. Or perhaps the wound was not so dreadful as she had imagined. Surely no more than a scratch . . .

But as the last of the bandaging fell away, Rosalind emitted a cry of dismay. The wound was amazingly healed over, but still raw, red, and ugly. Rosalind could not fool herself. Even with the passage of time, there would always be a prominent scar left to mar the whiteness of her shoulder.

She felt her throat tighten and swallowed thickly, adjuring herself not to be ridiculous. She should be thankful merely to be alive. What did a scar matter? It was not as though she would ever be unveiling herself to Sir Lancelot anyway, feeling his tender caress, his gentle touch. Not as though she possessed enough beauty to charm the man, even if he were still alive and capable of loving her. Which he wasn't.

The entire situation was—was all too absurd and hopeless. Despite her best efforts, Rosalind felt a few tears escape to splash down her cheeks. Resting her arm upon the dresser, she buried her face against it, quietly indulging her despair.

Lost in her misery, she never felt the slight stirring in the air, didn't realize she was no longer alone until a deep voice called softly.

"Milady?"

Rosalind sat up with a start, blinking away her blur of tears. The sound seemed so close, directly behind her, yet she saw no reflection other than her own in the mirror.

She twisted on the chair, coming halfway about before she gazed up at him, a towering figure of a man, scarce more than an arm's length away. A mail-clad warrior with midnight hair and weary face, sad smile, and haunted eyes. As ephemeral as the candlelight and yet somehow more solid and real than the very castle walls.

A glad cry breached her lips. Sir Lancelot's dark eyes glowed warmly, but his smile of greeting froze into a stunned expression. It was only then that Rosalind remembered her state of undress.

Gasping, she hastily crossed her arms over her bare breasts, clutching her hands to her shoulders. The movement seemed to snap Sir Lancelot out of his trance.

"I—I'm sorry, milady. Obviously, I wait upon you too early. I will just . . . just—" If a ghost could have stumbled, Sir Lancelot would have done so as he backed away from her.

"Oh no!" Rosalind cried, fearing he meant to vanish as suddenly as he had come. She started to rise, nearly causing her nightdress to tumble off the rest of the way. She shrank back down.

"Please don't go," she whispered, even though her face seemed to have turned to fire.

"But, milady—" Sir Lancelot began, only to check himself with a frown. His own embarrassment vanished as he focused on her face, and Rosalind realized the tracks of her tears must be clearly revealed to him in the candlelight.

She was more mortified to have him catch her weeping than half-naked. She would have dashed her tears aside, but moving her hands from their present position was unthinkable. All she could do was duck her head.

To her dismay, Sir Lancelot knelt down in front of her. He peered up at her, his eyes so intent with concern, it was nearly enough to make her start crying all over again.

"Milady," he said, his voice a gentle balm. "I had hoped to find thee in much better spirits this evening."

"I—I am. Now that you are here."

"Yet you *were* weeping. Why didst thou so?"

"No particular reason. Only something too trifling to mention."

"Tell me," he insisted.

Rosalind squirmed, feeling more embarrassed than ever. "If—if you must know, it was because I suddenly realized I—I am going to be left with this dreadful scar on my shoulder." She forced her lips into a lopsided smile. "You see? I told you it was mere foolishness."

Sir Lancelot did not look as though he thought so. He demanded, "Let me see thy wound."

Rosalind shook her head, horrified by the mere suggestion of such a thing. "Please."

There was no way he could have forced her to comply with his request, but neither was there any way she could resist the plea in his eyes. Slowly, reluctantly, she inched her fingers down her shoulder until her wound was revealed. It struck her as being even larger and more ugly than she remembered.

She hardly dared look at Sir Lancelot, but she found no revulsion in his eyes, only a deep sadness. He raised his hand, his fingers drifting over the region of her wound.

She could not sense his touch, but she tingled with a powerful warmth all the same. As though all of his regrets, his comfort, his caring flowed directly from his soul into hers, leaving her trembling.

" 'Tis a most grievous wound, milady," he said. "How much I wish it could have been inflicted upon my own tough hide instead of thy gentle frame. But if you think such a scar will mar thy loveliness, thou art much mistaken. Yours is the sort of beauty that shines from within."

She offered him a wobbly smile. "I thank you, sir, but like most women, I fear I am foolish enough to wish for more outward signs."

"That, thou hast, too, in abundance." His thick dark lashes fluttered as his gaze drifted over her face, the column of her neck, the soft swell of her bosom.

Rosalind realized she had allowed her arms to relax, nearly exposing her breasts again. She should have moved promptly to re-cover herself, but she couldn't seem to stir, held fast by the look on Sir Lancelot's face.

Was it truly possible, she wondered? To find such awe and hunger, such reverence and longing simmering in this magnificent man's dark eyes?

Her hands dropped limp to her side, and she thought she saw a tremor course through her gallant knight. She scarce knew how long they remained that way, Sir Lancelot kneeling at her feet, herself perched on the edge of the chair, barely breathing. Like two lovers woven into an ancient tapestry, caught spellbound in a moment of sweet desire that could never fade, never be fulfilled.

Sir Lancelot was the first to rouse himself. Struggling to his feet, his great spirit seemed to tremble as he turned away from her.

"You—you had best robe thyself before you take a chill, milady."

Rosalind made no move to do so. She stretched out one hand toward the wall of his back, her heart aching with impossible womanly longings toward this man she so adored, whose touch she could never hope to feel, whose love could never be hers. Only when her hand passed through him did she snap back to her senses. She pulled up her nightgown and eased it back over her shoulders with shaking fingers.

When Sir Lancelot came around to face her again, she might well only have imagined the passion she had seen raging in his eyes.

"I crave your pardon, lady," he said. "I should not have stared at you thus. 'Tis only that it has been a very long time since I gazed upon charms such as thine."

" 'Tis all right," Rosalind assured him, attempting to recover her own composure. Though she blushed to confess it, she said, "I did not mind you looking."

"Because I am only a ghost?" he asked with a sad smile.

"No, because . . ."

Because I love you.

Rosalind swallowed the imprudent words just in time. She fidgeted with the lace on her nightgown in order to avoid his eyes. "Because you are a man of great honor, and I know you would never harbor any wicked thoughts about me."

Sir Lancelot flinched. "You accord me far too much credit, milady," he muttered.

Rosalind glanced up at him in surprise, wondering what she could have said to make him look so grim, but he was quick to rally behind one of his blinding smiles.

"In my eagerness to see you again, I fear I have managed to discompose us both with my untimely arrival. Allow me to greet thee in more proper fashion."

He swept her a courtly bow. "I bid thee good evening, my fair Lady Rosalind."

"Good evening, sir." She rose to her feet and dropped a demure curtsy, her primness barely concealing the quiver of delight that shot through her. He had been *eager* to see her again?

Stepping back, he subjected her to a more thoughtful scrutiny this time. "Despite your distress over thy scar, it pleases me to see you so much on the mend. I trust you have been well looked after during my absence?"

"Oh, yes. Everyone here has been most kind except . . ."

"Except?" Sir Lancelot prompted when she hesitated.

Rosalind fretted her lower lip. She had not meant to pounce upon her noble hero with her distressing tale the moment she clapped eyes upon him, but she couldn't seem to help herself. She would have flung herself headlong into the comfort of Lancelot's strong arms if it had been possible.

The only thing checking the urge was her realization she would pass right through her bold knight and likely end by cracking her head against the wall.

She burst out instead, "It's that descendant of yours. Lance St. Leger. He's done the most dreadful thing."

Lancelot's mail-clad shoulders heaved with an almost martyred resignation. "What now?"

"He has asked me to marry him!"

Sir Lancelot looked rather nonplussed for a moment. Then he exclaimed, "Ah, by St. George. Is there no end to the man's villainy?"

Rosalind's mouth twitched in a reluctant smile, realizing herself how absurd her complaint must sound. But she went on earnestly, "Truly, sir. His proposal was most distressing and unwelcome."

In her agitation at the memory, she took a restless turn about the room. "I suppose Lance meant well enough. He was likely trying to save my reputation, and he seemed genuinely disappointed by my refusal. I might even have felt a little sorry for him except for his reprehensible behavior since."

"But I haven't even been near—I—I mean, what else has the varlet done to you?"

"Nothing directly, but my maid has carried reports to me of what has been going on belowstairs. Jenny told me that she saw bolts of cloth being delivered for my bride clothes, and Lance kept his meeting with the lawyer and the vicar as though he intends to force me to marry him."

"He could hardly do that, my dear," Sir Lancelot soothed.

"N-no." Rosalind agreed reluctantly. But he could do other things, she thought. Those things that rendered her so weak and breathless in his arms, threatened to strip away her very reason. She had this inexplicable fear that if she ever did surrender to Lance's seduction, she would somehow be lost . . . lost to her beloved Sir Lancelot forever.

Not that she at all belonged to him now, she was forced to remind herself. No, only in her own heart.

She turned to her gallant knight in sheer desperation. "Is there nothing that you can do to stop Lance?" she pleaded. "Could you not find some way to spirit me far from here, hide me away in some peaceful little cottage?"

"No, my dear," he said. "I cannot help you escape, and I am not sure that I would, even if I could."

His words stunned Rosalind. "Why not?"

"There is the matter of the legend. If you are indeed fated to be Lance's bride—"

"You told me you were not certain you believed in that yourself."

"I am fast learning to have an entirely new respect for the traditions of the St. Leger family," Sir Lancelot replied. "But setting the legend aside, milady, there are more practical considerations here. The question of your reputation and your dire circumstances. Lance St. Leger may be a worthless rogue, but he could provide you with a home, a secure income, and I believe he would do his best to make you happy."

"I know that everyone else seems determined to push me into a loveless match," Rosalind said with a tiny catch in her voice. "But I thought it was your solemn vow to rescue damsels in distress. I thought you were my friend."

"Ah, my dear Rosalind, so I am." He smiled at her so tenderly, it hurt. He moved toward her with hands outstretched, only to check the futile gesture.

"Milady," he said gently. "I only want to see you kept safe."

She shrank reproachfully away from him. "Safe! I don't want to be kept safe. All my life I have been tucked away in some bower reading about romance and legends while the world slipped away from me. I am weary of it."

She realized she must sound like a petulant child, but she couldn't seem to help herself, some long-suppressed rebellion swelling inside her like a painful tide.

"Just once, I would like to find a legend of my own. Some small bit of passion and excitement and—and adventure."

"You don't think that Lance might be able to supply those things? He has a reputation for—"

"I know all about Lance's reputation," Rosalind said bitterly. "Oh, I will admit that the man is possessed of a dangerous kind of attraction, and he can even be kind upon occasion. But he has no belief in chivalry, magic, and dreams. He simply isn't . . . isn't—"

"Isn't what, milady?" he asked.

She raised her head to look at Lancelot, unable to suppress the yearning in her voice.

"He isn't you," she whispered.

"No, Lance certainly isn't me," he said with an inexplicable bitterness. "Forgive me, milady, I can no longer pretend to misunderstand the nature of your feelings toward me. But I assure you, I am most unworthy."

Rosalind flushed hot with shame, realizing she had betrayed herself. She had ever been too impulsive, too transparent in her emotions. She had clearly distressed Sir Lancelot with her unrequited love. The man was far too chivalrous, too noble to willingly hurt any lady.

"I am sorry," she stammered. "I never meant to burden you with—with an affection I know you cannot possibly return."

"Ah, milady! All such tender feelings died in me a long time ago when I dishonored myself for the sake of the wrong woman." He hesitated for a long moment before going on. "But if by some miracle, my life and heart could be restored to me, then they would belong entirely to thee."

Rosalind stilled, scarce daring to breathe, her heart torn between hope and disbelief. She was certain she could not have heard him right.

"Are—are you saying that you could love me, too?"

"Aye, milady, until the day I—" He checked himself with a wry smile. "I will love you through all eternity."

Rosalind stumbled toward him, her arms outstretched, her pulse hammering in her ears. Sir Lancelot's hand came up to meet hers, their fingertips seeming to meet in a shimmer of light, unable to touch, yet touching each other in a way that mattered far more. A gentle communion of heart and soul.

Sir Lancelot could not kiss her, but he caressed her with the dark tenderness of his eyes, and she felt flowing from him that which she could scarce believe.

"You . . . you *do* love me," she murmured.

His mouth trembled with a smile as full of wonder as her own. "Aye, lady. From the moment I first set eyes upon you."

"Oh, sweet heaven!" Rosalind released a tremulous, half-laughing breath, her eyes misting with a joy too strong to be contained. "Then nothing else matters."

Lancelot's smile faded to sadness, and he drew his hand away. "Not so, lady. My love for thee can afford you nothing. You must still plight your troth to Lance St. Leger."

Rosalind's own hand fell limp to her side, her overwhelming happiness clouded with painful bewilderment. "You say you love me and yet you would *still* see me wed to another man?"

"There is no other choice, lady." Sir Lancelot spread his hands in a helpless gesture. "Look at me. I am only a ghost, a mere shadow of what was once and can never be again. There is no way I can care for you as I would wish to do."

"But if I married Lance, wouldn't it be like Arthur and Guinevere all over again?" Rosalind suggested timidly.

"That would appear to be my destiny, lady. Always cursed to love another man's wife."

"No, I cannot do such a thing to you. Or to Lance either."

"If you are worried about wounding St. Leger, milady, don't be." Sir Lancelot spoke with unusual harshness for him. "I can assure you he has no such tender sensibilities you need trouble about."

Rosalind stirred uncomfortably, but she feared Sir Lancelot might be right. After all, she had told Lance that she loved another, and it clearly had made no difference to the man. He still seemed ruthlessly determined to marry her.

Lancelot's voice gentled, his hand drifting along the fall of her hair, the gesture rife with his own sense of futility and desperate longing. "There has been little good in Lance. But this proposal he has made to you . . . it is the best and most honorable thing he's ever done in his entire wretched life. I should so like, at least one time, to be able to look upon his face with some pride. I beg you, milady. Allow it to be so."

Rosalind wrung her hands together, feeling as though her heart were being torn in two. She found it difficult to deny Sir Lancelot anything, especially when he looked at her so, his eyes an aching torment of love, despair, and tenderness. Yet what he was asking of her was nigh impossible.

"If I was wed to Lance," she argued, "how would I ever see you? How could you come to me each night?"

"I could not. This would have to be farewell."

"No!" Rosalind's chest tightened with alarm. She clutched at Sir Lancelot in terror that he might vanish before her very eyes. Her hands passed through him, only adding to her sense of desperation.

"But, milady, it would be far better for you if I—"

"No!" she cried again, even more fiercely. "I would die if I lost you now!"

Lancelot stared back at her helplessly. It was hardly possible for a ghost to sigh, but he emitted a sound full of weary resignation.

"Very well," he said. "I will continue to visit thee. But you must promise to wed Lance at once."

"How can I do that when I love you so?"

"Milady, I have had so many regrets to torment me. Let not the night that I drifted into your heart become another of them. If I were forced to see thee embark upon a life of poverty, cast off and alone, it would be more than I could bear."

Rosalind could see the truth of his words, writ in every agonized line of his noble countenance.

Sir Lancelot continued to urge, "Your marriage to Lance would not diminish what we feel for one another. It would become a kind of courtly love like the troubadours used to sing of."

"C-courtly love?" Rosalind echoed.

"Aye, a rather popular fashion in my time, though I could never see precisely why. A lady properly and respectably wed to some lord, giving him heirs, tending his castle, a most practical arrangement, while her heart was bestowed upon some knight who performed courageous deeds in her honor for no more repayment than a smile."

Rosalind nodded dreamily. "A love that was ever destined to remain pure and chaste, unfulfilled. But it would be more than enough."

"Would it?" Sir Lancelot cast her an odd enigmatic glance.

"Oh yes, was there ever a higher form of love?"

"Mayhap not." Lancelot smiled ruefully. "Then I will swear never to forsake thee. And in return, you will promise to do as I ask."

Rosalind wrestled with her own doubts for a moment longer. But there was no resisting the plea in Lancelot's expressive eyes, the painful knowledge there was little else she could do for her love's weary spirit, condemned to an eternity of wandering the earth. Just this one thing that might bring his noble heart a little ease. Perhaps the only way that they could remain together.

"A-all right," she said in a small voice.

"I will marry Lance St. Leger."

CHAPTER THIRTEEN

*L*ight flickered where there should have been none, in the tower high above the ancient castle keep, the oldest and most mysterious part of Castle Leger. The chamber where the great sorcerer lord, Prospero, had once spun out his days, striving for forbidden knowledge, casting his wicked spells.

But tonight the chamber was haunted by another restless spirit. Lance St. Leger drifted through the thick stone walls, seeking the place where he had abandoned the encumbrance of his body a few hours before.

The lantern he'd left burning flung out its feeble glow in an effort to hold back what remained of the night, illuminating the tower room with all its medieval trappings. The chamber itself seemed frozen in time, the dark wood of the small desk, the heavy cord-bound chests, the cupboard containing strange parchments and tomes gathered from the far corners of the globe, the mysterious vials and vessels of the alchemist's art—all appeared to be waiting the return of the lord and master rumored to have perished by flame so long ago.

Lance's body reposed upon the bed whose massive posts were carved with intricate symbols reminiscent of the interlacing of the ancient Celts. Flinching, he hesitated only a moment before committing himself to the shock of rejoining. Spirit returned to flesh. He had not been gone that long this time, so the jolt was not as great. A shudder, a gasp for air, and his eyes flew wide as he snapped out of his self-induced trance.

His breath slowly rising and falling, he lay immobile for a long time, simply staring up at the fiery St. Leger dragon painted upon the wooden canopy above his head, still not feeling comfortable in his own skin.

But then he supposed snakes didn't. That's why they were always shedding them. If only he could as easily have shucked off the guilt engendered by this night's work. He had accomplished what he had set out to do, persuaded Rosalind to marry him. But his victory was a hollow one.

He sat up with a low groan, the heavy mail coat weighing him down as though he'd been left bound and shackled. But he supposed he'd better get used to the sensation of stiff muscles and aching back. He'd condemned himself to these chains of deceit for a good many nights to come.

It was no more than he deserved after what he'd done to his poor Lady of the Lake: fed her even greater lies, continued to confuse her, tampered ruthlessly with her all too trusting heart.

And how she did trust and love this ridiculous phantom he had created. Even Lance hadn't realized how much so until tonight, when she had made that extraordinary gesture, her slender white arms falling to her side, exposing both her charms and vulnerability. The scar that distressed her so much, the creamy slope of her shoulders, the small perfect globes of her breasts. All shyly revealed to her hero.

Except it hadn't been any gallant knight who'd knelt at her feet as she thought. Only a lying, rather jaded rake who'd assessed and sampled far too many women in his time.

Then why had Rosalind been able to move him so? She'd stirred in him a purity of longing that had seemed to burn directly from his soul to Rosalind's. Unfortunately, now that he was rejoined to his body, it wasn't the spiritual part of his anatomy that was being affected by the remembrance of her naked beauty. Desire coursed through his veins with a power that went strong and deep, setting up an ache in his loins, actually bringing a fine sheen of sweat to his brow.

Awkwardly swinging his legs over the side of the bed, Lance gulped in several breaths, fighting against the overwhelming sensation. He wanted the woman. God, how he wanted her with a desire that went beyond reason, beyond any sense of decency. And the most damnable part of all this was—he didn't see how he could have her, not even after they were married.

Not with Lancelot du Lac filling her head with all those damn fool notions of courtly love, pure and chaste worship from afar. Levering himself stiffly to his feet, Lance caught sight of his own image in the polished steel surface of a shield mounted upon the rough stone wall.

No, not his image, Lance thought bitterly, but his hated rival's, Rosalind's noble lover. Sir Lancelot was reflected back to him in a phantom blur of chain mail, flowing dark hair, and intense eyes.

"You treacherous bastard," Lance muttered. "You were supposed to bow yourself gracefully out of the lady's life tonight. You were supposed to woo her for *me*, not you!

"*Oh, milady, if my life and heart could miraculously be restored to me, they would belong entirely to you.*" Lance mimicked himself savagely. "What the devil did you think you were doing, spouting such nonsense?"

"No, lad," an amused drawl came from the shadows behind Lance. "The more accurate question *is* who the devil are you talking to?"

Lance spun around, his pulse giving an uneasy thud. A familiar spectral figure lounged in the open arch of the tower room, the circular stone stair behind him spiraling away into darkness. But Lord Prospero cast an unearthly glow of his own, his cloak swirling off one shoulder, his scarlet tunic almost iridescent as he regarded Lance through the exotic slant of his eyes.

Recovering from his shock, Lance felt his heart drop in dismay. Bad enough to be caught behaving like a lunatic running around in chain mail, addressing his own reflection. But by that mocking devil, Prospero . . .

Lance let out a mouth-filling oath. "You! I hoped I had seen the last of you."

"Did you?" Prospero gave a laconic smile as though Lance's hopes were of no particular interest to him. "Then you shouldn't be clanking around, playing at knights and dragons in my tower. Haven't you gotten a little old for such games?"

Lance flushed hotly. "I only rested on your bed for a while. I didn't think you'd have much use for it anymore."

"True enough." Prospero abandoned his negligent pose, shifting away from the arch. "However, my private library is another matter."

He pointed an accusing finger in the direction of the cupboard. "Some of my books and documents are missing."

"Are they? My brother probably borrowed them. I told you he is attempting to delve into your history."

"That lad should learn to tend to his own business. You will tell him to put my books back at once," Prospero commanded.

"Tell him yourself," Lance snapped. "Why don't you fly back out of here and go plague Val for a while? I did what you wanted. I got your blasted sword back."

"I've seen it." Prospero's mouth thinned with displeasure. "There's a chip missing from the crystal."

"So what? The sword is safe. Isn't that good enough?"

"You are a St. Leger, boy, and you *still* seem to have no comprehension of the power that lies in that crystal, even the tiniest fragment. If that shard were to fall into the wrong hands—"

"That missing shard is very likely at the bottom of the Maiden Lake," Lance interrupted. "And if you think for one moment I'm going to wade back into that infernally cold murky water, you should be haunting Bedlam. You're obviously mad as well as dead. If that crystal fragment is so important to you, use your own sorcery to fetch it and leave me alone!"

Prospero's brows arched in haughty surprise. "By all the gods, you are in a surly humor this eve. No doubt it's the chain mail. I never saw the attraction of the stuff myself."

"Maybe you would have if someone had ever tried to hack you in two with a sword."

"A man of wit and intelligence could always find more clever ways of avoiding such an untidy end."

"Aye, such as being roasted alive."

Prospero scowled, but Lance glared right back. In his present mood, he didn't give a damn for Prospero's anger, even if the sorcerer were to reduce him to a pile of cinders. Chafing under the ghost's mockery, Lance struggled to shed his ridiculous disguise, slamming the coat of mail against the stone floor.

With a muttered oath, Prospero made an irritated gesture and levitated the chain mail into the air. He flicked open one of the heavy trunks and folded the armor neatly inside before slamming down the lid.

Clad only in his rough wool tunic, Lance spun around to face Prospero, only too ready to cross swords. But a thoughtful expression had settled into Prospero's eyes, replacing his earlier one of annoyance.

"What's amiss, lad?" he asked quietly.

The unexpected gentleness of the question took Lance somewhat aback.

"Nothing," he muttered, stalking over to the little wooden desk and fidgeting with a quill that had been abandoned there. With but a flick of one finger, the sorcerer floated the pen from Lance's grasp.

"This appears to be the sort of 'nothing' that drives a man to distraction." Prospero studied Lance through narrowed eyes. "And I mistake naught, you bear the unmistakable sign of a St. Leger whose blood is on the rise, seething with that inescapable urge to claim your one true mate."

"Don't be ridiculous," Lance snarled, rubbing the back of his neck. Damn, his skin did feel overwarm, almost feverish.

"I don't see why you torment yourself, lad," Prospero went on as though Lance hadn't spoken. "I believe your lady is already here, ensconced safely in your bed, waiting."

"But not for me," Lance burst out. "She—"

He checked himself, but he felt a strange need to continue, drawn by the hypnotic quality of Prospero's eyes, the wisdom of centuries that seemed lined deep into the sorcerer's bearded countenance, the hint of compassion that was almost fatherly.

It brought to mind thoughts of Lance's own father, so far away and unreachable. But when had Anatole St. Leger ever been anything else, Lance thought, an odd lump rising to his throat.

Even if his father had been home, it would have been unthinkable to seek out his help and advice. How could Lance go to the dread lord of Castle Leger and reveal that he had yet again proved himself to be unworthy as Anatole's older son and heir? Report of his present behavior could only disappoint and grieve the father Lance admired so desperately.

But Prospero . . . If even half the rumors were true, he had been exactly like Lance, wild and reckless, a liar and a rogue. Who better to understand a scoundrel than his own kind?

Lance sank down despondently on top of one of the large chests. Chin propped on his hands, he told Prospero all the grim details of the deception he'd practiced on Rosalind Carlyon.

"And now she's pledged to marry me," Lance said gloomily. "But she doesn't want me. She wants *him*."

He expected Prospero to burst out laughing at the absurd situation, a man setting himself up to be his own rival. If it was happening to someone else, Lance feared that he might have roared.

Although there was a suspicious twinkle in the sorcerer's eyes, Prospero replied solemnly enough, "Well, lad, your problem seems to have a very simple solution."

Lance flung up one hand in weary protest. "Don't advise me to tell her the truth."

"Why ever not?"

"Because she completely adores Sir Lancelot. If you could but see the way her eyes glow whenever he appears. She becomes radiant. If I cease being Sir Lancelot, I'll never see her face light up like that again, and I've rather grown to like it."

It was a difficult admission to make. Like it? Hell! He'd come to depend upon Rosalind's smiles, need them, crave them as much as he did the taste of her sweet lips.

"Ah, so you have fallen completely in love with the young lady," Prospero mused, stroking the tip of his lustrous beard.

"No, it's not that. I only—" Lance began his instinctive bluster only to falter, for once unable to continue with his denial. Not even to himself.

A dozen images of Rosalind flashed through his mind. Her wide-eyed wonder over anything that hinted at legend, her fierce courage as she'd fought to save his sword, her valiant optimism even when confronting the bleakest aspects of her own life.

His Lady of the Lake with her earnest chin, snub nose, and melting blue eyes. A barefoot enchantress, forever clad in a simple white nightgown and a soft cloud of dreams.

Milady . . . I will love you through all eternity.

The voice that echoed through his head was the courtly one of Lancelot du Lac. But the words—Lance was staggered to realize. Those words had come straight from the heart of Lance St. Leger.

"Damn!" Lance breathed, stunned. "I *do* love her. So much. I'd willingly die for her."

Prospero smiled. "Then I suggest you tell her, lad. Not me. And—er—without the chain mail this time."

Lance half stood up, his heart quickening with hope as he considered the possibility, only to come to his senses and sink immediately back down again.

"I can't," he groaned.

"Why the devil not?" Prospero asked with a hint of impatience.

"Because my love for her doesn't change anything," Lance said miserably. "I've given her a legendary knight, a perfect hero. If I take Sir Lancelot away, what am I supposed to offer her in his place? One very imperfect man?"

"You'd be astonished at the number of flaws a woman will tolerate in a man as long as she feels she is loved and cherished."

Lance only shook his head in stubborn disbelief, and Prospero made a sound that was very like an exasperated sigh.

"Ah, you mortals. I will never understand why you seek to turn something as simple as love into such a complicated business."

"If you think it's all that simple, then you've obviously never been in love."

"Very likely I haven't," Prospero agreed affably. "I chose my wife for far more mundane considerations of ambition and greed."

Despite his own turbulent emotions, Lance glanced up at Prospero in awed astonishment. "You married? And without the aide of a Bride Finder?"

"There was no such thing in my day. I was the first St. Leger lord, remember? I had to rely on my own wits." The mighty sorcerer's mouth twisted in an expression of rare self-deprecation. "Clever lad, that I was, I selected an honest lass of plain face and exceedingly large fortune."

"But there is no record of her in any of our family documents. She's not buried in the St. Leger tombs beneath the church."

"That is because my Agnes had the good sense to remarry after my death.

To a simple worthy man who was too sensible to hunger after forbidden knowledge, who gave the poor woman more peace than she ever knew as my bride."

A pensive look stole over Prospero's usually arrogant features, and his gaze seemed to turn inward, sifting through some memory that was clearly stained dark with regret.

His brooding silence lasted so long, Lance felt loath to disturb him, but his curiosity won out.

"Your pardon, my lord. But do you think that is possibly why you ended up being burned at the stake?" Lance asked. "Because of the St. Leger curse for marrying the wrong woman?"

"No, boy. I managed to curse myself without the aide of any legend."

Prospero flexed his shoulders, appearing to give himself a brisk mental shake. "But enough of ancient history. We were discussing your future. If you cannot bring yourself to abandon this masquerade of yours for the sake of love, then do it for a far more practical reason. Your life. This night drifting of yours is dangerous. Far more than you can possibly know."

"Oh, yes, I do." Lance shoved to his feet with a dismissive shrug. "My own sire frequently cautioned me.

"He who possesses great power must use it wisely." Lance imitated Anatole St. Leger's stern voice. "If I ever separate from my body for too long, if I am not rejoined before the sun is fully up, then very likely, I'll die."

"Die? You'll wish that you had, boy!"

The unexpected fierceness in Prospero's voice startled Lance. He stared at his ancestor in surprise as Prospero went on grimly, "The fate you'll endure is one far beyond your worst imaginings. Caught forever somewhere between heaven and hell, watching all that you knew fade and disappear before the relentless march of time. While you continue relentlessly on, unable to live out the rest of your life, unable to die either, an endless eternity of nothing but drifting."

For a moment Lance was deeply shaken by Prospero's words; then he gave an uneasy laugh, certain the wily sorcerer was only seeking to frighten him into abandoning his masquerade as Lancelot du Lac.

"How could you possibly know what would happen to me?" Lance scoffed. "There's no St. Leger recorded that ever possessed a power remotely like mine. Who do you know that suffered such a dire—"

Lance froze, the answer writ clearly for him in the depths of Prospero's despairing eyes, the eyes of a man already damned.

"My God!" Lance murmured. "It was you. You were once a night drifter the same as me."

Prospero said nothing, swirling his cloak more tightly around him as though seeking to shroud himself back in the aura of mystery that had ever enveloped his life.

"Just remember what I told you, boy."

And before Lance could even blink, the sorcerer was gone. A cold chill worked through him as he remembered how close he'd already skirted to Prospero's shadowlands a time or two.

Caught forever, somewhere between heaven and hell . . .

Lance shuddered. A daunting prospect, and yet even the threat of such a dark fate paled before the other discovery he had made tonight. Now that he had finally realized the nature of his feelings for Rosalind, nothing else seemed to matter.

The power of his love for her filled him with awe, the kind of wonder he had not experienced since his days as a dream-ridden young man. If the only way he could continue to hold a place in Rosalind's heart was as a phantom hero, a night drifter, then so be it. His lady was worth any risk.

Gathering up the lantern, Lance made his way carefully toward the circular stone stair, turning his back upon the tower room.

And on Prospero's warning as well.

CHAPTER FOURTEEN

A soft summer rain pattered against the tracery of St. Gothian's arched windows, the misty gray sky casting a pall over the church's serene interior, even the smiling cherubs carved into the baptismal font looking somewhat subdued.

The village church was a small one, the nave barely able to accommodate more than a hundred souls, but the pews seemed dismally empty this morning with only a handful of the Castle Leger retainers, family, and friends gathered to witness the wedding of Lance St. Leger to Lady Rosalind Carlyon.

Crisp and starched in his intricately tied cravat and best blue frock coat, Lance stood with his trembling bride before the altar as the Reverend Josiah Gramble intoned the marriage service in that sonorous voice that had been known to put more than one parishioner to sleep. Although it was hardly the custom, Lance kept his arm firmly banded around his lady's waist.

To support the poor child who was still recovering from a most grievous wound, many of the onlookers thought. Only Lance was fully aware of the fear that governed his action, the apprehension that if he released her, Rosalind might change her mind and flee back down the aisle.

Ever since the morning Rosalind had crept belowstairs and informed Lance in a barely audible voice that she had reconsidered his marriage proposal, he'd wasted little time in rushing her to the altar.

Scrambling to procure a special license, Lance had put the vicar on alert, not even waiting for the dressmaker to stitch up Rosalind's new garments.

Her wedding clothes consisted of items he'd plundered from his sisters' wardrobes: Leonie's sprigged muslin gown, Phoebe's straw bonnet, Mariah's delicate lace shawl.

Not the elegant sort of apparel Lance would have chosen to shower upon his bride, but he had to admit the simplicity of it became Rosalind's slender figure, her winsome face. She had been transformed from a sad young widow . . . into a sad young bride.

Clutching a spray of wild heather in her gloved hands, she appeared pale and frightened, wearing what Lance had come to think of as her daytime look. She was so different from the vibrant, smiling woman who greeted Sir Lancelot at night that Lance felt an uncomfortable stirring of conscience. There was still time to put a halt to this, stop the wedding and tell her the truth.

He didn't know what unkind fate had designated Rosalind to be his chosen bride. He should release her, give her half his fortune and simply let her go.

But even as the thought occurred to him, Lance's fingers tightened about her waist. For the first time during the ceremony, Rosalind lifted her gaze from the stone floor and peeked up at him. One look at her innocent face and Lance's good intentions crumbled to dust. Everything he'd been searching for his entire restless life shimmered there in her lake-blue eyes. Lost honor, lost hopes, lost dreams.

When the time came to make his vows, Lance did so in a voice that wavered and cracked with emotion. One final blessing and the Reverend Gramble closed up his prayer book with a complacent smile.

It was done for good or ill. Lance and Rosalind were now man and wife. She trembled, but she stood quite still as Lance ducked beneath the brim of her bonnet to bestow a chaste kiss upon her soft mouth.

He'd meant it to be no more than a reverent peck, but Rosalind's lips clung to his with an unexpected warmth and sweetness that startled him, caused his heart to thud with an unreasonable hope.

But when he drew back, her eyes were closed. He saw that dream-ridden expression on her face and knew what she had been doing. Pretending that he was Sir Lancelot du Lac.

And why not? Lance thought bitterly. It was what his perfidious rival, himself, had advised her to do when he'd drifted into Rosalind's bedchamber only last night.

Her eyes fluttered open, and when her gaze focused on Lance again, it was painfully obvious that all such pretty imaginings had come to an end. Before

Lance could clasp her hand and try to offer some words of reassurance, they were both set upon by Effie Fitzleger bounding out from her pew.

"Oh, I declare!" Effie cooed, still dabbing at her moist eyes with a lace-trimmed handkerchief. She had sniffed her way through most of the ceremony, though not, Lance suspected, out of any sentimental reasons, but more because of her chagrin at another wedding that was not her own.

She enveloped first Lance, then Rosalind in a moist hug, pouring out breathless congratulations. For all of Effie's reluctance over her role as Bride Finder, she took as great a pride in the matches she made as her grandfather had done before her. Val's quieter felicitations were almost lost in Effie's noisy exuberance.

"I trust you will both be very happy," he said, clasping Lance's hand.

"Thank you, Val. Now that I am safely leg-shackled, perhaps you can stop worrying about me so much."

"I would hardly presume to do that anymore," Val replied, withdrawing his hand as quickly as it had been offered. His light tone was as forced as Lance's smile.

A tension had lingered between them ever since the afternoon they had quarreled over Rafe Mortmain. Too much said that day and even more left unsaid. Lance had been far too stiff-necked to apologize, and for once, amazingly, his brother had failed to do so.

He had thought that Val would have made some effort to mend their quarrel, as he always did. Especially today of all days, when Lance would have welcomed Val's familiar warmth and support.

"Val, I—" Lance began awkwardly, only to be drowned out by one of Josiah Gramble's booming laughs.

Effie was flirting outrageously with the portly vicar, Rosalind caught like a quiet shadow in between them.

"Ah, Miss Effie, so when is the next St. Leger wedding to be?" Gramble teased. "I trust I'll be given a little more notice next time, dear lady."

"Never fear, sir. I am still quite fatigued by my last bride-finding effort. You know the delicacy of my constitution." Effie tittered and fluttered her fan before her eyes. "Thank the heavens, I won't be called upon to make another match for a long, long time."

Lance observed Val wince. Lance reminded Effie tartly, "You are forgetting something. What about my brother?"

"Yes, indeed, poor Valentine," she said with an airy shrug. "I see no great urgency there. In fact, there may not be a bride waiting for him."

Lance stiffened at her words, even more so at Val's reaction. He merely hung his head. Had St. Valentine gotten so meek, he was unwilling to speak up, even for his own happiness?

Even Rosalind was driven to protest. Casting a sympathetic glance at Val, she pleaded, "Oh, Miss Fitzleger, surely you must be wrong."

"I'm afraid not. It happens, you know. Not every St. Leger is destined to be married. Valentine is likely meant for other more noble things, a career as a dedicated doctor with no time for a wife." Effie's bonnet feathers fluttered as she bobbed and smiled at Val. "I daresay you'll end up a merry old bachelor like your cousin Marius."

Marius? The unfortunate St. Leger whose chosen bride had died in his arms? Lance nearly choked on his indignation. He started to deliver an angry rebuke, but with her butterfly-like lack of concentration, Effie had already drifted on to another topic, Rosalind's new clothes.

"Now, my dear," she said, patting Rosalind's hand. "Mrs. Bell may be handy with a needle, but the woman has no taste. Before you let her set a stitch for you, you'd best consult me."

Lance fumed, but he realized this was hardly the time or place to take Effie to task. Turning back to his brother, he assured Val in an undertone, "Don't pay any heed to her. You know what Effie is like. I'll have a word with her later."

"There's no need for you to bother."

"All she requires is a little persuasion to take up her bride-finding duties. I'm sure if I promise to buy her some expensive trinket, she'll—"

"Let it be, Lance." Val cut him off with a sharpness that surprised Lance. "Effie is very likely right about me."

"Right?" Lance exclaimed. "The whole reason I'm standing here at the altar myself is because I went to consult the Bride Finder on your behalf. What happened to the sleepless nights you were moaning about, the restless misery of a St. Leger who knows his time has come to mate?"

"It seems to have gone away."

Gone away? Lance gaped at his brother. His own nights of late had been pure hell, tossing and turning, burning and aching with his need to make love to Rosalind. The only peace he found was in his trancelike state when he was masquerading as Sir Lancelot.

And Val's urge for a bride of his own had simply gone away? Lance would liked to have known just how the devil Val had managed that. But before Lance could question him further, Val brushed past him.

A lull in Effie's unending chatter afforded Val the opportunity to inch his way forward to congratulate Rosalind and claim a brotherly kiss.

Lance's troubled gaze continued to rest on his brother, noting a subtle change in Val that alarmed him. The same gentle smile, the same quiet manner, but Val seemed to rely more heavily on the use of his cane, a defeated slump to his shoulders.

As though he'd given up on more than finding a bride. Given up all hope of mending his differences with Lance as well. In his own guilt and bitterness, Lance had oft told himself that was exactly what he wanted, this estrangement from Val. Now that he seemed to have achieved it, he had to fight against a panicky sensation of being cut adrift.

He might have gained a bride, but in this past week, he had a hollow feeling that he had lost both a brother and a friend. Lance had invited Rafe to attend the ceremony. He hadn't really thought he'd come, but a part of him had hoped.

Thrusting these melancholy thoughts aside, Lance forced a smile to his lips as he greeted the remainder of his wedding guests, the retainers who had served Castle Leger for many years, knowing Lance as both man and boy. His faithful headgroom, Walters, the old butler, Will Sparkins, who'd often hoisted Lance up high, giving him a ride upon his lanky shoulders despite the fact Will had one wooden leg owing to a terrible accident in his youth. Will's plump wife Nancy brought up the rear, beaming and calling down fervent blessings upon her young master, whom she still seemed to think of as the little scamp who was forever stealing biscuits from her baking jars.

Even as Lance accepted their earnest congratulations, his eyes were drawn toward the back of the church, to a silent figure who'd escaped his notice before. A tall man seated in the shadowy recesses of the very last pew.

Lance's spirits lifted. Escaping his well-wishers as quickly as he could, he made his way down the aisle, his shoes ringing out against the worn stones carved with names, the monuments to other St. Legers long dead and buried beneath the church floor.

Entirely forgetting where he was, Lance called out eagerly, "Rafe! Damn your eyes. So you made it after all. I thought—"

Lance's enthusiastic greeting faltered and died as the shadowy figure stood up, stepping out of the pew and into the gray light filtering through the lancet windows.

It wasn't Rafe, but a far older man, tall and lean. Dr. Marius St. Leger, his father's cousin. He had to be about the same age as Anatole St. Leger, but Marius had always seemed far older to Lance. Perhaps it was because of his hair that had turned prematurely silver or the hollows carved deep in his gaunt cheeks accenting the intensity of his eyes, eyes of such burning brilliance they seemed to be consuming the man from within.

Lance had never felt quite comfortable in Marius St. Leger's presence, but he did his best to conceal his dismay.

"Marius," he said. "What—what a surprise."

"Not a disagreeable one, I trust. I hope I am not an unwelcome guest?" Marius offered him a wry smile. "I assumed my invitation must have gone missing."

"Uh, actually, I didn't extend any invitations, and I wasn't aware you'd returned to the village. I heard that you'd gone north to help Frederick St. Leger's wife with her confinement. But if I'd known you'd come back, of course I—I . . ."

Lance faltered. He was lying, and Marius would certainly know it. That was the thing about the man that had always rendered Lance so damned uneasy—Marius's unique St. Leger gift to delve deep into another man's heart and discover what less than noble emotions lay hidden there.

Still, he felt compelled to stammer out excuses until Marius took pity upon him with a soft laugh.

"It's all right, lad. It's not me you have to worry about offending. Your parents are the ones who are going to have your hide when they return to discover their oldest son celebrated his wedding in their absence."

"I know," Lance said regretfully. Madeline St. Leger would scold, then laugh and shake her head in that practical way of hers. Disappointed, but forgiving him just as she'd always done when he'd been caught in some scrape.

It was Anatole St. Leger who would never understand. Like everything else about the man, his love story with Madeline Breton was the stuff of legends. No doubt his father had won his mother with but one smile, one flash of his compelling eyes. Just as the Bride Finder tradition proclaimed it should be.

Two hearts brought together in a moment, two souls united for eternity.

The dread lord of Castle Leger would be pained to discover that his son had managed to make a disaster of what should have been a perfectly simple courtship. Pained, but given that it was Lance, hardly surprised.

Lance fetched a deep sigh. "I couldn't help it, Marius. If I hadn't rushed Rosalind to the altar, I might have lost her."

He winced. He'd hardly meant to blurt out such a confession, especially to a man who was, after all, his father's closest friend. He locked his arms over the region of his heart, a gesture he'd seen many other people compelled to make when in Marius's presence. But it was clearly a futile one.

Marius rested his hand on Lance's shoulder, peering down at him with that all too penetrating gaze.

"I don't know what this is all about, but I sense something amiss between you and Rosalind, something that is rendering you mighty guilty. But whatever it is, Lance, trust me. You could have done nothing worse than if you had allowed your lady to slip away from you."

Marius's intense words surprised Lance until he remembered the reason for them, observing the doctor's lean features haunted with memories of his own mistake, the one that had altered the course of his life forever.

Lance shifted uncomfortably, almost wishing that Prospero had told him nothing of Marius's sad history, how his delay in claiming his chosen bride had cost him so dearly, his only chance for love perishing along with his most unfortunate lady.

Lance felt as though he ought to say something, offer some gruff word of sympathy. Yet Marius did not appear to be asking for any. There was a quiet resignation in the older man's eyes.

He gave Lance's shoulder a light squeeze, his hand dropping back to his side. "I am glad to see you wed, both you and your bride safe and sound. I was deeply distressed to hear of your misadventure by the Maiden Lake and shocked as well. That any thief could have been so bold as to lay hands upon the St. Leger sword."

"How did you—" Lance broke off, scowling. "Oh, yes, of course. *Val.*"

"Don't be vexed with your brother. He has been much concerned about you, and he needed to confide his fears to someone." Marius hesitated, then asked, "Have you made any further progress in apprehending the villain?"

"No, but no doubt Val has regaled you with his theories on that score, too."

Marius nodded but said nothing, allowing Lance full opportunity to let the matter drop. But Lance had difficulty doing so. Standing before him was the one man who could possibly lay Val's doubts about Rafe Mortmain to rest.

He hated to ask Marius, but he couldn't seem to stop himself.

"And—and what is your opinion of Rafe Mortmain? I don't suppose that you ever . . . ever—"

"Tried to look into his heart?" Marius sighed. "Mine is not a talent I care to use if I can avoid it. Go prying into a man's secrets and you frequently discover things about him you'd as soon not know. But . . . yes. At Val's request, I did attempt to employ my power on Rafe."

"And?"

"Rafe is not an easy man to read, but he reminds me strangely of a dog Caleb St. Leger used to own."

"A dog?" Lance echoed incredulously.

"Aye. Do you remember that beast Caleb used to call Cannis? Part tame, part wolf, the poor creature never seemed able to make up its mind what it was supposed to be. Until the day he turned on Caleb and nearly took off his hand." Marius shook his head sadly. "I still recall how that great hulking cousin of yours wept like a babe when he was obliged to put that animal down."

Lance had been quite young at the time, but he remembered the disturbing incident himself all too well. He frowned. "I don't quite see what that dog has to do with Rafe."

"Only that Rafe is the same, torn between being part wolf, part tame." Marius went on somberly. "You should have a care, Lance, about being too close to the man the day he finally makes up his mind."

The doctor's words rendered him more uneasy than he cared to admit. At times, he had himself sensed that tug in Rafe, a wrestling with some inner darkness. But unlike Val and the rest of the St. Legers, Lance was not convinced that the wolf in Rafe would finally triumph.

Thanking Marius somewhat stiffly for his advice, he said, "Now I best go see to my bride. Although she is well recovered from her wound, she still tires easily. If you would care to join us back at Castle Leger, we are serving a rather modest wedding breakfast."

Sketching Marius a curt bow, Lance turned and walked away, leaving the doctor staring after him with a worried frown. Marius settled back on the pew to wait. After Lance had departed, flinging his own cloak about Rosalind to protect her from the rain, Marius soon found himself alone at the back of the church.

Only one of the other wedding guests had lingered behind. Val limped toward him, the tip of his cane clacking out an echo in the now empty church.

Val peered down at Marius and without preamble demanded, "Well? Were you able to speak to Lance about Rafe?"

"I did."

"And did he take heed of your warning?"

Marius gave him a sad smile. "No. Did you really expect him to?"

"I realize Lance sets no value at all upon my opinions. But I truly thought if you were to intervene . . ." Val trailed off, his shoulders sagging at what he recognized had been a forlorn hope. Marius had always been his teacher, his friend, like a second father to him. Save for Anatole St. Leger, there was no one whose advice he valued more. But Val supposed he'd been quite foolish to imagine his hard-headed brother might feel the same.

Val flexed his hands restlessly on the top of the cane. "Then there is only one thing left to do. I will simply have to find some proof against the bastard myself."

He saw Marius tense. "I trust you will be very careful, Valentine. Such a course could be exceedingly dangerous."

"I'm not afraid of Rafe Mortmain," Val said fiercely. "But no doubt like everyone else, you think me capable of wielding nothing more forceful than a pen or this infernal walking stick."

"You know better than that, my young friend," Marius admonished him gently. "I am fully aware of your capabilities. Perhaps the danger I apprehend lies more between you and your brother. It has given me great sadness to see how estranged the pair of you are. Lance regards Rafe Mortmain as a friend. If you were the one to jeopardize that friendship, I'm not certain Lance would be able to forgive you for it."

"I'm already well past Lance's forgiveness," Val said bitterly. "I don't see how I could possibly make matters any worse."

Marius cast him a grave look. "I pray that you are right."

By the time Rosalind reached the solitude of her bedchamber, the rain was falling in a heavy downpour. She removed her damp bonnet and shawl, draping them carefully upon the dressing table to dry. They were garments she had borrowed from sisters she had never seen, but Rosalind felt as guilty as though she'd stolen them.

Stripping off her gloves, she stared down in dismay at the expensive gold ring that now encircled her finger where Arthur's more modest one had once been. She had passed through her entire wedding like a woman walking through some vague and disturbing dream. But now the reality of it struck her more forcibly than the deluge battering against her windows.

Sweet angels in heaven! What had she done? She had actually gone through with it, married Lance St. Leger.

It had all seemed so simple, so reasonable that velvet night Lancelot du Lac had whispered his words of passion and reassurance in her ear, spinning out for her the romance of courtly love, a bold knight to adore and serve her, a husband for propriety and convenience.

But it was different in the somber gray light of day, when one stood before God and the vicar and solemnly pledged to honor, cherish, and obey that self-same husband, keeping herself only to him for the remainder of her days.

Rosalind shivered, rubbing her bare arms, exposed beneath the muslin gown's short puffed sleeves. It was not as though she'd actually deceived Lance. When she had accepted his proposal, she had informed him again that her love would always belong to someone else, another man that she could never hope to marry.

Lance hadn't even cared enough to ask the name of his rival, for which Rosalind had been extremely grateful. She could have just heard herself trying to explain to someone as cynical as Lance that not only had she fallen in love with a ghost, but it was his own ancestor, the legendary Lancelot du Lac.

Fortunately Lance's only concern had been getting the wedding over and done with as soon as possible, no doubt so that he could forget all about her and return to his own rakehell pursuits. And yet . . .

Rosalind twisted her wedding ring with a troubled frown. Lance had been so gentle and patient when he'd escorted her to the church that morning, so understanding of her nervousness. He had reminded her again that it was a marriage in name only. He would never even attempt to touch her if she didn't wish it.

She had never expected such chivalry from him, any more than she had expected him to take his own vows in that voice that had trembled and broken. Almost as if . . . as if he really meant them.

Ridiculous, she told herself. Lance didn't love her any more than she did him. And it wasn't as though she was planning to ever dishonor her marriage vows by giving her body to another man, only her heart. But realizing that did little to quiet her conscience.

She could hardly bring herself to face her own image in the mirror. The unhappy young woman with the slightly bedraggled ringlets framing her pale face seemed like a stranger.

Rosalind bent closer to the looking glass, seeking some trace of her former serenity, that sweet innocence she had always deplored. Was it only her imagination, or had her mouth become a trifle hardened, a certain slyness creeping into her eyes? Was her blush far more shameless?

Rosalind continued her anxious examination until she was interrupted by a knock on the bedchamber door.

"Come in," she called out distractedly, not even troubling to think who it might be. Her heart jumped when the door creaked open and her new husband stood poised on the threshold.

"L-lance!" Rosalind jerked back from the mirror as guiltily as though she'd been caught rouging her cheeks for a tryst with some lover.

He'd been smiling when he'd started to enter, but he froze. "Are you all right?" he asked with a quick frown. "You didn't end up taking a chill from our mad dash through the rain, did you?"

"Oh, n-no. I'm fine," Rosalind stammered. Of the two of them, she feared it was Lance who had received the worse of it, protecting her with his own cloak when the gentle rain had turned into a torrent.

His curly-brimmed beaver had done little to shield him, his dark hair still damp and disheveled, giving him the appearance of a warrior returning sweat-soaked from the heat of some fierce battle.

His frock coat had likely been ruined, Rosalind thought with a twinge. He'd discarded it, but even clad only in his shirtsleeves, breeches, and embroidered waistcoat, he still cut an elegant figure. Overwhelmingly handsome, disturbingly virile. His mere physical presence was enough to send a feminine jolt through her.

She inched toward the door, thinking it was probably not wise to linger with him in the bedchamber. Promise or no promise.

"I only needed a moment to freshen up," she said. "But no doubt Nancy will be eager to serve up our wedding breakfast. We should probably—"

"There's no hurry," Lance interrupted, not budging from the doorway. "Val and Marius haven't even returned from the village yet. And I would like a few moments alone with my bride."

"O-oh?" Rosalind's hand fluttered nervously to her throat, her heart tripping over itself with a strange mingling of alarm and anticipation.

"Not for anything like *that*," Lance was quick to disclaim.

"Oh." Rosalind ducked her head, mortified to realize she sounded almost disappointed.

"I did promise you and—and even if I hadn't . . . Well, I would hardly try to—at least, not before breakfast."

Lance was actually stammering, something Rosalind had never heard him do. She glanced up, surprised to discover the arrogant rake appearing more uncertain than she had ever seen him.

He fortified himself with a deep breath. "Actually, I need to see you because of something I forgot to do, something I neglected to give you."

Lance stepped into the room, closing the door while his other hand dropped to the sheath he had buckled about his waist. A familiar gold hilt protruded from the leather scabbard, the mesmerizing crystal sparkling even in the bedchamber's subdued light.

Rosalind felt herself blanch. It was a testimony to the unsettling effect Lance had on her that he could have appeared at her door with the St. Leger sword strapped to his side and she not even notice. Until now.

As he unsheathed the magnificent blade, her heart sank, knowing what was coming, dreading it.

He balanced the heavy blade across his palms and cleared his throat. "It has long been a custom for the heir to Castle Leger to present his bride with this—"

"Oh no, please," Rosalind said, backing away. "I don't want it."

Lance appeared discomfited by her reaction, but he hastened to reassure her, "I know what you must be thinking, Rosalind. That this damned thing already put you in enough danger. But I'll give you a chest, the one I always kept the sword locked away in, and I promise you there is no thief in the world who'd ever dare breach the walls of Castle Leger."

"That's not what I'm afraid of."

"Then what is it, sweetheart?"

Sweetheart? Rosalind flinched. When had Lance taken to calling her that? She hastily retreated another step.

"I can't take the sword because I know what your giving it to me is supposed to mean. Your brother told me."

"Thank you, St. Valentine," Lance muttered. "Always so helpful."

He made another attempt to approach, only to utter a frustrated sound when Rosalind skittered farther out of reach.

"Rosalind, this is only another of my family's blasted absurd customs. It doesn't mean a damn thing."

"Yes, it does! If you give me that sword, it means you surrender your heart and soul to me for all eternity. That would hardly be appropriate in our case. You should—should . . ."

Should do what, Rosalind thought, faltering to silence. Save the sword and someday give it to the woman he would love, his true chosen bride? But that was supposed to be her. And now that he had married Rosalind, Lance could never surrender the sword to anyone else.

Rosalind pressed her hand to her brow, her head spinning with distress, guilt, and confusion.

"Please," was all she could whisper.

Lance hesitated for a long moment, but then he withdrew the sword with a heavy sigh.

"Very well," he said. "I can't say as I blame you. If someone offered me a heart and soul like mine, I wouldn't want them either."

"Oh, no!" Rosalind cried in dismay. "I didn't mean—"

But Lance hushed her with a light touch to her lips. "As usual, my dear, I was only teasing you."

Then why was there something sad, even a little wistful about the way he slid the sword back into its sheath? Rosalind watched him, feeling more wretched than ever, not even knowing what to say.

She was relieved when Lance broke the awkward silence. "I should leave you to finish brushing your hair or whatever you were doing there at the mirror. I trust you have everything you need here to make you comfortable?"

"Y-yes." Rosalind attempted to smile. "You have been very obliging, sir."

Lance winced strangely at her words. "Later, I'll send my man around to clear the rest of my things out of this room."

"Oh no! There is no need. After all, this was your room first. I could easily take another."

"No, I've already found myself a comfortable chamber—up in the old tower. I want you to have this room. It overlooks the garden and besides—" Lance shot her a warm wicked look from beneath the thickness of his lashes. "I like imagining you in my bed."

Rosalind blushed hotly, her gaze skittering from him to the bed and back, scarcely knowing where to look.

He chuckled, reaching for her hand. "My dear, you really are going to have to grow accustomed to my teasing or—" He checked himself with a frown. "My God, Rosalind. You're freezing."

Was she? Rosalind didn't seem to be aware of anything but the heat of Lance's fingers curling around hers.

"Why didn't you summon your maid or one of the servants to light a fire in here?" He ran his hands lightly up her bare arms, and she shivered uncontrollably at the warmth of his touch.

"It's the damned dress," he said scowling. "Not exactly suited for a wedding day in the rain. I should have found you something else."

Rosalind tried to pull away, to assure him that she was all right, but once she had started trembling, she couldn't seem to stop. And it wasn't the dress, or the chill in the room. It was everything. The entire pretense of this mock marriage, the tearing of her heart in two. Desperately in love with one man, and yet undeniably physically attracted to another.

Her throat knotted and her eyes filled with tears. She ducked her head, embarrassed to display such weakness before Lance. But it was too late. He'd already seen. He peered down at her with such concern as only made matters worse.

"Come here," he said huskily, drawing her into his embrace.

Rosalind went reluctantly, stiff and unyielding at first. But it was impossible not to melt into the strength of his shoulder, the comfort of his arms straining her close. Rosalind suddenly realized how cold she was, had been for a very long time—perhaps ever since Arthur had died and left her so all alone.

Of course she'd had her memories to warm her, and now there was Sir Lancelot. To adore her, to love her, to caress her with the dark fire of his legendary eyes. But sometimes . . . Rosalind deplored her own weakness . . . sometimes a woman desperately needed to be touched and held.

She nestled her face against Lance, the tears she'd been holding back all morning spilling down his waistcoat. He cradled her in his arms, murmuring incoherent words of comfort and endearment in her ear. It almost sounded as though he was apologizing to her for something, but exactly what he begged her pardon for, she was unable to tell.

It hardly mattered. The mere rumble of his voice was soothing, and Rosalind felt the weight of her despair begin to ease. She blinked out the last of her tears and yet was strangely reluctant to quit the security of Lance's arms.

"Your shoulder's wet," she informed him with an apologetic sigh as she struggled to regain command of herself.

"Is it, sweetheart? Then just shift yourself a bit. There's a dry one on the other side."

It wasn't the sort of tender remark Sir Lancelot would have made, but so like Lance, Rosalind was forced to laugh. She drew back with a tremulous chuckle.

His arms still encircling her waist, Lance bent to whisper his lips against her forehead, then beneath each eye, kissing her tears away. Rosalind made no effort to resist. After all, he was merely trying to comfort her.

She was unable to say at what moment comfort turned to something else, each brush of his lips becoming a little more insistent, his arms tightening around her. Rosalind felt her pulse skitter, but Lance was her husband now, she reminded herself. It was his right to kiss her if he wanted to.

She closed her eyes, trying to follow the advice Sir Lancelot had given her. Pretend that this was her gallant knight embracing her. But it was so difficult to imagine anyone but Lance kissing her this way, coaxing her lips apart, his tongue seeking a bold intimate mating that swept all reason before it, like flower petals scattered by a powerful wind.

His mouth claimed hers in one hungry kiss after another. Kisses that tasted of her salt tears, sweet summer rain, and Lance's own masculine heat. Kisses that filled her with a fierce exhilaration, making it nigh impossible to breathe, impossible to think. She had to wrap her arms around his neck and cling to him, or she feared she might have swooned at his feet.

"Rosalind." He whispered her name in a husky rasp of desire. His hands roamed feverishly over her, sending dark shivers up her bare arms, sparking a rush of warmth that spread through her like a wildfire.

Lance held her hard against him, as though he were unable to get her close enough. When the St. Leger sword interfered, he yanked at the buckle of the scabbard, heedlessly tossing his ancestral weapon down to the carpet.

When he reached for her again, Rosalind came readily, molding her body to his with an eagerness she should have found shameful. Fully aware of the desire that hardened his own lean frame, all that was woman in her helplessly responded to it.

Her muslin gown seemed to chafe her, even that thin fabric a frustrating barrier to the fierce longings that Lance aroused in her. When he began to fumble with her laces, she was not demure at all, shifting position so that he could proceed more quickly.

It was Lance who stopped. Turning her back to face him, he rested his brow against hers, his breath coming quick and unsteady. She could feel his entire body shuddering with suppressed need.

"Rosalind, I—I'm sorry," he panted. "I swore I wouldn't touch you. I don't seem to be much good at keeping promises."

"That's all right," Rosalind whispered, her own breast rising and falling. She fidgeted with the button on Lance's waistcoat. "It wasn't a promise I ever expected you to keep."

"You didn't?" Lance drew back, staring down at her.

"N-no." Her cheeks fired as she realized she had undone his topmost button and her wayward fingers were straying toward the next one.

"I am now your wife," she said, assuring herself as much as him. "It's my duty to submit to you."

"Your duty!" The passion roiling in Lance's eyes seemed to freeze. Rosalind was fully prepared to melt back into his embrace, but to her bewilderment and chagrin, Lance's hands fell away from her.

He stepped back looking like a challenged knight who had just been struck across the face with a steel gauntlet.

"Your *duty*," he echoed again, fairly seeming to choke on the word. "My dear Rosalind, I've never in my entire life made love to a woman for that reason. And I'll be damned if I'm going to start with my own wife."

"But—but—" Rosalind faltered, wrapping her arms about herself, feeling cold and bereft again.

Lance didn't even seem to hear her weak attempt at protest. Snatching up his discarded sword, he muttered, "If you ever find that you want me for some other reason, you know where to find me."

He stalked from the bedchamber, slamming the door behind him. Rosalind simply stood there as confused by his behavior as she was ashamed of her own. Her body still ached with frustrated desire when she should have been glad to see him go.

A few moments more and they would have been naked, tumbling about the sheets like a pair of scandalous St. Legers who couldn't even keep their hands off each other long enough to eat breakfast. And she didn't even love the man!

Then why did she have this inexplicable urge to go running after him?

Midnight seemed to take forever in coming. The hall clock had barely struck twelve as Rosalind stumbled her way through the dark and unfamiliar house, seeking the back door that led out into the gardens.

Wrapping a heavy cloak about her shoulders, she stepped out into a night that was still overcast. A wind tumbled in, rough and salty from the sea that battered against the bottom of nearby cliffs, the stiff breeze causing the trees to sway, sending showers of rain-wet rhododendron petals down upon her.

Rosalind plucked a few from her hair and raised up her hood to shield herself. Even this enchanting garden seemed dark, cold, and lonely on a night like this. Alive with too many mysterious rustlings, snappings of twigs, unidentified shadows.

As dark clouds scudded across the face of the moon, Rosalind shivered, wishing she were snug back in her own bedchamber. But it no longer seemed fitting to receive Sir Lancelot in the same room where she should have bedded her husband.

She had left a note upon her dressing table, directing the ghost to come find her in the garden. Huddling deeper beneath her cloak, Rosalind prayed that he would do so and soon.

The rest of her wedding day had been a nightmare, the celebratory breakfast stiff and strained. Rosalind had dreaded even facing Lance again, but he had treated her with such studious politeness, she had to fight against an unreasonable urge to smash the creamer over his head.

She supposed she had wounded his pride when she had offered to submit to him out of duty. No doubt the arrogant rake thought that every woman ought to just melt in his arms. But she *had* been melting. He could have seduced her in a heartbeat, and any man as experienced as Lance must have realized that. So why had he stopped? What more did he want from her?

Surely not love. He had made clear his lack of interest in that from the start, just as she had made it plain her heart was already taken.

It was Sir Lancelot that she loved. She was certain of that if nothing else. And any doubts she had would vanish as soon as she gazed upon his beloved face again.

She took to pacing along the garden's graveled pathways as much to keep warm as to quiet her agitation. As the wind tugged at her cloak, each minute began to seem an hour. But just when she began to despair, the clouds shifted away from the moon and she saw him. Her phantom lover, tall and stalwart in his chain mail and dark tunic, waiting for her at the end of the path.

Rosalind flew toward him with a glad cry, her hands outstretched. But her joy-filled greeting was not returned. Lancelot stood with his arms locked across his massive chest, no welcome in his eyes, only a thunderous disapproval. Daunted by his scowling expression, Rosalind came to an abrupt halt.

"Milady," he said. "Why ever did you bid me meet you out here on such a dismal night?"

"Why, I thought it would be romantic," she faltered.

"Romantic? Stumbling around this garden in the dark? Do you have any idea how dangerous it is? Did you know this path eventually slopes straight down to the edge of the cliff?"

"No, I didn't." Rosalind flinched at his rough tone. She would have thought her kind Sir Lancelot would have found a gentler way of warning her. "But I didn't know where else to meet you. It hardly seems proper to continue receiving you in my bedchamber now that I am married."

"Such scruples no doubt do you credit, milady," Sir Lancelot said tartly. "I hope they'll keep you warm as well when we're standing out here some eve ankle deep in snow."

Rosalind cast him a reproachful look, longing to snap that it needn't worry him. He wouldn't feel it. He was dead. But she swallowed the remark, horrified by how close she was to quarreling with her adored Sir Lancelot. And she simply couldn't bear that, not after the distressing scene with Lance.

Despite the wind whipping at her face, she gazed up at him, pleading, "Please don't be vexed with me. It's already been such a dreadful day."

Lancelot winced, something dark flashing in his eyes, leaving Rosalind to wonder what she could have said that caused him such pain. But the grim planes of his face slowly softened to that expression of tender adoration that never failed to soothe her heart.

"Forgive me, milady. I did not mean to sound surly. It has been a trying day for me as well."

He was indeed looking pulled down, weary with despair. The same way he must have appeared when he first acknowledged his hopeless love for Arthur's queen, Guinevere.

Rosalind's heart ached with remorse as she remembered she had not been the only one to suffer from this wedding day. Once more Lancelot was obliged to stand aside and see the woman he adored bestowed upon another. And Rosalind could not even take his hand to comfort him.

All she could do was stretch her fingertips close to his ghostly ones, feeling not his touch but all his pain and frustration, his regrets and love becoming her own.

When the wind whipped back her hood, sending tendrils of hair tangling across her eyes, Lancelot insisted they move to a location that was at least a little more sheltered. He urged her to a secluded bench behind a stand of trees where even the moonlight barely penetrated.

She could scarce make out Sir Lancelot's features as he settled himself beside her. But perhaps that was just as well. He looked far too much like her husband. And she was finding the resemblance particularly disturbing tonight.

They sat for some time in silence, made mournful by their own melancholy thoughts and the haunting whisper of the distant sea. Sir Lancelot finally said in the voice of a man determined to be cheerful, "So you have now become Madame St. Leger."

"Yes," Rosalind agreed glumly. But she attempted to describe her wedding day to Sir Lancelot as favorably as she could.

". . . and it was a very pretty little church. All things considered, the wedding came off far better than my first one did."

"It did?" Sir Lancelot sounded inordinately pleased to hear that.

"Oh, yes. My first wedding was also conducted in some haste. Arthur was so busy with the upcoming elections to Parliament, he was quite distracted. He told all his relatives to meet us at the wrong church, and he entirely forgot the ring." Although Rosalind chuckled at the memory, she was unable to prevent the wistfulness from creeping into her voice. "I had always hoped that if I ever did remarry that the second time would be different. I'd hoped—"

"Hoped what, milady?" Sir Lancelot urged when she hesitated, feeling embarrassed and foolish.

"Oh, for . . . for sunshine and ribbon favors, bridesmaids and flower petals. All those ridiculous things women dream of on their wedding day. A beautiful dress and a church overflowing with family and friends."

"Why didn't you tell me?" Lancelot burst out. "I—I mean Lance. I'm sure he would have given you whatever you desired."

"I know." Rosalind sighed. Whatever his other faults, Lance was unfailingly generous. "But it wouldn't have mattered. No matter how perfectly the wedding was arranged, it still would never have been real and true. It was bad enough as it was, with Val, Marius, and Effie being so kind. Having to accept all their wishes for a long and happy marriage under such false pretenses. I felt quite wretched with guilt."

"Whatever do you have to feel guilty about, milady?"

Rosalind peered at Sir Lancelot's shadowed features in astonishment, surprised that he, of all men, should ask her such a thing.

"Because they all think of me as Lance's chosen bride, that he and I are two halves of some great love story. And here I am, already being unfaithful to him." Rosalind twisted her hands beneath her cloak. "Now I understand what you meant about being so tormented with sin that it keeps you wandering the earth. I daresay I'll end up the same when I die."

"My dearest funny little Rosalind!" Lancelot's voice vibrated with a tender amusement. "You still know nothing of sin, milady. And you have nothing in the world to feel guilty about. Leave that to your husband. Lance understood the situation well enough when he married you."

Rosalind wished she felt as certain of that. She couldn't seem to stop remembering the way Lance had stalked from the bedchamber, the hurt pride, the frustrated longing in his parting words.

If you ever want me for any other reason, you know where to find me.

Rosalind stood up abruptly, no longer finding the concealing darkness so soothing, for at times, Sir Lancelot's voice even sounded discomfitingly like her husband's.

She took a few steps down the garden path, Sir Lancelot drifting after her. She heard him stumble over his next words as though he was finding them very difficult.

"Milady, I never desired that you should be thus tormented. All I wanted was your happiness. If you ever feel the need to end our liaison, if the day comes that you prefer your husband over me, I would certainly understand and—"

"No, no! That will never happen," Rosalind cried hastily. Almost too hastily, she realized, cringing. She whirled about to face Lancelot, seeking to reassure him.

"It is you I love. Only you. Forever and ever."

Her declaration brought a forced smile to his lips, but even in the moon-shadowed darkness, she could see there was more of pain than pleasure in it.

Rosalind felt guiltier than ever. This was all her fault that her poor Lancelot felt obliged to offer such a heroic sacrifice. All her foolish talk of sin and remorse . . . It was ruining what precious little time they had together.

Summoning up her brightest smile, she urged Sir Lancelot to speak of something other than her unfortunate marriage. They spent the next quarter hour strolling the garden path together while her gallant knight poured out enough words of love and adoration to have enthralled any lady.

But perhaps it was the wildness of the night, the shifting of the clouds, the restless call of the nearby sea. . . . All seemed to settle into her very blood, stirring in her a strange dissatisfaction. A hunger for something beyond mere words.

Even while she huddled close to Lancelot's side, her gaze was drawn to the shadow of the old castle keep looming in the distance, the topmost tower where a single light still glowed from the narrow windows.

Rosalind's pulse quickened. Did that mean that Lance, too, was still awake? Perhaps dejectedly locking the St. Leger sword away in his trunk? Or pacing, as restless as she, plagued by far too many unspoken wishes and unfulfilled desires?

Rosalind trembled in the darkness, trying to focus attention on her beloved Sir Lancelot. But for the first time since the noble phantom had drifted into her life, it was difficult to keep her thoughts from straying far away.

To a distant tower bedchamber. To the oft infuriating, and far too seductive, man that sheltered there. And to the wedding night that might have been.

CHAPTER FIFTEEN

*R*osalind crept along the corridors of Castle Leger, a small wooden box tucked under her arm. The folds of her dove-gray gown rustled about her ankles. Jenny had industriously removed all the black trim, replacing it with a soft icing of lace.

No longer a widow, but not truly a wife either, Rosalind thought glumly. She still felt very much like a tentative guest in this household as she struggled to find her way toward the older section of the castle.

She believed she must be on the right track, for the wooden beams and stonework in this hallway seemed of far more ancient construction than the rest of the house. The narrow windows lit her path with slivers of afternoon sunlight, and she picked her way over the uneven floor, adjusting her grip on the box.

It contained a few odds and ends of Lance's possessions that had been overlooked when his valet had removed Lance's things from her bedchamber. Rosalind had listened intently all morning for any sound of her husband's voice. But when he had failed to put in an appearance, even at the breakfast table, she had packed up his belongings, resolving to take them to him herself.

Perhaps she was seeking him out simply because she was so restless, unable to settle herself to any task, even pouring over her beloved books of Arthurian legends. But she supposed that might be a natural consequence of the uneasy night she had spent.

She had not lingered long in the garden with Sir Lancelot because her gallant knight had insisted she return to the house before she caught her death in the damp night air. Much to her disgust, she had meekly complied.

She was a woman who had once believed she was willing to die for love, but when put to the test, it seemed she would not even risk catching a cold.

Rosalind winced, knowing that was far from the truth. The real reason she had been so eager to leave was because her wayward mind insisted upon drifting off to Lance. He was starting to occupy far too much of her thoughts like a disturbing puzzle that defied solution. At times he seemed to be nothing more than a shallow rake, with not a notion beyond his own pleasure.

Then at other times, she believed she'd seen a hint of something deeper in Lance's dark eyes, something that went beyond the surface of his wickedly charming smile. Glimpses of a man who could be sensitive and compassionate, even caring if he chose. Or was she merely starting to confuse him with her beloved Sir Lancelot, since that was who she so desperately wanted him to be?

The farther Rosalind traveled down the narrow corridor, the more she realized how foolish she was being. She could not even be sure of finding Lance. And if she did, he might be less than delighted to see her, the woman who had both rejected his sword and failed to come to his bed.

Her footsteps faltered, her courage all but failing her when she came to a formidable door barring her way. It was an ancient one, weathered with the passage of centuries, sturdy English oak fitted into the stone archway adorned with some sort of heraldic device.

Rosalind peered upward, a delicious shiver working through her. The painting depicted a fiery dragon rising out of a lamp of knowledge. Vermilion wings outstretched, a mythical beast with golden eyes peered down at Rosalind like the ferocious guardian to some magical realm.

At the base of the lamp was something inscribed in Latin that Rosalind was unable to translate. A warning for her to stay away? Or words beckoning her to some wondrous and unexpected adventure?

She was haunted by a strange feeling that if she didn't pass through the door, she might never know. Rosalind hesitated a moment before she reached for the iron handle and turned.

For such a heavy-looking door, it creaked open rather easily, and she stepped inside. The sun streamed through arched windows, the light diffused into soft rays that gave the ancient keep an aura of being spellbound, a place summoned from the mists of a faraway time.

The walls towered over Rosalind, rough stonework adorned with fading tapestries that seemed woven of a hundred legends and tales of days gone by:

stories of brave knights and their squires, ladies fair and troubadours, bold kings and jesters.

The long oak banquet table seemed to be still awaiting their return, the torchères set into the wall only needing rekindling as page boys scurried to light them.

"Ohhh," Rosalind breathed, so entranced it took her a moment to realize she was not alone. Then she spotted the two figures at the far end of the great hall, her husband and some dark-haired youth, engaged in a bout of sword-play with weapons that appeared to be fashioned of wood.

Stripped down to his breeches and shirt, the sweat-stained linen clinging to his muscular chest, Lance wielded a mock sword, trading blows with a slender boy.

No, not a boy, Rosalind realized in astonishment as Lance drove the youth back toward the center of the room, continuing their combat in front of the massive fireplace. Lance's opponent was a small thin girl of about twelve, scandalously clad in a white shirt and breeches. Her mass of dark gypsy hair was tied back in a queue, her lean face flushed and determined as she swung wildly at Lance with her own wood carved weapon.

"Varlet!" the girl growled. "Your dastardly carcass will soon be lying dead at my feet."

"Only in your wildest dreams, Sir Bedivere." Lance grinned, circling her, getting in several good whacks, which caused his opponent to squeal and skitter backward.

Rosalind hesitated just inside the door, reluctant to interrupt but too fascinated to retreat either. She had seen Lance in different guises. Polished and starched, cravat tied to perfection, not one hair out of place, such a picture of masculine elegance, he was intimidating. Or else disheveled just enough to exude that disturbing aura of sensuality, his eyes hazy with a languid heat.

But never had he appeared less like a dangerous rake than at this moment. Looking so natural and relaxed, one hand poised on the lean plane of his hip while the other was a blur of movement with the sword. Several dark strands of hair fell across his brow, his handsome face flushed with an enthusiasm that was almost boyish.

Too absorbed in the game to notice Rosalind's arrival, he deflected several more of his opponent's thrusts. Then with a movement so subtle, only someone watching closely could have detected it, Lance allowed his guard to waver, and the girl struck home.

He staggered back with a guttural cry, clutching his chest and dropping his sword. While the girl squealed in delight, he went off into paroxysms that would have done a Drury Lane actor proud. Clutching at the edge of the banquet table, his features contorted in mock agony, he sank down flat on his back. With one final burst of spasms, Lance flung his arms wide and went still.

"Oh! You're dead. You're very dead and I'm the best," the girl crowed, waving her sword and doing such a joyous dance around Lance's supine form that Rosalind couldn't restrain a laugh.

She clapped her hand over her mouth to stifle it, but it was too late. Alerted to her presence, the girl stopped in midskip and spun around glaring.

"Aha! Methinks I spy an intruder in the castle, m'lord." The girl took a menacing step in Rosalind's direction, lowering her sword, looking so savage, Rosalind almost forgot it was a toy the child brandished.

Rosalind backed warily toward the door, clutching the trinket box in front of her like a shield.

Lance stirred, his eyes flying wide at the sight of Rosalind. He sat up so abruptly, he banged his head against the side of the table.

Stifling a curse, he struggled to his feet, rubbing his temple. "Uh, no, Sir Bedivere. 'Tis no intruder. 'Tis my fair lady Rosalind."

"Aha! One of Effie's blasted chosen brides!" The girl advanced closer.

"Now, Kate—" Lance hastened to intercept her. To Rosalind's immense relief, he wrenched the sword from the girl's hand.

She continued to glower at Rosalind for a moment, then shrugged. "Oh, well, since she married you instead of Val, she may live for all I care."

"How generous of you," Lance drawled.

"In fact, I feel quite sorry for the poor lady, having a devil like you for a husband."

"Brat!" Lance thwacked the girl's bottom with the flat of the sword, but he gazed down at her with an obvious affection. "Stop being impertinent and go make your curtsy to the lady."

Nudging the girl in Rosalind's direction, he cast Rosalind a smile over the child's head. "Rosalind, this little hoyden is Effie's adopted ward, Kate."

Effie's ward? Rosalind could not conceal her start of surprise. Kindhearted as Effie could be at times, Rosalind could not imagine the flighty woman in the tender role of mama. In all her chatter, Effie had never even so much as mentioned the girl's name.

Instead of curtsying, Kate sketched Rosalind a graceful bow. "How do you do," she said, her gaze sweeping over Rosalind with an unabashed look of assessment.

Returning the child's frank stare, Rosalind smiled and curtsied. "How do you do, Miss Fitzleger."

"Bah! I'm not Miss Fitzleger. I'm only Kate. I don't have a surname because I'm a bastard."

"Kate!" Lance groaned, rolling his eyes at the girl's frankness.

But beneath the child's bluntness and bravado, Rosalind detected a fragile pride, an almost brittle vulnerability.

"I think Kate is a lovely name," Rosalind said gently, extending her hand.

But the girl skittered away from her touch like a wild colt, apparently unaccustomed to kindness from strangers. She sauntered back to Lance. "Perhaps now that you have someone else to fight with you, you'll let me go see Val."

"Kate, I already told you," Lance said in a voice of strained patience. "Val is locked away in the library, busy with his studies."

"I can always climb in through the window." A mischievous glint sprang to the girl's eyes as she darted away from him.

"No, damn it, Kate," Lance said charging after her. "If Val sees that I've let you wear breeches again, he'll—"

But he was too late. Kate had already whisked out the door, tugging it closed behind her. Lance drew up short with a muttered oath, although he looked more amused than irritated.

When he turned back to Rosalind, she stammered out an apology. "I'm sorry. I didn't mean to drive the child away."

"It's quite all right. Kate ought to be at work on her lessons. Val usually helps her, but he's been strangely preoccupied this morning, and Kate was looking so forlorn, I attempted to keep her amused." Lance glanced ruefully down at the toy sword he grasped in his strong hands. "Effie lets the girl run wild, and I fear I'm just as bad. But Kate simply is not the sort of girl to sit quietly with her stitching, you see."

His dark eyes appealed to Rosalind, as though he were an advocate pleading Kate's case before the bar. And Rosalind had an odd feeling this likely wasn't the first time Lance had done so.

It was a rare thing that any gentleman would attempt to understand a wayward girl like Kate, let alone surrender his morning to the entertainment of a neglected child.

It astonished Rosalind even more that Lance would do so, a man who professed to have no interest in children, not even in fathering his own. She had married the man yesterday morning, but she was struck by how very little she really did know about him.

The realization made her feel suddenly shy in his presence. She fidgeted with the box tucked under her arm, wishing that Kate had stayed. She suddenly found herself quite unprepared to be alone with Lance. Despite the

vastness of the great hall, they seemed drawn far too close together, too intimate. One step more and she could have brushed the damp tendrils of dark
hair back from his brow, could have clearly marked the hard delineation of his
muscles beneath that sweat-stained shirt.

She supposed it must be natural to feel some of this awkwardness, a bride
encountering her husband for the first time the morning after their wedding
night. She was far too conscious of the passion that had not been shared, the
consummation that never had been.

Lance did not seem quite at his ease either, but he swept her a magnificent
bow, flourishing his sword. "I am remiss in my manners, milady. You honor
my castle with thy fair presence. Is there some boon I can perform for thee?
But name it, and I will ride to the ends of the earth."

He was teasing her, but a gentle light had softened his laughing eyes, tugging at Rosalind's heart.

Perhaps it was the setting, the surroundings of a great medieval hall that
could well have passed for the ancient court of Camelot. But it was as though
the spirit of Lancelot du Lac had been again made flesh, brought back into the
sun. A modern knight in his linen shirt, skin-tight breeches, and leather
boots.

Rosalind blinked to banish the painful image. She simply had to stop com-
paring the two men. It was unfair to both of them.

When she remained silent, Lance prompted in a more normal tone, "Was
there something you wanted of me, Rosalind?"

Was there? Rosalind struggled to remember, finding herself nearly lost in
the dark seduction of his eyes. There was no trace of the resentment she had
feared she might find. Rather he smiled at her in a hopeful way, his entire face
alight as though he'd been gladdened by the mere sight of her.

If you ever want me for any other reason, you know where to find me. . . .

Her heart quickened with an involuntary response, and she was forced to
remind herself of why she had come.

"H-here," she said, producing the box, extending it toward him.

His brows arched upward in inquiry, but he cast the sword aside, accepting
the small case from her.

"What's this? A belated wedding gift?" he teased. "My dear, you shouldn't
have."

"I didn't," Rosalind murmured. "It's merely some of your things that I
found left behind in my bedchamber."

A fleeting disappointment clouded his features, but he flicked open the lid
of the trinket box and sifted through the contents, holding up a few watch
fobs and a stray quill pen that wanted mending.

"It was good of you to make the effort to return all this to me," he said. "But these things could just as easily have been discarded."

"Oh no," Rosalind protested when he started to close up the lid, certain that his inspection had been far too cursory. She stole timidly to his side, delving into the box herself. She brushed a masculine handkerchief aside to unearth the items he must have overlooked: several bronze military decorations attached to loops of crumpled velvet ribbon.

Rosalind pressed them anxiously into Lance's hand. "I am certain you will want to make sure these are kept safe."

But instead of appearing relieved at the recovery of such valuable items, Lance merely pulled a wry face.

"These things? I assure you they were handed out to every officer who managed to survive the battle of Waterloo."

"T-they were?" Rosalind faltered.

"Aye. Did you imagine that I'd won them performing some bold and glorious deeds?"

Rosalind felt a telltale blush steal into her cheeks, for that was exactly what she'd done. When she had first stumbled across the medals, she had spent many delightful moments imagining what courageous actions her husband might have performed to receive such honors.

Lance dropped the medals back into the box and chucked her lightly under the chin. "Don't go trying to make a hero out of me, my girl. You'll only end up disappointed."

Very likely he was right, Rosalind thought sadly. But as he moved to dump the box unceremoniously down on the banquet table, she was beset by an inexplicable urge to argue the matter.

"You are named for a legendary hero," she reminded him, "perhaps the greatest one who ever lived."

"My mother's notion, not mine. If I could have spoken up at my own christening, I would have warned them what a mistake was being made. I'm not even that good with a sword."

"You're not?" Rosalind was hard-pressed to conceal her disappointment. "You appeared to be doing quite well when I first came into the hall."

Lance snorted. "Against a little girl. If I faced an opponent with any real skill, that death scene I played out would have been genuine. Unlike my friend, Rafe. Now he's the very devil with a rapier. The only person I've ever known who could have been his equal is my brother."

"Val?"

Her surprise must have been evident, for Lance grinned. "Oh, I assure you St. Valentine was once quite a bold man with the blade before . . . before—"

Lance fell silent, his smile fading.

Before whatever accident had left Val lame? Rosalind wanted to prompt. But she had been at Castle Leger long enough to know that was a subject never spoken of. Any mention of the injury was enough to make Val's gentle eyes sadden, Lance's darken with some emotion even more painful.

Rosalind wished she could ask Lance about it. It might help her better understand her husband, but Lance was already moving away from her. He retrieved the wooden swords to put them away, and Rosalind trailed after him, intrigued to note that these mock weapons were given such a place of honor, mounted upon the keep wall beneath a collection of far more lethal-looking relics: Medieval broadswords, daggers, even a pike or two.

For mere toys, the wooden ones were magnificent pieces of workmanship, the hilts finely carved in an elegant scrolling design. Peering closer, Rosalind noticed that a name had been scratched along one of the blades in an obviously boyish burst of enthusiasm.

"Sir Lancelot," Rosalind read aloud.

Lance shrugged and explained, "My brother and I were always coming to blows over which sword belonged to whom. So we marked our names on them. That one was Val's." He indicated the toy weapon he had fit into the mountings next to his own.

But the name neatly carved on the blade's surface was different from what Rosalind expected. Not Valentine but . . .

"It says Sir Galahad," she murmured. Then comprehension broke over her. She raised wondering eyes to Lance's face. "You and your brother used to play at being Knights of the Round Table?"

A faint hint of color crept into Lance's cheeks. "Uh . . . I'm sure it must have been Val's notion," he said rather sheepishly. "My father had the wooden swords made for us when he caught us attempting to tug the real ones down from the wall."

"But there are five of them." Rosalind pointed in puzzlement to three more of the intricately fashioned toy blades fastened upon the wall.

"Aye, those belonged to my sisters. St. Leger ladies are not the sort to remain content playing the damsel in distress. Ah, no! Leonie always insisted upon being King Arthur. She's a rather domineering wench, fancying herself in charge of everything. And Phoebe was our gallant Sir Gawaine. Then that last sword there belonged to Mariah, our little mouse. She liked to pretend to be Don Quixote."

"*Don Quixote?*"

"Er, yes. Mouse tended to get her stories a little mixed up."

Rosalind smiled, but she ran her fingers wistfully over the hilt of Lance's toy sword, well able to imagine the delightful revels the St. Leger children must have had. The old hall must have echoed with youthful shouts and laughter, so different from the silence of her own girlhood, wandering the solitary paths of her garden with only imaginary friends for company.

"How I envy you, Lance St. Leger," she murmured, "having a brother and so many sisters. It must have been wonderful being part of such a large family."

"Your family now," he reminded her, leaning idly against the wall, watching her. "You are quite welcome to all of them."

"You are very generous with what you love, sir."

"No, merely careless," he said dryly. But an odd expression filtered through his eyes, something akin to regret. After a brief hesitation, he straightened and asked, "Would you like to see them?"

"Who?"

"The rest of my family."

"Y-you mean they've returned?" Rosalind froze, panic-stricken at the thought of encountering these sisters she had never met. And Lance's parents . . . Her hand fluttered nervously to the neckline of her gown, and Lance chuckled, hastening to reassure her.

"No, I was only referring to their portraits. They are displayed on the far wall over there."

"Oh." Rosalind emitted a deep sigh of relief. "Yes, I'd love to see them."

Lance offered her his arm, and she diffidently linked hers with his, resting her fingertips against his sleeve. He led her to the far wall, whose towering surface was indeed covered with paintings of generations of St. Legers.

Her attention claimed by the portraits, she was completely unaware of the hungry way Lance's gaze rested on her profile.

He was damned if he even knew what he was doing, dragging Rosalind over to see a musty collection of family paintings he himself had always found rather boring. But he was desperate enough to resort to any ploy, any excuse to get her to stay with him, to linger when he could see the sunlight striking off her golden hair, when he could be something more than a mere shadow, when he could at least reach out and touch her hand.

It both awed and dismayed him to realize how much power she already had over him, this slender slip of a woman with her dream-ridden eyes. The power to raise his hopes, to touch his heart, to stir his desires past bearing.

When Rosalind asked him a question, he bent eagerly to hear, taking pleasure in the mere sound of her voice. Unfortunately it was not a query he could answer. She wondered about the identity of a dashing cavalier in one of the paintings, but Lance couldn't recollect the names of over half these people.

There were enough tales and legends behind these portraits so that he could have captured Rosalind's interest easily for the rest of the afternoon. Val certainly could have done so. For the first time in his life, Lance regretted knowing so little of his family's history.

The only ancestor he was truly familiar with was Prospero. Too familiar, Lance thought grimly. Considering his past encounters with the sorcerer, Lance wasn't even willing to risk invoking his name.

Instead he steered Rosalind toward the more contemporary portraits. He felt her fingers tighten on his arm, and he began to realize with what trepidation she regarded all these in-laws that she had never met.

But he wasn't sure the portrait of her father would reassure her. Framed against a dramatic backdrop of sea-lashed cliffs, Anatole St. Leger stared out of the three-quarter length painting with fierce dark eyes, his ebony hair drawn back into a severe queue. The artist had done nothing to mitigate the harshness of his features, including the pale scar that streaked his forehead, capturing well the dread lord's towering stature, his aura of unchallenged authority.

"This is my father," Lance said, his voice rough with that painful mingling of emotions his sire aroused in him—pride waging with despair of ever being able to live up to being the son of such a man.

"What a remarkable countenance," Rosalind murmured in admiration, although she clung a little closer to Lance as she studied the formidable portrait.

"Aye, it's a pity I'm nothing like him."

She shot him an incredulous look. "Lance, you're practically the man's image."

It was Lance's turn to look incredulous, wondering if perhaps his Lady of the Lake required spectacles.

But she continued to insist, "You both have the same hair, the same eyes, the same hawklike nose, although I do have to admit that your face is more— more—"

"Lacking in character?"

"No." She blushed deeply, ducking her head. "I was going to say handsome."

"Thank you, my lady, although I doubt my mother would agree with you."

Rosalind returned to her earnest inspection of his father. "He looks very stern," she said anxiously.

"He can be," Lance admitted, although he'd often observed the way Anatole St. Leger's eyes could soften when he gazed at his wife or lifted one of his daughters onto his knee or tousled Val's hair. Far different from the steely look he trained upon his older son. But Lance reckoned he'd given his father more than enough reason for that grim expression.

Draping his arm across Rosalind's shoulders, he attempted to reassure her, "*You* need never be afraid of my father. No doubt you may have heard some of the folk hereabouts call him the dread lord of Castle Leger, but it is a title more of respect because he takes such fierce care of the people on his lands. He's the perfect master, completely infallible. I've only heard tell of him ever making one mistake in his life, and that was when he predicted our butler Will Sparkins would father a dozen children."

Lance grinned. "Actually Will sired thirteen."

"Your father makes predictions?" Rosalind asked, her eyes widening. "Like—like an oracle?"

Lance winced, wishing he could bite out his own careless tongue. This was a subject better off avoided. But if Rosalind didn't hear about it from him, she very well might from someone else.

"Er—yes, my father has been known to have these inexplicable visions of the future which tend to come true."

Anyone else would have stared at him as though he'd run mad or were only jesting. But a lady who could believe that she'd fallen in love with the spirit of Lancelot du Lac apparently was capable of accepting almost anything.

Rosalind merely gave a solemn nod at Lance's words. "I had heard gossip in the village that many of the St. Legers possess unusual abilities."

She ran her hand lightly over her shoulder that had been injured. "Val has some unique gift for healing, doesn't he?"

"Aye," Lance agreed, although he was uncertain if Val's ability to absorb another's pain was less of a gift than a curse.

"And what about you?" Rosalind asked, gazing innocently up at him.

Lance flinched, mentally cursing himself because he should have anticipated the question. But he made a quick recovery. "Oh, I don't have any talents that are of particular use to anyone," he hedged, and made haste to turn the discussion back to Anatole St. Leger.

"Besides his visions, my father also has this uncanny ability to sense the whereabouts of anyone in the castle. A damned inconvenient thing when one is sneaking about, hoping not to be caught out in some mischief."

"Which I imagine you often did."

"Too often. I recall more than one summons to my father's study to account for myself."

There must have been a certain edge to his voice, for Rosalind asked timidly, "You do not get on well with your father, then?"

"No, but I fear it is more my fault than his, although I never defied him outright except when I wanted to go into the army."

"Your father did not wish you to do so?"

"No." Lance grimaced, thinking that was putting it mildly. He retained all too clear a memory of their thundering quarrels on the subject, the distress it had caused his mother.

"Cornwall is not the entire universe, sir!" Lance had raged, pacing like a caged lion before the desk in his father's study. "There is a huge world out there, and before I'm too blasted old, I would like to see some of it."

"Perhaps if you knew more of this world you speak of, you wouldn't be so eager, boy," his father had growled.

"And what do you know of it? You've never been five miles beyond Castle Leger in your entire life."

His father had shot him a warning glare, and Lance had known he was bordering upon intolerable disrespect, but he was too beside himself in his frustration to care.

"You can't even give me a good reason why I shouldn't be allowed to go. It's not as though you've had one of your visions predicting that I'll come to some disaster."

"No," his father had conceded reluctantly. "Nothing so clear as a vision, only this powerful feeling."

"A feeling," Lance had sneered in scorn.

"I couldn't imagine what the blazes he was talking about," Lance mused. "I remember demanding, 'What the devil do you think I'm going to find out there that is so terrible?' And my father's reply made no sense at all."

"He said, 'It's not what you're going to find that alarms me, lad. It's all that you stand to lose.' "

Lance scarce realized he'd been speaking aloud until Rosalind prodded softly, "So what happened? Did you run away?"

"No, but my father must have realized I was planning to do so, or else my mother interceded. He finally relented and bought me my commission. But the day I rode out of Castle Leger was the unhappiest I'd ever seen him." Lance sighed. "Because as usual, he was right."

"Then . . . you did lose something?"

"Everything," Lance said hoarsely. Honor, dreams, and self-respect. Any chance he'd ever had to be considered worthy of being Anatole St. Leger's son forfeited forever. Snapping himself briskly out of the past, he made haste to change the subject, drawing Rosalind's attention to some of the smaller portraits.

"Of course, my father keeps the one of my mother in his own study. But there are my sisters." Lance indicated a trio of oval framed paintings of smiling young women with bright eyes.

"The red-haired chit with the imperious expression is Leonie. The Lioness, I call her. And next to her is Phoebe, cuddling one of her beloved cats. The last one, the girl with the soft brown curls is Mariah, our little mouse, and I'm certain you recognize Valentine."

Lance pointed out the portrait of his brother, Val as usual posed in the library, looking dreamy-eyed, the inevitable book clutched in his hand.

Rosalind crept closer, scrutinizing all the paintings, especially the ones of his sisters. She admired their beauty and also the skill of the artist.

"My father painted them," Lance informed her.

"Your father!"

"Aye, I know," Lance chuckled. "Astonishing isn't it? He appears far more likely to wield a battle-ax than a brush. But I assure you, he's amazingly talented."

"You don't have to assure me. The portraits speak for themselves," Rosalind murmured. "And where is yours?"

"I don't have one. I'm afraid I was always too restless to stay still, even long enough for my father to make a preliminary sketch."

"But . . . but isn't that you?"

Lance had started to move away, but he came over to see what Rosalind was talking about. She pointed to a lone painting set in a rectangular gilt-trimmed frame, an addition to the wall that Lance had not noticed since his return home.

He stalked closer, his eyes narrowing at the image of the young man posed proudly in all the glory of his scarlet regimentals. *His own image.*

Lance's breath hitched in his throat. It was like looking into a mirror and seeing the years stripped away in a manner that was both painful and poignant. Peering into his own young arrogant face, brash with all the foolish confidence of an eighteen-year-old who believed he could charge out into the world, conquer Napoleon's entire army, and be back home in time for tea. And at no greater cost than a few smudges to his uniform.

Stunned by the discovery of the portrait, Lance could only stare in dumbfounded silence.

"So you never posed for this?" Rosalind asked.

"No."

"Someone painted it from . . . from memory?"

"Aye." And there was no doubt who that someone was, as incredible and unlikely as that possibility seemed.

"My father must have done it," Lance said, frowning in bewilderment. "Although I can't imagine why. Most likely to please my mother, I suppose."

He continued to regard the portrait in amazement until an interruption occurred. The heavy door leading to the keep creaked open, and one of the footmen appeared, obviously looking for Lance. He excused himself to Rosalind as he stalked in that direction to see what the young man wanted.

Rosalind remained where she was, studying her husband's portrait, thinking about both Lance and the man who had painted it. She mulled over everything Lance had said about his relationship with his father, and she had no difficulty believing the two would frequently be at odds with each other. Two such strong-willed, hard-headed men, the clashes would be inevitable.

But no matter what Lance claimed, there was one thing Rosalind could not be brought to believe. A painting such as that had never been accomplished by a man who was disappointed in Lance, but by a father who so cherished his son that he could produce a likeness that remarkable merely from the reaches of his memory.

Anatole St. Leger had captured all of Lance's strength, vitality, and reckless courage. And something more . . . Stroked into the face of that dark-haired soldier was an innocence that was almost heartbreaking. All the earnest nobility of a young knight setting out to slay the dragon and win his lady fair, his eyes shining with a hundred hopes of love, success, and glory and the confidence that every last one of those dreams would be fulfilled.

So what had happened to change all that? Rosalind wondered. To change Lance from the idealistic young soldier to the world-weary man with his cynical eyes and self-mocking smile. From the lighthearted boy who had once romped in this hall playing at knights with his brother and sisters, into the jaded rake who seemed to deliberately distance himself from his entire family.

"Rosalind?" Lance's voice broke in on her troubled thoughts. She tore her gaze away from the portrait to discover he had returned to her side with an apologetic smile.

"I'm afraid I have to go. Mr. Throckmorton, our steward, is waiting for me in the library. A matter of some estate business."

Rosalind nodded her understanding, but she was surprised by the depth of her disappointment. She had been more at ease with Lance during these last few moments than she ever had been before.

No teasing, no mocking, no playing the wickedly seductive rogue, he had been more open and honest with her, offering her perhaps a rare opportunity to know the real Lance St. Leger.

But . . . a matter of business. Rosalind sighed, knowing too well from her late husband what that meant. A pat on the shoulder, a kiss to the cheek, and a "run along and amuse yourself, my dear."

Curtsying to Lance, she turned to go when she was arrested by Lance calling her name.

"Rosalind?"

She came about to face him. Her usually brash husband appeared almost diffident as he asked, "Er . . . unless—I don't suppose you'd care to come with me?"

"On a matter of business?"

"It's nothing very tedious. Only about some cottages on the estate that are being rebuilt for some of our tenants. Perhaps you would care to favor me and Throckmorton with your opinions on the subject."

"My opinions?" she asked, certain he had to be jesting.

But he appeared quite in earnest despite the way he teased, "Yes, yours. You do have them, don't you?"

"I—I'm not certain," she murmured, a little stunned. "No one ever asked me before."

"Well, I'm asking you now."

He certainly was, and with such a warmth in his eyes, her heart missed a beat. She was flattered by his request, but she really ought to return to her room and rest or she'd likely be too tired to meet Sir Lancelot in the garden tonight.

"I—I thank you, but—" she stammered.

"But you have something more important to do than waste the rest of the afternoon with your worthless rogue of a husband," Lance filled in with a wry smile. But he looked so disappointed, Rosalind hastened to reassure him.

"Oh no. There is nothing else I would rather do."

And she was rather stunned herself to realize she was speaking the truth.

It was well past midnight when the ghost of Sir Lancelot du Lac abandoned his vigil in the garden. Forgetting his lady's scruples, he drifted impatiently toward her bedchamber to discover what was keeping her so long.

And found Rosalind fast asleep. Lance's mouth curved in a tender smile at the sight of her head nestled into her pillow, her sweet face looking tired but contented, lost deep in some land of gentle dreamings.

She'd clearly intended to keep their rendezvous. Moonlight spilling through the window revealed her gown, shoes, and cloak all neatly laid out. But after her maid had left her, Rosalind must have been too exhausted to stay awake. Hardly surprising after the busy afternoon they had spent.

Lance hovered over Rosalind for a moment, debating whether to wake her. She'd no doubt be chagrined in the morning to discover she'd slept through her chance to be with her noble hero. He felt a sharp twinge of conscience at the thought of her disappointment.

But at some point today, he was not quite certain when or how, he felt that he'd gained a small advantage over this phantom rival he'd created, and he was damned if he was going to surrender it. Perhaps not tonight, or even to-morrow . . . but soon, he hoped, he could finally lay the ghost of Sir Lancelot to rest.

With a last longing glance at his sleeping lady, Lance smiled and drifted quietly from the room.

Chapter Sixteen

*T*he summer drifted by in a soft warm haze, a succession of golden days that Rosalind never wanted to end. A gentle breeze teased the tendrils of her hair as she stole into the garden as had become her habit each morning.

Armed with a basket and the sturdy pocketknife that Lance had given her, Rosalind flitted between the flowering beds and bushes, taking fresh cuttings to fill the vases in all the drawing rooms, strolling those same paths that she often did at midnight when the garden was a place of moon-spun shadows, rustling with a darker kind of magic.

It was far different in the light of day, rhododendrons, azaleas, and blue-bells all unfurling their petals to the brilliance of the sun. As different as the two men who had become such an integral part of her life these past few weeks. By night, she had her gallant Sir Lancelot with his tender declarations of love, his sympathetic ear, ever ready to listen to her chatter of all her adventures.

And she was having plenty of those . . . by day with her roguish husband, Lance, leading her on countless forays out into the rugged beauty of the Castle Leger lands. Flirting, teasing, sometimes quarreling, more often they laughed together like a pair of unruly children.

The result of their latest expedition darted past her skirts, a small black-and-white hunting spaniel stumbling over his own feet in his earnest pursuit of a butterfly. The puppy had been acquired from the kennels of her husband's second cousin, Caleb St. Leger.

Sir Pellinore, as Rosalind had dubbed him, was Lance's most recent gift to her. Or should she say Sir Lancelot's? Sometimes Rosalind was not quite sure.

It had been her noble knight that she had confided in, during their late-night strolls through the garden, that she had never had a dog or even a kitten of her own, her anxious mama fearing that contact with any sort of livestock might somehow be injurious to her daughter's health.

Then Lance had swept her off the next day to Caleb St. Leger's to inspect his kennel's latest litter. Of course, this had not been the first time something of that strange nature had happened, Rosalind thought with a bemused frown.

There had been the time she had complained to Sir Lancelot that all her shoes were ill-suited to some of the rugged walks Lance led her on. The very next day, Lance had whisked her off to be fitted for a sturdy pair of boots.

And then there was the night she had wistfully mentioned to Sir Lancelot that she had never accomplished her goal of visiting Tintagel. By the end of that same week, she had found herself strolling through the ruins of King Arthur's birthplace on her husband's arm.

A series of peculiar coincidences? Rosalind didn't think so. In fact she could only imagine one explanation, strange as it was. Somehow . . . the ghost of Sir Lancelot had found a way to woo her through her husband.

As she cut off several more rhododendrons to drop into her basket, Rosalind kept a wary eye on the pup. Pellinore had a penchant for trouble. When the little dog showed signs of angering a very large bumblebee, Rosalind dropped her basket and scooped the spaniel up into her arms.

"That is no questing beast you are meddling with there, Sir Pellinore," she scolded. "Unless you want to end up with a swollen nose, I'd advise you to leave that bee alone."

Undaunted by her mock severe tone, Pellinore merely licked her chin, bathing her face with a warm blast of puppy breath. Settling herself onto a stone bench, Rosalind attempted to cuddle her squirming burden in her lap.

She and Lance had scarce been parted since their wedding day, and she was finding his absence this morning rather melancholy, missing him as much as she did Sir Lancelot those rare nights when she had been too ex-hausted to keep their midnight rendezvous. It was rather a heady experience now, having two dashing men in her life, even if one was only a phantom.

"Is it really so wicked and wrong of me to wish that things could go on this way forever?" Rosalind whispered into the little dog's fur. She often feared that it was, but she could not see how she could ever get along without either of her two gentlemen.

What would she do without her Sir Lancelot, who adored her so, sharing with her all her stories and dreams of long-ago Camelot? Or her wicked rake of a husband who seemed to have dragged her out of her ivory tower, sweeping her headlong into a world of more possibilities than she could have ever imagined? Each day with Lance sparkled with some fresh discovery, many of them about herself.

She was a good horsewoman, Rosalind had been stunned to realize. Born to the saddle, Lance proclaimed. Although she had blushed at his praise, she attributed her newfound skill more to the fact that for once in her life she had been mounted upon a horse with more spirit than a fat, sluggish pony. Unlike those few times she'd ridden with Arthur, Lance was not always grabbing at her reins and cautioning her to be careful.

And Lance respected her opinion. That thought more than any other filled Rosalind with a warm glow. He was forever encouraging her to assert her views. Timid at first, she had gained in confidence, making such practical suggestions for the renovations of the tenants' cottages that even Castle Leger's crusty old steward had nodded in approval.

"So you see, Pellinore, I am not just a dream-ridden little fool," Rosalind murmured in an awed tone, holding up the wriggling puppy and peering into his black button eyes. "It turns out that I am a rather clever woman."

"I am sure he quite agrees with you," an amused voice called out.

Rosalind gave a start, embarrassed to be caught sharing confidences with her dog, but she relaxed when she glanced up to meet her brother-in-law's smiling eyes. Rosalind rose to meet Val as he limped down the path. Pellinore nearly leapt from her arms, his plumy tail slapping her sides as he strained eagerly toward the young man.

"I am afraid this rogue barely stays still long enough to be agreeable about anything," Rosalind said. "Have you been introduced to Sir Pellinore yet?"

"I fear we became well acquainted yesterday afternoon." Val indicated the tip of his cane, which now bore the unmistakable sign of teeth marks.

"Oh!" Rosalind flushed guiltily. "I—I am so sorry."

Val merely shook his head with a wry smile, scratching the puppy behind one silken ear, reducing the little dog to a state of panting bliss. "No great matter, I assure you, my dear. There have been many times I've been tempted to gnaw on the infernal thing myself."

Which was as close as Val would ever come to complaining about his injury, Rosalind realized. This dry jest. But the evidence was there, feathering his brown eyes, tiny lines that spoke of a pain borne too often alone.

Rosalind had become familiar enough with her brother-in-law to tell when he'd passed a particularly bad night, enough to know that Val would not want to be pitied or even have his exhaustion be remarked upon.

So she forced a smile to her lips. "In the future, I believe Sir Pellinore had better be confined until he learns to behave himself in polite society."

The spaniel was scrabbling to be free of her grasp, but she didn't dare release him when the little rogue did not have her full attention to keep him out of mischief. Scooting past Val, she carried Pellinore toward the house and summoned one of the footmen to take charge of the dog.

When she returned to the garden, she discovered that Val had righted the basket she had dropped, picking up the flowers that had tumbled out. Stiffly but gallantly, he returned the basket to her.

"It's pleasant to have the house filled with flowers again," he said. "I've missed that while my mother has been gone. It was one of the first things she did every morning."

"I hope she won't think that I have been encroaching or—or trying to take over—"

"Not at all. I know my mother will be delighted with you."

His words warmed and reassured Rosalind, but she couldn't help thinking that Madeline St. Leger would not be so delighted by the state of her younger son. So pale, so worn down. Val must have always been a quiet man, Rosalind thought, but a new silence seemed to have settled in his eyes since that day in the church when Effie had made her infamous pronouncement regarding Val's chosen bride. A silence of sorrow and resignation.

How often when Rosalind had ridden off with Lance, laughing and jesting, had she caught a glimpse of Val at the window watching them go. Even at that distance, she could sense his wistfulness and his despair, making her want to defy the St. Leger legend and play matchmaker herself for the gentle Valentine.

Hoping that her solicitude was not too transparent, Rosalind sank back down on the bench, patting the seat so that Val would feel free to do likewise. He eased himself down beside her, flinching a little as he took his weight off his stiff leg.

His knee must be bothering him worse than usual, and yet Rosalind noted that he was attired for riding in a buff-colored frock coat and buckskin breeches.

"I would enjoy having your company for a while," she said. "But I fear I detain you. You were going somewhere?"

"Uh . . . no." Val stared down at the tip of his cane, poking at a stray weed with it. "Only into the village."

"Oh! I'm pleased to hear that."

"Why? Was there some errand you need me to execute for you?"

"No, I am merely glad to see you getting out of the library, away from your studies for a while." Rosalind bent impulsively toward the flower basket, which she had settled near her feet. "Perhaps I should fashion a small nosegay for you to take with you."

"Whatever for?"

"Oh, one never knows." Rosalind gave an airy shrug. "Perhaps you might stumble upon some lovely young lady who—"

"In Torrecombe?" Val looked almost tenderly amused, but he gave her an admonishing shake of his head. "I don't think that likely, Rosalind. Not according to Effie Fitzleger."

"Effie could be wrong."

"Our Bride Finder has always been infallible, my dear. Didn't Effie know immediately that you belonged to Lance?"

"Y-yes," Rosalind conceded, but she could hardly tell Val that she and Lance were not the great love match the legend proclaimed. Oh, she had grown unexpectedly attached to her husband. Very attached indeed, she thought, a warm flush rising to her cheeks.

But history was full of examples of lovers who had found each other without the aide of a Bride Finder, Rosalind longed to point out. Tristan and Isolde, Antony and Cleopatra, Romeo and Juliet. Unfortunately she could not seem to think of any examples that hadn't ended in terrible tragedy.

It hardly mattered. She could tell from the guarded expression that had settled into Val's eyes, this was not a subject he wished to discuss.

"At least let me send you off with this," she insisted. Plucking up a particularly bright yellow primrose, she threaded the stem through the buttonhole of Val's riding coat.

"There." She smoothed out the fabric. "I always think a flower in the lapel makes a gentleman look very dapper."

Val laughed ruefully. "Thank you, my dear, but I think it would take a great deal more than a flower to accomplish that for me."

"Nonsense. You look perfectly dashing," Rosalind proclaimed. "I've often tried to do the same for Lance, but the odious man persists in keeping whip points tucked through the buttonhole of his riding coat."

"Speaking of my brother, where is the bold Sir Lancelot this morning?"

Rosalind flinched. It always disconcerted her to hear Val refer to his brother that way, the title she reserved for her noble phantom of the night. But she composed herself and replied, "Lance had an engagement with his friend Captain Mortmain."

"Indeed?" Val's shoulders stiffened perceptibly.

"You disapprove?" she asked.

"I don't think that Lance should be neglecting you to spend time with that—with Rafe Mortmain."

"I could hardly expect Lance to sit in my pocket," Rosalind said. "And besides, he has not called upon his friend since our marriage. I think Lance merely wanted to heal the breach before it grew any worse."

"Oh, by all means. Certainly Lance must do his best to make amends to Captain Mortmain." The unexpected bitterness in Val's voice took Rosalind aback. He must have realized it, for he moderated his tone as he asked, "Have you been presented to this dear friend of my brother's?"

"Once, when Lance and I were out riding."

"And what did you think of Rafe Mortmain?"

"Why, he seemed perfectly gentlemanlike and—and—" But beneath Val's hard stare, Rosalind felt obliged to confess, "Actually he made me a little uneasy, though I can't think why. It's something about his eyes. They were like—like—"

"Like a wolf's eyes?" Val filled in.

"No. But very cold and empty. As if he truly wished to be amiable, but he didn't quite know how. There is even something rather sad and forced about his smile. He—he—" Rosalind broke off, smiling apologetically. "I fear I am making no sense at all. Captain Mortmain is a difficult man to comprehend, but Lance seems to hold a very high opinion of him."

"There is something you need to understand about my brother, Rosalind," Val said hesitantly, as though choosing his words with great care. "Lance may give the impression of being a man all too familiar with the ways of the world, the darker side of human nature. But he is not as cynical as he appears."

"I know that," Rosalind said warmly. These past days had given her more than one glimpse of the man behind the rakehell facade. "He pretends to be so callous and uncaring. But Mrs. Bell, the lady who has been stitching up my new gowns, told me the most remarkable tale."

Val's lips twitched with a slight smile. "All about how Alice Bell was the wife of one of the privates in Lance's company? And when her husband died fighting in Spain, Lance made sure she found safe passage home. Not only that, but he set her up in her dressmaking business so she would have a respectable way of making her own living."

"Yes!" Rosalind exclaimed. "And Lance will not even permit her to thank him!"

"There is nothing Lance hates worse than that. I have seen how he tosses aside the letters that come from all the others."

"*Others?* There have been more?"

"An entire ledger full. Sometimes I think my brother charged himself with the care of every widow and orphan in his regiment."

"Lance said that he believes war is far harder on the women who—" Rosalind checked herself with a bewildered frown. No, it had been Sir Lancelot who had said that. Or at least she thought so. Sometimes she ran a grave risk of getting these two men of hers desperately tangled in her mind.

Val looked uncomfortable. "Lance was annoyed enough when he realized I had stumbled upon his secret. I don't think he would appreciate my sharing it with you."

"Don't worry. I shan't tell him," Rosalind was quick to assure Val. "Heaven forbid that anyone should suspect that Lance St. Leger might possess a kind heart. It would quite ruin his wicked reputation."

Val smiled. "You *do* understand my brother rather well, I see."

"Yes, I believe so. After all, he rescued me, too. You might say that I am but one more of his unfortunate widows."

"No." Val laid his hand over hers. "You cannot believe that, Rosalind. You must see how completely he adores you."

Rosalind blinked. It was Sir Lancelot who adored her. Lance merely . . . merely—she was not exactly certain how Lance did feel about her.

"I believe he has grown fond of me," she said cautiously.

"*Fond* of you? That is far too tame a word for my brother. When Lance cares about someone, he doesn't do it by halves. He loves in the same neck-or-nothing way he rides his horse, surrendering his heart completely with absolute faith and trust.

"A noble trait," Val added gravely. "But unfortunately it can make my brother a very easy man to betray."

As easy as slipping out into the garden for a moonlit tryst with another man? Rosalind winced. She withdrew her hand from beneath Val's, feeling suddenly too guilty to meet that good man's honest gaze.

She was relieved when a footman strode into the garden to inform her that Effie had come to pay her a call. Excusing herself to Val, Rosalind gathered up her basket of flowers and hastened inside.

As he watched Rosalind vanish into the house, Val realized he must have said something inadvertently to distress her. He'd only been trying to find some gentle way to warn her about the danger that Lance's friendship with Rafe Mortmain presented.

But he was glad now that he had resisted the temptation to say anything more. Rosalind seemed to have put all memories of that terrible night when she'd been attacked behind her, and perhaps it was better that way.

Telling her his suspicions about Rafe could only frighten her and there was nothing that she would be able to do but worry. Val feared he had been doing enough of that lately for everyone.

Val's one consolation had been Lance's preoccupation with his new bride. His brother spending every waking moment with Rosalind had kept him far away from the Mortmain bastard and out of any more possible danger.

Rosalind's innocently imparted information about Lance resuming the friendship had been a disagreeable jolt to Val. Calling upon Rafe to . . . how had Rosalind put it . . . *to heal the breach before it grew any worse.*

"And what about the one with your own brother, Lance?" Val longed to demand. But he forced himself to set such bitter thoughts aside. This was hardly the moment for indulging in petty jealousy and hurt feelings.

For once in his sedate, boring life, Val thought grimly, the time had come not to think but to act.

Damn his blasted leg, Val cursed under his breath as he guided his horse over the rocky ground. This was poor timing for his infernal knee to flare up. Even such a gentle mount as his old roan mare jarred his old injury until he was forced to grit his teeth. But he couldn't allow a few aches and throbs to keep him from his appointed rendezvous—not in the village, as he'd regrettably been forced to lie to Rosalind, but in a far more isolated spot on the Castle Leger estate.

Clenching his jaw, Val urged his horse up a heather-strewn hillside capped by a towering mound of granite. Like a piece of Stonehenge that had gone astray, this stone monument had stood for centuries, bearing silent testimony to a people long since vanished, druids or perhaps some culture even more ancient and mysterious.

A hole had been worn through the center of the standing stone large enough for a man to crawl through. As boys, he and Lance had often heard it rumored that visiting the stone could work miracles on all manner of illness, but they had paid little heed to such gossip. Too busy tearing about the countryside, playing at knights and dragons, they had thought of the stone as nothing more than some evil wizard's tower to be charged and conquered. Perhaps because in those days, he and Lance had been in the full vigor and innocence of their youth with no need for any sort of cure. Not for shattered knees or broken dreams.

But such thoughts only filled Val with bittersweet regret for that carefree time when he and his brother had been the best of friends, a time that was gone and could never come again. Sweeping all such painful remembrance behind him, he cantered to the summit of the hill.

Slowing his horse, he peered toward the mammoth stone and the person he had come to meet. Jem Sparkins's sturdy farm horse was tethered to a nearby tree, the strapping lad hovering beneath the shadow of the stone.

Jem's position as ostler at the Dragon's Fire Inn had made him the ideal choice for Val to recruit as a fellow conspirator. Young Sparkins had been able to keep a sharp eye on all of Rafe's comings and goings these past weeks, and Jem had reveled in his role as spy upon "that pernicious Mortmain devil."

But Jem's enthusiasm for the venture seemed to have waned. He glanced up at Val's approach, looking less excited than tense. Val didn't even attempt to dismount. When his leg got this bad, there was no guarantee of being able to climb back into the saddle again.

He reined in the placid mare instead. Gazing down at Jem, Val barked out his question in a single anxious word, "Well?"

Jem shuffled his feet and sighed. "Tonight . . . I heard Captain Mortmain tell Mr. Braggs that he means to go out tonight."

Jem's shoulders sagged, but Val scarce noticed. He was filled with a fierce elation. This was what he had been waiting to hear these past few endless weeks. For a customs officer who was supposed to be patrolling for smugglers, Rafe had been staying frustratingly close to his room, affording Val no opportunity to conduct a search. But now, at last . . .

Val leaned forward eagerly in the saddle. "And you are certain you will have no difficulty getting me the spare key?"

"No, I know where old Braggs keeps them, but—" Jem fetched another deep sigh.

"But what, lad?" Val asked with a trace of impatience.

Jem plucked nervously at some of the taller croppings of heather around the stone before blurting out. "I wish you would reconsider this whole thing, sir. It was one thing when we were just keeping watch over that Mortmain, but for you to actually try to sneak into his room . . . It's a terrible risk, Mr. Val."

"Aye, but it is my only hope of finding some proof against that villainous bastard. As long as we make sure Mortmain is gone, I should be safe enough."

"Aye, but Mr. Braggs'll still be about, won't he? And let me tell you, sir, I don't trust him much more than a Mortmain. That old Braggs is something of a rum customer himself. The Dragon's Fire just isn't the respectable place it used to be when Mr. Hanover was landlord there."

Jem twisted his large, ungainly hands. "All I'm trying to say, sir, is perhaps we could use some help with this search. If we told Mr. Lance what we—"

"No!" Val snapped.

"Or even your cousin Caleb," Jem went on, raising his eyes to Val in a desperate appeal. "Please, sir, I still feel bad enough about what happened that night to Lady Rosalind when I left her alone in those woods. And you say that Captain Mortmain is the same one who attacked her ladyship. What if he comes back early and catches you in his room?"

"Then I shall deal with him," Val said. "Or do you think me no more capable of defending myself than a fragile young woman?"

"Oh, er—ah, no, sir." Jem stammered. But it was obvious that was exactly what the boy thought.

And why should Jem believe any different, Val mused with a grim twist of his lips. After all, who was he, but Val St. Leger, the crippled scholar, clearly destined by fate to be a doctor, a healer, and a celibate one at that. Never a soldier, a hero, a lover. Only St. Valentine, not the bold and dashing Sir Lancelot.

A raw bitterness surged through Val, mingled with a sense of frustration, a sharp envy of his own brother. He gripped the reins hard, struggling for mastery over these emotions that had always troubled him . . . emotions that were hardly to be expected of a man named after a saint.

Locking such disturbing feelings back into the darkest corner of his heart, where they belonged, Val focused his attention on young Jem's face. The poor boy was looking so miserable that Val regathered his patience and gentled his voice.

"You are right, boy. What I'm proposing to do is dangerous. Mortmain has already threatened my family more than once. No matter what Lance says about that accident out at the lake when he was a boy, I believe Rafe was responsible for my brother nearly drowning. And now he's attempted to steal the St. Leger sword, shot my brother's bride. I believe it will only be a matter of time before Rafe strikes again. A wolf's nature doesn't change simply because you attempt to befriend him, and I need to find some way to prove that to my brother before it is too late."

Even if Lance hates me for it, Val thought bleakly.

He went on, "But if you are having second thoughts and no longer wish to help me, I perfectly understand."

"No sir!" Jem said fiercely. "I will get you that key. Only you . . . you will be very careful, won't you, Mr. Val?"

"Aye, lad. I promise."

Jem still looked far from happy, but he squared his shoulders and attempted to smile. "I suppose it will be quite an adventure, won't it? Like when I was little and sometimes you let me play with you and Mr. Lance. I was your squire and you was that knight with the funny-sounding name."

"The saintly and perfect Sir Galahad," Val murmured. "But no one ever asked if that was who I wanted to be."

Val saw that his words only confused the boy. He swiftly agreed on a time for their next meeting, and then, wheeling his horse about, he rode off feeling suddenly very tired.

All this watching, waiting, and endless suspicion could wear a man down. But one way or another, the threat of Rafe Mortmain was finally going to be settled, Val thought grimly.

Tonight.

CHAPTER SEVENTEEN

*T*he tide was out, the restless sea pulling back from the rocky shore like an untidy traveler, leaving behind a scattering of pearly shell fragments, seaweed, and driftwood in its wake.

Rosalind picked her way carefully through the debris. Shoes and stockings stripped off, she dipped her bare toes in the foam, the icy water in marked contrast to the heat of the sun beating down upon her.

She shivered at her own daring, knowing she would never have acted in such scandalous fashion before, skirts hitched up past her ankles, her hair tangled about her shoulders like a wild gypsy. That was one of the advantages of keeping company with a man who was a rogue himself. Nothing ever shocked or alarmed Lance. She never had to weigh her words or her actions when she was with him, which gave her a freedom she doubted few other respectable women ever experienced.

She stole a glance to where Lance strolled a few paces away from her, idly tossing pieces of driftwood out into a surf that was sun-dappled and glassy smooth. She couldn't help but admire the play of muscle beneath the stretch of his linen shirt, a casual display of strength Lance wasn't even aware of.

They had spent an agreeable afternoon together, exploring the inlet at the base of the cliffs beneath Castle Leger. Just another pleasant outing like so many that had gone before. Or it should have been.

But the things that Val had said to her that morning kept drifting back into her head, as relentless as the ebb and flow of the waves.

You must see how completely he adores you. . . . When Lance loves someone, he doesn't do it by halves.

Lance adore her? It could not possibly be so. He was incredibly kind to her and attentive, frequently flirting in that wicked way of his. But love her?

Rosalind could never believe that. Because if she ever did, it would change everything. It was one thing to steal off every night to the phantom embrace of a gallant lover when one's marriage remained only a convenience, when one's husband was cynical and indifferent.

But if Lance ever came to truly care for her, he would—what had Val said . . . *surrender his heart with absolute trust . . . making him so easy to betray.*

Pretending to shield her eyes from the sun, Rosalind tried to make a surreptitious study of Lance's face, looking for any sign that what Val had told her might be true. She had done so more than once this afternoon, but this time Lance caught her at it.

"Rosalind!" he laughingly complained. "What is the matter?" He ran his hand self-consciously along his jaw. "You keep staring at me so that I'm beginning to wonder. Do I have crabs crawling out of my ears, or is there merely a bit of shaving soap I missed?"

"Oh, n-no. Nothing like that," Rosalind reassured him with a quick smile. She averted her eyes. "I wasn't staring. I was merely woolgathering."

"Daydreaming about Merlin's cave?" Lance closed the distance between them, brushing back some of the tendrils the salt breeze persisted in tangling across her face. "I am sorry I was unable to find it for you."

Rosalind gave a tiny shrug. They had spent a portion of the afternoon exploring the base of the cliffs for any hint of the legendary cavern where the sorcerer Merlin supposedly had been imprisoned by the evil Morgan le Fey. But Rosalind had not truly expected to find anything. It had been enough somehow that Lance was willing to help her search for something she knew he did not believe in.

Had he done it merely to indulge one of her whims as he so often did with little Kate? Or had he been inspired by some deeper affection? Rosalind hardly dared look into his eyes for fear of the answer.

"I'm almost glad we didn't find the cave," she said. "Perhaps there are some things that ought to remain hidden."

Like whatever tender feelings a certain rake might be concealing behind his roguish smile. Rosalind turned abruptly away, preparing to head back up the beach to where she had abandoned her shoes and stockings. She winced a little when she stepped on a stray shell, and Lance swooped her off her feet, cradling her high in his arms.

It was a playful gesture, with Lance doing much groaning about her weight, threatening to drop her with every step. She was forced to laugh, fling her arms around his neck, and cling hard.

But their play had an undercurrent to it that Rosalind was keenly aware of. The feel of her own softer frame pressed to the unyielding strength of his chest, a heat that pulsed between them that had nothing to do with the blaze of the sun.

Lance lowered her slowly to her feet, sliding her body down the length of his as though he were reluctant to release her. She was trembling a little as she sat down upon a large rock to put her shoes and stockings back on. Lance gathered up a stray garter she had missed, dangling the delicate pink garment before her eyes.

"Need any help?" he murmured wickedly.

"No, thank you, sir," she replied with a severity she had to feign. Lance was only flirting with her, as he did so often. The man was far too much of a rogue to help himself, but he didn't mean anything by it.

She dusted the sand from her feet as best she could, knowing he would have averted his eyes if she insisted. The mystery was why she didn't ask him to, why she sat there shamelessly easing the silk stocking up over her knee, fastening her garter with quivering fingers. Almost as if she were trying to tempt the man.

To distract herself as much as him, Rosalind sought for something to talk about, *anything*.

"You never said how your breakfast with Captain Mortmain went this morning."

"Well enough," Lance murmured, his too intent gaze following the progress of her second stocking being smoothed over her bare calf. "I trust you did not miss me too badly."

"Oh no," Rosalind replied airily. "Val kept me company. We had a pleasant chat, although for some reason, I fear your brother doesn't approve of your friendship with the captain."

"Val is far too caught up with the past. The Mortmains have always had a black reputation for villainy, especially where the St. Legers are concerned."

Rosalind tugged hard to pull her walking boot back on. Observing her struggle, Lance bent down to help her as he continued, "Everyone has always been too ready to condemn Rafe, merely for the infamy of his name. Giving the man a chance is one of the two best things I've ever done in my life."

"What was the other one?"

"Why, marrying you, of course." Lance pressed the heel of her boot into place, smiling up at her. The warmth in his eyes caused her heart to miss a beat.

She attempted to flirt, forcing her voice to remain light. "You are very gallant, sir."

"You weren't always wont to think so," Lance reminded her with a laugh as he braced her foot on his knee, lacing up her boot for her.

"Perhaps I simply didn't know you well enough then," Rosalind said.

"Oh? And what do you know about me now, my lady, which could possibly have changed your mind?"

"Well, for one thing, there is the way you helped all those women who were widowed during the wa—" Rosalind checked herself, horrified at what she'd blurted out, but it was too late.

Lance looked up from her boot, a faint crease between his brows. "Who the deuce told you about that?"

"Oh dear." Rosalind pressed her hand to her mouth. "I promised him I wouldn't say anything to you."

"*Him?* Of course," he muttered. "St. Valentine. Who else?"

"Please don't be vexed with your brother. He didn't mean to let the information slip, and such generosity is hardly something you should be ashamed of."

"It's nothing to be proud of either." Lance finished lacing her boot with a sharp snap. "I was merely paying off a debt I owed to the men who died fighting under my command, men far more gallant than me. I'm no hero, Rosalind. I told you that once before."

So he had, many times. Why did she seem to have so much trouble accepting that? Was it because of his extraordinary physical resemblance to Sir Lancelot? Or something sad she glimpsed in Lance's own face—the haunted look of a man struggling to find some missing part of himself, some long-vanished ideal?

He fell silent, concentrating on helping her with her second boot. Lance hated to talk about his time in the army, and Rosalind usually avoided the subject. But for once, she could not seem to do so.

As he struggled to undo a knot in her boot lacings, she leaned forward earnestly. "Lance, how did you really win all those medals? And don't try to fob me off with some wicked nonsense like you usually do, telling me you were decorated for bedding officers' wives, because I won't believe you."

Lance gave a wry laugh. "No, it was bedding the colonel's wife that nearly got me killed."

It was another of Lance's jests. It had to be. His lips were quirked, but his eyes weren't smiling.

"You seduced your commanding officer's wife?" she asked, unable to conceal her shock.

"Aye. It's not a very pretty story, m'dear." Lance's fingers stilled on the lacing. "But perhaps you have the right to know. It would certainly end any illusions you have about my grand military career."

Rosalind was tempted to tell him that she didn't have the right to know anything. But she kept silent because she badly needed to know what had transformed the idealistic young soldier in that portrait into the man who knelt before her, trying so hard to remain encased in his cynical armor, no longer able to believe in anything, least of all himself.

Lance finished lacing up her boot and helped her to her feet. They strolled back down the rocky beach, side by side beneath the shadow of the towering cliffs.

He began hesitantly, "You've already seen that painting of me in the old hall, a painfully accurate reflection of the arrogant young ass I was."

Rather she had seen the innocence, the almost heartbreaking eagerness, the dark eyes dusted with dreams. But Rosalind didn't attempt to argue with Lance's assessment of himself. She merely nodded.

"The day I left Castle Leger, I charged out into the world with less good sense than Don Quixote. I suppose I'd spent too many hours with Val, playing at being Sir Lancelot. But I had these ridiculous notions in my head that I would perform all these heroic deeds, cover myself with glory.

"Unfortunately the regiment I joined was encamped at Brighton for the summer. Ostensibly for training, but more often for parades, reviews, and other saber-flashing nonsense that left far too much time for idle young men to get into mischief. My opportunity came at a military ball. That was when I first saw her."

Lance paused to fetch a deep sigh. "Adele Monteroy, my commanding officer's wife. She was one of those women who could dazzle every man present simply by entering the room. Witty, graceful, charming."

Rosalind felt a strange hot prickling in her heart, the emotion so foreign to her, she scarce recognized it for what it was. Jealousy. But over a woman she had never even met? How absurd. She sought to quell the disturbing sensation, concentrating on what Lance was saying.

"Over half the regiment was in love with Adele. There was no particular reason she should have even noticed a green young lieutenant like me."

Oh no, not much, Rosalind thought wryly, stealing a glance up at her husband's handsome profile.

"But Adele singled me out for her smiles, and I was quite besotted."

"And she also fell in love with you?"

"I believed so. It was my only excuse for engaging in an illicit affair with a married woman. I tried to content myself to worship her from afar, but my blood ran a little too hot for that, and Adele was . . . most receptive. I convinced myself that I had managed to find my one true love without the aide of the Bride Finder. By some tragic misfortune Adele was already wed, but I didn't doubt that could be taken care of as soon as I explained the situation to her husband."

"You *told* the colonel?" Rosalind exclaimed in horror.

"Aye. It seemed the only fair thing to do. I marched straight into Monteroy's quarters and begged his pardon for loving his wife. I was fully prepared to offer him satisfaction on the dueling field if he required it."

Lance grimaced. "I truly was a stupid young clunch, wasn't I?"

Rosalind shook her head, imagining instead the boy that Lance had been, so fiercely proud, so earnest, charging into that colonel's tent, stumbling over himself to do the right thing. Her heart quailed for him.

"What happened?" she almost dreaded to ask.

"Oh, Monteroy merely laughed in my face and sneered at me to get out. I wasn't the first young fool his wife had lured into her bed. But at least the others had the wit to be more discreet.

"Naturally I took exception to this unflattering way of speaking about my angel. I would likely have milled Monteroy down if his aide had not been present to restrain me. I could have ended up court-martialed and shot for striking a superior officer. Instead I spent time in the stocks until I cooled my hot head."

Lance spoke lightly enough, as though these memories meant little to him, no more than a source of amusement at his own folly. But it was obvious from the way he flinched that the recollection of his youthful humiliation still had the power to sting.

"As soon as I was released, I went straight to Adele," he continued. "I was afraid the colonel might turn his anger against her. But what I found was hardly a damsel needing my protection. More like a fire-breathing dragon. She was absolutely furious. She demanded to know what I was trying to do, ruin her? Didn't I understand how the game was played?

"The *game*," Lance repeated with a mirthless laugh.

"Apparently I didn't understand, but I learned quickly enough when she replaced me in her bed with a cavalry captain, a great swaggering idiot, but one who had enough sense to keep his mouth shut both in and out of bed. And not plague her with a lot of nonsense about eternal love and running away together.

"I was hot-blooded enough that I might have challenged the captain over her, but he wasn't worth the bother. Suddenly nothing seemed worth it anymore."

That cynical light crept into Lance's eyes, the look that Rosalind had always hated. But now that she understood the cause of it, she wrapped her hands gently about his arm instead. "You must have been quite brokenhearted."

"Oh, I daresay I was. To have dishonored myself for a woman like that. It was hardly behavior to be expected of Anatole St. Leger's son. That more than anything tormented me, the thought of how disappointed my father must be—" Lance broke off, attempting to shrug. "Well, one tends to take these things too damned serious at the age of eighteen. I was miserable enough to have blown my own brains out. But it was quite unnecessary because there were plenty of others willing to do that for me. Our regiment was finally ordered into action in Spain, and I realized I had acquired a powerful enemy."

"Napoleon?"

"No, Colonel Monteroy. He really didn't mind that I had slept with his wife, but the fact that I had nearly created a scandal—that apparently was unforgivable. He made sure that I was always ordered into the thick of the fighting, hoping that I would be killed."

"Oh, Lance!" Rosalind shuddered, her fingers tightening convulsively on his arm.

He patted her hand. "It was quite all right with me, my dear. I was far too ready to oblige him, completely reckless, not caring whether I lived or died. But I seemed to lead a charmed life. It was always the poor sods in my company who were obliged to follow me that took the pistol balls. Always someone else paying the price for my sins. Even my own—"

Lance checked himself with a bitter smile. "In any event, now you must understand that it was no great virtue in me to help the wives of those men I widowed. It was the least I could do."

Except that Lance would have felt obliged to help those women under any circumstances. No matter how callous he pretended to be, it was not in his nature to see anyone in distress or want and simply turn aside. It stunned Rosalind to realize that she knew her husband far better than the man seemed to know himself.

Her heart ached as she kept thinking of the young soldier he had once been, his eyes shining with dreams of love and glory, only to meet with disillusionment and betrayal.

She now understood why Anatole St. Leger had been so afraid for his son. What was it he had said to Lance?

*It's not what you're going to find that alarms me, lad. It's all that you stand to
lose.*

"*Then you did lose something?*" Rosalind remembered asking Lance.

And Lance's bleak reply, "*Everything.*"

Which he had, innocence, trust and dreams, all notions of self-respect and
honor. She couldn't help wondering if that was the same thing that had happened to her Sir Lancelot, when he had first gone riding into Camelot, a young
knight eager to win renown by serving a famous king, only to tragically lose
his heart to Guinevere instead.

Was there some sort of curse on the name, that all men who bore it
were doomed to a romance with a married woman that could only bring them
dishonor and pain? She saw the same emotions simmering in Lance's eyes
that so frequently tormented her gallant knight. The guilt, the self-loathing,
the regrets.

Rosalind had never even been able to comfort Sir Lancelot by so much as
the touch of her hand. But Lance ... Her heart aching for him, she could not
resist flinging her arms about his neck in a fierce hug.

Her impulsive act clearly surprised him, but he was not slow to respond,
stealing his arms about her waist.

"What's all this?" he chuckled, until he caught a glimpse of her face. Rosalind blinked very hard, but she could not keep back the stinging of her tears.

"Rosalind," he murmured, capturing one bright drop with the pad of his
thumb before it had a chance to fall. "Good lord, woman, I never meant to distress you with this absurd tale of mine. I thought you far more likely to despise me than weep over me."

Rosalind vigorously shook her head. "If I was going to despise anyone, it
would be that evil Adele woman. How could she—"

But Lance silenced her, resting the tip of one finger lightly against her lips.
"Adele was many things, shallow, thoughtless, selfish, but hardly evil. I was not
her victim, my dear. I made my own choice.

"And when a man chooses passion over honor, he deserves to pay the
consequence."

It was exactly like something Sir Lancelot would have said. But Rosalind
found that less disturbing than Lance seeking to defend Adele Monteroy. Was
it possible that in some small way he still cared for her? The thought pained
her to a degree she would never have expected.

"Was she very beautiful, this Adele?" she asked wistfully.

"With you in my arms, how am I supposed to remember?"

"Lance!" Rosalind protested against his teasing. She didn't want him to flirt with her, not at such a moment. But as she raised her eyes to his, her breath stilled.

He wasn't flirting. Never had she seen the man look so intently serious.

"Adele was lovely, seductive, but it was a common sort of prettiness. She didn't have the kind of face that a man is destined to remember forever, even in his dreams." Lance skimmed his fingers down the curve of her cheek. "A face such as yours."

"One with a snub nose and freckles?" Rosalind asked with a wry smile.

"Especially the freckles." Lance dusted a light kiss across the bridge of her nose. "And the hair of gold." He kissed her crown.

"And those eyes," he murmured, brushing his mouth against her eyelids. "Those impossibly blue eyes forever urging a man to attempt impossible things, to be far more than he ever imagined he could be. You've already caused me to forget so much of the pain of the past. And coaxed me to recall other things instead."

"Like what?" Rosalind asked shyly.

Lance's gaze drifted past her, seeming to encompass the rugged beauty of the land around them, the sweep of sea, sky, and rocky shore, the castle perched high above them on the cliffs.

"I've begun to remember just how much I used to love this place," he said. "What I cannot seem to recall is why I was ever so eager to leave. Not with you here."

"But I have not even been that good a wife to you," Rosalind faltered, her conscience stabbing her with the memory of all those moonlit trysts. "I have never even come to—to your bed." She blushed hotly.

Lance cupped her face in his hands. "That doesn't matter. Oh, I want you, Rosalind. Make no mistake about that. Very badly, but not until you are ready. I could wait for you forever, lady, if need be."

He peered down at her, the look in his eyes warm, caressing, and so familiar, for she had often seen just that same expression on Sir Lancelot's face. Whenever he told her that he loved her.

Trembling, Rosalind drew away from Lance, no longer able to deny the truth. Val was right. Lance did adore her. She stared down at his boots, not able to look at him, not knowing what to say, stunned not so much by Lance's declaration but by the tide of emotion that swelled in her own heart.

The realization that some place, at some time during these past few giddy weeks, she had fallen in love with Lance as well.

*   *   *

The hands of the clock inched relentlessly toward midnight, but Rosalind was still in her nightgown, the dress and the shawl that she had selected for her meeting with Sir Lancelot laid out upon the bed.

The air drifting in through her bedchamber window was growing brisk, and Rosalind paced over to the casement to close it, wondering how all her golden summer days had dissolved into this.

This single dark night in which an agonizing decision lay before her. Leaning against the window frame, she peered up at a sky so relentlessly overcast, even the moon did not dare show its face. There was a tension in the air as though a storm were brewing. Or was the turmoil all in her own heart?

How had she ever gotten herself entangled in such a situation, one that many women would have envied, two bold handsome men in love with her, a circumstance she herself would have once thought romantic?

But it wasn't romantic. It was perfectly dreadful because someone was bound to end up brokenhearted. She wasn't the sort of woman who could return the affections of two different men.

She had always loved her gallant Sir Lancelot, first as the legend and then as the sad, gentle phantom who had drifted into her life. But at some point during this whirlwind of a summer, she had fallen in love with his descendant as well.

Not with Lance St. Leger, the wicked rake who had no doubt charmed so many other women. But with the man who had once been the eager young soldier in that portrait, who took time to engage in mock sword fights with lonely little girls, who rescued penniless widows and pretended it was nothing.

The man who'd bought her a puppy and sturdy boots, and whisked her away to visit Tintagel. Who was able to make her laugh, make her blush, make her skin tingle with the mere brush of his hand. The man who'd encouraged her to speak her mind, to recognize in herself strengths she'd never known existed.

But Sir Lancelot needs you, a voice whispered sadly in her mind. Her lonely knight, his entire world vanished into the mists of time. His love for Rosalind was surely all he had.

But what about Lance? her heart argued in return. Her bold soldier, returned from the wars, his body unscathed, but so many permanent scars left upon his heart. A heart that was just now beginning to mend. And all because of her, Lance had implied.

Lance needed her, too . . . and what was more, she needed him. She was not a phantom herself, but a woman of flesh and blood with very human desires. To be held, kissed, and touched. To be caressed and loved . . . to have a child planted in her womb. And those were things that only Lance could give her.

Rosalind pulled away from the window and trudged over to where she had laid out her gown for her midnight rendezvous. She fingered the soft folds of her India muslin shawl, another of Lance's gifts to her, and her heart ached, feeling as though it were being torn in two.

She dropped the shawl and strode resolutely to her bedside table, where she kept a small portable writing desk. Sinking down on the edge of the bed, she lifted the desk's wooden lid, drawing forth pen, ink, and a sheet of vellum.

Rosalind tried to console herself. Sir Lancelot had never truly been hers. He had always seemed to belong more to Guinevere and long-ago Camelot, to the timeless love story that spanned the ages.

If only she had not gotten to know the man behind the legend, the weary warrior, so gentle and compassionate, daunted by the mistakes of his past. She wondered what he would do without her love. Continue to wander through time, seeking the redemption that had eluded him?

Rosalind could only hope that Sir Lancelot would find it, the peace that he so desperately sought. The legends claimed that someday King Arthur would return, the once and future king. And perhaps Lancelot would be back at his side, his most trusted knight and friend.

Rosalind had to believe that, or she would never get through this letter. Steeling her heart, she dipped her quill into the ink and began to write.

My dearest Lancelot,
*   With that generosity of your noble spirit, you once told me if the time ever came that I preferred to be with my husband . . .*

Somehow she managed to finish the letter without bursting into tears. When she failed to appear in the garden tonight, she knew he would come looking for her. She laid the letter out on her dressing table where he would be certain to find it.

Then donning a wrapper over her nightgown, Rosalind snatched up the candle and stole out of her bedchamber. Before she was tempted to change her mind.

CHAPTER EIGHTEEN

$\mathcal{T}$he night breeze whispered through the narrow tower windows, tickling Lance's bare back as he stripped down to his breeches, preparing to don his disguise. Another midnight, Lance sighed. And another backache from lying abed, stretched out in chain mail. But he was growing resigned to wearing the blasted stuff.

I could wait for you forever, lady, if need be, he had told Rosalind, and Lance was surprised to realize that was true, although it was damned hard at times fighting his very natural masculine urges.

But something strange had happened to him since he'd met Rosalind, a sense of peace stealing into his restless heart the like of which he'd never known before. He'd even been able to talk to her about things he'd found too painful to remember, the way he'd dishonored himself over Adele Monteroy, the waste and destruction that he witnessed on the battlefield. The regret he felt over those days, the guilt was still there but softened somehow, as though he'd finally found the forgiveness he'd so long sought in Rosalind's eyes.

He'd still been unable to speak of the dreadful thing that had happened between him and Val, but perhaps in time he'd even find a way to lay that torment to rest.

Thoughts of his brother caused Lance's gaze to drift toward Prospero's bookcase, and he noted with a wry smile that the empty spaces on the shelves were now filled. The sorcerer had reclaimed the books that Val had borrowed. *Again.*

Much to his frustration, Val had to keep marching back to the tower to retrieve the volumes, never suspecting that he was engaged in a tug-of-war with an irritated ghost.

Prospero had even spirited away the manuscript Val was working on. Last eve, Lance had returned from his night drifting to discover the sorcerer poring through the pages of Val's history of the St. Legers to see "what that infernal whelp has been writing about me."

Strangely, Val didn't seem to have missed the manuscript yet. Lance would have to make certain it was returned to him and finally tell him what was going on. Tell his brother a few other things as well.

Perhaps it was Rosalind's influence on him, with all her notions about heroes and idealistic quests, but Lance was experiencing this strong urge to charge out and set things right with the world. His own, at least.

Only this morning, he thought he'd done much to mend his friendship with Rafe Mortmain. Perhaps the time had come to reach out to his brother as well, heal the scars that had been left on both of them that terrible day on the battlefield.

Tomorrow . . . But now, unfortunately, it was time to resurrect his phantom rival, give Rosalind one more night with her hero. Lifting up the trunk lid, Lance dragged out the heavy chain mail. He was reaching for the black wool tunic as well when a sound carried to his ears. A muffled exclamation, a skittering as though someone had dislodged a chunk of the ancient stone.

Lance spun around, peering toward the arch that led to the circular stair, the regions below shrouded in darkness.

"Prospero?" he said hesitantly. His ghostlike ancestor usually tended to herald his arrival with a far more dramatic flair. Nor was the great sorcerer obliged to come trudging up the tower stairs, which was the direction the sound came from.

Lance heard a determined footfall, and now he could see light flickering up from the darkness below.

"Lance?" a soft voice called.

Good lord! Rosalind.

Lance froze for a moment, the damning evidence of the chain mail clutched in his hands. Then he whirled about to toss it in the chest and missed. The heavy trunk lid slammed down, nearly catching his fingers, and the mail coat slithered to the floor with an appalling chink.

Lance had only enough time to nudge the metal garment beneath the bed before Rosalind appeared. Perhaps it was the lateness of the hour, the mystery that had always surrounded the stroke of midnight at Castle Leger, or the magic that clung to the sorcerer's tower alone.

But as Rosalind emerged from the darkness, she looked more like some fairy creature than a mortal maid. His lady come from those enchanted realms beneath the lake to weave her spell upon him. The candle she carried haloed the pale oval of her face, her hair cascading over her shoulders in ripples of gold, her lithe figure draped beneath gossamer hints of white nightgown and folds of cloudy blue robe.

Lance felt himself stir with immediate response. But it was a yearning of the heart as much as the body.

"Rosalind? What is the matter, my dear?" he asked as soon as he could summon up his voice. "Why aren't you—"

Waiting down in the garden for Sir Lancelot, he nearly blurted out. Lance checked himself just in time.

"Why aren't you in bed?"

She made no reply, drifting farther into the tower with the subdued silence of a sleepwalker. But perhaps he was the one asleep, merely dreaming all this. She paused before the iron candelabrum where he had a full set of candles ablaze.

She extinguished her own, placing the half-melted taper carefully upon Prospero's desk, and Lance noticed the way her hand shook. A slight tremor that betrayed her as being no vision, no fairy born maid, but a woman, warm and real.

Lance's blood quickened as she crept closer, so near, he could almost feel the soft, swift draw of her breath stir the dark hairs matting his chest.

She ducked her head, her voice so muffled, he had to bend down to hear her.

"Lance, you told me if I could ever think of a reason to come to you besides duty that—that . . ."

She faltered, unable to go on, but Lance was already anticipating what she might be trying to say, although he scarce dared believe it.

He noticed that his own hand was less than steady as he crooked his fingers beneath her chin, forcing her to look up. What he saw shimmering in her blue eyes caused his heart to go still.

The same hunger, the reflection of all that he had been feeling all these endless nights of waiting. But he hardly trusted his own perception.

"And have you found another reason, my lady?" he asked hoarsely.

Rosalind nodded. "I want you," she said in a low whisper. She placed the palm of her hand over the region of his heart, which was just as well, Lance thought. For his heart had begun to pound so hard, her gentle touch seemed to be all that was restraining it in place.

Now was the time for him to murmur those tender words of love that came so easily to Sir Lancelot du Lac. But all he could do was close his fingers over hers, holding her hand fast to his chest for fear that if he let her go, she might melt away and disappear back into the darkness.

Sir Lancelot might be able to pour out his heart to Rosalind, but Lance's throat had gone dry. He couldn't speak. All he could do was act.

Bending down, he brushed his mouth over hers in the most tender kiss he'd ever bestowed on any woman, the one that he'd always reserved for Rosalind alone. Her lips clung to his, her hand stirring beneath his, sliding up, around his neck.

Gathering her close, he buried his face in her hair, murmuring her name, embracing her with gentleness and reverence like the miracle that she was.

This was the moment he'd waited for, prayed for, almost despaired of. Rosalind was finally here, in his arms, wanting him as he wanted her.

He was tempted to ask her why, what had happened to bring her seeking him tonight instead of Sir Lancelot. But it was far too dangerous to question a miracle. It might simply vanish.

He strained her close instead, realizing that now if ever was the moment to tell her the truth. Ah, but sweet heaven! For far too long now, Sir Lancelot had stood between him and his lady.

Was it so wrong of him to want to take no risks, to banish all thought of his rival? To seize upon this one night to make certain first that Rosalind was well and truly his?

Lance drew back to peer into her eyes, soft with affection and trust, hazy with desire. All he managed to croak out was, "Rosalind, are you certain this is what you want?"

She answered him by reaching up to kiss him, the first time *she* had ever done so, a timid brush of her lips against his. But to Lance, it was the sweetest kiss he'd ever known.

Then she undid the belt of her wrapper. In a whisper of silk, the garment pooled to the floor and Lance's mouth went dry. Even the pale glow of the candles was enough to render her delicate nightgown all but transparent, her womanly silhouette a tantalizing shadow beneath the gossamer fabric.

Swallowing hard, he lifted her into his arms and placed her carefully in the center of Prospero's massive bed. Legs tucked beneath her, Rosalind sat up, gazing about her in awe and fascination at the mysterious and intricate carvings on the newel posts.

"This bed was fashioned by my ancestor," Lance murmured as he sank down beside Rosalind. "The wicked sorcerer Prospero. It is said that all those strange symbols represent a spell he wove so that any lady he ever carried to this bed became lost to his enchantment, driven wild with desire."

Rosalind shivered. "The people in the village believe that his ghost still roams this tower some dark nights."

"Perhaps he does." Lance ran his fingers through the length of Rosalind's hair, experiencing a pure sensual delight in the silken texture. "But you need not worry that he would ever disturb us, sweetheart. He may be a scoundrel, but he has his own code."

"Like you?" Rosalind smiled.

"Aye . . . like me." Lance sealed her lips with his kiss, easing her down onto the bed. Her golden hair fanning out, she nestled her head against the pillow with a soft sigh, even that innocent gesture fraught with a powerful seduction.

When her hand slid up his bare arm, his entire frame shuddered with desires too long repressed, and he had to fight hard to contain his fierce urges. He'd always prided himself upon his self-control as a lover, his ability to keep his own passion in check until he'd thoroughly satisfied his partner.

That was perhaps the only real thing he'd ever had to offer Rosalind, his skill in bed. He knew he would have to proceed slowly with his Lady of the Lake and so he did. Breathing soft, careful kisses along her temple, the curve of her cheek.

Rosalind snuggled trustingly closer, but she peered up at him with a troubled frown. "Lance . . . are you going to be a gentleman?"

"Of course, sweetheart," he reassured her with another soft kiss.

"Don't be."

Her blunt words caused Lance's eyes to fly wide.

A rosy blush stole into Rosalind's cheeks, but she met his gaze unflinchingly as she said, "I want you to be completely wicked, just like your ancestor Prospero. Weave your dark spell over me."

Burying her fingers in his hair, she drew his mouth down to hers for a more insistent kiss. It took little coaxing from her lips to rouse the heat in him. With a low groan, he kissed her back with increasing fierceness. Her hands roved over his back, timidly at first; then her caresses grew more confident, bolder, and Lance's mind reeled beneath the realization.

His innocent little widow, his dreamy-eyed Lady of the Lake was seducing him! Caught up in the fire of their kiss, all notions of self-control and practiced lovemaking seemed to crumple away like a fragile ledge beneath his feet, hurling him into a maelstrom of passion.

He fumbled with the lacings of Rosalind's nightgown, feeling as eager as a clumsy young boy again. As though this were his first time with a woman, as though she were his first love.

Which was exactly what she was, Lance thought. His first *true* love and his last. Now and always. He captured her lips, their tongues mating in a kiss that tasted of heat, desire, and forever.

He'd always suspected that hidden beneath the prim trappings of Rosalind's widowhood lurked a passionate woman. He'd often teased her about it, but even he had never imagined the depths of fire she was capable of.

She met his eagerness kiss for kiss, caress for feverish caress, never shrinking from his boldness until he eased her nightgown off her shoulders. Only then did she flinch, seeking instinctively to cover the scar that so embarrassed her.

But Lance tugged her hand away, pressing his lips to the spot in a kiss that was equal parts fire and tenderness. Rosalind quivered beneath the pressure of his mouth.

"Is—is that for medicinal purposes only?" she attempted to jest, but her breath was coming far too quickly.

"No," Lance replied with a wicked smile. Allowing his mouth to trail lower, he peeled away the nightgown to her waist. Baring the soft round globes of her breasts, he fastened his lips hungrily to one rosy crest.

Arching beneath him, she gave a soft gasp, digging her fingers into Lance's back, surrendering herself completely to the sensations he was arousing in her. Before she scarce realized it had happened, Lance stripped her nightgown away, then his breeches.

They were naked in each other's arms, flesh pressed to flesh, heart to heart. Rosalind responded eagerly to his embrace, hardly recognizing herself in this woman who kissed so fiercely, loved so boldly.

No longer a dreamy-eyed girl or a proper widow, she seemed to have become a complete wanton, transformed into a seductress beneath Lance's awakening touch. He caressed and kissed her in intimate ways that should have shocked her but only caused desire to coil ever tighter, so sweet, so hot, it became an unmerciful ache.

She ran her hands feverishly over his smooth, hard-muscled frame. Sir Lancelot and the garden suddenly seemed so far away, only a distant dream.

Only this was real, these kisses, these caresses, this passion she shared with Lance, both hot and tender. She was like a woman who had been abruptly awakened from a daydream, no longer looking wistfully out of her window as the world passed by.

She was no longer reading about legends of passionate love but finding one of her own. A legend of a lonely widow lured away from her books, out of her garden, and into the heart and arms of a battered soldier, a rogue, a rake, a vulnerable man. Who needed her, wanted her as she did him. With a yearning that pierced her flesh and her heart as well.

When Lance finally sought to join with her, she opened to him, trembling and eager. They moved and breathed as one. Hearts pounding in unison, they swept each other to a shattering fulfillment. Only to have the desire, the hunger for each other flare anew before flesh had a chance to cool or pulses could stop their mad race.

The candles burned low and guttered out, and still they found each other again in the darkness. Again and again. Time no longer seemed to have any meaning. Rosalind was not certain how many hours or lifetimes had gone by when they at last collapsed, spent in each other's arms. Lance continued to hold her so close as though he never meant to let her go.

Rosalind snuggled her face into the damp heat of his shoulder, both awed and amazed by all that she had experienced in Lance's arms, saddened by only one thought. It could not have been the same for him. He'd known so many other women, so many other lovers before her.

Though she half dreaded the answer, she couldn't help whispering, "Lance, was I able to please you? I—I mean did I do all right?"

"All right?" Lance groaned. "Lady, if you had been any more all right, I fear I would be dead."

His chest quivered, and she feared he was laughing at her. She struggled up onto one elbow to peer earnestly down at him, but his face was only a blur in the darkness.

"It is only that I know you've had so many other women," she said. "And I even expected after we were married that you would still be tempted to—to—"

"Seek out someone else's bed. Lady, I shall consider myself fortunate if I am man enough to keep you satisfied."

But the teasing drawl faded as Lance reached up to cup her cheek, his touch tender as his voice as he said, "Rosalind, I freely admit I've been no saint in the past. But there is another part of my family's legend that claims that when a St. Leger finds his chosen bride, he can never be unfaithful, never love another again.

"I never fully believed that. But after tonight, I know it's true."

Lance drew her down for a kiss, and Rosalind issued a deep sigh. Soothed and reassured, she nestled back in his arms.

Feeling replete, more content than he had ever imagined possible, Lance cradled her close, savoring the feel, the pure joy of her in his arms. Even with all the passion they had shared, the endearments he'd whispered, it suddenly occurred to Lance he had never told his lady exactly how much he adored her. Not as himself, Lance St. Leger.

Some accomplished lover, he thought with a grimace. He shifted toward her, prepared to remedy his neglect at once, but when Rosalind's head lolled against his shoulder, her breath coming in a soft blur, he realized his lady had fallen sound asleep.

He suppressed a wry chuckle. Well, he'd waited this long to break such astonishing tidings to her. He supposed his vows of love could keep a little longer. At least until the morning.

Shifting the coverlet carefully up over her, he deposited a tender kiss on top of her head. Lance burrowed into the pillow and was soon lost in sleep himself.

But not the deep, satisfied rest he might have expected. He tossed and turned, troubled by a vague sensation of unease. A haunting premonition of disaster, a feeling that solidified into a cold stab of fear that wrenched him wide awake.

Val! Something terrible had happened to his brother.

Lance sat bolt upright, sweating, heart pounding with the most irrational sense of alarm. Fighting his way from beneath the covers, he leapt out of bed, his feet striking the cold floor.

He staggered across the room, stumbling through the darkness toward the arch that led to the stairs. He was halfway there when he brought himself up short, pressing his hand to his brow, swaying a little with dizziness and confusion.

What the devil was he doing? Getting ready to charge naked through the castle and do what? Rush to the aide of a brother who was either tucked up safe in his bed or in the library slumped over one of his infernal history books.

Val would look at him as if he'd lost his mind, which he very likely had. Lance ground his fingertips against his eyes, trying to rub away the last groggy remnants of sleep that still clung like the webs of a nightmare.

Yes . . . nightmare. No doubt that was what had jarred him out of his sleep. Some disturbing dream about Val that he could not remember now that he was fully awake. But it must have been a damned bad one to have such a powerful effect on him. He was still trembling, and he felt so blasted cold, a chill that went far deeper than the marrow of his bones, all the way to his heart.

Shivering a little, Lance crept back to bed, tunneling beneath the covers. He lay down beside his lady, and even in her sleep, Rosalind instinctively melted into his arms. Lance held her close, grateful for her warmth. But the strange feeling the dream had induced persisted, and it was a long time before Lance could allow sleep to reclaim him.

CHAPTER NINETEEN

*R*osalind was the first to awaken the next morning. Her eyes fluttered open. With a deep yawn and a languid stretch, she blinked, for a moment confused by her unfamiliar surroundings. Then her gaze fell upon the dark head nestled on the pillow, and she smiled softly, memories of last night flooding back to her.

She reached out to stroke Lance's cheek, now roughened by a faint stubble of beard, several unruly strands of dark hair straggling across his brow. Even asleep, the man was dangerous, the very picture of a seductive rogue. So different from the gentler aura that Sir Lance—

Rosalind tried to check her thoughts before she even conjured up the name. Sir Lancelot . . . how had he fared last night while she had been deliriously swept away by Lance's passionate embrace?

What had her gallant knight thought when he found that painful letter of farewell she'd been obliged to leave for him? Had he understood or had he been completely devastated?

No, she couldn't think about any of that just now. It hurt far too much. Rosalind scooted closer to Lance, longing to kiss him awake, wanting, needing to lose herself in his loving once more.

But he looked so exhausted, poor darling, dark bruises smudged beneath his eyes, his breath issuing in heavy sleep-blurred sighs. Rosalind forced herself to retreat back to her own side of the bed.

It must still be quite early. She closed her eyes, but she was far too wide

awake to doze off again. Tossing restively on her pillow, she took closer stock
of the tower room than she had been able to do the night before.

It was the first time she had ever slept in a sorcerer's bedchamber, she
thought with a tiny shiver. Pale sunlight streamed through the windows, illuminating many objects she found intriguing, a collection of strange vials atop
a wooden shelf, a bookcase groaning under the weight of mysterious-looking
tomes.

Rosalind slipped from beneath the covers, the sight of those books an irresistible lure. The raw morning air sifted over her skin, raising gooseflesh. She
was obliged to scramble back into her nightgown and wrapper before turning
her attention to the bookcase.

But as she examined the volumes on the shelf, her shoulders slumped in
disappointment. She could not find a single one written in English, most of
them inscribed in foreign tongues she could not hope to understand. She
moved on to the small writing desk. There perched atop the scarred mahogany surface rested an unbound manuscript, not of any ancient parchment
but of modern vellum, the title page penned out in a neat hand.

The True and Curious History of the St. Legers.

Rosalind stifled a soft exclamation as she recognized Val's manuscript. She
had seen him working on it in the library only the other day. But what was
Lance doing with it up here in the tower?

So many pages. She ran her thumb alongside the thick stack. Knowing
what she already did about the St. Leger family, she was certain those precisely inked lines of Val's must contain an absolute treasure trove of strange
stories, enough wondrous tales to satisfy even her legend-hungry heart.

She fingered the top page wistfully, wondering if it would be a great breach
of Val's privacy if she were merely to skim a chapter or two. She seemed to remember that Val *had* told her that as soon as he was finished, he would allow
her to read it. Would it be so terrible if she took just a tiny peek now?

She stole an uncertain glance at Lance. Her husband had burrowed deeper
beneath the covers and looked unlikely to wake for some time. Rosalind
stared down at the manuscript, resisting temptation for a moment longer before surrendering.

Scooping up the pages, she perched on top of an ancient trunk to take advantage of the light filtering through the windows, and settled in happily to
read.

It was obvious immediately that the history was far from complete. Val told
her he'd been having trouble gleaning enough facts on his early ancestors.
Rosalind had been so tempted to tell him about his family's extraordinary

connection to Sir Lancelot du Lac, but that would have been awkward, explaining the circumstances under which she had obtained her information.

Val's chief concern was the elusive Prospero. The opening pages describing the great sorcerer were still rough, with many gaps, incomplete sentences, and crossed-out lines. Rosalind skimmed ahead until an intriguing segment on the St. Leger sword caught her eye.

. . . according to legend, the infamous crystal was once part of a much larger stone, employed in some devilish invention of Prospero St. Leger's that went horribly awry. There was a hideous explosion, and all that remained was the single piece of crystal which is now embedded in the sword.

The weapon itself is magnificent, of strong tempered steel and a hilt of pure wrought gold. But the sword derives its strange power entirely from that fragment of crystal.

The mystic stone has always meant something different to each man that possesses the great weapon, a reflection of his own unique St. Leger power. By tradition, the heir to Castle Leger surrenders the sword to his chosen bride upon their wedding day, along with his heart and soul forever.

There have been a few recorded instances where the bride herself has been visited by a surge of arcane power, able to share a portion of her true love's own unusual abilities as long as she clasps the sword. . . .

Rosalind shuddered, remembering the times she had so innocently handled that mighty weapon. Dear heavens! If she was indeed Lance's chosen bride, anything might have happened, according to what Val had written. She could have experienced some terrifying flash of the future or sent objects flying or—or—

Rosalind checked her alarmed imaginings, reminding herself that Lance possessed none of these powers, so she could not have shared them, sword or no sword. Lance claimed that he had no unusual St. Leger ability. But no, Rosalind frowned in an effort of memory. That was not precisely what her husband had said.

He had faltered, *"Oh, er—I don't have any talents that are of any particular use to anyone."*

Rosalind's gaze shifted thoughtfully toward the man slumbering upon the bed. She had once thought Lance St. Leger the most arrogant person she'd ever met, but she was coming to realize quite the opposite. He was modest, even disparaging about his heroic actions during the war and all the good deeds he had performed after.

Might he not be likewise dismissive toward any more unusual talent he had inherited? Rosalind sifted through the pages on her lap, wondering what

Val might have to say about his brother's abilities, if Val had gotten that far in his chronicles.

He had. Rosalind pounced upon Val's account of the present-day St. Legers: Anatole, with his glimpses of the future; his daughter Mariah, who sometimes obtained visions of the past; Val, with his healing gift for absorbing another's pain; Marius, who could probe the secret emotions other men kept locked in their hearts; Caleb, who apparently had the ability to communicate with four-legged creatures.

Scores of St. Legers with talents, both wondrous and strange. But Rosalind skimmed over them, looking impatiently for the one name above all others that she sought.

Of all the supernatural gifts inherited by the St. Leger family, none has proved more amazing and terrifying than the power of Lance St. Leger.

Rosalind's eyes widened in disbelief the further she read. Surely what Val described here had to be impossible. How could any mortal man separate from his own body, send his soul drifting out in the night, turning into a phantom version of himself?

A phantom version of Lance St. Leger . . . *Sir Lancelot* St. Leger. Rosalind felt her heart go still, dark suspicion crowding into her mind. Impossible, painful suspicion that would not be banished no matter how hard she tried.

It couldn't be true. It simply couldn't be. Her gaze roved desperately around the room as though seeking reassurance from somewhere, anywhere. But what she spied was the glint of metal beneath the bed, the sunlight, like prying fingers, catching at the tip of some pooled garment all too hauntingly familiar.

The manuscript page fluttered from Rosalind's numb fingers. She sat there for a long time before she could rouse the courage to move, to creep across the room. Crouching down, she tugged out the discarded garment she had spotted, the metal links of the shirt heavy in her hands. The mail shirt of a long-ago warrior . . . or a gallant knight.

Rosalind's heart constricted. It was as if she had just stumbled upon some cherished memento of a lover she had lost, a valiant hero felled in some great battle. Except Sir Lancelot hadn't died. He had never even existed. At least not *her* Sir Lancelot, the tender friend she'd rushed to meet on so many warm summer nights. He'd never been anything more than a jest, a deception, a St. Leger illusion.

She clutched the mail shirt to her, pillowing her cheek against the steely links, as cold as all her foolish imaginings seemed to have grown.

It was at this unfortunate moment that Lance rolled over, stirring awake. His eyes fluttered half-open and he peered drowsily up at her.

"My lady," he murmured. The husky voice was Sir Lancelot's, the seductive smile purely Lance St. Leger.

Rosalind felt something snap inside of her, her heart pierced clean through by a hurt and an anger the likes of which she'd never known.

"You despicable villain!" she cried.

"What?" Lance's eyes flew wide as he came more fully awake. He struggled to a sitting position. "Rosalind, sweetheart, what ever is the—ooof."

He gave a sharp gasp as Rosalind slapped the full weight of the chain mail against his bare chest. He looked bewildered, so confused for a moment that she experienced a wild hope that she would yet discover she'd made a mistake.

But as Lance clutched at the metal shirt, glancing down to see what she had hit him with, a flush of guilt spread across his cheeks that condemned him more surely than the coat of mail.

"Oh, lord," he groaned, stealing a stricken glance up at her.

Rosalind balled her hand into a fist and pressed it hard to her lips to keep from either hitting him or bursting into furious tears. She wasn't sure whose betrayal hurt her the most, that of the man who had made love to her so tenderly, so passionately in this bed last night, or that of the one who'd pretended to be her heroic friend, always listening to her woes with such gentleness, such compassion. That was the worst part of fancying oneself in love with two different men, she was fast discovering. They both could break your heart.

"How could you do this to me?" she choked, remembering all the misery she'd gone through before coming to Lance, wrestling with her agonizing "choice," practically tearing herself in two.

"How could you make such a fool of me, getting me to believe that—that—" Rosalind whirled away from him, unable to continue, scarce able to bear the sight of him. She stumbled toward the tower stair, only wanting to escape back to the solitude of her own bedchamber.

But Lance scrambled out of bed and managed to block her way, a formidable barrier of naked hard-muscled man, but his hands were achingly gentle as he reached for her.

"Rosalind, please, my dearest, you've got to let me explain."

"Explain?" She shrank away from him. "Exactly what is there to explain?"

"About that chain mail—"

"Oh, I believe its purpose is clear enough to me, *Sir Lancelot*. Just another one of Lance St. Leger's little jests."

Lance flinched as though she'd slapped him. "Rosalind! You can't believe that. Surely you know me better by now."

"Which one of you?" she responded bitterly. "You or Sir Lancelot?"

"Rosalind, I'm sorry. I know how badly I must have hurt you, and God knows, I've no right to ask anything from you. But please, if you would but stay, give me five minutes."

Rosalind didn't want to give him anything. She wanted to sweep imperiously past, but her way was barred by more than the breadth of his powerful shoulders, by the intent expression in his dark eyes.

Damn him! she thought, swallowing thickly. After what he'd done, what right did he have to stand looking at her that way, so sad and wistful?

But she had no choice except to comply with his request. Her knees had begun to tremble so, she was not sure how long they would continue to support her. She backed away from Lance and sank rigidly down atop the ancient chest.

Keeping a wary eye on her, Lance paced back toward the bed, hunting for his discarded clothing. Not merely because it was less than dignified to conduct such a grim discussion naked, but to give himself time to think what the deuce he was going to say to her.

But as he scrambled into his breeches, he feared that centuries might not be enough for that, to help him find the right words to repair the damage he'd done, to soothe away the raw hurt he saw shimmering in her soft blue eyes. He cursed himself a thousand times over for not having found the courage to tell her the truth himself, in some gentler fashion.

Shrugging into his shirt, Lance felt like a warrior girding himself for battle, the most important battle he'd ever waged in his life: to win back his lady's trust, perhaps even her heart.

He approached Rosalind, manfully bracing himself for the hail of her fury or the gentle rain of her tears. He was not as prepared to find her so pale, so quiet, her delicate features set into such a stony expression, it alarmed him.

He crept toward her, his bare foot trodding on a discarded sheet of vellum. He bent to pick it up, frowning when he saw what it was, a portion of Val's history of the St. Legers.

One paragraph in particular seemed to leap out at him.

Lance St. Leger possesses the uncanny ability to ease himself into a deep trance, a deathlike state in which his spirit leaves his body and goes drifting through the night.

Lance pulled a grim face, realizing it was not the evidence of the chain mail alone that had tripped him up.

"Thank you, St. Valentine," he murmured.

Rosalind shot him a reproachful glance. "Don't you dare try to blame your brother for any of this."

"I don't. Believe me, Rosalind, at this moment I am cursing no one but myself. It is just that I didn't want you to find out the truth like this."

"You didn't want me to find out at all!"

Lance started to deny it but found that he couldn't, not entirely. He realized that a part of him had been cowardly enough to wish that Sir Lancelot would just fade into the twilight, no more than a pretty memory, no questions asked.

He sighed and gathered up the strewn pages of the manuscript, restacking his brother's precious book carefully back on the desk.

Rosalind had her arms locked tightly over her breasts, her face averted. Lance knelt down on the stone floor, directly in front of her so that she would be forced to look at him. After a brief hesitation, he reached for her hand.

She did not try to resist, but her fingers rested cold and unresponsive within his.

"Rosalind," he began. "I never meant for my posing as Sir Lancelot to get so far out of hand. God knows that hurting you with it was the last thing I ever wished to do. It all began as merely an accident."

"An accident!"

"Aye, that night we'd first met I'd been attending that fair in the village, masquerading as a knight for a mock tournament. It was also the night the St. Leger sword was stolen from me. I was still wearing my costume when I went out drifting in search of the weapon. You see, when I put myself into the trance, my shade or whatever the devil it is that leaves my body, tends to assume the appearance of how I looked when I went to sleep."

He scanned Rosalind's face desperately for any sign that she was listening to him, at least trying to understand. Her expression was not encouraging, but Lance forced himself to continue.

"That was how I came to stumble upon you at the inn, looking like I was the ghost of some knight of the Round Table."

Rosalind's lips thinned. "Not *some* knight. Sir Lancelot du Lac. You told me you were Sir Lancelot."

Lance winced. "Yes, I did. But Rosalind, you have to understand, you caught me drifting. I had pledged to my father that I would never reveal my strange ability to anyone outside of the family. I have managed to keep so few of my promises to him. It seemed desperately important that I honor at least that one."

"That explains the first night, Lance. But what about all the others? Why did you let the deception go on and on, filling my head full of such nonsense, telling me that you—" Her voice broke, and Lance thought that she would weep, but Rosalind compressed her lips tightly together, steeling the delicate line of her jaw.

He squeezed her hand, caressing those soft fingers, trying to chafe some warmth into them, the comfort he seemed unable to convey.

"I don't know," he murmured. "I hardly understand myself what possessed me to continue such a masquerade, long after I should have told you the truth."

He gave a shaky laugh. "Hell, I almost wish it were Sir Lancelot here with you now instead of me. He always seems better at knowing what to say to you."

Rosalind wrenched her hand from him. "Oh, stop it, Lance!" she cried. "There is no Sir Lancelot. He is you."

"No, he's not." Lance shook his head sadly. "Just a dream I created for us both. You were a damsel in distress, and you needed a hero, the kind of hero I always wanted to be, a knight in shining armor, and you looked at me as if that was exactly what I was . . . and for a little while, I could pretend, too."

Rosalind raised her eyes to his, her expression now more sorrowful than angry. "Do you know what really hurts most of all in this, Lance?"

"That I never told you the truth? Not even last night. Rosalind, I wanted to. I was simply too afraid that—"

"No, that's not it." She pushed to her feet, brushing past him. "It has nothing to do with Sir Lancelot. It is the way you made me feel when you were Lance St. Leger. That I was this strong, capable woman. That you respected me, my opinions, my intelligence."

"Rosalind, I do."

"No, obviously you don't, and why should you? A dream-ridden little fool too ready to believe in anything, a silly schoolgirl cherishing a *tendre* for someone who didn't even exist."

"Rosalind!" Lance moved toward her, trying to take her into his arms, but she slipped away from him, shaking her head.

"It's all right. I've grown up at last. You don't have to bother pretending to be Sir Lancelot anymore. You don't even have to pretend that you love me."

Before he could stop her, she bolted from the chamber, disappearing beneath the arch and down the curving stone stair. But not before he'd glimpsed the disillusionment, the self-loathing darkening her eyes. Emotions he was all too familiar with because he'd experienced them in full measure himself. The day he'd realized what a fool he'd been over Adele Monteroy.

Lance started to go after Rosalind, only to bring himself up short, feeling sick. His sweet Lady of the Lake . . . what on earth had he done to her? And would he ever be able to make it right?

He'd found a taste of heaven in Rosalind's arms last night. But trust Lance St. Leger to find a way to turn it into hell.

Perhaps all that Rosalind needed was a little time to be alone, to cry out her hurt over his deception, to think, to compose herself. But Lance didn't seem able to give it to her.

Good God! His lady didn't even realize how he felt about her. He paced outside her bedchamber door, which remained closed in his face, locked against him.

Lance strained to listen through the thick wood, thinking he might have been relieved to hear some muffled sobs. But this terrible silence was starting to unnerve him.

He knocked again, pleading for perhaps the dozenth time. "Rosalind, please, just let me in. I won't try to touch you. I only want to talk you."

No response. Not even a "Go to the devil."

Lance hammered louder. "You have to listen to me, Rosalind. Please? You have to at least let me tell you how much I love you. I lied to you about a lot of things, but never about that."

Nothing, only that relentless silence.

His fear and desperation caused his patience to thin. Crouching down, he bellowed through the keyhole, regardless of what servants might be passing by to hear.

"Blast it all, Rosalind. If you don't open this door, I swear I'm going to drop my body right out here on the floor and drift through the wall. I don't care if it is daylight."

Before she could respond or Lance could even start to act on this threat, he heard the stately stump of Will Sparkins's wooden leg as the St. Leger butler approached, no doubt drawn by all the commotion Lance was raising, but he didn't care.

"Rosalind!" Lance rattled the doorknob in pure frustration.

"Master Lance—"

"Not now, Sparkins," Lance snapped. "As you can see, I am a bit preoccupied at the moment."

"Master Lance, please."

Something in the older man's voice caused Lance to look around. Despite the grim accident in his youth that left Will Sparkins with one missing limb, Lance had never seen the family retainer ever look other than cheerful and serene. But his deep-set eyes peered at Lance from beneath his thatch of gray hair with such an unusually grave expression that Lance's hand froze on the doorknob.

"Sir, you are wanted belowstairs, immediately."

"What the devil's the matter?" Lance demanded.

"Something has happened to your brother."

"Val? Good God, don't tell me he fell asleep with his candle burning and nearly set his pillow afire again." But despite his impatient words, Lance experienced a frisson of unease.

"No, sir. Master Valentine has been shot."

"What!" Lance's hand fell away from Rosalind's door. He stared at Will Sparkins as though the older man had lost his mind. Val shot? That was ridiculous, unless Val had been attempting to clean a loaded pistol. His brother knew nothing of firearms, and he cared about them even less.

"Are you telling me there's been some sort of accident?"

"No, sir." Will swallowed thickly. "There was apparently a confrontation last night between Master Val and that Captain Mortmain."

Lance felt his veins turn to ice. Rafe and Val had fought a duel? No, that was equally impossible, Lance sought to reassure himself. He'd put a stop to any such nonsense that day in the library, when he'd warned Val to stay away from Rafe.

And he'd had breakfast with Rafe himself only yesterday morning, smoothing things over between them. Rafe would not have shot his brother. He couldn't have.

His heart beginning to thud uncomfortably fast, Lance shoved past Will. He never noticed Rosalind's door crack open as he headed for the stairs.

Will stumped after him, trying to keep up as Lance fired anxious questions over his shoulder. "Where was Val hit? How bad is it? Where have you taken him?"

"In the stillroom sir, but—"

Lance didn't wait to hear more. He raced down the stairs, leaving Will far behind, a sick feeling of dread curling in the pit of Lance's stomach.

A dread as cold as that vague nightmare that had inexplicably awakened him last night. No, not a nightmare. More like a chilling premonition of what might await him.

Lance charged down the narrow hall that led toward a small chamber off the kitchens. A throng of servants were assembled outside of the stillroom, grim footmen, frightened housemaids, and even Will's oldest son, Jem, the lad who worked at the Dragon's Fire Inn.

The boy came about at Lance's approach, tears beating dirty streaks down his thin face. He was sobbing so hard, Lance could barely understand him.

"Oh, Mr. Lance. S-sorry. Should have stopped him. Sh-should never have gotten him that key."

But Lance ruthlessly shoved the incoherent boy aside, his heart now hammering with a fear so sharp, it was almost painful. He pushed his way into the barren recess of the stillroom, an austere chamber he'd hated since his childhood, associating it with the agony of broken bones and bitter medicine.

Val had been laid out on the wooden table, and Lance drew up short at the sight of him. He'd often thought in recent years of his brother as fragile, but Val looked even frighteningly smaller, as though he had shrunk.

Lance stumbled toward him, concealing his alarm behind a low growl. "Damn it, Val. What nonsense have you been about? Do you think I want to be digging a bullet out of you before I've even had my break—"

He broke off, seeing that his brother's eyes were sealed closed. So pale, so still, Val's features were smoothed out in a terrible serenity for a man whose waistcoat was covered with dried blood.

"Val!" Lance bent over him, urgently calling his name, sharply patting his cheek. Val's skin felt so damned cold.

A wild panic shot through Lance, but he quelled it, snapping out fierce orders to the hushed throng behind him.

"Why the blazes are you all standing around? Has Dr. Marius been sent for?"

"Master Lance—" It was Will Sparkins. Panting, the older man had finally caught up to him. But why the devil wasn't Will doing anything, except standing there regarding Lance so mournfully?

"Somebody fetch me some water and some bandages."

"Master Lance—" Will quavered.

"Move!" Lance began fumbling with the layers of Val's blood-stiffened clothes himself.

Dimly he was aware of the servants shuffling back and someone slipping to his side. Rosalind, a soft presence in this harsh room.

She took one look at Val. Her eyes misted with tears, but Lance sensed they were no longer from the hurt that he had caused her.

She tugged at Lance's arm, trying to pull him away from the table. "Lance, please. There is nothing you can do for Val."

She gazed sadly up at him, whispering what they all realized but no one had the courage to tell him.

"Lance . . . your brother is dead."

CHAPTER TWENTY

*L*ance cradled his brother in his arms, his chest heaving with the strain of Val's inert form and the weight of his own heart, heavy enough to break beneath its load of grief and rage.

His throat constricted with unshed tears and a fierce cry of denial trapped deep inside of him. Rosalind's sad words continued to echo through his mind as he half dragged, half carried Val toward the ancient castle keep.

Lance, there's nothing you can do for Val. Your brother is dead.

No. No . . . no!

With a ragged breath, Lance managed to shift Val enough to shove open the heavy door. Kicking it closed behind him, he carted his brother into the vast chamber and laid Val out as gently as he could upon the oak banquet table.

The silent stone walls all around him seemed to echo with memories of days gone by, so clear they were painful. Sounds of two boys thwacking away at each other with wooden swords, calling out laughing challenges.

Lance clutched at his brother's hand, those same healing fingers that had often reached out to him, that comforting touch Lance had as often rejected. That gentle hand now so still and cold. Lance blinked back a fierce burning of tears.

"Damn it, Sir Galahad, you can't do this. You haven't even found the Holy Grail yet." Lance's throat constricted. "Bloody hell, Val! You haven't even found your chosen bride. What do you want to do? Go wandering through eternity all . . . all alone?"

Lance's breath hitched in his chest, and he felt himself in danger of coming completely undone. He stepped back from his brother, struggling to regain command of himself to do what he had come here to do. His one last desperate hope.

He stalked toward the portrait wall, all those generations a blur before his eyes. He sought out the one painting that had always dominated the others, the man that had begun all this St. Leger madness.

"Prospero?" Lance called hoarsely.

Those mysterious slanted eyes seemed to stare back at him from the depths of the portrait, colors still vivid even though the painting had once nearly been destroyed during a grim confrontation between his father and the sorcerer.

According to the family legends, the portrait had been miraculously mended by one who'd always possessed far more power than any mere mortal.

"Prospero?" Lance called again, his gaze flicking around the towering walls. The wily sorcerer came and went as he pleased, never answering anyone's bidding. But it had to be different this time.

"Prospero!" Lance's voice gained with the strength of his desperation. "Answer me, damn it! I need you."

A chill swept through the hall, but Lance barely noticed it. He already felt so infernally cold. Prospero emerged from the depths of his own portrait, but with none of his usual flair. Even his iridescent scarlet tunic had lost some of its luster or was it merely that the entire Castle Leger seemed suddenly enshrouded in a mist of gloom?

"Well, boy?" Prospero demanded, his unnerving gaze fixed intently upon Lance's face.

Lance released a shuddering sigh, not certain whether to thank God or the devil for Prospero's appearance. At the moment he didn't really care which.

Lance stumbled toward the sorcerer. "You've got to help me. It's my brother. He—he—"

"I know." Profound sadness robbed Prospero's face of all its customary arrogance.

"Then you see what has to be done."

Prospero's thin dark brows arched questioningly.

"You have to use your power to help him," Lance went on, his voice roughened with impatience and despair. "Bring Val back."

Prospero cast him a glance of such deep pity that Lance instinctively shrank from it. With rare gentleness the sorcerer said, "I fear you greatly overestimate my powers, lad."

"You say that?" Lance cried. "The mighty wizard who's always boasting of what he can do. Well, here's your chance to prove it. You mended that infernal portrait of yours. Now, I'm asking you to mend my brother."

"A man is far different from a scrap of canvas and a wooden frame."

"Then summon up a stronger magic, damn it."

"I'm not God, boy, although there was a time I was arrogant enough to think I was. But even I cannot pick the locks on the gates to heaven."

"Then you are refusing?"

"To raise your brother up from the dead? Perhaps I'm not making myself clear. It's not that I won't help you. I *can't*."

"Then what use are you and all your vaunted powers?" Lance choked. "What good have you ever done for this family?"

"None," Prospero replied quietly, bowing his head. "None whatsoever."

Lance stared at him, his heart burning with anger, all the more powerful because it was fueled by his grief. He advanced on Prospero, fists clenched, wanting to smash the blasted sorcerer's face. Wanting to hurt someone, anyone. Most of all himself.

"Then why don't you get the devil out of here," he roared. "And don't bother coming back."

But Prospero had already complied, vanishing into the wall, the sad wisdom in his mysterious dark eyes haunting Lance as he faded from view.

Silence descended, heavier than any Lance had ever known. The welcome heat of his anger went out like the last flicker of a dying fire, leaving nothing but a cold heart and the ashes of despair. The chilling finality that he was now forced to accept.

There truly was nothing to be done. Val was gone.

And never in his life had Lance felt so alone.

Rosalind hovered outside the keep, the dragon painted above the threshold keeping guard over the door through which Lance had vanished what seemed a lifetime ago.

She was still reeling from the shock of Val's death herself, but she'd scarce been able to shed a tear, her grief for her gentle brother-in-law all but swallowed up by her alarm over Lance.

Savagely snarling at everyone to get away from him, he'd scooped his brother up in his arms, bearing Val off to the old keep. Shutting himself away in there with his brother's body, allowing no one to enter. Rosalind was terrified that grief had caused Lance to lose his very reason.

Her fear was shared by the rest of the household, no one knowing exactly what to do, all of them looking to her, from Will Sparkins to the youngest scullery maid.

Rosalind had wanted to plead with them, try to explain. She was not accustomed to this sort of thing. She had experienced death before, but in its gentler form, nothing this terrible and violent. When she had lost her parents and then her husband, she had been the one sheltered and comforted, permitted to do nothing but grieve. No one had ever expected her to be strong.

But they were all clearly expecting it now. Will Sparkins had even begged her. "Please, my lady. You've got to go to Master Lance, help him. You're the only one who can."

Rosalind's heart had quailed, knowing that was untrue. After what had passed between them this morning, she doubted that she had any influence at all over Lance. But as she had glanced from Will to the rest of the household, all those sorrowing, frightened eyes regarding her hopefully, she'd realized she had no choice. She had to try.

Nodding weakly, she had set out for the old keep, only to lose her courage when confronted by that formidable door, closed so firmly in her face, shutting her out. Just as Lance had always succeeded in doing, even when she'd flattered herself that she'd known him best.

This was no time for nursing wounded feelings or hurt pride over the masquerade that Lance had practiced upon her, Rosalind adjured herself. Indeed, all of that had dwindled into insignificance in the face of this greater tragedy.

But she still could not help feeling that the man who'd managed to deceive her so completely was a stranger to her. She didn't know Lance at all, not really. Then how could she possibly know what to say to him to ease his overwhelming sorrow?

But she kept recollecting his face as she'd last seen it. Wild, grief-stricken, desperate enough to do himself harm. Gathering up her nerve, she fumbled for the key that Will Sparkins had slipped to her.

Her fingers were trembling so badly, she could hardly fit the heavy iron key into the keyhole. But it proved unnecessary. The knob shifted, the door suddenly easing open with a low creak.

"L-lance?" Rosalind said tremulously, taking a timid step forward, expecting to find him awaiting her. Whether ravaged with grief or furious at her for intruding, she had no idea.

But when she stepped across the threshold, she was astonished and a little frightened to find no one on the other side of the door. It was as if some invisible hand had reached out to let her in.

A cold chill swept through her, and she thought she heard a low voice rasp in her ear.

"Help him."

Or was that merely the promptings of her own heart which had begun to pound unmercifully hard? Her gaze darted around the vast chamber, searching for Lance.

She was almost relieved to see him sitting quietly in one of the chairs, hunched over, his back toward her as though keeping vigil over his brother's body, Val laid carefully out on the table before him.

But as she dared steal closer, she was horrified to realize Lance was weeping. Sobs all the more terrible because they were so silent, racking his entire body.

She had never seen a man weep before, not even her own gentle papa. Watching Lance give way to such an unheroic weakness made her feel hollow, her heart squeezed too tight with uncertainty and fear.

Rosalind pressed her hand to her mouth, her own throat knotting. It seemed hardly right she should be witnessing this. Lance would surely not want her seeing him in such a distraught condition, and she had not the least notion how to ease his suffering.

She paused, on the verge of creeping quietly away again when Lance lifted his head, his strong, handsome face streaked with tears. He groped for his brother's hand, saying in a broken whisper, "Oh, God, Val! Please . . . take the pain away."

That ragged plea lodged itself deep in Rosalind's heart, and she stared at Lance as though seeing him for the first time. No legendary hero. No battered soldier. Not even the rogue who'd first charmed then deceived her.

Simply a man who needed her love desperately. More than anyone had ever needed her before. With a strength and a calm unlike any she'd ever known, she walked straight over to her husband and placed her hand on his shoulder.

"Lance?"

He started violently at her touch, glancing up with dull, reddened eyes.

"Give it to me," she murmured.

"What?" Too dazed by his grief to understand, he attempted to wave her away.

But Rosalind persisted gently.

"Your pain," she said, holding her arms out to him. "Give it to me."

He stared at her numbly for a long moment. Then with a fierce cry, he wrapped his arms about her, burying his face in the folds of her skirt.

Afternoon shadows stretched across the tower chamber, an unnatural hush settling over Castle Leger, that solemn stillness only the presence of death could bring.

Rosalind perched on the edge of the sorcerer's brocade-draped bed, watching the man she had held in her arms this past hour, soothed, caressed, and comforted. Sharing their grief in a fierce mingling of tears. Never had she felt so close to Lance.

But now . . .

A terrible calm had descended over her husband, in its way almost as frightening as the previous wildness of his grief. He had allowed the servants to bear Val away so that he could be readied for burial. And Lance likewise appeared to be preparing himself.

Rosalind anxiously tracked his movements as he stripped off his shoes and dragged his heavy riding boots out from under the bed. Unshaven and unkempt, he brushed back strands of disheveled dark hair from his eyes, then jammed his foot into the worn, battered leather.

Rosalind scooted closer to where he had plunked himself down on the side of the bed. Mere inches separated them. Then why did she have this panicked feeling that he was somehow in danger of slipping far away from her?

"What are you thinking?" she asked. He glanced round at her and attempted to offer a tender smile, although it was clear that it cost him an effort.

"About Val." It was the first time Lance had even brought himself to speak his brother's name to her. Surely that was a good sign.

If only Lance's voice hadn't sounded so grim. "I was thinking that there was only one thing Val ever dreaded. And that was not finding his chosen bride. Ending up wandering through eternity, unloved and alone. And that is exactly what has happened to him."

"No!" Rosalind reached out to give Lance's hand a gentle squeeze. "No matter where he's gone, Val will always have our love."

"Your affection would be a great joy to him, my dear. Mine, however, never did my brother much good." Lance bent down, thrusting his foot into his other boot.

Rosalind's heart sank, for this was exactly what she had feared, that sooner or later Lance would get around to heaping recriminations upon himself for what had happened to Val.

"Lance," she murmured, "you must not blame yourself."

"For crippling my brother, then getting him killed?"

She only wanted to comfort him, but his unexpected words brought her up short. "C-crippling him?"

"Aye." Lance's mouth twisted bitterly. "Just another charming fact about myself that I neglected to tell you, my dear. I was the one responsible for Val's lameness."

"But it was some sort of accident, surely?"

"If you can call my trying to fling my own life away on the battlefield an *accident*."

"Val followed you into battle?" Rosalind asked in bewilderment. "I never knew he'd been a soldier, too."

"He wasn't. Val only followed me because—because—" Lance rose abruptly from the bed, dragging his hand wearily over the haggard planes of his face.

"Val has—" Lance winced painfully as he corrected himself. "I mean *had* this uncanny ability to know whenever I was in trouble, no matter where I was. As though there was some strange link between us, perhaps because we were twins and St. Legers. He described it as a piercingly cold sensation that would settle right here."

Lance pressed his hand over the region of his heart. "I never experienced anything like it myself until last night. Perhaps because St. Valentine never got himself into any kind of trouble before."

A fleeting smile touched Lance's mouth as if at some tender recollection of his brother, but the softer expression was gone in a heartbeat as he continued, "Unlike Val, I simply dismissed the premonition I had about him, rolled over, and went back to sleep. But Sir Galahad always came riding to my rescue."

"He followed you all the way to Spain?" Rosalind asked in awe.

"Aye, but that's hardly surprising. Because that was during the time that Colonel Monteroy was still my commanding officer and wanted me dead, and I was doing my best to oblige him. After one particularly reckless assault on the French, I finally did manage to get myself shot. A pistol ball that shattered my knee. They probably would have had to amputate my leg to save me.

"Not that I would have let them," Lance added. "Because all I wanted to do was die, and I thought I was finally going to get my wish. And then before the cannon smoke of the battle had even cleared, *he* was there. Appearing miraculously out of nowhere like some ministering angel. Reaching for my hand."

Lance stared down at his own strong, calloused fingers, lightly rubbing the pad of his thumb over his knuckles as though he were still feeling his brother's touch.

"You know what Val's healing gift was like," he said. "You've experienced it yourself."

"Yes. Oh, yes," Rosalind murmured, her hand straying to her shoulder, knowing she would never forget the sensation of her terrible pain being lifted away from her, the golden warmth that had replaced it, seeping into her through the medium of Val's gentle fingers.

"Val's extraordinary gift was different with me," Lance continued, "somehow stronger and more powerful than it had ever been. He took my hand, and I could feel my pain being absorbed into him. Too much of my pain, more than even he could bear. I tried to make him release me, but I was too damned weak.

"No matter how I begged or cursed him, he simply wouldn't let go. He kept holding on and on, and something went terribly wrong." Lance paused, his throat muscles constricting. "And when he was done, there wasn't a trace of my injury left, no blood, no scar. Not on me, but Val . . .

"Well, you've seen what it did to him," Lance concluded hoarsely.

Rosalind could see too clearly what that wondrous and terrible healing had cost her husband as well. Lance claimed he bore no scars from the incident. Only because his wounds had never healed.

They were still open and raw, finding expression in the darkness roiling in his eyes, the guilt and self-loathing that ravaged his features.

He was crushing his own hand, gripping his fingers so tightly, his knuckles were turning white, and Rosalind doubted he was even aware of doing so.

She hurried over to him, laying her hand over his, kneading his fingers until he eased his hard clasp.

"Lance," she said. "Whatever Val did for you, he did it out of love. He would not have wished you to torment yourself this way."

"I know that," Lance replied dully. "All he ever wanted was for me to forgive myself."

"Then do it now," Rosalind pleaded, laying her fingers alongside his cheek.

He caught her hand, pressing a brusque kiss into her palm. "I can't."

Lance turned abruptly away from her, and she heard him mutter in a voice almost too low for her to hear, "There's only one thing I can do for my brother now."

Rosalind felt her veins turn to ice, for she knew all too well what he meant. "You are going after Rafe Mortmain?"

Lance didn't reply, but he didn't have to. The answer was written in every rigid line of his steely frame as he stalked over to the peg where he'd hung his riding frock and shrugged himself into it.

Rosalind fought to quell her rising sense of panic. "Of course, you are the acting magistrate, and Captain Mortmain will have to be arrested. Dueling is illegal and—"

"A duel?" Lance snapped. "My brother was crippled and he scarce knew one end of a pistol from the other. I don't know what sort of confrontation took place between Val and Rafe. But it was no duel. It was cold-blooded murder."

"Then Captain Mortmain is obviously a very dangerous man, and you'll have to round up a large party of men to go with you."

"No! This is entirely between me and the Mortmain." Lance brushed past her, and Rosalind watched wide-eyed as he stalked toward the wooden writing desk. A long leather case rested upon it that Lance had had one of the footmen fetch to him earlier.

He flicked it open, and Rosalind recoiled when she saw what lay nestled against the silk lining: a rapier, more slender and graceful than the St. Leger sword, but equally as deadly.

"This belonged to my brother," Lance said. "It seems rather appropriate that I use it now."

"No!" Rosalind's fingers closed desperately over Lance's as he reached for the hilt. "Have you run quite mad? Didn't you tell me that Captain Mortmain is far more skilled with a blade than you are?"

"He always has been, but this time I'll have to do better, won't I?" Lance shook her off, gently but firmly, and drew the rapier out of its case. "When you challenge a man, my dear, the choice of weapons is his. And Rafe will never be stupid enough to opt for pistols."

"Then don't challenge him at all," Rosalind cried. "You can't bring Val back by throwing your own life away. Lance, please! This is honorable nonsense."

Lance's mouth thinned into a self-mocking smile. "Ah, but this is what a hero is supposed to do, isn't it? Avenge his brother."

"Not like this," Rosalind choked. She watched in helpless horror as Lance strapped that lethal blade to his side. Her heart thudding, she scrambled to get between him and the door.

"I won't let you go charging off to get yourself killed. Do you hear me, Lance St. Leger? Do you?"

She thumped her fists against his chest as though she could pound some sense into the man. But Lance caught her wrists, sweeping her into his embrace instead. She held herself rigid for a moment, then collapsed against him in a flood of tears.

She had wept so hard for Val, she thought she had cried herself out. But she found she had plenty more tears left for this frustrating, stubborn man she'd once believed so cynical.

Lance St. Leger had a code of honor so impossible, no man could live by it.

But he could very well die.

Rosalind clung to him, sobbing into his coat while Lance murmured soft words in her ear that did little to reassure. How could any man sound at once so tender and so inexorable?

"Shh, sweetheart," he whispered, cradling her close. "Everything will be all right. Just pretend I'm a knight that you've sent off on a quest."

The saddest sort of quest any man could ever have, Lance thought bleakly. To kill a friend.

But he had to stop thinking of Rafe that way, just as he had to steel himself against the distress he was causing his lady. Both could only weaken his resolve.

Pressing one last fierce kiss to her lips, Lance thrust Rosalind away from him. And then he was gone.

CHAPTER TWENTY-ONE

$\mathcal{T}$he sun faded into the shadows of twilight, a day that had seemed shrouded in darkness giving way to a night that promised to be just as bleak. Clouds drifted across the face of the rising moon, the wind blowing in from the sea, brisk and sharp.

Lance was forced to rein his gelding to a cautious trot. Not only did the gathering gloom impair his vision, but as he urged his mount forward, he ventured ever closer to dangerous ground.

Lost Land . . . the place had long ago been christened by the local fisher folk, a stretch of coastal property that was barren and isolated. The home of the once proud and treacherous Mortmain family, both their evil and their hatred of the St. Legers passing from generation to generation like an infection in the blood.

Lance had never wanted to believe that. Rafe was different, he'd always insisted, never listening to Val's warnings. But it had appeared that Val had been right all along, and now his innocent brother had paid the ultimate price for Lance's blind, trusting folly.

Thoughts of Rafe's betrayal dogged Lance through the falling night, piercing him as deeply as the death of his brother. His jaw hardened as he sought to deaden his heart to all such feelings of pain and loss. He'd left that tender, more vulnerable part of himself far behind, back at Castle Leger in the warm embrace of his sorrowing lady.

The gelding shied as something darted across the path ahead, some night creature taking cover beneath the shelter of a withered bramble bush. A rodent or weasel perhaps.

Lance drew rein as he sought to soothe his mount, bring it back under control.

"Easy, Blaze," he murmured, reaching down to pat the gelding's sleek neck, able to feel the beast's tension, the same that thrummed through Lance's own veins.

He tried to pierce the darkness ahead, study the layout of this most unfamiliar territory. As close as the property was to the St. Leger holdings, Lance had never dared set foot on Mortmain land during his boyhood.

Anatole St. Leger was not the sort of father to raise a hand to any of his children. But he'd threatened to take a rod to both Lance and Val if they ever disobeyed him by stealing off to investigate Lost Land. One look at his father's grim face had been enough to assure Lance that the dread lord meant what he said.

Lance had always thought his father's command unreasonable, born out of that St. Leger superstitious wariness of anything connected with the Mortmains.

But as he cleared the next rise, he was no longer so sure. Enough moonlight filtered from behind the cloud cover, enabling him to see just how wild this land was spread out before him, lonely and bleak with an unmistakable aura of decay. Stunted, dying oak trees stood as grim sentinels to the blackened ruins of a burned-out manor house, the crumbling walls etched starkly against the night sky.

With none of the dramatic grandeur of Castle Leger, the low-lying valley seemed to shuffle ignominiously down to meet the sea. Just beyond the dunes of drifted sand and sea grass was the cove, the black waves lapping against the shore, frothing like a hungry predator.

The place was unwarmed by any hint of life. The local folk avoided Lost Land like the plague, claiming the ruins were haunted by the spirits of those Mortmain devils who, one and all, had come to a bad end.

Except ghosts seldom required the use of lanterns. Lance's eyes narrowed as he could see one bobbing now, flickering behind the blasted-out windows of the manor house.

When he had discovered that Rafe had fled the Dragon's Fire Inn, tracking him out here had almost seemed a forlorn hope to Lance. Rafe had never come near this place before, claiming no interest in any part of his Mortmain heritage. But in the end, it seemed the wolf was bound to return to its lair.

Riding in closer, Lance saw Rafe's horse tethered just outside the ruins. He dismounted himself, lashing the gelding's reins to the skeletal branch of a salt-blasted oak. He wasn't some infernal knight charging up to strike the shield of an honorable foe in challenge, or even a local magistrate come seeking justice.

Only a man hell-bent on vengeance. Until he knew exactly what the deuce Rafe was up to, Lance reckoned he'd be better off approaching quietly.

Lance crept stealthily, working his way toward the ruins, keeping to the shadows as best he could. Crouching low, he darted forward, ducking behind a portion of crumbling wall. Lance craned his neck, peering over the blackened stonework.

Destroyed by fire decades ago, the manor had ceased to resemble any place that had ever been inhabited, the roof nothing but a canopy of darkened sky. A mass of fallen stonework marked where the great hearth in the main hall must have been.

No welcoming fire blazed there now or ever would again; the only light came from the lantern that Rafe had managed to hang from a twisted bit of iron jutting out from the wall.

The lantern's glow flickered eerily over Rafe as he paced, his dark multi-caped cloak slung about his shoulders. From time to time, he paused to glance through a gaping hole in the far wall, peering seaward, almost as though he expected rescue from that quarter, some phantom ship to appear on the horizon that would spirit him away.

Impossible. No one but a madman would anchor any sort of vessel near Lost Land's inhospitable shoreline, the jagged reefs of the cove treacherous enough by day, let alone by the dark of night.

Rafe shifted his cloak to consult his pocket watch and then sank down, perching himself atop a pile of rubble, his aquiline features stilled in that brooding expression Lance knew far too well.

Lance stared, searching Rafe's countenance for . . . what? Some sign of the evil, the depravity that everyone else had recognized and Lance had never been able to see?

Rafe still looked too damned much like the man he'd cracked a bottle with only yesterday, sharing a laugh, a jest, a few reminiscences over past foolish escapades. The same man who'd wrung his hand in an unusually hard clasp, his mouth twisting in a melancholy smile as though Rafe had known even then that it might be the very last time they parted in friendship.

Lance felt a hard lump rise in his throat, and he swallowed it, blotting out Rafe's features, conjuring up the gentle image of his brother instead.

Making no further effort to conceal his presence, Lance stood up and climbed through the tottering opening, all that remained of the manor's imposing front door.

When his boot struck up a spray of pebbles, Rafe started from whatever dark reverie absorbed him. His head jerked up and he paled at the sight of Lance, like a man confronted by a phantom melting out of the darkness.

But apparently Rafe Mortmain was far too accustomed to dealing with the ghosts of his past. He rose unhurriedly to his feet as Lance advanced upon him.

"Well, Captain Mortmain," Lance grated, making a contemptuous gesture toward the broken walls that surrounded them. "Welcome home."

"Lance," Rafe murmured.

"You act as though you were expecting me."

"No. I was rather hoping never to see you again."

"I'll wager that you were. Considering the fact my brother was found dead this morning lying facedown in the lane."

"I know. I . . . I'm sorry."

Damn the bastard for being able to sound as though he meant it!

"Not half as sorry as you're going to be that you killed him," Lance grated.

Something dark, unreadable flickered in Rafe's eyes. "You think that I was the one who murdered the noble Valentine?"

"Are you telling me you didn't?" Lance demanded.

Rafe gave a harsh laugh. "No. Why would I bother trying to do that?"

His mouth compressing in a taut line, he said, "I think you'd better do us both a favor, Lance. Get back on your horse and get the devil out of here."

Pivoting on his heel, Rafe turned and stalked haughtily away from Lance, exactly as though he were the lord of this tumbledown pile of ruins, dismissing some unwanted guest.

Lance felt a flicker of uncertainty, the stirring of a hope so desperate it was painful. He stalked after Rafe, saying, "Blast you, Mortmain. This is no time for any of your stubborn pride. Jem Sparkins told me that you caught Val searching your room last night. And the chambermaid at the inn said you had a violent quarrel. You nearly knocked my brother down the stairs."

"Aye," Rafe drawled. "My usual response when a man is threatening to beat my brains out with his cane."

Lance started to retort that Val would never do a thing like that, but he hesitated, frowning. Like most gentle people who seldom lost their tempers, he knew that Val could be rather explosive when he was goaded too far.

"What happened to set Val over the edge like that?" Lance asked. "Did he find something in your room?"

Rafe hunched his shoulders in a contemptuous shrug, turning his back on Lance. Lance seized the collar of his cloak, wrenching him around.

"Damn it, Rafe. You've got to tell me the truth. What really hap—" Lance broke off, feeling his face drain of all color. He'd tugged with such force, he yanked Rafe's cape half off, exposing the ghostlike white of Rafe's shirtsleeves. And something more besides.

A leather cord dangled from his neck, the object attached to the end glittering against the dark folds of Rafe's waistcoat. A shard of crystal. Even in the weak light of the lantern, the fragment of mystic stone gleamed, taunting Lance.

Lance's hand fell limp to his side. He stared directly into Rafe's eyes for a long moment, eyes that blazed back at him with a strange mingling of guilt and defiance . . . the eyes of a stranger.

Lance swallowed hard, despising Rafe Mortmain, despising himself even more for still being vulnerable to these sensations of shock and betrayal. The brief hope he'd dared to entertain shattered him with the same ruthless force Rafe had used to hack the shard of crystal from the St. Leger sword.

Rafe's hand closed over the glittering fragment, tucking it back out of sight beneath his shirt.

"I'm sorry you had to see that," he murmured.

"So am I," Lance said. "Is that what Val discovered when he searched your room last night?"

Rafe nodded.

"Right before you killed him." Lance's eyes clouded with the image of the bloodstains he'd discovered in the narrow lane behind the inn, the place where Val had crawled in his effort to escape, to find help. The place where his brother had died, alone.

All the grief, the raw emotion Lance struggled to suppress broke through in an angry surge. He knotted his fist and drove it hard into Rafe's jaw. Rafe staggered back, clutching his face, but Lance scarce felt the pain spiking up his hand.

He stripped out of his riding coat, flinging it to the ground, his lips forming into a cold sneer. "I trust you will spare me the usual formalities of issuing a challenge."

Lance unsheathed Val's rapier, holding up the gleaming blade to the light. "As you can see, I anticipated your choice of weapon."

Rafe didn't stir so much as a muscle, even at the sight of the deadly length of steel. "I've already done you enough wrong, Lance." he said tersely. "I have no intention of fighting you."

Lance leveled the tip of the rapier directly over Rafe's heart. "Then prepare to be cut down with as little mercy as you showed my brother."

Rafe's gaze flickered hesitantly from the sword to Lance's face. Whatever he saw there caused him to retreat a step. With an expression of more resignation than anger, he stripped down to his shirtsleeves and drew forth his own weapon.

Lance braced himself as Rafe faced him, rapier poised in the same sort of mocking salute that he'd always used to begin their pretend battles. Only this time their blades came together in a deadly hiss of steel.

They fought in grim silence. Every muscle tensed, Lance thrust and parried, meeting each lethal flash of Rafe's weapon with a fierce challenge of his own. Lance strove not to make his usual errors, the reckless lunges that would enable Rafe to emerge the victor. The cost of such mistakes this time would be far too high.

As he circled Rafe, seeking an opening, he felt neither fear nor anger, his heart encased in ice. More detached from his own body than when he night drifted. As though this were no more than a bad dream or a destiny far older than these ruins. St. Leger against Mortmain, condemned by some ancient feud to duel to the death, throughout all time.

Only Lance never seemed to have known that or accepted it, until now. The lantern light threw eerie shadows upon the tumbledown walls, the silhouettes of two men engaged in a desperate battle to kill or be killed.

Lip curled back in a savage sneer, Lance drove Rafe hard, taking a vicious satisfaction when he saw Rafe's energy begin to flag. The Mortmain was tiring, no longer fighting with his usual cold precision.

Lance forced him ruthlessly back, honing in for the kill. In a blur of movement, it was over. Rafe stumbled over a piling of rubble and fell. Lance struck his blade from his hand.

He loomed over Rafe, leveling the tip of his sword at his enemy's throat. Rafe stared up at him, his chest rising and falling quickly, but not from any fear.

"Go ahead," he snapped. "Finish it."

Lance hesitated. Perhaps because in that instant he realized that he hadn't won because of his own skill or because of Rafe's exhaustion. Rafe simply didn't care whether he lived or died.

Lance knew the emotion too well not to recognize it in another man's eyes. He tried to think of Val instead, steeling his hand to drive the blade home.

If only Rafe would close his blasted eyes, stop staring up at Lance with that look of dark desperation, reminding Lance too much of the wild lost boy Rafe had once been.

Lance tightened his grip on the hilt, but the sword had begun to waver in his hand.

"What's the matter, St. Leger?" Rafe taunted. "It's your destiny, isn't it? To destroy all the evil Mortmains."

Perhaps it was, Lance thought grimly. A part of his heritage as inevitable as the legend of the chosen bride—

No! An image of Rosalind's sweet face forced its way into Lance's mind, and he was revolted he'd even made such a comparison. The love he felt for his gentle Lady of the Lake—that was true destiny, pure magic, but this . . .

Lance stared at Rafe sprawled at his feet, helpless beneath the blade of Lance's sword. This bad blood between the Mortmains and St. Legers was no more than the brutal stupidity that Lance had always known it to be.

Rafe had had a choice. So had Val . . . and so did he, Lance thought. Never even in his days as a soldier had he derived satisfaction from killing, and Rafe Mortmain had nearly goaded him into that.

Lance lowered his sword, feeling sickened. He glanced down at his one-time friend with a wearied sigh. "Maybe you simply aren't worth the bother, Rafe."

Rafe struggled up onto one elbow, his brow furrowing with confusion and disbelief. "You're going to let me go?"

"No. As acting magistrate, I'm arresting you. I'll take you back to Torrecombe. You'll receive a fair trial."

"A fair trial for a Mortmain? In Torrecombe? You might as well hang me now and—" Rafe broke off, tensing, his gaze shifting to some point in the darkness beyond Lance.

Lance heard the crunch of a footfall and then Rafe's alarmed cry. "Lance!"

Lance spun around just as there was a deafening explosion. He felt the deadly whisper of a pistol ball hiss past his ear. But before he could even react, the burly figure behind him charged.

The heavy butt of the smoking pistol cracked hard against the side of Lance's skull. He felt his sword dropping from his nerveless fingers. His knees buckled as he swayed, his head swimming with blinding pain and confusion. He attempted to focus on the coarse, heavy features of his attacker.

Silas . . . Silas Braggs, the landlord of the Dragon's Fire. What the devil was he doing here? Rushing to the aid of Rafe Mortmain?

But that notion wasn't half so bewildering as the thought that seeped into Lance's mind as he sagged to the ground, losing consciousness.

Rafe had tried to warn him.

*   *   *

Lance's head tossed to one side as he struggled to make his way back to consciousness—a difficult journey, since the path was barred by the hideous pain throbbing behind his temples. But he fought the darkness, compelled by a strong sense of urgency, of danger.

He tried to move, open his eyes, but the world was a blur, dipping and rocking around him. A wave of nausea hit him, and he had to close his eyes, gulping in a shuddering breath.

But somewhere beyond the swaying darkness, beyond the ache pounding through his skull, there was a voice, insistently calling his name.

"Lance? Lance!"

He winced as he felt something pressed to his brow. A cloth cold and damp, soothed away some of the dark webs that clouded his mind. His lashes fluttered as he risked opening his eyes again, tensing at the sinister shadow looming over him, only to relax as his vision cleared and he saw who it was.

Rafe . . . it was Rafe bending anxiously over him, dabbing a cold compress against his forehead. Despite his pain, Lance's mouth wobbled in a relieved half smile. His gaze drifted past Rafe, woozily taking in the rest of his surroundings.

He was lying on a narrow hard bed, in a cramped austere chamber with a low-beamed ceiling. The only other furnishings were a chair and a small desk bolted to the wall. A lantern swayed overhead, the entire room swaying along with it.

And not merely from the reeling in his head, Lance realized with a jolt. He was in a cabin . . . a cabin on the deck of some ship.

But how the blazes did he get here? The last he remembered he had been at Lost Land, the walls of the ruined manor towering above him. And he and Rafe had been . . . had been—Lance's gaze drifted back to the man bending over him, recollection striking him with as much force as another blow to the head.

He tensed, struggling to bolt upright, a feat made difficult by more than his throbbing head. Lance realized he was bound, both hand and foot, tightly lashed with a rough cord of rope.

Rafe's hand clamped on his shoulder, thrusting him back down. "Easy, Lance," he purred.

He turned away from the bed long enough to fetch a glass of some amber-colored liquid.

"Here. Drink this," he commanded, easing his hand behind Lance's neck in an effort to raise him up.

But Lance resisted, clamping his jaw shut.

"It's not poison, only brandy," Rafe said with a hint of impatience. "Drink it. It will do you good."

"I didn't think 'doing me good' was high on your list of priorities, Mortmain," Lance said hoarsely. He raised his hands instinctively to take the glass himself, only to utter a frustrated oath at his restraints.

"Sorry about the necessity for that," Rafe said. "But I wasn't about to risk fighting you again or finding myself overpowered and marched back to Torrecombe for that *fair trial.*"

Lance winced at both the sarcasm of Rafe's words and the dull throb in his head. He was forced to submit to Rafe's ministrations, sipping at the glass Rafe held to his lips.

Lance choked a little as the fiery liquid spilled down his throat, but the brandy flooded through his veins, warming him, and he felt a little better.

Enough to study Rafe Mortmain through narrowed eyes, taking in his disheveled state. Rafe looked pretty damn near as bad as Lance felt, his waistcoat torn open, a trace of blood on his white sleeve.

Lance remembered clipping Rafe on the jaw, but that didn't explain those bruises that darkened Rafe's cheekbone or the purple swelling beneath one eye.

"You look like some dockside ruffian," Lance muttered.

"Thank you," Rafe said dryly, forcing Lance to take another sip. He shifted the compress, studying Lance's skull. Lance winced when Rafe touched a particularly tender spot.

"That's quite a lump you've got there, St. Leger. But I daresay you'll live. You've got an incredibly hard head."

"You should know," Lance retorted. Beneath the open neckline of Rafe's shirt, he could still see the leather cord, the fragment of crystal that condemned Rafe as the masked brigand who'd knocked him out cold on the beach the night of the masquerade. But it wasn't Rafe who'd assaulted him this time, Lance suddenly recollected.

Silas Braggs . . . Lance's eyes darted around the cabin as though he half expected to find the oily proprietor of the Dragon's Fire lounging there, leering at him.

But he and Rafe were quite alone.

"Where is that bastard Braggs?" he demanded.

"You don't have to worry about him."

As Rafe held the glass to his lips again, Lance noticed his knuckles were raw and bruised. He glanced from Rafe's hand back to his swelling eye and comprehension flooded him.

"You fought with Braggs, didn't you? If you hadn't warned me when he took that shot, I'd be dead."

Rafe said nothing.

"You stopped him from killing me. Why, Rafe?"

"Damned if I know," he growled irritably. "Now will you shut up and drink the rest of this?"

Lance obeyed. As soon as he'd drained the glass, Rafe lowered him to the pillow and stepped away. He reached for the bottle refilling the glass for himself. He tossed the liquid down his throat with a dark impatience.

Lance studied him thoughtfully, this man he'd once been so sure was his friend, then equally convinced had become his enemy. Only to have Rafe save him from Silas Braggs. But he was still Rafe's prisoner. And what had happened to Braggs? What the devil did he have to do with any of this?

Lance closed his eyes again for a fleeting moment, his head swimming with too many unanswered questions. He felt as though he were groping his way through some dark netherworld where nothing made sense any longer.

"How did we get . . . out here?" Lance ventured, although he didn't have the damnedest notion yet where out *here* was. Was this ship already under way, leaving the coast of Cornwall far behind? Or merely still rocking at anchor off the dangerous shore at Lost Land?

The pitching movement of the ship seemed rough to Lance, but he knew damned little about boats. That had always been Rafe's milieu.

Easily bracing himself against the sway of the deck beneath him, Rafe sank down on the chair, stretching out his long legs although the narrow cabin barely permitted such a thing.

"We reached the ship by longboat, of course," he said. "And a blasted tricky maneuver it was, too. That cove adjoining my ancestor's fine piece of property is a cursed nuisance to navigate in the dark, and I'd forgotten how damned heavy you are to move when you're out cold, St. Leger. It took two of my men to do so. I should have remembered that time you passed out on me when we were carousing with those redheaded wenches at Penrith, and I was obliged to cart you home."

No, Lance was tempted to retort, Rafe should have remembered that Lance had been his friend, willing to defend Rafe Mortmain against the entire world, including his own brother.

But Lance swallowed the bitter remark, asking instead, "And just whose ship is this, providing you with such a timely rescue?"

"Mine."

Lance snorted, then winced, the harsh sound of derision causing his sore head to throb. "Since when do you own a ship?"

"Since I needed one in my current business."

"What business? You're a riding officer."

"No, I'm a smuggler," Rafe replied coolly.

Lance's jaw dropped open, but only momentarily. He snapped it closed, muttering, "I should have guessed as much. You patrolled these coasts for a long time without ever arresting anyone."

"Which I could have done easily." Rafe gave an amused chuckle. "An inept lot they were, your local rogues led by that fat idiot Braggs."

"Well, at least that explains Braggs's part in all this." Lance shifted painfully on the bed, the better able to stare at Rafe. Considering everything else that Rafe had done, Lance hardly knew why he should care about reports of any further infamy.

But he frowned. "So you unmasked the smugglers and then . . . did what? Instead of apprehending them, you cut yourself in for a share?"

"No," Rafe retorted. "I took over. Lost Land, you must admit, makes a far more discreet location to land contraband goods than Torrecombe in the dead of night. Braggs was never exactly pleased to have me assume command, but I did the dolt a great favor."

"Aye." Lance sneered. "If you are a smuggler, it must be a great convenience to have the customs officer for your partner."

"Don't sound so disgusted, Sir Lancelot. I doubt that I'm the first government official to abuse my post."

"No, but I thought you were a cut above the rest, Rafe. Not quite that common."

Lance doubted anything he could say would have the power to sting Rafe Mortmain. Not any longer. He was surprised to see Rafe flinch, although the expression was smoothly masked over.

Rafe moved calmly to pour himself another drink, and Lance reflected that they might well have been chatting in quite the old way over a bottle of port, down at the Dragon's Fire.

Except that he was Rafe's prisoner. The stolen piece of crystal glittered around Rafe's neck, and his brother's blood was on Rafe's hands.

It couldn't alter anything that Rafe had done, couldn't possibly help Lance to know. But he felt as though he had to ask all the same.

"Why, Rafe?"

"Why what?" Rafe took another swallow of his brandy. "Why did I become a smuggler? Well, it's not as lucrative as it used to be during the war, but—"

"Damn the smuggling! I don't care about that. But the rest of it . . . what you did to me, to Rosalind, my brother. Betraying my trust." Lance could not keep the raw edge from creeping into his voice. "Why, Rafe? Damn it, *why*?"

Rafe drank his brandy, silent for so long, Lance thought he didn't intend to answer. At last his mouth hooked into a slightly bitter smile. "Perhaps it was my destiny. For as long as I could remember, people have been watching me and waiting. For my bad blood to emerge. For me to transform into the villainous Mortmain I was expected to be."

Rafe shrugged. "How could I possibly disappoint everyone?"

"Not *everyone*, Rafe," Lance reminded him sharply. "I never waited for that. I never expected it."

Rafe stared moodily into the bottom of his glass, swirling the dregs. "No, you didn't. You persisted in believing the best of me, even when I gave you cause enough to suspect otherwise. Sometimes I think all I've ever known of friendship, I learned from you."

He fixed his gaze on Lance with an intent brooding expression. "How is it possible to have felt so—so close to another man and yet envy him so much? And I did envy you, St. Leger. So fiercely, it was like a poison eating at my soul. Not your wealth or your land. But your heritage . . .

"Not a legacy of cursed villains and the scum of the earth. But legends of . . . of heroes and magic and love. And that incredible blade with its alluring stone."

"The St. Leger sword?"

"Aye, that damnable magnificent sword." Rafe sighed bitterly. "All that magic, all that power and you treated it as though it meant nothing to you. That night of the fair, you flashed it around as though it were some toy made of wood and paste."

Lance squirmed. His behavior didn't excuse what Rafe had done, but he flinched with shame.

"So I decided to steal the sword," Rafe went on. "After all, I reasoned, what the devil would you really care? I simply waited for my chance. When you set off up the beach alone, I came up behind you, and you know the rest."

Rafe straightened and fished a small pouch from the pocket of his waistcoat. He dumped out the contents into his hand and almost defiantly slapped the objects down on the table where Lance could see them: his missing watch and signet ring.

"I took these as well in an effort to divert your suspicion. To make you think you'd been set upon by a common footpad. I always meant to find a way to return them to you."

"Just as I suppose you eventually meant to give back the sword," Lance said coldly.

A ghost of a smile touched Rafe's lips. "Believe it or not, I did. From the moment I had that sword in my possession, it . . . it didn't feel right somehow. So awkward and heavy in my hands.

"And that crystal . . . that's a damned peculiar stone, St. Leger. Brilliant, mesmerizing, playing tricks with my mind." Rafe seemed unable to restrain a shudder. "You will probably laugh when I tell you this—"

"I doubt it," Lance interrupted. "I seem to have lost my sense of humor, Mortmain."

Rafe grimaced but continued, "When I was staring into that crystal, somehow all I could think of was . . . you.

"Not as you are now but the way you were that long-ago summer we were boys. A mere scrub of a brat, forever tagging at my heels."

Rafe sighed. "Lord, how I wanted to hate you. That was the one legacy my mother left me, the only thing she'd ever bothered to teach me . . . to hate St. Legers. And yet there you were, beaming up at me like I was your long-lost brother or something. Flying out with your puny fists at anyone who dared taunt me for being a Mortmain. You were so damned honorable even then, Sir Lancelot. With all these notions of what was right, fair, and just."

"Am I supposed to be touched by these recollections, Rafe?"

"No." Rafe ground his fingertips wearily against his eyes almost as though he wished he could discard the memories himself.

Lance certainly wished he could do so. It would make hearing all this so much easier, he thought bitterly. If he could just forget that he and Rafe had ever been friends.

Rafe went on gruffly, "In any event, the sword made me feel so damned strange, I decided to give it back. I did break off a small fragment of the crystal to keep for myself. I—I don't know why. Perhaps because that's all I ever wanted . . . just a small piece of all that you had and took for granted.

"I didn't want to be caught with the sword in my possession, so I hid it in the storeroom at the inn until I could think of some plausible way to get it back to you. Unfortunately in the meantime, Lady Carlyon somehow stumbled upon my hiding place."

"So you tracked her out to the Maiden Lake that night and shot her." Lance glared at him. He might be able to pardon Rafe for being tempted to steal the sword, but what he'd done to Rosalind . . . that was unforgivable.

"I never intended to shoot her," Rafe muttered.

"You aimed a loaded pistol at a woman. What did you expect to happen?"

"I expected her to be reasonable when I told her to hand over the sword, damn it!" Rafe shook his head, scowling. "But I swear, she would have fought me to the death. Somehow I think she set a higher value upon that sword than either one of us."

"She did," Lance said, the hard set of his mouth softening in spite of himself as he remembered Rosalind's fierce conviction that she had found Excalibur.

In a tone of grudging admiration Rafe continued, "The little fool actually attacked me with the sword, tried to knock the pistol out of my hand. The damned thing went off just as you arrived and I fled. I never even knew I'd hit her until I heard the gossip in Torrecombe the next day."

He added quietly, "You have no idea how relieved I was to hear that she was going to be all right."

"But obviously not relieved enough to have told me the truth."

"Told you the truth?" Rafe gave a bark of incredulous laughter. "That I'd stolen your sword. That I'd shot the woman you planned to marry. What would you have done, Lance? Clapped me on the back and said, 'That's perfectly all right, Rafe, old fellow. These little things do happen.' "

"No," Lance retorted. "But I've made enough mistakes myself, I would have tried to . . . to understand. Instead you made me feel guilty for suspecting you. I even quarreled with my own brother, defending you, and that is what goaded Val into conducting his investigation. I'm as much responsible for my brother's death as you are."

"No, you have no cause to blame yourself, Lance, or to believe any of what I'm telling you." Rafe heaved a dark bitter sigh. "And there is no reason I should care if you do. But listen well because I have no intention of repeating myself.

"*I didn't kill your brother.*"

Rafe was right. Lance had no cause to believe him, and he didn't.

"It was you that Val fought with last night," he said. "The chambermaid saw you."

"Aye, I caught the saintly Valentine going through my room. He uncovered everything, the evidence of my smuggling partnership with Braggs and this." Rafe drew forth the crystal shard, dangling it from the end of the leather cord.

"And you still claim that you didn't—" Lance began hotly.

"Yes, I do. I'll admit we exchanged some high words. There was even a scuffle, and I ejected your brother rather forcibly from my quarters. He left, I believe with the intention of summoning enough men from the village to have us all arrested."

"And you expect me to believe you just let him go!"

"That's right, I did. I didn't care who he fetched. I'd already made up my mind to be gone, shake the dust off my boots from this damned part of the world forever."

"Then who killed my brother?"

Rafe answered by shoving to his feet and drawing a knife from his boot. As he stalked forward, Lance shrank back, instinctively bracing himself.

But Rafe's mouth snaked in a cold smile. "Don't be alarmed. I merely want to show you something."

Bending down, he sawed through the cords that bound Lance's ankles, then hauled Lance to his feet. Lance swayed dizzily for a moment, fighting against the roil of the ship and the stiffness of his own legs, numb from having been bound. He would have fallen to his knees, but Rafe braced him until he was able to stagger forward.

Rafe prodded him out of the cabin and up to the deck. Lance shrank back momentarily at the blast of raw wind that struck his face, carrying with it the salt mist of the sea. His eyes struggled to adjust to the mysterious moonbound world that was Rafe's ship, strange men moving about in the shadows, the rigging creaking overhead.

Lance stumbled forward until he was able to brace himself against the nearest deck rail, the ship pitching so beneath him, he was certain they must be far out to sea.

But as he peered through the darkness, he was amazed to be able to make out the shore's distant outline. They were still riding at anchor, and for one moment Lance knew a wild impulse to try to jump ship, swim for it.

But with his hands still tightly bound, he'd sink like a stone before he even cleared the wake of the ship. Besides, Rafe was already upon him again.

Hauling him around, Rafe barked over the wind, "There! Look up there!"

The command bewildered Lance, and he was slow in responding. Rafe seized his chin and forced Lance's head up for him. The wind whipping his hair across his eyes, Lance squinted, at first seeing nothing but the intricate crisscross of rigging and the towering mast of the ship.

Then some of the clouds shifted from the face of the moon, the pale light silhouetting a grotesque object hanging from one of the spars. The bulky shape of a man. As the wind tugged at the dangling body, twisting at the end of a stout rope, Lance saw who it was.

Silas Braggs, his thick neck snapped to one side like a broken marionette.

"There, Sir Lancelot." Rafe growled in his ear. "I give you the man who killed your brother."

"My God," Lance said hoarsely, recoiling. He'd seen men hanged before, in the army: deserters, murderers, rapists. And if Rafe was telling the truth and Braggs had killed Val, no doubt the man deserved such a fate.

The sight still sickened Lance. But Rafe gazed dispassionately at Braggs's swaying form, not a ripple of emotion marring his smooth handsome features.

"My own brand of justice," Rafe said with a grim satisfaction. He averted his gaze back to Lance. "But don't flatter yourself I did it for any sentimental reasons. Out of respect for the lamented St. Valentine or . . . or because I feel that I owed anything to you.

"I gave Braggs a command. Your brother was to be left untouched. And no one crosses a Mortmain."

Rafe uttered these last words so softly, Lance almost didn't hear them over the roar of the wind and waves. But it was enough to send a chill up his spine.

"You're a dangerous man, Rafe," he said. "My uncle Marius once told me that. He said you were like some creature part tame, part wolf."

"The wise Dr. Marius. He's right. I've been wrestling with my own particular wolf for years." The hard set of Rafe's mouth wavered into an expression, wearied and sad. "And I've gotten so damn tired, Lance."

"It never had to be this way, Rafe. And it's still not too late for you to turn back from this course you've chosen," Lance said desperately. "If you've told me the truth, Braggs can be proven as Val's murderer. And as for your other crimes, the only one who knows about them is—"

"Is you," Rafe cut in. "Are you really prepared to pardon me for all I've done?"

"I . . . I don't know," Lance was obliged to admit. "But a very wise man once tried to counsel me that one of the hardest things a man has to do is forgive himself."

Rafe stared back at him, his eyes as black and roiling as the night, and Lance imagined he could almost see the man wrestling with his own inner demons.

A clap of thunder sounded, and both Lance and Rafe involuntarily shifted their eyes skyward, where the clouds had begun to assume a more ominous hue.

One of Rafe's burly seamen called out, "Dirty weather comin', Cap'n."

When Rafe made no reply, the man ventured, "Shouldn't we weigh anchor?"

Rafe studied the sky a moment longer, his jaw setting in a grim line. "Aye," he said almost more to himself. "Lost Land has never been a good place to ride out a storm."

Striding away from Lance, he began to issue some curt commands that sent his men scrambling. He almost seemed to have forgotten about Lance until the burly seaman jerked a thumb in Lance's direction.

"And what about 'im, sir?"

Rafe paused to gaze back at Lance. Across the deck, through the billowing darkness, their eyes seemed to meet and hold, and in that one moment, Lance felt as though everything they had ever been to each other, their friendship, his very life was weighed in the balance.

Then Rafe turned away. "Put him down in the hold."

"No!" Lance's heart sank and he tried to resist. But it was a useless proposition, weakened as he was by the blow to his head, his hands still tightly bound.

Two hard-muscled seamen dragged him below deck and tossed him into some dank storage chamber at the bottom of the ship. As the hatch above his head was slammed closed, Lance was swallowed up in darkness.

He wasted the first few minutes in a futile struggle to loosen his bonds that left his wrists raw and aching. Rafe had simply done too good a job of trussing him up. No doubt some damned kind of sailor's knot.

As for trying to find some sharp object to cut himself loose . . . Curse it all, Lance thought, he couldn't even see his own hands in this black hellhole.

He managed to wriggle into a sitting position, bracing himself, panting against a sack of grain, even that much effort causing his head to throb.

He felt the ship pitch and shudder around him, movement growing rough. Did that mean they had finally gotten underway, or was the storm starting to break? He listened desperately for any sounds of what was going on up above, but could hear nothing beyond the roar of the waves, the creak and groaning of the timber.

He sighed, contemplating his prospects, none of which seemed too good at the moment. He tried to console himself that if Rafe had meant to dispose of him, he'd have done it before. He wouldn't have saved him from Braggs.

But it would be an easy matter to toss a man overboard when they were far out to sea. Was Rafe capable of doing such a thing—killing Lance in cold blood?

Despite all that Rafe had done, Lance still didn't want to believe that. But he kept remembering the dark conflict in Rafe's eyes, remembering Marius's soft words of warning.

"Rafe is . . . torn between being part wolf, part tame. You should have a care, Lance, about being too close to the man the day he finally makes up his mind."

He had believed in Rafe Mortmain once, to his great cost, Lance reflected sadly. He could no longer afford such trust, or he might well end up dead before morning.

And for a man who'd once been so eager to fling his life away, Lance discovered that it was now very precious to him because of his Lady of the Lake.

He thought of Rosalind and wondered what she was doing now. Still weeping and worrying over him, her lovely blue eyes reddened and drenched in tears?

Lance smiled sadly to himself in the darkness. Was he the first fool ever to risk his life over some damn idiotic battle, some quest for vengeance, some stupid notion of honor, only to realize when it was too late, that it hadn't been worth it? That nothing was as important as being able to find himself back in his lady's gentle arms?

He'd never even been able to tell Rosalind how much he loved her, never had a chance to make amends for his dreadful deception. But it could not be too late for all that, Lance resolved grimly. He would not allow it to be.

He was a St. Leger, blast it, and one that had never been held back by any earthly constraints before. His heart quailed a little at the prospect of using his power now, his spirit drifting off, leaving his body behind, bound and helpless at the bottom of this ship. At the mercy of Rafe Mortmain.

Yet what choice did he have? Lance argued with himself. One of his uncle Hadrian's ships might be anchored near Torrecombe, able to sail in pursuit of Rafe, intercept him. Lance would only drift long enough to alert someone as to his predicament. And to see Rosalind, tell her how much he loved her, assure her he was going to be all right.

His decision made, Lance eased his head back against the burlap sack. Willing himself to relax, he closed his eyes, coaxing his mind down . . . down into his own special brand of darkness. Where all aches, all pain, all physical awareness ceased. Where he became lighter and lighter, like a ship tugging at its moorings, his spirit buoyed upward, pulling clear of the encumbrance of his flesh.

He hovered for a moment, staring back at the huddled mass that was his own inert body. Then Lance drifted upward, the decks of the ship no more than a phantomlike blur. He streaked faster, having no wish to draw notice to the strange apparition he had become. Hurling himself up into the dark of night, impervious to the roar of the wind, the cold lash of the rain, the sizzle of lightning. All things that he could not feel.

But he could sense the raw power of the storm. A flagh, the fisher folk had always called it, this sudden fury of the elements that had brought more than one ship to grief.

Hovering at the edge of the cloud cover, Lance paused to risk one look back, and what he saw filled him with alarm. The *Circe* was in trouble, floundering, being driven mercilessly back toward the reefs of Lost Land.

Lance hesitated, realizing he'd just made a terrible mistake, abandoning his body back there in a ship being tossed about as helplessly as one of those toy boats he and Val had once sailed upon the Maiden Lake.

Should he go back, rejoin to his body, attempt to get free, get himself out of that hold before it was too late? But it already was.

As though shoved by a mighty dark hand, the *Circe* dashed up against the rocks. Lance watched in helpless horror as the mast caved in, the ship breaking up, preparing to take all hands down with it.

Including the body of Lance St. Leger.

CHAPTER TWENTY-TWO

osalind had long ago abandoned any thoughts of sleep even though it was well past midnight, the clock upon the mantel chiming out the early hours of a day that had yet to dawn. She wandered through the confines of the library, peering out the rain-drenched long windows.

The gardens beyond were usually a place of moonlit magic, fragrant flowers, and gentle breezes. But the storm that had passed over had left bent tree branches and broken petals in its wake, the sky still black and cloud-ridden, blotting out all trace of the moon and stars.

Rosalind bit down upon her knuckle to still her fears, her worries about her husband having been caught out there in that storm, lost in his dark quest for vengeance alone.

No, not alone, she sought to reassure herself. Not long after Lance had ridden out, she had stopped her useless flow of tears and summoned every able-bodied male she could find, grooms, stablehands, even the footmen.

Mounted them all up and commanded them to go in search of their master, ride with him even if he ordered otherwise. Stop Lance from fighting and clap that dreadful Rafe Mortmain in irons.

Rosalind had never read about any heroine doing such a thing in any of the old legends. Interfering with her knight's bold venture, attempting to stop his duel, sending out a rescue party. Lance would likely be angry with her.

But she didn't care, Rosalind thought defiantly. This wasn't some fairy story about knights or heroes or foolish sighing maidens. This was about

Lance St. Leger, the man that she loved, and all she wanted was him back home. Safe.

She would have led the searchers herself if she hadn't been needed so badly at Castle Leger. Just as the men had been saddling up, a distraught Kate had arrived at the house, the young girl demanding to see Valentine.

What she'd heard couldn't be true, Kate had declared fiercely. He couldn't be dead. Not her Val. Rosalind had stared sorrowfully at the child's tear-streaked face and then gathered Kate up in her arms.

It had been like trying to comfort a hurt sparrow, its broken wings beating wildly to be free. But in the end, Kate had subsided, sobbing her grief out against Rosalind's bosom.

Long after the men had gone, Rosalind had comforted and rocked the young girl, stroking Kate's hair until at last she'd fallen into an exhausted sleep.

She'd tucked Kate up into her own bed. It was not as though she would be requiring the use of it, Rosalind thought, wearily rubbing the back of her stiff, aching neck. She would never be able to rest until Lance had returned.

But in the meantime, there surely must be something more useful for her to do than pace and worry. Rosalind turned away from the windows, her wearied gaze shifting thoughtfully back to the library desk.

It occurred to her that a note should be dispatched to Effie, despite the lateness of the hour. Effie very likely had no notion that Kate had run off to Castle Leger. Not that that was anything unusual.

But as scatterbrained as the woman was, she would likely be distressed come morning when she discovered Kate missing. Rosalind would dash off a note to her explaining.

And there were other letters that needed to be written as well, so many of the St. Legers as yet ignorant of the tragedy that had befallen them. Marius, who'd loved Val like his own son, was off somewhere, attending the bedside of some critically ill patient. The doctor would have to be summoned home and told.

And then there was Val's immediate family, traveling abroad. His fierce proud papa, his sweet practical mama, and those three younger sisters whose bright faces had smiled at Rosalind from their portraits. What a sad and difficult letter that would be, Rosalind thought, what grief it would bring to that family so far away.

Removing this terrible burden from Lance's shoulders was the least Rosalind could do. Moving the candle closer, she settled resolutely behind the desk, trying not to let her gaze linger upon the volumes strewn across the wide oak surface.

Val's books. His medical texts, his precious well-worn history of Cornwall cracked open as though he meant to return to it at any moment. Rosalind could not bring herself to reach out and close the cover, that simple action somehow too hard, too final.

Swallowing the knot in her throat, she slid open the desk drawer, briskly rummaging for some vellum and a quill. Her fingers struck up against a soft fold of cloth instead. She drew the garment out into the light, frowning in puzzlement when she saw what it was.

A woman's lace cap. *Her* lace cap, the same one she'd lost so long ago on that first day at Effie's, the one Lance had claimed he'd been unable to find.

Why, the teasing rogue! He'd had the cap all along, tucked away here in this drawer like some knight hiding away a token he'd dared steal from the lady he adored.

Rosalind smoothed out the folds of the cap, her lips curving in a tremulous smile as she recalled all the romantic words of love that Lance had poured in her ear under the guise of Sir Lancelot. Strange, but somehow the thought of Lance's deception no longer had the power to hurt her.

She remembered with a pang how Lance had knelt at her feet this morning, trying earnestly to explain.

"You were a damsel in distress, and you needed a hero, the kind of hero I always wanted to be, a knight in shining armor, and you looked at me as if that was exactly what I was . . . and for a little while, I could pretend, too."

Her heart welled with tenderness, saddened that a man like Lance could have ever felt the need for such pretense. All that time she had thought that the ghost of Sir Lancelot was attempting to woo her through Lance St. Leger.

How foolishly mistaken she'd been. It had been quite the other way around, Lance trying to woo her the only way he knew how, because he never thought he was worthy enough. The man who could be so generous and forgiving with everyone but himself. Decorated for his courage, praised for his compassion, always destined to be a hero . . . in everyone's eyes but his own.

Rosalind folded up the cap with trembling fingers, realizing she had never been in love with two men.

Only one, and she closed her eyes, fiercely praying for Lance to come home safe so she would have the chance to tell him so.

"Rosalind?"

She heard a voice call her name, and her eyes fluttered open in disbelief. Was she only imagining what she so desperately wanted to see, Lance standing before her, but an arm's reach away?

She had never even heard him come in, and yet there he was. Her battered knight had come back to her, weary but unharmed and still very much alive. Her heart flooded with joy and gratitude to discover that her prayer had been answered.

With a glad cry, Rosalind leapt up to fling herself into his embrace. She hurled herself at Lance, only to stagger forward, feeling nothing . . . only the eerie whisper of his spirit brushing against hers, filling her with confusion.

She passed straight through him, catching herself just short of stumbling against the hearth. Rosalind blinked, gripping the mantel to get her bearings. Realizing what had just happened, she spun around, frowning at Lance.

Damn the man! He was drifting again.

"What are you doing, Lance?" she cried. "You don't have to pretend to be Sir Lancelot anymore."

"I'm not. Rosalind, I—"

"No, not another word," she scolded. "I haven't spent all this time pacing the floor and worrying to have you return as a wretched ghost. So you just re-join to your body or whatever it is you do and then put your arms around me."

"Rosalind, I can't. My body . . . is gone."

Rosalind stared at him. She gave an uncertain laugh, positive that this had to be more of his wicked teasing. "You're always losing everything, Lance St. Leger. Your gloves, your riding crop. But surely not even you could misplace your own . . ."

Her voice faltered to silence at his grave look. He wasn't teasing. There was something very different about his eyes, so still and solemn and sad, no trace of his usual irrepressible twinkle.

"Perhaps you had better sit down, my dear," he suggested gently.

"No!" Rosalind's heart gave an apprehensive thud. "Just tell me what happened."

Lance's shoulders sagged, but he complied, relating the entire tale of his confrontation with Rafe Mortmain. But before he could even reach the end, Rosalind had tensed with alarm, interrupting him.

"Sweet heaven, Lance! The ship was foundering? We've got to hurry. Send someone to help, to get you out of there."

She actually took a frantic step toward the door, but she was arrested by the sound of Lance's voice.

"Rosalind, it's too late. The ship went down, taking me with it. By now I expect that I am somewhere at the bottom of Lost Land's cove."

She came slowly around to face him. "Are you trying to tell me that you . . . that you are—"

Dead.

She couldn't even bring herself to say the word, but she didn't have to. She could read the truth in the weary lines of Lance's face, the infinite sadness of his eyes.

Both her heart and mind rebelled. No! He couldn't be dead, lying buried fathoms deep in a cold unfeeling sea.

He was here with her. She could see the love shining from his eyes, hear the tenderness in his voice. This was no ghost of Lancelot du Lac standing before her, too perfect and unreal in his glinting armor.

This was her Lance with his half-open shirt and scandalously tight breeches, with his all too seductive mouth and dark strands of hair drooping over his brow. That same thick luxuriant hair she'd buried her fingers in when they'd made love, those same strong hands that had held and caressed her, that smooth sun-bronzed skin. Surely all she had to do was reach out to feel the warmth of his touch.

Rosalind stretched trembling fingers toward him. With an achingly wistful look, Lance met her halfway, resting his palm against hers as they had done on so many of their moonlit trysts.

She could not feel his warmth, the strength of his hand no matter how desperately she tried. But as before, she experienced that wondrous communion of their souls, all his love and longing spilling into her. And his regrets as well for the life they would never be able to share. All the passion, the kisses, the caresses. And the children that would never be born, the union of their love.

"Oh, L-lance," she whispered brokenly.

"Rosalind, I'm sorry," he murmured. "I'm so sorry."

Rosalind winked hard, battling back her tears. The man was dead, and he was apologizing to her? Lance was more concerned for her distress than with the thought that his life was over.

But that was so like her gallant knight that Rosalind's heart fairly ached with love and tenderness toward him. She forced herself to smile, digging deep inside of herself for a well of strength that she never knew she possessed. Because Lance was going to need her strength, all her courage more than he ever had before.

He was with her still, would be forever. A St. Leger miracle. More than other women who lost their husbands were ever granted, Rosalind reminded herself.

She attempted to stroke the hair back from his brow, her heart breaking anew as she realized she could no longer even offer him that small loving gesture.

"It will be all right, Lance," she assured him. "I loved you once before as a ghost. I can do it again."

He tried to return her smile, caught at her hand, clearly wanting to draw her fingers to his lips. A hopeless wish. His hand drifted back to his side with a look of resignation.

"I'm afraid my condition is a little more permanent this time, my dear."

"I understand that, but—"

"No, Rosalind, you don't understand at all. Prospero tried to warn me what would happen if I was night drifting and something happened to my body before I could rejoin, if I did not die a natural death."

"Prospero?" she echoed, wide-eyed. "The sorcerer?"

"Aye." A hint of grim humor touched Lance's mouth. "You needn't look at me that way, my dear. I'm not mad, only dead. Believe me when I tell you that Prospero's ghost has visited me in the old tower upon more than one occasion.

"That is if you can describe what he is by the mere word 'ghost.' In addition to his other powers, he was once a night drifter, just like me. Able to separate his spirit from his body safely as long as he rejoined before the sun came up. The same rules that bound me."

A chill worked through Rosalind. She was not certain she had the courage to hear the rest of this, but she forced herself to ask, "What happened to him?"

"Prospero was drifting when his body was destroyed. Ever since then he's been trapped here on earth, not truly alive and not truly dead. Caught halfway between heaven and hell, that is how he describes it. A drifter for all eternity."

Rosalind's mind reeled, unable to comprehend such a horrible fate, unable to accept that the same thing had happened to Lance. But she tipped up her head, squaring her chin. "It doesn't matter. Whoever you are, Lance St. Leger, whatever you've become, I love you. Nothing has changed."

"Everything has changed." His eyes dropped and he seemed unable to meet her gaze for a moment. Then he said softly, "Rosalind, I . . . I am going to have to leave you."

She stared at him in dismay. "L-leave me? What are you talking about? If Prospero could stay here all these centuries, then surely you can do the same."

"A castle can only accommodate so many ghosts," Lance explained with a fleeting smile. He immediately sombered, "And I believe it would be for the best if I go."

"For the best that I never see you again?" Rosalind cried. "I am still your wife, Lance. Your chosen bride. According to the legends, we are not to be parted, not even in death."

"That is no longer true. When you die, you are going to be an angel in heaven, not trapped here on earth forever with a sinner like me. And I thank God for that!"

"Then I shall take great care not to die," Rosalind argued desperately, "so that we may be together for as long as possible."

"And spend your life wedded to a mere shadow? No, my dear. I sought to rescue you from being a widow, not to condemn you to such a state until the end of your days."

Lance shook his head, the gesture tender but so inexorable. She studied his face with growing alarm, realizing he had made up his mind to this course before he had ever drifted back to her. The set of his jaw was inflexible, his mouth firmed with a steely resolve she recognized all too well.

Her hands fluttered helplessly, wanting to shake him for such stupid nobility, to fling her arms about his waist, hold him fast, prevent him from going anywhere. But neither was possible.

She had only one weapon at her disposal, one hope of being able to dissuade him. Rosalind sank down upon the chair and promptly burst into tears.

Lance groaned, "Ah, Rosalind, please . . . don't do that."

He dropped down to one knee before her in that gallant pose that had always come naturally to him. He could not gather her hands into his as he so clearly wanted to do, but with Sir Lancelot's tenderest voice, he attempted to brush back the veil of her sorrow.

"Milady, please listen to me. You are still so young, with so much of your life before you. Only think of all the things you have not done, have not seen. You still have to travel to Glastonbury, figure out if it was the site of Camelot."

"I don't care about b-blasted Camelot," Rosalind choked.

"Then what about marriage, children? I hope that someday you will find someone else who—"

"I could never do that!" Rosalind shot him a reproachful glare through the haze of her tears, wounded and appalled that he could even suggest such a thing. "No matter where you are, I belong to you forever. Effie said so."

"Our Bride Finder was obviously much mistaken." Lance's mouth twisted ruefully. "How could an angel like you be destined for a rogue like me? Hurting and deceiving you at every turn. You should have a husband more like my brother Val was. Good, kind, honest, a true gentleman."

"I don't want a gentleman," Rosalind sniffed. "I only want you."

But Lance ignored her anguished words, continuing resolutely, "And when you find this man, I hope he'll give you the kind of home that you deserve. Full of laughter and sunshine and a large boisterous family that will adore you.

"But you needn't feel pressed to marry again until you are ready. I've left you well provided for. A very handsome settlement in my will. You'll be a rich woman, my dear."

"H-how can you even talk to me about settlements when you are planning to—to abandon me?"

"And I don't want you wearing black for me," Lance rushed on. "You know how I detest the color. No ridiculous mourning beds, brooches, or rings. None of that funereal nonsense. If you must remember me at all . . . then just remember me as this rogue you met at an inn, masquerading as a great hero. A foolish fellow who . . . who would have liked to be your knight in shining armor but could never quite manage. . . ."

Lance's voice wavered at last, and he shoved to his feet, fairly flinging himself away from her. Rosalind leapt up in a panic, terrified he would vanish before her very eyes.

She clutched at him, the gesture all the more desperate because it was so useless. She cried out his name, struggling to find some words to move him, to deter him from his purpose.

But all she could do was whisper brokenly, "Lance, please . . . please don't leave me."

She gazed up at him, pleading with the full force of her heart. Lance stared back at her, no longer able to keep the despair or the longing from his eyes.

"And remember one more thing," he said hoarsely. "I told you many lies when I pretended to be Sir Lancelot, except when I said I love you, Rosalind. I will forever." Lance bent slowly toward her, bringing his mouth to hers.

Her lashes still damp with tears, Rosalind closed her eyes to receive his kiss. She could not feel the warm sweet pressure of his mouth, but his passion poured into her like a brilliant white light, warming her, filling her with a love strong enough to last an eternity.

She issued a deep sigh, but when her eyes fluttered open, he was gone.

"Lance!"

She rushed toward the window. Flattening her palms against the cold panes, she peered out into the gardens beyond. But there was nothing out there except the rustling darkness, the same that she felt stealing over her.

She sagged against the windows, overwhelmed by the sense of her loss. But she was not even given the time to collapse to the carpet and sob out her grief in peace.

She became dimly aware that someone was knocking at the library door. When she didn't answer, the door creaked open and Sparkins stumped into the room.

The elderly butler was still fully dressed, and from the haggard look of him, it was obvious that he had spent the night after the same dire fashion as she, roaming the house and worrying.

It was equally obvious from the look in Sparkins's eyes that some fresh crisis had arisen.

"My lady, I am sorry to—"

But Rosalind made a weak gesture, attempting to wave him off. She no longer had any strength left to deal with anyone else's problems.

"Mr. Sparkins, please. I—I need to be alone just now."

"But, my lady, I thought you'd want to know. The men have returned from searching for Master Lance."

"Oh," Rosalind said bleakly. "I am sure they all must be—very wet and tired. If you would see to them—"

"Yes, my lady. I've already roused the cook to dispense hot tea, and we've put Master Lance to bed in the green chamber."

Rosalind nodded numbly, starting to push past Sparkins to seek out her own bedchamber, where she could allow her heart to break in private.

But she froze, the sense of Sparkins's words penetrating her grief-fogged mind.

"W-what did you say?" She spun about to face the elderly butler.

"I said that the men found Master Lance, and he's in a very bad way, my lady. I don't know what that Mortmain devil did to him, but we put the young master to bed and—"

Will Sparkins got no further because Rosalind seized him fiercely by the front of his waistcoat.

"That's impossible," she cried, "because Lance has been lost at sea. His body is at the bottom of Lost Land cove. He told me so himself."

Sparkins stared at her in such a way that made Rosalind wonder if she looked as wild as she sounded.

The butler laid his hands over hers, gently easing her grip. "No, my lady. The men found Master Lance lying near the old ruined manor. Wet, unconscious, but still alive. Those young fools should have fetched him into the nearest cottage, but instead they dragged him all the way back home and—"

"Take me to him at once," Rosalind demanded, unable to believe Will, certain that the old man had run mad. Or perhaps she had, maddened by such sudden impossible hope that her heart threatened to burst, it had begun to pound so hard. She was trembling so badly, she was obliged to depend upon Sparkins's arm for support.

But when they reached the upper hall, she released him and rushed ahead. Darting into the green bedchamber, she drew up short, hitching in her breath at the sight.

Barnes, Lance's valet, hovered over someone stretched out on the bed, stripping a damp shirt away from the supine body of her husband.

It was Lance, as she'd seen him only moments ago, his dark, disheveled hair plastered to his brow. But this was no ghostly apparition. A soft cry escaped Rosalind, and she swayed from the shock, feeling as though she was about to faint. However, this was no time to indulge in such foolish weakness. She gave herself a brisk shake, then staggered across the room.

The valet moved respectfully aside as she sank down on the edge of the bed beside her husband.

"Lance," she whispered hoarsely, afraid to touch him, dreading to find this was all some sweet, tormenting illusion. Slowly she reached trembling fingers toward his chest. Her hand did not pass through him but came to rest on solid, hard-muscled flesh.

His skin was cold to the touch, but if she pressed hard enough she could feel it, the faint rhythm of his heart.

"He . . . he *is* still alive," she murmured wonderingly. "He didn't drown."

"No, my lady." Will Sparkins hovered behind her, peering down at Lance past her shoulder.

"The master appears to have taken something of a knock on the head," Barnes ventured in a worried tone. "We cannot seem to rouse him."

"Never mind," Rosalind said with a tremulous smile. "He'll be all right."

Just as soon as her night-drifting rogue got himself back—But the joy coursing through Rosalind came to an abrupt halt as the horrible realization struck her.

Lance would have no way of knowing his body had been found, no reason to come back. In his cursed noble quest to set her free, he had likely already drifted far away from Castle Leger.

And there was nothing she could do but sit helplessly by his bedside, waiting for the sun to come up and feel Lance's heart still to silence. Lose him for the second time.

No! Rosalind thought frantically. She couldn't have this hope held out to her, only to see it dashed. There had to be something she could do to save her husband, to summon his restless spirit back here before it was too late.

If only she could . . . if only—Rosalind caught her breath, memory striking through her like a shaft of lightning, like the answer to a fervent prayer.

Memory of those words that Val had written in his manuscript. *By tradition, the heir to Castle Leger surrenders the sword to his chosen bride upon their wedding day, along with his heart and soul forever.*

There have been a few recorded instances where the bride herself has been visited by a surge of arcane power, able to share a portion of her true love's own unusual abilities as long as she clasps the sword.

Was such a thing truly possible? Rosalind wondered. Could she figure out how to use the crystal to turn herself into a drifter, soaring out into the night until she found her husband?

She didn't know, but she had to try. She stole a glance toward the clock on the wall, realizing how precious little time she had left until dawn.

She felt Will tugging at her arm, trying to ease her away from Lance.

"Please, my lady. I know you must be pure exhausted. Allow us to tend to the master. I've sent my son Jem to look for Dr. Marius. Mr. Barnes, if you would be so good as to fetch more blankets and—"

"No!" Rosalind wrenched away from Will's grasp. "Forget Dr. Marius and the blankets. Just send someone to fetch me the St. Leger sword."

Sparkins and Barnes exchanged a dubious glance as if doubting her sanity, but Rosalind had no time to argue or explain.

She gave her foot an imperious stamp. "Don't stand there gawking at me. Bring me that sword and hurry!"

Lance sent his spirit hurling out into the night, drifting somewhere between the thick cover of black clouds and the cold light of the distant stars. Leaving Cornwall far behind him, his home, his land, and his lady . . . all lost to him forever.

But the whisper of the sea dashing against those rugged cliffs, that strange magic that had ever been woven into the walls of Castle Leger, the sad echoes of Rosalind's sweet voice all seemed to call to him relentlessly.

Lance, please . . . please don't leave me.

Lance sought to dam up his ears, cursing himself for ever having gone back there in the first place. He feared he'd only made matters worse for his Lady of the Lake. Far better to have let Rosalind believe that he'd merely drowned.

He'd been too blasted selfish to stay away, needing so desperately to see her winsome face, if only for one last time. But now he had to fight with all that was in him to resist the temptation to return.

He brought Rosalind enough misery in the brief time they'd been together. He'd be damned before he ruined the rest of her life by haunting her until the end of her days.

Damned? Lance gave a bleak laugh. He certainly was that all right. He gazed despairingly out across the sea of black clouds, the seemingly endless stretch of darkness.

"So this is eternity," he muttered.

"No, boy," a sad voice replied. "Only yours and mine."

Lance should have been startled to find that he was not alone out here, but he wasn't. It was as though in some odd way he'd sensed Prospero's presence before he ever came about to face his ancestor.

Mantle flowing off his broad shoulders, the black-bearded sorcerer stalked toward Lance through the billowing clouds.

"I tried to warn you, lad."

"So you did," Lance agreed. "Then you already know what happened to me?"

"Aye, I could sense it. I told you that every time you drift I can feel you tugging at the border of my shadowlands." Prospero scowled, resting his hand heavily on Lance's shoulder.

Lance winced in surprise. "I can almost feel you, too."

"That is because you are close to passing over. As soon as the day breaks, your connection to your past life will end completely, and I will become the only thing real in your world."

Now, there was a daunting prospect, Lance thought, retreating a wary step. Alone forever with the sorcerer he'd raged at and insulted.

"Uh, Prospero, about all those things I said to you yesterday—"

But his ancestor silenced him with the haughty gesture of one hand. "You were distraught with grief. Besides, do you think that I would ever heed the ravings of a mere mortal?"

Yes, he would, and he could be wounded by them, Lance realized, studying Prospero through narrowed eyes. Perhaps it was because he was so close to passing over himself, but he seemed to have acquired the ability to pierce the sorcerer's inscrutable aura. He could see clearly that beneath the flash of all that posturing Prospero was but a man as uncertain and vulnerable as Lance himself.

"I'm sorry," Lance said.

Prospero folded his arms across his chest, trying to appear indifferent to Lance's words of apology.

Lance continued. "If we are going to spend eternity together, we are going to have to make some effort to get along."

Prospero's mouth twitched, the taut set of his lips softening into a reluctant smile. "I suppose so."

A silence settled over them, deep and vast as the dark sky itself, as though both men had paused to contemplate the unbearable bleakness of their future.

Lance finally asked, "So what happens now?"

"What happens?" Prospero arched one dark brow at the question. "We drift."

"Aye, but I mean will it seem the same to me as when I was alive? Will I notice the passage of time?"

"Sometimes each second feels like an eternity. And then at others, decades can flash by in the blink of an eye."

Decades? Lance felt his soul freeze at the thought of everything he had ever known melting away with the years, Rosalind vanishing into the mists of time, where he truly never would be able to look upon her again.

He experienced an almost overwhelming desire to go hurling back toward Castle Leger and had to fight with everything in him to resist it. If there was only some way he could continue to be near Rosalind, watch over her without her being aware of it.

Lance turned anxiously to Prospero. "You have the power to render yourself invisible, do you not? Is there any way you could teach me to do that?"

"Perhaps, given enough time."

Lance gave a bitter laugh. "I have nothing but time."

"Aye, lad, but the question is, if you had such a power, what would you do with it?"

Lance didn't reply, but he didn't have to. Prospero seemed too well able to read the desire locked away in the back of his mind.

"It would not be a good idea," Prospero admonished him gently, "to keep such a vigil over your lady, witness all the sufferings, the pain and sorrow mortals fall prey to. To see her age and eventually die. Believe me, you will experience enough torments and regrets without that."

"Nonetheless, I—" Lance began, only to break off in dismay as he saw a faint light beginning to shine through the roiling pool of black clouds.

Dawn . . . the herald of his last day as a man, the beginning of his endless days as a drifter, an eternity without Rosalind. Prospero spoke of torments and regrets, but it seemed to Lance that was all his life had been, one long regret. He would have cast aside his very soul for a second chance.

But then . . . that was exactly what he'd already done. Now he could only watch helplessly, despairing as the light began to spread toward him, a light whose warmth he would never know again.

He tried to brace himself, meet his fate with some semblance of courage and resignation.

"Well," he murmured, trying to sound as though the sight meant nothing to him. "There is the sun."

"Hardly," Prospero said. "It is still a bit too early for that."

"What else can it be?"

Prospero cast him an irritated look. "I have been around for a few more centuries than you. I think I know enough to tell what time—"

The sorcerer checked himself with a muttered oath, staring toward the light himself with a puzzled frown. It was piercing the clouds with a brilliance that was blinding, dazzling Lance's eyes to a degree that he imagined he was seeing things . . . a lady garbed in white, her silken hair tumbled around her shoulders, her fragile hands gripping the hilt of a mighty sword. The crystal embedded in the pommel sent out rays of light that rivaled the sun.

Lance felt himself sinking to his knees right there in the misty clouds, staring in awe. Now he knew how dazzled Arthur must have felt when the enchantress rose from the Maiden Lake, bringing him Excalibur.

But that golden hair, those eyes of purest blue, that sweet mouth—this wasn't Arthur's Lady of the Lake. She was Lance's very own.

"Rosalind," Lance whispered. He was dreaming. He had to be. But if he was, he prayed never to awaken. "Prospero, is there part of this new existence of mine you haven't explained to me? Do you ever have visions?"

"That is no vision, lad," the sorcerer replied grimly. "That is indeed your lady. She's using my sword to share your ability to drift, and the power of the crystal has drawn her straight to you."

Prospero's words snapped Lance out of his dazed state. He drifted toward Rosalind, his soul flooding with unrestrainable joy merely to see her again. But it mingled with his horror at what she'd done, all that she was risking in her innocence even now.

"Rosalind," he shouted. "What are you doing here? Go back!"

But she only smiled at him with such a radiance, it was nearly his undoing. "I've come to bring you home." Keeping a careful grip on the sword with one hand, she stretched the other one out to him.

Lance shuddered, longing to reach for those gentle fingers, but all he could succeed in doing was pulling her spirit into the darkness of his own world. The temptation was so strong, he was forced to draw back from her.

"Rosalind, my dearest, you've got to go back before it's too late. You know that I can't—"

"Yes, you can." She beamed at him. "Lance, we've found you. You didn't sink to the bottom of the sea. You're tucked up safe in bed. All you have to do is return with me to Castle Leger."

Lance could only stare at her outstretched hand, stunned by her words, by what she appeared to be offering him. Life, love, hope, another chance. Surely a miracle too incredible to be true.

He stole an uncertain look back toward Prospero.

"You heard the lady," Prospero said gruffly. "It seems that you've been rescued."

"But I saw the ship go down. I was tied up in the hold. It's impossible that I could have been saved."

Prospero's mouth curled in a wry smile. "When you've existed as long as I have, you'll realize that nothing is impossible."

Lance turned wonderingly back to Rosalind, still hardly daring to believe it. He reached tremulously for Rosalind's hand, and he could feel the warm glow of her love, could suddenly see tomorrow shimmering in her eyes. All those endless days they would now have together.

His heart flooding with joy, Lance could have drifted there forever, content just to gaze at her.

But Prospero's sharp warning snapped him out of his trance. "It's almost dawn. You'd best hurry, or I'll end up plagued with both of you for the rest of eternity."

The sorcerer's words alarmed Lance so that he thought only of getting Rosalind home safely. He prepared to drift off at once, but she hung back. She peered at Prospero with a timid curiosity.

"Will you not come with us, sir?"

Prospero swept her a magnificent bow. "Alas, my lady, I fear I have no young vigorous body, no life to return to."

"But you could come back to your tower room as you have always done before."

Only Rosalind would courteously invite a ghost to haunt her home, Lance reflected with a tender smile. But her gentle suggestion shamed him because he should have thought of it himself. He'd had enough of a taste of Prospero's world to understand what a dark lonely existence the sorcerer must have led all these centuries.

"Aye, sir, do come with us," Lance seconded Rosalind earnestly. "I know that I ordered you to stay away from Castle Leger, but I didn't mean it."

Prospero drew himself up with a thunderous look. "As if I would heed any commands of yours, you young whelp. I only returned because you were making such a cursed nuisance of yourself, getting into so much trouble. Now that you have a strong woman to take you in hand, perhaps I might have a little peace.

"Please God, I shall not be plagued again with any of you blundering St. Legers for at least another century." Swirling his cloak haughtily over one shoulder, Prospero turned to go.

Lance took a hesitant step after him. "But, sir—"

"Go on! Get the devil out of here," Prospero growled. His voice softened a little as he added. "And I trust that from now on you will remember my warnings about drifting."

"I won't forget them. Or you, my lord." Lance reached out and caught at the sorcerer's hand in an impulsive clasp. But the dawn was almost upon them. There was nothing that he could do for Prospero. Lance turned and drifted back toward where Rosalind was waiting for him.

Prospero remained where he was, a tall imperious figure even in the vastness of the towering sky. He risked one glance as the young couple drifted away, vanishing into the clouds. Only after Lance and Rosalind had shimmered out of sight, leaving him alone in the predawn darkness did Prospero gaze down at the hand Lance had touched.

The mighty sorcerer's fingers trembled. It was as close as he had come to feeling any real human contact in centuries.

But there was no use repining for what could not be, Prospero adjured himself. He had no body, no life to return to, he'd told that lovely young woman. But perhaps that was not entirely the truth, he thought with a melancholy smile.

Perhaps he'd simply never found anyone who loved him enough to lead him back home.

Lance stirred against the pillow, wincing. His rejoining had been the most difficult he'd ever endured, but he rejoiced at every throbbing muscle, every stiff joint, every ache, every pain that reassured him that he was alive.

He shifted up onto one elbow to peer down at the woman sprawled upon the bed next to him. Rosalind's long lashes rested against the creamy curve of her cheeks, her eyes closed fast like one lost in a deep sleep.

She still had not roused, but Lance was not alarmed. He remembered the first time he had ever drifted, how long it had taken him to pull out of his trance.

This was Rosalind's first time and her last, Lance resolved. He gently pried the St. Leger sword from his lady's grasp and set it carefully out of her reach. Bending over her, he pressed a kiss to her brow, reveling in the warm feel of her skin and of the sunlight pouring through the bedchamber windows.

His heart swelled with love and gratitude for this miracle he'd been granted, though he still did not understand how it had come about. He'd been left bound fast, unconscious in the hold of a sinking ship.

Lance could think of only one possible explanation for how he'd gotten free. Although he would never have admitted as much, his rescuer had to have been that old scoundrel Prospero. Who else but a sorcerer would have had the power to loosen his bonds and transport him safely back to shore?

But did it even matter who or how? Lance thought, only grateful for this second chance he'd been given. He hovered over his sleeping lady, stroking his fingers through her silken hair, the sunlight striking off the golden strands and his ring.

His ring? Lance drew his hand back, amazed to discover his signet ring thrust back into place on his finger, the same ring he'd not worn since the night of the robbery. The one that he'd last seen spilled out on a table in a ship's cabin, along with his pocket watch.

His heart giving a startled thud, Lance eased himself away from Rosalind and scrambled in search of the garments his valet had stripped off him. The damp clothes had long since been removed by the efficient Barnes, but the object that Lance sought was still there, propped upon the dresser.

His pocket watch, a little worse for wear, waterlogged, the hands stopped dead, gritty with sand. Lance cupped it in his palm, stunned by the realization that washed over him like a pounding wave.

He hadn't been saved by the magic of any sorcerer, but by a man who was all too human. Who must have made a supremely superhuman effort, risking his own life to drag Lance out of that hold, somehow managing to convey him safely to shore.

For the second time, Rafe Mortmain had saved him from drowning. Rafe hadn't gone down with the ship. He was still alive out there somewhere, and Lance was fiercely glad of it. For wherever his friend was, wherever he'd gone, Lance knew.

Rafe Mortmain had once more managed to subdue his wolf.

*L*ance dressed himself and slipped quietly downstairs. Rosalind was still fast asleep, exhausted by all that had happened in the past twenty-four hours. Although Lance longed for nothing more than to be able to take her into his arms, lose himself in her sweet warm passion, he was content to wait because they had all the time in the world.

The future stretched out before him, more bright and shining than it had been the day he'd ridden off to find glory as an arrogant young soldier. But one part of his past remained to be dealt with, one sad duty left to perform.

He had to bid Val farewell.

Lance crept into the long gallery and dismissed the solemn young footman who kept vigil there. He needed to be left alone with his brother.

As was the St. Leger custom, Val had been laid out in the ornate drawing room upon a bier decked with flowers. Later he would be borne through the sorrowing village and settled to rest in the St. Leger tombs beneath the church.

Lance moved toward the bier, his heart constricting anew at the sight of his brother's still form, dressed in his finest frock coat. The lines of Val's face were smoothed into such a look of peace, that single stubborn curl as ever drooping across his brow. He seemed to have found rest from his pain at last, his healing hands folded upon his chest.

Lance swallowed hard, fiercely winking his eyes. It was a moment before he was able to speak.

"Val, there has always been this strange link between us, no matter how hard I tried to break it. So I'm hoping you'll be able to hear me, even from as far away as heaven.

"Once long ago, you reached out to heal me, and far more than my body, I realize now. But there is something I never told you about that day. You saved more than my leg. You saved my life as well."

Lance was forced to draw in a deep breath before he could go on. "Even though I cursed you for it, after you had made such a sacrifice for me, I was never able to be quite so reckless, so selfish as to deliberately try to cast my life away again. It forced me to become a better soldier, a better officer, thinking less of myself and more of my men. And I was honored because of it."

Lance gazed down at his brother, his voice cracking from the force of the love he'd felt for this gentle man yet never had been able to acknowledge. "But all those medals for valor should have gone to you. I can't imagine any greater courage than to take another man's pain and make it your own. Yet you never asked for any honors. You didn't even want my gratitude. All that you ever demanded was that I forgive myself.

"I don't know if I ever will be able to do that, Val. Not entirely." Lance fetched a deep sigh. "But I promise you I will try."

"Thank you," Val St. Leger murmured. "That is all I ever wanted to hear." His eyes fluttered open, and he raised himself slowly to a sitting position.

Lance's mouth fell open, his heart kicking violently against his ribs. More stunned than when Silas Braggs had dealt him that blow to the head, Lance staggered back from the bier, tripping over his own two feet. He might have fallen down entirely if he hadn't tumbled into a chair.

Lance stared at Val, his mind reeling. He had to be dreaming, or else he'd finally run mad. His brother . . . his *dead* brother was calmly plucking flower petals from his frock coat and smiling at him.

"Don't look at me as though I were a ghost, Lance."

"Aren't you?" Lance croaked.

"I don't believe so." Val patted his hands cautiously over his own chest. He gave a wide yawn like someone stirring awake from a particularly deep sleep. Climbing unsteadily down from the bier, he hobbled over to a gilt-framed mirror mounted on the wall.

Peeling back the layer of his frock coat and lifting up his shirt, Val examined the bare planes of his chest. There wasn't a mark on him.

Still dazed, Lance managed to get to his feet and stumbled toward him, peering at his brother's smooth flesh.

"But . . . but you were shot," Lance said numbly. "I saw the wound myself."

"Aye. Amazing, isn't it?"

"Amazing? It's bloody impossible."

"Actually, no, it isn't." Val tucked his shirt back inside his breeches, frowning at his own reflection as he attempted to straighten his frock coat. "I discovered some time ago that I have the ability to put myself into a trance even deeper than yours. Except I don't drift. Whenever I sustain an injury—not one I've absorbed from someone else, but one of my own—I can shut my body down until it heals itself.

"Of course, I've never tried it before with something as serious as a bullet wound." Val shrugged. "But after Braggs shot me, I didn't have much choice."

Lance could only nod stupidly, scarce able to absorb what Val was saying, scarce able to believe that his brother was . . . was *alive*.

He ran his hands down the length of Val's arms, touching his hand, feeling the warmth that pulsed through Val's skin. Lance began to shake, feeling nearly unmanned by the force of his joy.

His brother was alive! The brother he had wept over, prayed over, nearly run mad with grief over—

Lance's flood of happiness and relief received an abrupt check as the sense of Val's words finally struck him. He stiffened with sudden outrage.

"You've always been able to do this, put yourself into such a healing trance? Why the blazes didn't you ever tell anyone?"

"Mother and Father know about it."

"Well, they're not here, are they?" Lance snapped. "You damned fool, I could have walled you up alive beneath the church floor."

The very idea of such a thing was enough to make Lance shudder, but Val didn't appear particularly concerned.

"Oh, I doubt if it would have ever come to that. Even though I didn't feel quite up to moving about, I could feel myself starting to stir out of the trance as early as this morning."

"As early as—" Lance choked, his brows crashing together in a mighty scowl. "Are you telling me you were conscious when I first came into this room?"

"Well, er—yes," Val said, somewhat sheepishly. "I suppose that I was."

"Then why the devil didn't you give me some sign of it?"

"I intended to, but—" Val's mouth crooked in a slight smile. "You started speaking, and what you were saying was so interesting, I felt obliged to let you finish."

The black look that Lance shot his brother would have sent any other man scurrying for cover, but Val merely stood there, smoothing his cuffs.

"Do you have any idea of what it is like," Lance rasped, "to be so torn up over someone you're afraid you're going to lose your mind?"

"As a matter of fact, I do, Lance," Val retorted. "I've experienced a similar sensation every time I've stumbled across your body when you were off drifting.

"When we were boys, I used to sob over you, certain this time you must be dead. Only to have you spring up all of a sudden crying out, 'Got you, Val!' "

Val's mouth thinned. "Well, perhaps I have waited years to be able to say this to you."

Val looked at him with the most wicked smile Lance had ever seen cross his brother's saintly features.

"*Got you*, Lance," he said softly.

Lance blinked, sucking in a deep breath as though he'd been punched. He'd wept like a babe over his brother, and this was all that Val had to say to him? Got you?

A blind rage exploded inside Lance. Before he'd even had a chance to think, he doubled up his fist and let fly. He connected solidly with Val's jaw, knocking him down.

Lance was immediately horrified by his action. His brother had returned from the dead and instead of clasping him joyfully in his arms, he'd hit him. Hit his poor crippled brother who'd just recovered from a terrible wound.

Lance hunkered down, peering at him anxiously. "Oh God, Val, I'm sorry. Are you much hurt?"

Nursing his injured jaw, Val glanced at him with a dark look that Lance should have remembered from when they were boys. With a savage snarl, Val caught him completely off guard, tackling him so hard, Lance's head cracked against the marble floor.

"Ow!" Lance cried indignantly, but he had no chance to say more before Val socked him in the eye.

And the fight was on.

Punching, gouging, and wrestling, they crashed around the elegant parlor, banging into furniture, shattering vases. Battling with the kind of anger and frustration that only two brothers could turn against each other.

The parlor door flung open, and Lance was dimly aware that the commotion he and Val were causing had brought some of the servants running. Someone shrieked, and one of the housemaids fainted dead away.

But Lance was too caught up in the struggle, his furious attempt to throttle his one and only brother. Val, however, was far stronger than Lance would have ever imagined.

He held Lance at bay, and as Lance fought back, a strange exhilaration surging through him, one elated thought pounded through his brain.

He had his brother back again. The realization seemed to strike Val, too, and it became hard to maintain the fierce combat, anger dissolving into breathless laughter.

They tumbled to the carpet, and Lance managed to get Val pinned beneath him, but just barely.

"Surrender, St. Valentine," he panted.

"Be damned to you, Sir Lancelot," Val shot back, but he was by now too weak with laughing to fling Lance off.

Their eyes locked for a moment with a gruff affection neither was able to express. But then there never had been much need for many words between them, Lance thought. Not St. Valentine and Sir Lancelot.

Val grinned up at him, but the expression slowly faded, and it was only then that Lance realized how quiet the room had fallen. No shrieking house-maids, no shouting footmen.

"Oh, lord," Val muttered, his eyes fixing on some point beyond Lance.

A shadow fell over them, and Lance released his hard grip on Val's shoulders, drawing back to look behind him. He first encountered a pair of travel-stained boots attached to a towering frame.

Lance's dismayed gaze continued upward until he connected with fierce dark eyes set in a familiar weather-beaten face, framed by smooth wings of silver-tinted black hair drawn back in a queue. Lance felt his cheeks flood with a hot stain of mortification.

Anatole St. Leger, the dread lord of Castle Leger, had finally returned home.

The house was in an uproar, the main hall a clutter of the trunks, portman-teau, and bandboxes being unloaded from the coach, the evidence of the St. Legers' long stay abroad. A shy and bewildered Rosalind was swept into the noisy greetings and exuberant hugs of her new sisters-in-law, while Madeline St. Leger beamed and strove to restore some semblance of order.

There were servants to be soothed. The castle's retainers were a re-doubtable breed, accustomed to many strange sights, even the completely un-expected return of their master. But Val's recovery, a St. Leger actually appearing to pop back up from the dead, had proved too much for many of them. Even Will Sparkins looked pale and shaken. Madeline bustled about the household, attempting to spread her usual sense of practical cheer.

All that commotion seemed far removed from Anatole St. Leger's study set at the back of the house. The afternoon sunlight spilled over the dark linen-fold paneling of a chamber that bore a masculine aura as strong and austere as the man ensconced behind the desk.

Perched on the edge of his chair, Lance faced his formidable father across that expanse of mahogany. He reflected that Anatole St. Leger looked remarkably calm for a man who'd returned from a long journey abroad, only to find his two grown sons engaged in a bout of fisticuffs, tearing up the castle's best parlor like a pair of drunken alehouse ruffians.

Lance wondered if his father would be able to remain that way after he'd told him everything else that had occurred in his absence. Not a task that Lance relished, but he should have been accustomed to spilling out such confessions, he reflected.

How many times in his youth had he been summoned to this study to account for some mischief with a varying degree of dread, shame, and defiance. But it was somehow different this time.

Lance himself had demanded the interview, and he poured out his tale in a voice of quiet resignation.

When he'd finished, Lance didn't wait for his father to respond. He shoved to his feet, lifting the St. Leger sword into his hands. The sun glinted off the finely wrought gold hilt, the sparkling crystal.

Never had the magnificent blade looked more beautiful, Lance thought wistfully. He'd waited so impatiently for the day when he'd be able to thrust this sword back into his father's hands and ride out of here again.

But now . . . Lance approached his father's desk with a heavy heart. He steeled himself, knowing this was the only honorable thing to do.

Laying the sword down upon the desk, he said, "All things considered, sir, I think you'd better have this back again. To pass on to Val instead."

Anatole St. Leger's brow creased into a deep frown. He touched the hilt, studying the chipped crystal with a pained expression in his eyes.

Lance went on hurriedly, "After all, the St. Leger estate has never been entailed. There is no law obliging you to have me as your heir."

"No, there isn't." His father murmured. "At least no earthly one." He raised those fierce eyes of his, searching Lance's face with an intent gaze that Lance found uncomfortable. He turned away, pacing to the windows behind the desk. He heard his father vent a deep sigh.

"When I let you go away into the army, I'd always hoped that once you'd had a taste of the world, you would return feeling differently about your home. That somehow this land would come to mean to you all that it does to me."

"Good God, sir. It does!" Lance cried. And never more than now when he felt obliged to surrender all claim to it. Leaning against the casement, he could see the rocky sweep of the inlet below the castle, the sunlit waves breaking dark and golden against the shore. A land of hard, rugged, and impossible beauty. Lance felt his heart swell almost painfully at the sight.

He attempted to jest, "But I seem to have such a penchant for disaster, sir. I doubt Castle Leger could survive me as its master. Look at what havoc I managed to wreak in the short time you were gone."

"The castle is still standing, and Throckmorton informs me you've done a remarkable job looking after the estate."

"Aye, but what about the rest of it? The damaged crystal and—and my brother. Val was nearly killed."

"Considering the bruises on your face, Valentine strikes me as being remarkably alive," his father said dryly.

Lance touched the swelling beneath his right eye with a rueful smile and was obliged to admit that was true. But he sighed. "There is also the question of Rafe Mortmain. I failed to bring him to justice for stealing the St. Leger sword. He's escaped, and yet I have to admit that I am glad of it. Even though he has disappeared with that fragment of the crystal."

"The crystal is invested with such a strange power. Mayhap it will do the poor lad some good."

Lance spun about to stare at his father in astonishment. "Do Rafe some good? But sir, you've always hated and distrusted the Mortmains as much as Val does."

"So I have. To my shame." Anatole pushed away from the desk to join Lance at the windows.

They stood rigidly side by side, his father staring vacantly out as though at some memory he found not particularly pleasant.

"When your mother wanted to bring Rafe Mortmain to Castle Leger, I tried to resist the notion. Perhaps if we had found the boy sooner, when he was first orphaned, it might have been different, I argued. But he already seemed so wild, so hardened.

"The simple truth was I couldn't get past the fact that the boy was a Mortmain. But you know how persuasive your mother can be." The hard set of Anatole's mouth softened a little. "I can never say no to that woman.

"But from the time Rafe set foot across the threshold, I never gave the lad a chance. I kept an eye on him as I would have done had I brought some dangerous beast in our midst. And that day you nearly drowned in the Maiden Lake—"

"Father, I've told you so many times. That was an accident and Rafe saved me. Just as he did again when the *Circe* went down."

"I realize that now. But the first time, I fear that I merely used the incident as an excuse to send Rafe away."

Lance's eyes widened. "You, sir? You sent him away? I'd always thought that Rafe had run off."

His father shook his head sadly. "No, I bought the lad a berth on the nearest ship sailing back to France and sent him packing. All I could think of was my desire to keep my family safe from an evil Mortmain.

"But perhaps if I had ever showed the boy one tenth of the kindness that you and your mother did, things might have been different for Rafe. I fear I am as responsible for all these recent events as anyone."

Lance could only gape at his father, studying that stern, unyielding countenance, astounded to see the shadings of guilt, regret, and self-blame. Emotions that Lance was all too familiar with but had never expected to find reflected in Anatole St. Leger's eyes.

Becoming aware of Lance's intent scrutiny, Anatole gave a wry smile. "You never believed that I could make any sort of mistake, did you, son?"

"N-no, sir." He'd always been so convinced of his father's perfection, it had often been painful to reveal his own vulnerability to the man.

Even now Lance said hesitantly, "You've set a hard example to follow, my lord. Always so strong, so infallible. It was bad enough that you allowed mother to give me that impossibly romantic name, the name of a legendary hero. You have no idea what it has been like being the son of a legend as well."

"Try being the legend," his father said with a brief laugh. The sound had a rough self-mocking edge to it. "*The dread lord of Castle Leger.* All-powerful and all-knowing.

"*You* cannot imagine how terrifying it is to be set high upon such a pinnacle, expected to be so perfect, so wise, even by your own son." Anatole's mouth twisted ruefully. "From the day you could walk, you seemed to trail after me with so much hero worship, I was afraid to let you get too close. Afraid you'd fast realize your father was nothing more than a man, and a flawed one at that. Afraid that that admiring light in your eyes would fade and die."

His father shrugged his shoulders, appearing slightly embarrassed by his confession. "But that must sound ridiculous to you. You couldn't possibly understand."

"But I do," Lance murmured. He understood far too well because it was the same thing he'd done, distanced himself from his father for fear he'd be bound to disappoint. Anatole St. Leger might have chosen to hide his vulnerability behind a stern facade, Lance behind a quick laugh and a careless jest. But it staggered him to suddenly realize how very much alike they were.

His father moved back to the desk, toying with the hilt of the St. Leger sword.

"I have flaws enough, my young Lancelot," he said with a wearied sigh. "I've always had the devil of a temper, a tendency to prefer the isolation of Castle Leger. If I had had my way, I fear that I would have kept all my children cloistered safely behind these walls forever."

"I know," Lance said. "In fact, it surprised me exceedingly that after all these years, you yourself experienced this sudden urge to travel—"

Lance broke off, his eyes narrowing at the sudden way Anatole St. Leger averted his gaze, a distinctly guilty flush spreading across those high cheekbones.

"By God, sir!" Lance exclaimed. "You went away on purpose so that I would feel obliged to remain here at Castle Leger looking after things."

He should have been annoyed at his father's deception, but somehow he wasn't. Lance found himself smiling. "How the blazes did you know that I wouldn't simply shrug my shoulders and just ride off again as soon as you had gone? Did you have one of your visions?"

"No," Anatole said softly. "I simply knew my own son."

Far better than Lance had ever known his own father, it seemed. Lance stared at Anatole St. Leger as though he were really seeing him for the first time. Not some towering distant figure, some fierce lord of Castle Leger, but a man whose hair was graying at the temples, whose face was carved with deep lines put there by many of the same regrets that haunted Lance, including the regret that they had been so foolishly at odds for so many years. So much time wasted.

His father was aging, Lance realized with a pang. Anatole St. Leger was not immortal. He would grow stooped and old. The thought of his father's mortality left Lance feeling a little shaken and suddenly fiercely protective toward the man.

His father caressed the hilt of the St. Leger sword, regarding Lance wistfully as he said, "I've seen enough on my travels to realize how much things are changing. We won't always be able to remain as peaceful and isolated here at Castle Leger as I would like.

"The world will beat a path to our door whether I wish it or not, and it will take someone younger, stronger to deal with those changes. A man who has been out in the world more, a man like you, Lance. Castle Leger is going to need you. But if—if you don't want—"

"I have never wanted anything more, sir," Lance interrupted warmly, "than to be your son. To make you proud of me."

"I already am." His father came slowly around the desk and held out his hand.

Lance slipped his own into it, not the gesture of a worshipful boy to his father but a hard clasp between two men who had finally come to understand each other.

His father regarded Lance for a long moment and then suddenly pulled him roughly into his arms. His throat knotting, Lance returned the fierce embrace rife with all the feelings neither had ever dared express.

They drew apart almost immediately, both a little embarrassed by such an unmanly display of emotion. Blinking hard, Anatole waved Lance off, saying gruffly, "Good. That's settled, then. Now you'd best be off. If I know your sisters, I daresay they have quite overwhelmed that lovely young bride of yours with their exuberant attentions."

"Yes, sir. After all I have already put Rosalind through, it's a miracle she chooses to remain at Castle Leger."

"Women can be amazingly forgiving. Your mother taught me that."

"I cannot imagine she had much to forgive."

"Oh, you've no idea what a surly-tempered brute I was when she first came to Castle Leger. I terrified her once so badly that she actually ran from me and for a time took up residence with old Mr. Fitzleger."

"She did?" Lance asked almost diffidently. "I always fancied you and Mother were the very embodiment of the chosen bride legend."

"And so we are. But it took a deal of effort on both our parts. We St. Legers are blessed with a special gift, a Bride Finder who can unerringly lead us to a perfect love. But what we do with that love once it is found is entirely up to us."

"And I've made so many mistakes with Rosalind," Lance sighed.

"You can only do what so many of us hapless St. Leger men have done before you." Anatole St. Leger raised the crystal-adorned weapon from the desk. Laying it across his palms, he held it out to Lance.

"Take up your sword, Sir Lancelot, and venture bravely forth. To offer your heart up to your lady once more."

Lance's fingers closed over the hilt. "Thank you, sir."

With a respectful bow, he was almost out the door when his father's voice arrested him.

"And Lance, about that cursed fool romantic name of yours. It wasn't your mother that gave it to you. I did."

Lance's mouth fell open. He stumbled, nearly dropping the sword. But his father had settled back behind the desk, appearing quite unconcerned by the sensation he'd caused other than to remark, "Don't impale yourself on that thing, son."

"N-no, sir." Lance recovered himself. He started to go, only to hesitate once more. "Er . . . I don't want you to think that I am ungrateful to you, Father, for giving me such an unusual christening. But I hope you'll understand when I tell you. If I ever have a son of my own, I intend to call him John."

Anatole was still chuckling softly to himself long after Lance let himself out. Not so much over his last remark, but over the stunned expression on his son's face when he'd learned the truth about his christening.

It was good to be able to astound one's offspring occasionally, Anatole thought. It made a man feel less old, which was a pleasant thing. Especially when one's bones were feeling rather weary from travels that would never have daunted him as a younger man.

His return home had been eventful, to say the least. He leaned back in his chair, thinking he would be glad of a quiet moment. But his extraordinary sixth sense honed in on someone approaching the study.

That one person who always had the power to strip the years away from him and make him feel like a young fool again. His expression softened as the study door creaked open and his wife stole into the room.

Time had been kind to his Madeline. Barely a hint of gray touched her flame-red hair, and the lines that feathered her eyes were more those of laughter than grief.

Her green eyes were as bright as ever, although at the moment slightly clouded with anxiety. She had always known that he and Lance must sort out the difficulties between them, but Anatole fully realized how hard it had been for her not to intervene.

She hovered just inside the door, regarding Anatole hopefully. "Well? How did it go?"

"I believe we have our son back, madam." Anatole smiled slowly. "Sir Lancelot has come home. To stay."

Madeline gave a glad cry. Rushing around the side of his desk, she flung her arms around Anatole in a fierce hug.

He patted her hand, stretching up to brush a kiss on her cheek. "Lance has gone now to make peace with his lady, which is a good thing. He will need all of Rosalind's love and support to face what lies ahead of him."

Madeline's bright smile wavered. She peered intently into Anatole's eyes and faltered, "My lord, you have not had another of your dire visions, have you?"

"No, it requires no second sight to predict what lies ahead for our son if he continues on his present course. The most perilous and challenging task any man can face."

"What is that?" she asked anxiously.

"Why, madam, the raising of his own children."

Madeline's anxiety vanished in a trill of laughter. Anatole hauled her down onto his lap, and she wound her arms about his neck. They spent the next half hour behaving in a shocking manner not at all to be expected of two people who were destined to be grandparents.

Lance found Rosalind sitting on the bench in the garden. He suspected that his sisters had tactfully withdrawn at his approach, no doubt led away by the imperious Leonie.

He hesitated at the end of the path, content just to observe her for a long moment. She appeared so serene, her hands folded in the folds of her blue silk gown, her eyes lost in some soft reverie. The summer breeze teased a blush of rose to her cheeks, her hair drawn up in a crown of golden ringlets that exposed the slender curve of her neck.

She appeared different, as though the events of these past days had irretrievably altered her somehow. The dream-ridden girl he'd met that night at the inn was gone, and in her place, this quiet confident woman remained.

The realization made Lance feel strangely wistful, but as he approached, Rosalind looked up with a bright smile. She leaped up from the bench and met him halfway, her brow creasing with an anxious look.

"You've finished your talk with your father?" she asked. "How did it go?"

"Better than I had any right to expect. It seems he is still not ready to disown me." Lance attempted to jest, but his smile wavered. His hand dropped to the hilt of the blade strapped to his side. "I offered to give him back the sword, Rosalind. To surrender my inheritance to Val."

"Oh?" was all she said.

"I'm sorry. I should have consulted you first."

"No, of course not." She reached out to squeeze his hand. "Why should you?"

"Because it was your inheritance that I was prepared to give away, as well as that of our children. If my father had accepted my decision, I would probably have ended up back in the army, a soldier again, wandering the high roads."

"It wouldn't have mattered. I would follow you anywhere."

And so she would. She had already proved that, Lance thought. He gazed down at her, awed by the love shining from her eyes as he was by all that she had risked for him today.

"Val always said you would prove my salvation," he murmured, stroking the soft curve of her cheek.

Rosalind crinkled her nose impishly at him. "Your brother is an exceedingly wise man."

But for once Lance was unable to make light of something that so deeply moved him.

"How could you do something so amazingly brave, so incredibly foolish?" he chided her gently. "Do you realize what could have happened to you when you used that sword to come after me? You risked not only your life for me, Rosalind, but your very soul."

She caught his hand, pressing her lips to the back of his fingers. "I didn't care. I only wanted to be where I belonged. With you."

"With a man who has never done anything but deceive you? Pretending to be this legendary hero?"

Rosalind smiled at him, taking his face tenderly between her hands. "Oh, Lance, you dear silly man. You still don't realize, do you? You were never pretending. Lance St. Leger and Sir Lancelot, they are both you, my love. My teasing rogue and my gallant knight."

"Your gallant knight? You have no idea how much that is what I want to be for you," Lance said huskily. "I would willingly die for you, Rosalind."

"I don't want a man to die for me, Lance. I want you to *live* for me. To love me, to meet me for moonlit trysts in the garden, and mad gallops down the beach. To give me a house full of hunting dogs and boisterous children. To grow old with me by our own fireside."

Peering down into Rosalind's shining blue eyes, Lance felt his breath catch in his throat, for he realized his Lady of the Lake had not lost her dreams. They had merely changed. They were no longer of Camelot and some faraway time, but dreams for here and now. Of the love and the life they would share together.

With a low cry, Lance drew her into his arms, his lips claiming hers in a long passionate kiss. Her arms stole around his neck, and Lance would have been content to have remained lost in her sweet embrace.

Rosalind drew back to glance earnestly up at him. "You've got to promise me one thing. No more drifting again. Ever."

"Rosalind," Lance protested. "With you in my arms each night, how could you think that I would ever be tempted to—"

"Promise me," she insisted.

Lance smiled at her and then did better than that. Drawing forth the St. Leger sword, he dropped gallantly to one knee before her.

Blade poised across his palms, Sir Lancelot St. Leger offered up his sword to his lady, along with his most solemn vow.

"I pledge you my heart and soul, lady, for all eternity. I promise I will love you forever and go night drifting no more."